The MMRPG Apocalypse 2

The MMRPG Apocalypse 2

Jeremy Chambless

Published by Level Up in the United Kingdom in 2023

Cover illustration by Sippakorn Upama
Cover by Claire Wood

ISBN: 978-1-83919-567-9

www.levelup.pub

Chapter 1: When Insects are Worse than Elite Mobs

Early morning and the sun had just peeked over the horizon. It was a fresh day, and the best time for us to be adventuring into the unknown.

Our group was trapped inside the walls of a special game event by a crowd of players eager to kill us to get our gear. But we had a way out, a scroll with a group teleport spell on it: Close your eyes and count to five. Those were the instructions which were listed on the item. It also mentioned that the whole group would be teleported, but just to be sure I had everyone hold hands and close their eyes. Then we counted up to five together. It would be terrible if anyone was left behind, we had become a close-knit group: Thomas was our healer, with a superb sense of how to maximize cures without getting aggro; Alan was our tank and stoic in the face of the onslaught of our enemies; Lucas was like a rogue, who would enter battle from the flanks to get sneak attacks; Maria was an archer and so too was Jessica. Jessica was the true star of our group. We'd met soon after the apocalypse and she'd partnered me all the way up to our current level of 21.

Most of my time had been spent with Jessica and focusing on our own progress. The others I hadn't known so long but I had seen them in a crisis. Lucas was arguably the person I knew second best.

How would I describe him I wondered? Calculating? He seemed to be cautious in that he weighed most of his options pretty well. A good head on his shoulders and an eye for danger.

The rest...I couldn't be too sure. Alan put himself into the way of monsters without showing any fear, and I'd even seen a smile on his face when he stepped up. Adventurous? Daring? Thrill seeking?

Maria was timid, even a bit shy. There was an anxiousness to her that she tried to hide, but which had clearly come out during the Sphinx encounter. All of it was hidden pretty well behind a thorny exterior. I was probably leaning too hard into armchair psychology.

Thomas was...mysterious. He talked very little, never complained, and to me...it seemed like nothing mattered to him. I couldn't tell if he didn't care at all about what happened, or he was an expert at not showing it. Was this who he was? Or was he wearing a façade that never dropped?

After casting the teleport spell, I couldn't feel anything happen at all, but when we chanted 'five', the background soundscape around me changed and I felt warmer. I opened my eyes carefully and realized I was in a dense, jungle-like place. The entire area was over-run with rampant plant growth.

The humidity was awful and little insects buzzed around us while the nearby birds sang. "Where are we?" Thomas asked. If someone had said we were in the Brazilian rainforest I'd have believed them.

The spell's description was that we would land somewhere nearby...but the humidity was so intense and plant-life so rich that I'd question if whether we were on a different continent.

"I can see the dot for the Secret Shop on the map," Lucas said.

And sure enough, it was there, but was it our secret shop? "Can we be sure that's even the one we ported from?" Jessica also had the same thought. There was no indication at all where we were.

The term 'nearby' was loosely defined by the system, clearly. There was no sign of any human activity around here; the jungle was wild for at least this patch at least. "Can you lead the way, Alan?" I asked.

No one had any way to cut this dense foliage we were now trapped within so it was a case of hacking our way out.

"Towards the dot?" Alan asked.

"I don't see any other way."

"We've got nothing else to go on," added Jessica. "Hopefully, we'll eventually run into a road or some other sign of civilization."

"Come on then, the sooner we get out of this insect infected hell-hole, the better." Alan drew his sword and started chopping through branches and fronds.

I could feel preying eyes all around us as we walked. The chirping of the birds stopped abruptly, and I just knew that predators were lurking in the area. As far as I was aware, animal life had remained more or less the same after the apocalypse, with the only noticeable change an increase in how aggressive they were.

A deer was still a deer, a bear a bear, a wolf a wolf. None that I'd seen had become more powerful, but I hadn't done any due diligence. I doubted whether any of us had truly pushed into the dense wilderness that stretched for dozens of miles to the west of our hometown.

Another thought occurred to me. What if we were still near our point of departure like the spell had described? Perhaps a part of the Earth in the vicinity of the Special Vendor had vanished and been replaced by whatever this was. If that was the case, then whatever resided inside this jungle wasn't a naturally occurring animal, but something placed here by the system.

Branches cracked around us as predators stalked our movements. "Can you feel anything?" I asked Jessica. Despite constantly scanning the surroundings, and my Sixth Sense ability, I was coming up completely empty.

"No, I can't. It doesn't feel like there is anything near us." That just couldn't be a possibility, the movement in the underbrush was not up for debate. I heard it clear as day. We were being stalked by whatever it was that had taken a fancy to us. That or the jungle itself was alive.

"Let's get into a formation and keep moving forward," I said. "Alan and I will lead the front. Thomas, you remain behind us and everyone else behind Thomas." It was sort of a protect the healer type formation with Thomas remaining sandwiched between everyone.

Alan and I were the least likely to come into trouble if we walked upon something dangerous. With Bone Armor and my current HP I was close to Alan in terms of effective HP. He gave a nod and as we cleared the vines and branches in front of us and we stepped forward together.

Within twenty paces, the once solid terrain beneath our feet morphed into unsteady terrain and I studied the ground in front of me carefully so as to not plant myself face first into what looked and smelled like peat.

The trek through the jungle would have been a nightmare if it wasn't for my squad of summoned undead. The thick underbrush was overwhelming to say the least, and individually it would have been exhausting and tedious to struggle through it.

Even my abominations couldn't force their way through the vegetation by brute power, despite their strength. My two skeleton generals, however, along with several skeleton warriors took up the task to clear a way for us with their sharp blades.

Whatever was stalking us didn't give up, despite the strength we were showing as a unit. The bushes around us still shook and the occasional crack of a branch came from either side. Worst of all though were the bugs.

The mosquitoes tore away at us, "Gah, I wish there had been a repellent in the shop." Maria constantly swatted at her skin to fend off the biting insects. My concealing clothing was showing its value more so than ever before.

The long sleeves and almost trench-coat like clothing was keeping everything but my ankles and wrists protected. The bites to that area alone though were enough to drive me crazy with anger. I couldn't imagine just how the others were managing to hold up with this onslaught of pests.

Our surroundings slowly transformed into somewhat of a swamp, with a few paths of dry land surrounded by ankle-to-knee high water. Algae ranging from white to brown floated upon the surface. I immediately missed that mushy peat. At least it had kept my feet dry.

Dragonflies and other insects landed on pads of green before buzzing off into the dim light, and a stench of earthly decay filled my nostrils. The dense swarms of mosquitoes were thick enough it was possible to hear and see the clouds buzzing about.

"Can we change direction?" Jessica asked. Her face was scrunched into one of discomfort and the visible skin upon her arms and legs was already red with swollen bites. None of us were equipped to walk through water either.

We broke formation as a group and turning to the left I walked as far forward as I felt safe, I was looking for a possible path while also taking in the bushes and groves for signs of predators. Visibility wasn't great, but it was clear that the swamp continued for an unknown distance.

At least there was a path on the route we were on that we could take that would keep us above the water.

"Doesn't seem like it will be any faster or more rewarding to go around," Alan observed.

"As much as I don't want to travel through this, I have to agree with Alan," I said. "We can't be sure there will be a break in the swamp. If there isn't, we won't have any guarantee we'll have a path through like this one."

I didn't immediately set forward and instead waited for any objections. We were a group and while I had a lot of authority from my success at levelling, we shared the responsibility of calls like this one. In the end though, no one disagreed despite the reluctance on their faces.

We were stuck between a rock and a hard place, and the hard place ended up being the most logical solution. At least we could see what we were getting into here. No one could be sure it wouldn't be even worse if we set out to either side. There was the bonus of not having to forge a path through the swamp as well.

"I'll go first," I said trying to sound positive. I sent my skeletons on the path ahead, just in case the ground wasn't quite as solid as it looked. To my pleasant surprise though, their boney feet didn't sink into the dirt at all. The abominations, on the other hand, were too large for the path, so I just had them traverse through the swamp water carefully so as to not soak us in their wake.

The soil was spongy and each step caused sewage-like smells to be emitted that seared the nostrils. The thick trees growing from the knee-deep water were bleached by the sun, and were white and brittle and covered in algae that had no doubt remained from when the water was a higher level.

Even after an hour of walking nothing about the swamp had changed. The only thing letting us know we had made any progress was the sun slowly gaining distance in the sky. We were moving: time was passing.

My feeling that I was being watched by a predator slowly disappeared but that didn't offer any relief as my thoughts were now filled with the constant droning of insects, and the pressure of the sun pounding me from above. Our decision to sleep before transporting was the right one, no doubt. This would have been even more nightmarish after dark.

Every step through this murky land was arduous. My feet sank lower and lower with each step, and the peat gripped my ankles like panicked hands. I moved without much thought, only traveling where solid land took me.

My eyes spotted some swamp animals around, alligators mostly, but none so daring as to venture close. They stood locked in place like statues, their dark eyes peering with trepidation and curiosity. My abominations would take a relatively large step towards them, and the resulting wave that rushed ahead would send our admirers rushing away as if they had never existed.

"The map really is no help," Lucas complained. "I've been trying to get a grasp on where we are exactly and it's really just of no use."

"Well, at least it seems to be populating," Jessica chirped in from behind me. I checked. The map was completely blank ahead of us, but behind us and for a short distance on either side it had filled in with a small colored area illustrating the swamp. It was an interesting phenomenon, and potentially very helpful. At least we wouldn't get lost and – horrible though the thought was – could retrace our route to the jungle. Trees and ponds showed on the map in an animated fashion, even when I couldn't immediately see them.

"Was it doing this before?" I called over my shoulder. "I don't recall the map populating anything before…" Was this a new feature? Or if my theory that this might be a special game instance was right, perhaps it had unusual features including that of automating mapping.

"I was checking before," Lucas said. "This is definitely something new." I accepted his statement as fact and the conversation stopped there.

Finally, after we had walked another hour something changed.

"Look at the map!" cried Thomas and I did. There was something different there besides the mass of trees and the bending pond water. There was a structure, or was it a structure? I couldn't be sure.

"What is it?" Maria asked. "I'm still not very good with this map thing."

"I don't know," I confessed. There was a grey blob on the map, with a black dot. It looked like the entrance to some underground tomb. It was nearby, but I couldn't see it with my eyes; we must have come close enough for the map to show us its existence.

How had I not noticed this mapping feature before? Was I so negligent that I had never noticed this while we battled in the city streets? I shook that thought off almost instantly: Lucas said it was new, an extra feature either added when the Special Shop was implemented or because we were in a special zone. I told myself I should trust him.

"It doesn't look so inviting," Jessica said. "It's not natural, that's for sure."

"I agree." Lucas chimed in. A stone building or entranceway wouldn't be in this swamp naturally. "Can we just avoid it?"

"I think so too…" Maria said. She looked around nervously while rubbing her arms. The temperature was hot and humid, so the gesture definitely wasn't for warmth. She was clearly still shaken from her recent close encounter with death.

"I think it's worth the look," Alan said. "What if it's the location of a great treasure? We could all find skills and new equipment inside." His voice sounded so reassuring, but I wasn't reassured at all. No one could know what lay ahead.

I looked at the alligators in the distance, "This area doesn't seem to be too high level. A look might not be a bad idea."

"I'm for looking as well," Thomas said matter-of-factly. There was no excitement or fear upon his face, just a stoic expression, like nothing could affect him at all.

Everyone paused in deep thought. Treasure was enticing, but our lives were more valuable than any treasure…but then again treasure might help to keep us alive.

"…Just a look…" Maria agreed with a bit of hesitation.

"A small peek…" Lucas agreed reluctantly.

I turned to Jessica and gauged her reaction. Her eyes met mine and there was no fear or worry, just confidence, blind or not.

"I'm fine with checking it out." My answer came from her look, and she nodded to agree with me as well. "There doesn't seem to be any clear path that way though, so we'll have to wade through some water." Everyone's face immediately soured, "But think of the possible treasure." And my comment changed the mood immediately.

Chapter 2: Have we Found our First Dungeon Since the Apocalypse?

Distance wasn't easy to gauge on the system map, but the grey mark couldn't be more than a few minutes north of us, even in this slow-going terrain. Alan and I took to the front again while my abominations took each flank.

We did our best to find the shallowest water, but it was impossible to avoid soaking our footwear. I had to hold up the demonic garb to keep it from trailing through the murky dirty water. Thomas rolled up his jeans to his knees, which was enough to keep them from getting soaked when the water reached shin high levels.

A mere two or three minutes of walking through the swamp and we spotted the feature: inconspicuous at first, merely a mound of earth whose peak was some six or seven feet into the air.

The entrance was on the opposite end of us, and we had to circle around the mound before getting a good look at it. An arch of stones with a dark center was embedded in the earth. Each stone was dark and dirty, caked with a slimy layer of algae that appeared older than each of us. Vines twisted and slithered between every crevice giving it an ancient feel.

"This doesn't look like it's appeared here since the apocalypse; it could easily have been here for a century," Alan traced his hands carefully along the stone. The feel...the look, nothing was 'fresh' about it.

We walked behind him slowly as a group before standing just in front of the entrance. Being closer to the arch didn't help me see into it at all. Instead, the darkness just made me more weary and more anxious of what might wait beyond the arch. If it were a passage, then it felt like one that went on without end.

All that I could see were two or three steps of a staircase that led downward into the earth. What lay below, none of us could possibly know. Suddenly, there was flicker at the edge of my vision followed by a series of cracks like rolling thunder that made everyone jump with fright, "Jesus!" Lucas yelled.

Every single one of us turned back to look at the culprit, Maria, who was wiping fresh dirt from her hands. "What?" she asked innocently. "I just thought tossing a stone in would give us an idea of how deep it was..."

"A bit of warning would have been nice..." Lucas was wiping the sweat from his brow, and he received nods of agreement from his statement from nearly everyone. He was the closest besides Alan to the entrance, and had jumped nearly six feet in fright.

"So, did anyone actually hear Maria's rock stop?" I chipped in. In our fright not a single one of us was able to determine just how far down the tunnel the rock Maria had thrown went. What was clear though, was just how on edge everyone was.

Alan turned to Maria once again, this time urging her to chuck something else, "Get a bigger stone and ¾" he was cut off.

"Yeah, yeah." Maria sounded aggrieved, "Just a second ago you guys were chastising me..." Her voice trailed off into an inaudible mutter as her fingers pried out a melon-sized stone. "How's this?"

"A bit gentler this time..." Jessica urged, calmly. She, at least, didn't sound like she was filled with anxiety. Perhaps she and Thomas had their worries under control. Alan was clearly agitated though, and a bit fearful maybe.

Maria nodded at Jessica's suggestion and walked forward slowly before leaning forward and pushing the rock away from her, so that it hit the top stair and bounced down the staircase.

The cracking sound of thunder came again, but less intense this time. I listened intently as the stone tumbled away, each bounce knocking on the staircase like a distant drumming echoing outward and disappearing into the forest around us.

Although the principle was the same as tossing a rock in a well, I didn't hear any splash to allow me to estimate the depth... the rock kept tumbling until we could no longer hear the knocking. "How deep is that!" Face white, Alan looked more scared than the rest of us now. He would be at the frontlines if we decided to enter below.

No one answered his question, and instead Lucas countered with one of his own, "...What is it? Is this a dungeon?"

"That's...a likely possibility," I responded. This place was marked so clearly on the map: the atmosphere, the decrepit and uninviting look...it screamed danger...and adventure.

"Well, there's no indication that dungeons exist...and we've seen no announcement about them either." Thomas offered a different view. There was merit to every question asked, and none of them had clear answers.

There was only one answerable question currently to consider, "Do we dare go inside?" I asked with a sense of excitement. Dungeons could be great danger, but also great experience and rewards. The timing was bad, though.

We needed to return to our new fort and continue preparing for what was to come. Walking that distance when we didn't have our bearings? It could take up to two weeks. Two weeks was a long time in this new world, and a lot could change. I had given those people my word I'd keep them safe, and intended to keep it.

"How about just a look?" I asked. It was what we previously agreed upon. And knowing that Maria and Lucas had very little gear, I anticipated they would agree with me in the hope of getting good items. "Hands up if you are willing to see what it's like in there."

Only Alan failed to raise his hand. He looked at all of us, hesitant even to speak, there was a short silence before he voiced a complaint, "It's easy for you all to say…" His voice trailed off in a mutter, but I did manage to hear him muttering about the dangers of leading the front.

When his rambling had no effect on our desire to enter, he let out a sigh and gave us all a death stare before turning and facing the opening. "Just a look." His stern and serious voice wasn't all that reassuring, but everyone gave a few words of encouragement to give him that extra bit of courage.

One hand held that door frame while the other grasped the algae-covered stone. His head peered into the darkness and paused for a moment, "Can't see a damn thing." He complained. "Stay close behind me."

We huddled in a line behind him and, once at a time, entered into the darkness of the swampy pit. I had no choice but to cast Vast Shadows and park my squad of undead. They couldn't fit down this narrow corridor. That thought was slightly worrisome, but I bottled it up.

The darkness was overwhelming at first, but my eyes quickly acclimatized. There was nothing on the walls or the steps but more algae and dirt.

Alan swatted at cobwebs at the front with his spear, while his other hand sternly held his shield out front. The usual sturdiness with which he held it was gone, and instead I could see it trembling in his hand. "Careful, the steps are getting slicker." His voice was shaky and low.

There was a growing dampness as we traveled lower, and yet after about twenty steps there were no new features: just a narrow, dark descent that continued deeper with no sign of it ending.

The entrance behind us was the only source of light, and my visibility grew more and more limited as we continued. In almost pitch darkness, I guessed that the only thing allowing Alan to move forward was the knowledge that one stone step followed the next. A drip of water occasionally pattered onto the stone below, or splattered into a cheek or shoulder.

"Can you see anything?" Jessica asked. There was no doubt she was scanning the area for any enemies. If there were any, she would have alerted us already.

"Just what is this place…?" My hand traced the wall with curiosity, but came free with nothing but grime and a slimy substance.

"Just more steps" Alan whispered from below us. "Wait, I think we're coming to the end!" He said, "Stop, stop! Don't push!"

Everyone came to an as abrupt a halt as possible on these slippery steps. Hands grasped the wall and each other's shoulders in an attempt to keep from toppling over in one big mess. "What is it? What do you see?" shouted Maria from the back.

"Flat ground, there are no more steps." I could hear his spear tip tracing the ground slightly. The visibility was so bad he was basically walking blind and had no other option but to use the wooden spear as a cane. "It's just a hallway of darkness in front of me…" His face turned back and all I could see were his eyes, their moisture reflecting the barely visible entrance light.

"Well…we've come this far, should we go a bit further?" I asked. I was of the mind to keep going, but so far we'd seen nothing that suggested we were in a special – and potentially rewarding – dungeon. We were no doubt a decent depth underground. It was possible we could end up lost if this hallway turned into anything more than a single path.

"Let's just see what's at the end and make a decision then…" offered Jessica. We decided as a group, well…mostly.

"Are you alright Alan?" Lucas was directly behind our tank, and must have also sensed the discomfort he was facing.

"I forgot to mention…I don't really like enclosed spaces." His voice was shaky and uncertain. I suddenly realized that he had been struggling to make it this far, and we were only moving deeper into the darkness, with no end in sight. It wasn't monsters he feared, but the confinement.

"You're claustrophobic?" Maria asked.

"Very," Alan replied.

I spoke, "Let's just take a quick peek and turn around then." Everyone agreed. No doubt we all wanted to know what this was, what was located here. This was definitely out of the ordinary and must have some special reason for existing.

It took a while for Alan to begin moving again but at last I heard his spear scrapping on the floor and the clink of his step. Lucas began to move and then stopped, almost as if expecting something to happen. We were all expecting something…anything. But nothing happened.

A sigh of relief came from Alan, and then he started to move forward again. It was that next step that caused him to let out a yelp. "The ground just gave way a little, under my right foot!"

Then from all around, the sound of slow-moving stones, grinding deep within the walls of this pit filled our ears. "Turn around now and run!" Alan shouted frantically.

He was already at his wit's end, and the sudden commotion caused him to barge into Lucas who staggered against me. "Stay calm. We'll get out quicker without pushing. Turn back Maria please, lead us out."

To be fair to Alan, his panic stopped and we could begin climbing the steps. Unfortunately, it quickly became obvious there would be no easy exit.

The light atop the staircase, our ticket out, grew thinner and fainter, even though we were climbing fairly rapidly. It should have been getting lighter. It was then I realized what the stone moving commotion was. The entrance way was being sealed up, and soon after I had that thought darkness engulfed us completely.

My heart was in my throat, and the sound of Alan nearly hyperventilating drowned out all sounds except the droning mechanism of moving rock. I guessed he was on the verge of having a panic attack, but how could I offer any reassuring words? There was nothing reassuring I could say.

Alan hadn't been in favor of this journey below once he had seen the entranceway, and he had been dragged down from our nagging. If I tried to urge him to calm down and he exploded in anger, I wouldn't blame him for reacting that way.

Evidently, no one wanted to be the first to cut the tense atmosphere by saying something, and I was wondering what I could say to offer encouragement when lights suddenly appeared. The inside of the corridor began to glow as purple flames floated off the walls.

They started near the entrance and slowly lit up on each side one at a time before racing past us and into the distance. "What in the world—" muttered Lucas.

"This can't be re—" Maria stopped herself from even finishing that thought out loud. We weren't living in a logical world anymore.

"Is that a gate in the distance?" It seemed only Jessica was still fully in control of the situation. We all turned to look at what appeared to be a jail-cell type entrance about one hundred feet in front of us. What lay behind it, none of us could make out.

"Alan, are you okay?" I asked. There was only one path to take, and that was to keep moving ahead. We had to keep traveling deeper to get out of this place.

There was a moment before he responded, "Just a few moments... please." He was kneeling against the wall and calming his breathing.

"It's likely this pathway will open up into a bigger area. The system can't expect us to fight in such a narrow hallway," Lucas offered, patting Alan on the shoulder.

"I think so too." Jessica said. Everyone began giving their reassurances, and that little bit of hope seemed to give Alan some relief.

"Right..." Alan said. "It should definitely open up into a wider area." He pushed himself off the wall and took a deep breath before giving us all a glance.

"Everyone keep up your guard, we can't know for sure what lies ahead. There's no guarantee there aren't traps here as well," Lucas said.

"Once we can get into a more open area, I can summon one of my skeletons to lead the front," I suggested. "It should be able to trigger any traps for us. That way Alan can stay out of unnecessary danger."

"Does anyone have some extra potions?" Maria asked a bit timidly from behind. There was a shy interior underneath the thorny exterior she displayed. It was hard being a young girl in a world that was falling apart. Ghost Hand had been a cruel reality of a type that no doubt others still faced.

"I have a few extra," Jessica turned back and passed her three to keep hold of in case of emergencies.

I gestured at the door. "Let's take it slow, one step at a time. We can figure out our best course of action once we know what we're facing." Everyone nodded in agreement.

Alan picked up the shield and spear from the ground and steadied his shaking hands. "One foot in front of the other..." He mumbled beneath his breath. It wouldn't have been audible if there was any other sound besides the pattering of small water droplets.

Chapter 3: The Ancient Pit: Floor 1A

The metal bars ahead were as thick as half a grown man's hand. Algae covered everything the rust didn't. Dark spots shadowed holes beneath each bar, no doubt the ending place of the dirty water that constantly raced down them.

As for what was beyond the bars, there was no purple light, just a pool of black. It seemed to me that the sound of our hesitant steps would let us know if there was a door or solid wall somewhere ahead. Fortunately, the noise of our footfalls and clinking armor didn't echo back but instead vanished into the darkness and never returned. It felt like there was a cavity here—an opening that would finally give us some space to organize ourselves.

'Here goes,' Alan pushed at the metal gate and after some resistance it suddenly gave way and swung open, he staggered through and I hurried after him.

Just beyond those bars was a dark room, and only after we'd edged deeper inside did those purple lights flicker on and grant us any vision. I could see that the walls, flagstones and roof were made of very smooth stone and that we were standing in the middle of one side of a perfect square, about twenty yards across and twelve feet high. Especially interesting though, were the carvings along the other walls. If I hadn't known we weren't in Egypt, I have assumed that these were hieroglyphics.

Maria was the last to enter the room, and as she stepped through the gate, I looked back with sudden anxiety, not for her specifically, but with the expectation that a cell-door would magically appear and trap us inside.

"Should Maria go back outside? In case it's a trap? But I guess there's no need to trap us when we're already trapped." Lucas must have been thinking along the same lines as me. He spoke with a tone of self-deprecation. There was no way out for us going back so even if a door locked behind us, we still had to go forward.

"True, but where do we go from here?" Jessica asked. She moved closer to the walls and focused her attention there as though not expecting an answer from any of us.

"There must be something here," I said.

"Maybe it's a puzzle." Thomas spoke for the first time since we had been cut off from the outside world. "Solve the puzzle, exit this place?" It was an interesting theory, and no one had any better idea.

"What about you Alan? Any ideas?" I asked. My question was really asked to gauge his condition and find out how he was doing.

"I'm not sure," he replied, "but I definitely feel a lot better in here."

I couldn't see how…but I wasn't claustrophobic. We had gone from being in a small tomb to a slightly larger one. It made no difference to me in terms of the sense of being trapped under-ground. At least I could summon my squad of skeletons here if need be.

"These sort of look like alligators to me," Jessica suddenly said while pointing at the drawings upon the walls. Everyone turned to her and we grouped around the images.

20

"Why are they holding swords?" Maria asked. Soon we were all peering closely at the drawings upon the walls, and there was a lot to study. Although the wall on the side we had entered was smooth, the other three walls at least twelve feet high, covered in depictions of who knew what.

Bats, snakes, alligators, owls, insects, and even fish with alarmingly large teeth covered no end of illustrated scenes. The one pattern that stood out to me was that these stories were not peaceful ones. They all ended up the same way, with normal-looking humans being eaten alive, or chopped up, or devoured in a multitude of gruesome ways.

"Is this...telling us our fate?" Lucas asked from beside me. The images were slightly raised from the wall, like Braille on a page. As his hands slowly traced along the tail of an alligator, Lucas was deep in thought; eventually he reached the head. "This almost looks like a—" and then there was a click before he could even finish his sentence.

Lucas's hand had pressed against the alligator's eye and the entire room shook like an earthquake.

"What's happening?" Alan reacted strongly. "What did you do?" He rushed to the corner and we all followed.

I thought the entire room was going to collapse, and for a brief moment I battled with myself. Should I summon my minions in an attempt to shelter the collapse? I turned to Jessica and mumbled my thoughts.

Her calm eyes were reassuring, but a bit scary at the same time. Was her calmness at the cost of her usual emotional experience? For some reason I had the feeling she was losing part of her humanity and it scared me. She gave me a shake of her head and then directed my attention towards the far wall.

"That's a path…" Lucas with a steadily growing in excitement. "That's our way out!"

I was inclined to hurry down the dark exit while it was open and most of the others followed me across the room. But Alan stopped us with a thought.

"Isn't it possible that we get a choice? Shouldn't there be two more paths?" Given the layout of the room, he had a point. Perhaps each wall had a path in the middle of it.

"Let's get looking then," I said. And we split ourselves between the two other walls, carefully looking for any figure whose head could be pushed to open a secret exit. It wasn't hard once we knew what we were looking for. In less than five minutes we had three pathways available to us.

"What now?" Maria asked. There was really no way to tell if there was any difference between them, at least not from here.

"Splitting up isn't viable. Once we enter inside the pathways might close," Lucas said. "If we are trapped separately, our chances of survival drop dramatically."

"No one disagrees with that," I answered. "But how do we choose?" My first thought in response to my own question was a glance look to Jessica, who already knew what I wanted.

"There are no signatures. I don't sense any monsters nearby anywhere."

"Well that's our best chance at gathering information out the window," Lucas said.

"Does it matter? We can pick at random." Alan suggested.

"You'll be tanking, so it might not matter to us, but to you…probably." Thomas reminded him. Alan's face darkened and I couldn't help but give Thomas a look as if to say, now why did you have to go and say that…

Alan only pushed at Thomas's shoulder and gave a rare laugh. They knew each other before the apocalypse, whereas I wasn't familiar with the humor and banter that existed between them.

"What if the walls give us the answer?" Maria suddenly asked. "The scenes aren't the same on each."

"Right!" Lucas agreed, "I don't know why I didn't think of it before." He moved rapidly towards the nearest tunnel, and I almost felt the need to calm him down. "Where were the switches on this wall?"

"For that wall it was the fang of a snake," Jessica pointed.

"This one was the abdomen of a locust, or some sort of bug; don't know for sure." Alan had walked over to the opposite exit.

"Okay, and the other one was the eyeball of an alligator, or maybe a crocodile," Lucas finished. "So, it's possible the depictions indicate what we might be facing inside each pathway."

"Well, it wasn't strictly just those trigger creatures that were different," I pointed out. "There were other animals on each sliding panel that might have been different too."

"Right, so does anyone remember what was on each?" Lucas asked expectantly. A large portion of each wall was now gone, having slid aside to create an opening.

"I think this one was mostly insects," Maria said while pointing towards Alan's doorway. It was the one where the switch was the abdomen of a locust.

Jessica sounded thoughtful, "The snake fang wall was mostly reptiles. I think there were bat-looking creatures and other flying buggers as well."

"The alligator one had those weird sword-wielding amphibians, but there were also birds wielding polearm-looking weapons as well," Lucas said.

"Insects, reptiles, or weapon wielding demi-humans?" I asked aloud. "It's not an easy decision, so we should talk it out."

"Agreed. There's bound to be pros and cons of each pathway based on what the depictions showed," Lucas chimed in. "What do we think about the insect-based pathway?"

"Pass. I hate bugs," Maria said.

"Also pass, not doing bugs either," Jessica immediately followed up. I was flabbergasted, and almost expected them to high-five for their common dislike of multi-legged creatures.

"That's good and all, but does anyone have a real reason why it's a bad choice?" Lucas tried to make the discussion a more serious one.

"Poison," Thomas replied. "Could be lots of poisonous bugs. I can't cure poison either."

"Insects swarm, which might be hard for me to tank. Not only that, clouds of insects will make travel difficult depending on the terrain. Small, poisonous bugs sound like a nightmare," Alan added.

Lucas nodded. "Okay, those are good points. Poison truly would be a nightmare if we have no way to cure it reasonably. What about the second path?"

"I think the second path could be good." Jessica said. "Maria and I are both ranged. We should be able to deal well with any flying creatures."

"The rest of us are melee though. Mike would be almost entirely useless," Lucas said.

"There were snakes there and other reptiles as well," I added, "those could also end up being poisonous."

"And the third path?" Lucas asked. The was the original pathway he had opened by accident. "It seemed to have only demi-human creatures. Straight forward-looking brutes wielding swords and polearms."

"Well, we wouldn't be snuck up on by such enemies," Maria said.

I shrugged. "Jessica can sense nearby enemies, so that probably wouldn't be an issue. I think if we have to fight creatures like those, it would be more straightforward though. They use human weapons—combat should be more predictable."

"I like predictable," Alan said, "I'd rather block swords and polearm swings than deal with poisonous snakes and insects. Flying little buggers give me the heebie-jeebies." He started to rub his arms.

"They look more formidable though." Thomas said. "Judging by the humans they are devouring, those things could be seven-to-ten feet tall."

"Mike's minions should be an invaluable asset though. Even if these lizardmen are stronger, I'd prefer this path over the others," Alan said. Silence fell for a few moments. I felt that a more straightforward combat suited us. A stat check encounter was just up our alley. No one disagreed and Lucas gestured to the corridor he had opened.

"Gather close. We should enter together as swiftly as possible. The doorway might close and if anyone is separated... this may end up being your tomb," Lucas reminded everyone.

Maria frowned, "do you have to be so dramatic about it?"

"Sorry, that was a bit dark," Lucas agreed, "let's get our bearings and go from there."

"Agreed," I said, feeling that Lucas joining our ranks was paying off dividends now. It was heartening to have someone in the group who didn't mind taking up the reins and giving a lead to make sure we acted as team.

Not only that, the morale around the group had changed for the better. The gloom and downcast atmosphere disappeared. We now had a direction, and the goal of escaping this place felt tangible.

"Alan lead the front with Mike just behind?" Lucas asked.

"Sounds good," I replied, "unless the area is open enough, in which case I will lead with a skeleton general. In that case, wait while I summon my troops."

With that, Alan hoisted up his shield and walked to the doorway with all of us carefully behind him.

There was no breeze, no sign of anything in the blackness ahead, and it made me start to speculate on what might be there. As far as I could tell, we were walking into a small box with no openings anywhere. I couldn't help but look at the sweat on Alan's neck, and the hairs that had risen. No doubt he was having second thoughts right now.

"Let's move," Lucas said, and we walked forward as a unit. There was no sound, no smells, just darkness in every direction, and then suddenly, there wasn't. We didn't hear the sound of a door close, or of any stone mechanisms in the walls. We were suddenly somewhere completely different: a cavern appeared in front of us, lightly lit by purple spheres near the walls. The uneven pattern of the purple lights made it seem like they were outlining some huge, ghastly creature, but that was just my imagination.

Behind us, the path we had taken to enter was now gone, covered up by solid rock that was moist with water and covered in rich plant-life. "Where…are we?" Lucas was the first to speak as we all took in the scenery around us. It was nothing like the solid stone room we had left, which had been old stone, bland and brown. No, this place was like an underground swamp. Thick with flies and mosquitoes, it was so humid here you could feel the warmth on your skin.

Plants of all shapes and sizes dotted the distance—

"Mobs are spawning all around us" Jessica suddenly cut off my observations. "Seems like fresh spawns." Her voice was lacking urgency, so I knew they weren't currently rushing to our location.

She pointed with a finger and I saw a demi-human enemy at least eight feet tall: a fully upright alligator-like creature wielding a saber half the length of my torso. It was at least one-hundred feet away from us and also below us.

I now realized that we were currently at the top of a stone staircase that led down to the plant-covered cave floor.

"It looks like it will be wide and open enough to use your minions at least, Mike," Alan said. I could hear the relief in his voice. We couldn't be sure what would eat us here and what wouldn't. He needed my intelligence gathering potential at the front.

Visibility wasn't bad from so high up, but that would change as soon as we went down. There were thick and tall palm-like plants that would come up to our waist; oddly colored flowers; and ferns as tall as our shoulders. Some were even taller than Maria.

"Good job the lizardmen are tall, at least they stand out from all that vegetation," I joked.

"Any intel on them?" Lucas turned to Jessica.

"Child of Sobek, level twenty-four, Exceptional enemy." She was staring at the eight-foot-tall crocodilian-type demi-human in the distance. "There's one more mob type, but I don't have any visual on it so I can't see what it is."

"Can you feel anything about it?" I asked her.

"Seems to be around the same strength, so not much difference probably."

27

"That's...not low at all." Alan seemed to be sweating bullets now. Level twenty-four was three levels higher than both Jessica and I, and countless levels higher than the rest of our party. Personally, I had been expecting something easier given the cakewalk it was traversing the swamp.

"Maria, stay safe in the back at all costs," I said. She was our lowest level by far, "Alan you focus on defense and step in only when the party needs it. Let my minions tank whenever you can. Lucas, I trust your judgment so sneak in attacks whenever possible, Thomas you keep us topped up to the best of your ability." I didn't bother giving Jessica any instructions; she already knew what to do and was an expert at dealing damage without getting aggro.

I pulled my minions from Vast Shadows and we descended the stairs as a group. Like magic, the stairs behind us disappeared and a message became clear in my head.

The Ancient Pit: Floor 1A

"Woah, did everyone get that?" Alan asked.

"I did...and I guess that confirms our suspicions," I said. A bubbling excitement was filling me.

"Right, this is a dungeon," Lucas agreed, "we need to be extra cautious."

"I'll send a minion out front; Alan go directly behind. Jessica notify us if anything untoward appears." I gave that quick command and then sent my Zweihander-wielding skeleton general out.

His footing wasn't great on this uneven cave floor. Even worse, the stone was covered in a thin layer of moisture that seemed like it would never disappear in such a humid environment. Once we were at even level, the visibility was terrible, too.

28

A pathway was already carved for us between high cat-tails and grass I'd never seen. It was sharp and thin, and still had surprisingly high rigidity. Upon close examination, there were faint saw-teeth along the edges as well, which would definitely tear you up if rubbed the wrong way.

The plants and flowers were vibrant colors of purple and red, with hints of pink and yellow but I didn't see any immediate danger from them, and Jessica had given no warning about the vegetation. I felt a tension in me rise as we followed the path the dungeon had set before us.

Only the sound of our breathing and the clanking of my minions' armor could be heard. No one wanted to start a conversation in such a strained atmosphere. The feeling on the back of my neck was clear: this place was dangerous.

We moved in single-file behind my Skeleton General, the rest of my minions at the very back of the group and out of the way. There shouldn't be anything coming from behind, but at least they wouldn't hinder our visibility that way. It probably gave Maria some peace of mind too, with such a blockade behind her.

It became clear after passing the first bend that we were actually going even further down. The pathway in front of us was spiraling around and heading to a floor much deeper than this one. The issue though, was the path itself. It didn't continue as smoothly as I would have liked.

The bonus was that it didn't lead us to any enemies. Every enemy was on some platform far beyond us, or several levels below. Nothing short of jumping or taking a rope would get us to them, not that we would rush into harm's way without knowing what we were up against first anyway.

Chapter 4: A Pit of Death Encounter in our Dungeon Crawl

"Guys…There's a pit of alligators beneath us," Alan suddenly warned. He was the first to spot it being just behind my general.

"It's okay, follow the path. Just be careful," I said.

"GUYS…There is no path," Alan said even more loudly. We couldn't help but huddle together and see that the path ahead stopped, and all that was available to us was a single vine. A vine hanging from the roof, with the other end gathered in front of us at the end of a causeway. Looking down I saw a pool of hungry alligators, and about eight feet away on the far side of a wall that stopped the alligators coming out towards them, stood two of the lizardmen that Jessica had identified as Children of Sobek, armed with long sabers. The way out was a corridor beyond them.

It was obvious at a glance that we could only swing down to the lizardmen one at a time, but they definitely wouldn't be courteous enough to allow us to take turns and set up. Combat would begin as soon as the first person landed, and that person could only be me or Alan.

"I think I should swing down first," I suggested. "I can use Vast Shadows and then instantly summon all my squad on the other side. That should buy enough time for everyone to follow safely."

No one agreed or disagreed in that moment. Everyone else was fixated on the pool of sloshing alligators below. Crossing the gap didn't look like it was as easy as just a quick slide down the vine. There was definitely going to be some airtime involved to land clear of the pool of alligators.

"How about I put an arrow into one of them?" suggested Jessica. "They can't reach us from down there."

It was a nice daydream, to have a position on high level mobs that would allow us to pick them off safely. But this challenge was never going to be solved so easily. I shook my head. "They could back away into that corridor; maybe even get reinforcements. Two we can handle, but not many more. I'd rather we swing down and try to get what advantage we can from the surprise."

"I'm not really sure I can do this…" Maria said from behind. "I'm not good with heights."

Jessica was the first to encourage her. "You'll do fine. You've been adding strength and dex so you'll have no issue hanging onto the vine. You're stronger than you think."

"Right. And for this fight you can stay up here with Jessica using your bows until it's over," I pitched in. "Then it might be possible for both you and Jessica to go down together," I added. They were both petite, and the thick vine looked like it could hold quite a bit of weight. Honestly, in a game-sense it might not even be breakable. Someone had designed this encounter and it was pretty clear what they wanted to happen. Not that I was going to try and cut it or anything.

"What about you three?" I turned to Alan, Thomas and Lucas. "Any doubts?"

"No problem here," Lucas said.

"Me either," Thomas added.

"I'm not sure…" Alan held up his spear and bulky shield. The two items would definitely prove an issue.

"You can come across after me without your shield and someone can tie it on and send it to you after. Can you make the jump just holding your spear?" I asked.

He started to move the spear between his hands a few times, then worked it through two straps on his chest. "Shouldn't get in the way if we do it like that and I'll strap the shield to my back."

"I'll swing over first, Alan after. I'd suggest Thomas next in case we need a healer over there pronto. Safety first." I took a good look around the group, made sure to catch their eye and get a nod. Then I cast Vast Shadow and gathered up the vine.

I had talked a cool game, but as I held the vine and leaned towards the edge of the drop I found my heart beating wildly.

"Hold a sec," Lucas stopped me before I swung out over the edge. He pulled the vine from my hand and then tied two separate knots about five feet apart.

"For a single hand and foot, that way you won't lose your grip," Lucas smiled. "We also need to tie a cord around the vine, so we can pull it back to us." And he put his backpack on the ground and rummaged, producing a thin climbing rope. At last he was done and he patted me on the back. "Stay safe."

I firmly grasped the top knot in my hand and then lifted a single foot and placed it in the lower. A single push from my other foot would send me hurdling over the edge and towards the other side.

My mind filled with a sudden anxiety: what if this encounter was designed as a trap and the vine would simply give way and I'd plummet to the pool of reptiles below. The nape of my neck was drenched with a cold sweat and a tingling sensation filled all my limbs. I was frozen in place.

"Mike," it was Jessica's voice. I looked over my shoulder at her. "I've got your back." She had an arrow nocked.

And that was all it took for the fear to dissipate, for the jitters to subside. I pushed with all my might and watched the pit below shift in my view. I was only a brief moment in the air before I pushed hard from my foothold—two seconds of hang-time—and then I let go and landed on solid ground beyond the pool.

The two Children of Sobek in front of me let out guttural roars before I could even gain my bearings. I released Vast Shadows and my army of undead burst forth. I didn't even need to give the command for them to rush forward. My life was clearly in danger.

My squad swarmed the two lizardmen and gave me a moment of respite. Two arrows flitted across my vision.

"Mike!" I looked up to see Alan yelling. There wasn't even time to respond when he was hurdling at me with unimaginable speed.

"Alan...too fast!" I yelled.

"Too fast! TOO FAST!" he yelled back. There was no stopping him now. I braced myself to catch him as he swung past me and let go on the way back. I found myself flat on my ass, Alan on top of me. "Nice catch," he said embarrassingly.

"Go, go!" I struggled to get him off me. The Children of Sobek were no pushovers; my connection to a skeleton general had been lost, and a regular skeleton as well. A brief fifteen seconds and two of the squad were down.

Alan rolled over before unstrapping his shield from his shoulders and holding it ahead of him as he fell into line with my squad. He heeded my advice and stabbed out repeatedly from behind the screen of my undead warriors, never overextending himself.

As I concentrated on the battle, Thomas landed and patted me on the back. Then Lucas. We four had got across the pool of alligators in under a minute and a half. My undead warriors had held the fort long enough, but with heavy casualties on my side. These lizardmen were no pushovers, and they had remarkable strength and defense.

The swings of their sabers broke the guard of every one of my squad except the abominations, and they attacked with incredible fury. Even worse was the ability the lizardmen used when reaching low HP. When one of them was looking very wounded, it spanned in a circle—a standing death roll—and smashed and gashed my minions to pieces.

This ability was the bane of melee attackers, and with one of the Children of Sobek dead, I had only four of my squad remaining: my shield-wielding skeleton general; two abominations, and the one skeleton warrior lucky enough to be using a bow.

I had yet to use Summon Skeleton Mage, as we hadn't fought a single enemy since I had purchased it from the secret shop. But after this encounter I was planning to do so for sure. I needed to increase my ranged arsenal.

There was no doubt about how powerful these enemies were, and so I immediately reanimated the first Child of Sobek to fall, erasing one of my beloved abominations in the process. With that extra strength on our side, the second lizardman died much more swiftly, as to be expected. From up on the platform, Maria and Jessica poured arrows into the remaining mob nonstop, and Lucas could use Wind Slash from a safe range.

My heart finally slowed down after the lizardman performed his death spin and then collapsed. I reanimated this body too, as I was convinced these Children of Sobek were more powerful than my abominations. Dungeon monsters that were exceptional must be at least a step above monsters found in the open world, or at least I told myself that.

Unfortunately though, I needed to use a trump card to compensate for my losses. "Stand back, everyone." I cast Temporary Grave for the first time to replenish my regular skeletons. A murky mire of fog and death rolled over the cave floor.

Undead hands grasped the air and a deathly moan pervaded the area from every direction. Illusionary tombstones appeared and the stench of death filled my nostrils. If I had been unaware this was a skill, I'd have believed fully we were in a graveyard right now, one filled with ghoulish ghosts.

I cast Summon Skeleton, and then followed it up with Summon Skeletal Mage. Five beautiful skeletal mages appeared in front of me, 'beautiful' probably wasn't the right word—definitely wasn't the right word—but it felt right. Their eyes indicated their element. Each socket glowing with hues of deep red, icy blue, stormy yellow, shadowy darkness.

Not only that, Summon Skeletons raised another skeleton warrior. Unfortunately, it wasn't a skeleton general this time despite getting one every three skill levels before that. Was it possible + skills didn't affect the special attribute? Maybe it needed to be base level 9 on its own to get a new general.

As for Skeleton Mages, I could only summon two from the skill level, but with my being level 21 and having the necromancer passive, five was currently my maximum. I wouldn't be able to use Temporary Grave for at least another 24 hours, which was unfortunate, but it was well worth the sacrifice to add these minions to my army.

The growing issue was my MP. I had to cast Vast Shadows multiple times already today, resummoned two reanimated dead, and both Summon Skeleton and Summon Skeletal Mage. My MP was teetering on the brink of nil. I did have three points still available I could put into WIS and decided to do that for a bit more MP and Regeneration.

Name: Mike Reynolds [27] **Class: Necromancer Level:** 21 **EXP:** 9%
HP: 1085/1085 **MP:** 93/455
STR: 5 **Fear Resistance:** 5
AGI: 2
DEX: 5
VIT: 29 +14
WIS: 27 +23
Available: 0
Skills: [A] Summon Skeleton LV. 9| **[A] Summon Skeleton Mage LV.** 2| **[A] Decay LV.** 2| **[A] Reanimate Dead LV.** 3| **[A] Bone Armor LV.** 2 | **[A] Vast Shadows** | **[A] Temporary Grave LV.** 1 | **[P] Sixth Sense** | **[P] Bravery LV.** 2 | **[P] Mutated LV.** 2| **[P] Pain Resistance LV.** 2 | **[P] Skeletal Mastery LV.** 4| **[P]Intimidate Living** |**[P] Inner Calm LV.** 2 |**[P] Necrotic Vision**

I still hadn't fully recovered from the Sphinx encounter as it was. To spend over 250 MP in such a short time frame was unthinkable for me. Things would have to go much more smoothly as we continued or I would be out of gas before long.

"Everyone make it over in one piece?" I asked. While I had been reconstructing my undead army, Maria had taken the risk and swung over the alligators, to the welcoming arms of the three others below. Jessica had landed lightly on her own feet. From a glance it seemed that we had come through the encounter unscathed. Maria was still clinging closely to Jessica, and had a bit of jitters, but was unharmed.

Everyone else seemed to be taking in the moment, as it wasn't every day you got to swing over certain death. "Those gave a lot of EXP." Alan suddenly said.

"Actually, yeah," I echoed. EXP wasn't what I had looked at immediately, but I was currently at 9% now, so each mob had given me around 4.5%. That was a pretty remarkable number for a single mob shared among a six-player party. It was encouraging. If we could fight on through this dungeon, we all might come out of it with an extra level or two.

Chapter 5: How to Make Your Group's Tank Happy

Now that we had crossed the alligator pit trap, the question was what to do next? A short, dark pathway waited in front of us, quickly turning to the right and no one could see around the corner to know what was on the other side. There was no choice about where to go, the issue was when.

"I'll warn everyone now; my MP is dangerously low. I can, at best, re-summon my squad one more time," I said. "With that in mind, you all should decide if we camp here for now, or continue." Even being so low MP I was of the mind to continue.

We had battled only two enemies, and I didn't know if they were permanently gone or were on spawn timers. It was possible they could respawn on us in just a few minutes. It wasn't safe to sit on a spot where we knew mobs had patrolled or spawned before. "It's possible those two Children of Sobek will respawn atop us shortly, though." I voiced my thoughts aloud.

A tally of the group showed that I was the only one suffering from low MP; everyone else was at a reasonable level to continue. Fortunately, this time I wouldn't need to cast Vast Shadows. While my abominations could not fit into the corridors, now I sported two undead Children of Sobek who did.

It was tight fitting, but my squad managed to squeeze into the tunnel and as a group we pushed on into the darkness. Alan's claustrophobia started to act up, but the journey was quick. Thirty seconds and we were in and out.

This time, however, I wasn't expecting what we found.

The Ancient Pit: Floor 1

It seemed that our previous floor was merely an introduction for this new region. We weren't in a cave anymore, or at least I couldn't be sure if we were. It was…open. If I could see a sun in the sky I'd have believed we were outside.

A vast landscape appeared before us, swampy and dense and filled with plant-life and insect-life and goddamn mosquitoes. An entire ecosystem existed here, and I had not a clue as to which way to go.

The ground beneath us was that same spongy, peaty substance we'd been travelling through, and the occasional hard rock. Pools of water rested here and there with lily pads floating atop. Sun-dried algae added a bit of swamp snow from where the water must have once devoured the roots of ancient trees.

"More Children of Sobek all around," Jessica announced, "some patrolling and some stationary." It seemed I wasn't exactly spot on with my guess either. "Other enemies too, not Children or the other mob-type, new ones," she warned.

I glanced around the tree tops to see winged creatures, large and small staring at us hungrily. The occasional splash of water sounded, moving away from us into the depths of the swamp. Perhaps a frightened mob?

There was no wall behind us either, we were dead smack in the middle of 'Floor One' and I had no sense of where there might be an exit. "Where to now?" Alan asked. It was always the question on his mind. He was the tank, he was the frontline, and he needed to know.

"We pick a direction and walk till we hit an end to the floor?" Lucas suggested. "Then we follow the wall to the next room or the exit." It was a good plan as any, but it didn't exactly answer the question.

"We still need to pick the direction we walk in," I pointed out.

"Forward is a good direction," Alan said. Presumably he meant the direction we were facing when we landed, and that seemed to work for everyone. I sent a skeleton general to the front, the Zweihander-wielding one. There was no path here to follow, and he made quick work of the waist-high bushes blocking our chosen route.

Alan followed several feet behind, and it became apparent very quickly the previous floor had not prepared us at all for this one. Within just a few moments of walking, Alan received a rude awakening.

"Ahh!" Alan screamed. From behind him, despite the shorn vegetation, it was hard to see what was happening. Stepping to the side allowed me to see the scene, his wooden spear had pierced directly through a plant.

The petals of the bush were opening and closing like a jaw, over and over again, while trying to travel up the shaft of the spear. I directed my skeleton general to cut it in half, and it bisected it along the stem. Green goop poured out from within and the struggling ceased shortly after.

"What was that and what happened?" Lucas rushed forward. The whole conflict had taken only two or three seconds.

"The plant attacked me," Alan said. He held out his left arm, which had originally held the spear. The skin along his forearm was red and a bit bumpy, like a bad rash. "God, it fucking itches so bad," he complained.

"It looked like an over-sized Venus fly trap," observed Maria.

I nodded, "It completely ignored my skeleton general, which means it could sense that you were living. That or it couldn't sense my undead."

"I couldn't sense it, either," Jessica added, "doesn't track at all." It was unfortunate, but I had to conclude that there were plants, or traps, that my skeleton general would not be able to scout for us.

"Let me see your arm." Thomas pushed through our circle and grasped Alan by the elbow. He cast a heal, which only slightly abated the symptoms Alan was experiencing. "It almost looks like a chemical burn."

"Acid then, from the plant," Maria suggested. "It was going to digest you if it could have."

"Keep an eye on that arm and if anything about it changes tell us immediately," Lucas said and I understood why. There was always the chance Alan had been poisoned and the effect wouldn't trigger till much later.

"I'll stay with Alan at the front," I suggested. My skeleton general could still lead the front, but Alan and I could follow up, him on the left, me on the right. There was plenty of room here to move side by side.

I only truly appreciated the size of the floor after I got a good view of the swamp that was hidden beyond the tall bushes. Apart from a lack of breeze, it was exactly like being outdoors, the swamp stretched out to the horizon.

"I can't...see the end," beside me, Alan looked surprised.

"Me either." As everyone quickly came to join us and peered into the distance, there were several more murmurs about the size of the place.

Ahead of us were a choice of short, winding paths crisscrossing through the dirty swamp water. It would be possible to traverse the swamp without going into the water, but even then it did not feel not safe.

"There are mobs strewn all about," Jessica said, "most likely hidden in those pools." If that were true – and she was almost certainly right — it would be impossible to see anything coming from afar, and the possibility of being hit from behind or the flanks defeated the point of choosing a head 'straight-forward' strategy.

"I prefer we go around the swamp, even if it takes a lot longer," I said, "do we need to vote?" But immediately I got assent from everyone else: the decision was unanimous. No one wanted to be attacked from behind while trekking single file and with uneven footing, especially as we didn't even know what kind of mob the enemy might be.

We chose to go right and follow the border of the swamp with the region of bushes, which brought us quickly to our first battle.

"Three Children of Sobek," Jessica said. "They seem to be patrolling but I suggest we pull them now: we will have to fight them eventually."

She was right and since the mobs were moving across our route I quickly barked a game plan. "Jessica, Maria, you two utilize Entangling arrow, Quagmire Trap and Ankle Snare to completely hold the one on the right. Alan I'll trust the one on the left to you alone: as long as it doesn't go below half you won't have to deal with its death roll, focus on defense. Lucas and I will take down the third, Maria and Jessica can add damage to ours whenever possible."

A quick glance around confirmed that everyone understood. We moved to a more open area that suited us before prepping for battle. Jessica got the closest and laid a Quagmire trap before placing an Ankle Snare just behind. As the three Sobek walked across our line of sight, Maria charged up Explosive Arrow and then on my signal, "Go!" released it.

The fiery arrow collided with the ribs of a Child before exploding into a fiery mass. In response, the three lizardmen let out visceral roars before unsheathing their sabers and rushing directly at Maria.

"Hold!" Jessica yelled, "let them hit the Quagmire!"

Alan was prepped with shield and spear in hand while Thomas and Lucas waited to the side, ready to act. My squad of undead warriors were ready at a moment's notice as well. Battle was imminent.

The Quagmire Trap triggered, "Now!" Jessica yelled. Alan immediately cast Charge and intercepted the left-most Child. A Battle Shout followed immediately after as he swiftly backed away from the pack, shield raised.

Metal clanged as Alan retreated, half-kneeling, doing his best to take as little damage as possible. Thomas was positioned behind him and constantly prepared heals while canceling them at the last moment if they weren't needed.

My undead troops rushed forward and dog-piled the center Child while Maria shot out an Entangling Arrow on the third, which turned towards her, but hit the Ankle Snare shortly after. I hoped that the three combined CC abilities would have it locked in place for a long time.

The three mobs were properly separated now, which gave Lucas his opportunity. He joined my mass of undead warriors and used

Wind Slash from a safe distance. While my undead squad members were decent tanks, they didn't hold aggro like a real tank did. Lucas would most likely be the focus if he stepped into melee range.

This was the first battle in which I'd get to see my mages in action, and I was incredibly excited to see their white and boney hands glowing various colors as their elemental magic was launched. Lightning bolt, Ice bolt, Fire bolt and even a Shadow Bolt were cast every few seconds.

My expectations for the impact of this were high, despite the skill only being level two. In the future, after leveling, these magic bolts were likely to deliver significant damage. Regardless, even now damage was damage and the middle lizardman was suffering a constant barrage of magic bolts.

My two Reanimated Children of Sobek were also putting in massive work, and my decision to reanimate them was obviously the right one. Despite being weaker than their opponent, they were able to guard against the saber slashes and minimize their damage taken.

Not only that, they were doing big damage in return. In just under ten seconds, the middle Child of Sobek died. There was no opportunity for it to even death roll. One of Lucas' Wind Slashes cut off an arm, and the other was frozen in a block of ice from an Ice Bolt and then shattered by an Explosive Arrow from Maria.

"How are you holding up Alan?" I yelled as soon as our first enemy was put down.

"Fine! Leave me for last!" he yelled back. I had to admit, the constant banging and screech of metal on metal to my left worried me. Still, I trusted his judgment and turned my attention towards the Child of Sobek impatiently waiting for the timer of Ankle Snare to run down.

My undead squad washed over the pinned lizardman like a tide: the damage from my summoned troops, paired with Jessica and Maria unleashing their full fire power, meant the Child of Sobek could barely even start its death roll before it perished. Our damage was just too insane. If this was a game, I'd have grown bored already, but it wasn't. This was real life now, and I was determined to survive any way possible. The encounter ended almost anti-climactically, with us backstabbing the remaining enemy in mere seconds. My hunch was that whoever was behind the system had not anticipated anyone becoming this strong – it was partially dumb luck on my end that we had become so – and so the challenge of this pocket dungeon was not as tough for us as it would have been for most.

An item rested above the third corpse, which Alan scooped up almost on reflex. "It's a SHIEEEELD!" he yelled.

"Show us the stats," Lucas asked.

Steel Bulwark: An incredibly heavy shield that most attacks cannot penetrate.
STR +2, VIT +5, Attack Speed -10%

This drop was a perfect fit for Alan, who was already carrying an incredibly heavy shield as it was. This new one was definitely going to provide better protection, though.

"How does it feel?" I asked.

"Light as a feather." Alan laughed while barely managing to raise the Steel Bulwark above his shoulder. Another second like that and it looked like he would topple over. Our tank, however, was on cloud nine.

Chapter 6: The Danger of Pulling Trains When the Game is Real

Probably the typical party would find this place a nightmare, maybe even unclearable without serious grinding to gain levels. When I thought about that, I remembered Jessica and I had unused EXP potions available. These mobs weren't bad EXP at all, even when split among a six-person party.

Arguably, the potions could be better used if Jessica and I were to duo, but the dungeon's difficulty could ramp unexpectedly and then we'd be that imaginary party having to stop progressing in order to grind EXP. With that thought in mind, I realized the biggest growth in our group power would be via my party members, rather than myself or Jessica.

The others were level 16-18 range, Maria being level 16, Lucas 18, and both Thomas and Alan level 17. I flashed the potion in my hand to Jessica, which got me a confused look back. "Exp potions," I said. "Why don't we pass out at least one to each of them." My eyes glanced over the others who were still glowing from Alan's first item drop.

"We have six, so that's one for each of us," Jessica said. "We can save ours for a better time." I liked how easy-going, and even selfless she could be, and something of my feelings must have shown in my eyes, "What?"

"Nothing." I shook off my contemplation of my beautiful comrade. "Let's give them out and keep moving. It must be around midday right now, we need to find somewhere safe to camp for when we all get tired." Everyone else was still crowded around Alan and gawking over his new wear.

"One for each of you," I said while passing the potion bottles out.

Lucas held up the grey liquid with a confused look, "What's this?"

"EXP up potions, they give Increased EXP gain. It might be wise to use them if we start killing a lot of monsters."

"Is the boost time based, or does it run out after a set amount of EXP gained?" Lucas asked a good question. Many games made potions last a duration of time, but others might have their effect last for just a certain quantity.

"Honestly, I'm not sure. Never used one and it doesn't say in the description," I replied. The difference between the two though, was enormous. One meant the faster you killed, the more you were rewarded. The other meant regardless of how fast or efficient you were, you got the same benefit from each potion. It was easy to see which would be more 'fair.'

"What will you do with this thing?" I turned to Alan while nudging my foot into the tower shield previously used as his shield. It was a mess. The shield edges were chipped and bent. There were dozens of gashes digging into the metal frame as well.

"I'd like to say I'd keep it for sentimental val—" Alan started before Thomas started at him.

"Who are you kidding? You've never been sentimental a day in your life." Thomas laughed, "Just toss the thing."

"Yeah, I guess." Alan took one good look at his old shield on the floor then picked it up. He held it in both hands and then for some reason had the bright idea to spin in a circle to build up momentum before chucking it.

"Jesus Christ, a little warning!" Maria yelled at him after nearly being hit by the sweep of the shield. The rest of us made distance while Alan spun like a Child in death roll.

"Alleyoop!" With one final circle, Alan threw the shield as hard as he could and fell clean on his ass. His strength was impressive to say the least, as the car door had decent airtime. It hurdled towards the swamp and then landed in a small pool with a loud splash. The noise was nothing to scoff at, and every single person gave him a dirty look. "Whoops..." He started to scratch his head.

The door disappeared beneath the water with a gurgling bubble that rumbled through the air. There was no doubt that this was the start of a new chapter for Alan. He had been using the burnt and nearly destroyed car door since his journey started and it was clear he had wanted to mark the moment. But I was uneasy about having made a racket. And so were the others. No one could take their eyes off that little pool.

"Careful!" Jessica yelled suddenly. "From the front!" I was caught in a brief moment of confusion. The front was the swamp and that small pool, and I saw nothing threatening coming from that direction. The dark pool continued to seethe and bubble just as before, and only in that moment did I realize what had happened.

There was almost no time to react as a reptilian head nearly as thick as the pool burst forth. Snake-like, with black and brown splotches all over, the monster had green eyes that came to a point as sharp as any dagger. The creature's jaw was filled with razor-sharp teeth that curved like the claw of a bird of prey. Powered by a neck of pure muscle the snake sprang from the depths.

It towered over us a dozen feet high, looking at us like pests that had disturbed its cozy slumber. "Alan!" I yelled, but he was already getting to his feet, new shield in hand.

We were just about to engage when Maria's panicked voice drowned out everything else, "What...should I do?" I turned to her in that brief moment to see a tentacle-like appendage rip from her side and disappear into the swampy mud. Her hands clenched her side quickly, but her face was one of panic and pure confusion.

"Alan hold on defense while we retreat!" I yelled. There would be no battle, we needed to run or Maria would die. "Thomas, heal Maria!" No one but me had noticed exactly what happened, but as soon as the group turned to see her drenched in blood that was quickly flowing through her fingers, everyone understood. It was a sneak attack.

Jessica reached Maria even before me, as I frenziedly sent out my minions to deter this unknown enemy. Alan charged forth as well, feet nearly dipping into the swamp as he attacked as if enraged. He didn't have time to look back, but he could probably hear from our anxious cries that Maria's situation wasn't good.

A bandage was already in Jessica's hand as she haphazardly wrapped Maria as quickly as she could. Thomas sent a heal, and Lucas scooped Maria up without a second thought. "Hold that monster for just five seconds!" I instructed Alan.

The creature was spitting out green globs of goopy acid that sizzled upon his shield. There was no time for Alan to even open his mouth to respond. Any lapse in judgment might have him melting into a liquid goop.

"This way!" Jessica said. She was the only one who could lead us right now. There were enemies all around us, and she needed to maneuver us as best as possible through this part of the dungeon. She took off in a rush that almost made it hard for Thomas—me as well—to keep up with her.

Neither Thomas nor I had focused on STR, although we each had enough to get by reliably. We were slipping behind, and even Lucas—who was carrying Maria in his arms—gained considerable ground on us.

"Don't worry about us! Keep going!" I yelled ahead. Jessica was constantly swiveling her head back to see the situation, slowing her own speed. I did the same, just in time to see Alan rushing in our direction like a madman. He was red-faced yelling with his bulwark across his back, two hands behind his shoulders holding it up like a turtle shell.

The swamp creature continuously spit out gloopy acid balls that mostly missed, but occasionally landed on that thick board of a shield. Even he, with the massive weight on his back, was gaining on us—good news, truly.

The humidity here did nothing to stop the burning in my throat. I huffed like a man on his last breath, desperately trying to get any amount of oxygen into my body. My calves were spent; this swampy ground was hell to move through. Every step more arduous than the last with this muddy ground gripping so tight.

Things were looking better, until they weren't. It was an honest mistake, a slight miscalculation: Jessica was pathing for herself and Lucas, skimming through patrolling packs at the perfect interval to avoid triggering the mobs. The same could not be said about me and Thomas, and, in our wake, Alan.

I could not stop following Jessica and Lucas, quite apart from the giant snake chasing us, visibility was poor because of the bushes and the deep pools I was splashing though. It would be easy to lose sight of them. That might be a complete disaster, as I had no magical way to find their location again. Moreover, splitting up would bring about the most dangerous situation possible for all of us and it would probably mean Maria's life was forfeit, with Thomas unable to heal her wounds.

So I had to keep running in the wake of Jessica, even though mobs had moved dangerously near to her route. And the inevitable happened. The mobs inadvertently pulled were a pack of three Children of Sobek. As they charged after me I had no idea what would happen. I'd seen situations where monsters did de-aggro, but this was a dungeon. Would they trail behind us for eternity or eventually fall off?

No one could know, we were quite possibly the first humans to step foot into a dungeon in the world—a thought that may have been quite satisfactory ten minutes ago—and knew nothing of the rules. I couldn't turn and fight either, and so I kept running.

The Children of Sobek did fall behind surprisingly quickly; they were strong, but clearly that strength didn't translate into speed. The bad news though, was that they didn't stop chasing. They continued on our trail, and by the time Jessica had come to a stop—nearly five minutes of sprinting—we had another pack on our trail. Quite a train was developing, one that might already be too strong to face in battle.

Having caught up with Jessica at last, I would not have been surprised in that moment had I started coughing blood. My throat was dry, and cracked, and my mouth a thick paste. Nevertheless, I strained to force words. "Six...enemies. One minute." I forced out barely coherent gibberish.

My hands came to my knees as I almost collapsed to the floor, throat burning with every hack coming from my throat. My saliva was thick and the moisture in my mouth was non-existent. Sheer will forced me to stay standing. Every second was crucial, and my eyes scanned our surroundings intently. The location was important, terrain was important.

Jessica had brought us to a stone wall, presumably one of the borders of this first floor. A small cubbyhole was in front of us, merely three or four feet deep into the wall. Not enough to call it a cave, but enough to place Maria down inside. "What did you say?" Lucas asked as soon as he stood up from putting her on the flat rock.

Maybe the best decision was to keep running. The giant snake would arrive in moments and we didn't know how long that encounter would last, nor how strong of an enemy it was. The fact it attacked Maria through the ground was also problematic. Fortunately, it hadn't tried to do the same to Alan. Hindsight was twenty-twenty.

Splashing out of the swamp, breath rasping, Thomas pushed by me without a complaint, urging Jessica to move away so he could work his magic.

"Enemies. Coming," I said still struggling with my breathing. There was a commotion behind us a moment later, and I turned in fear, we weren't ready. Lucas drew his sword and held it in both hands, ready to strike.

The thick shrubs shook like a lion was inside and ready to pounce. My heart was in my throat as the figure burst through. It was Alan. "Six lizard guys right behind me…maybe twenty seconds," Alan said. He was breathing heavily, but not nearly as much as I or Thomas had been.

"Jessica, we need you!" Lucas called back. Looking deeply unhappy, she was pacing back and forth near Maria. Ever since she had trained her Expert Tracker passive skill, she had seemed confident. I'd even wondered if I'd ever see a panicked look on her face again. Well, it was there now. This wasn't good for the situation, but she was right to be desperate. Maria lay behind us dying, while a giant snake and six Children of Sobek rushed upon us and threatened to take our lives.

Chapter 7: Stuck Between Swords and a Hard Place

"Leave her! You can't help me," Thomas said to Jessica through a fit of coughing. "Maria's been healed as much as she can. Only time will tell if she makes it." There was only so much a Bandage could do. I could see that Maria's outer wounds were closed, but was she bleeding internally? If Thomas didn't know then none of us did.

Jessica shook her head in angry agreement. Her clenched teeth and fierce mouth were directed at no one but herself. She was the scout, the tracker, the information gatherer. By all accounts she should have 'felt' the enemy coming—at least that's what she seemed to be telling herself. I didn't feel that way though. It was simply impossible to find a route through the complex pathing of the mobs when we were so stretched out. And our train could have been even worse.

"Six Children of Sobek, fifteen seconds away at best." She looked up towards the horizon, a familiar stoic expression returning to her face. And that was far better than regret. At least I knew she had made a choice, that she was preparing herself for a do or die fight.

"What about that snake?" I had the passive Inner Calm, but I couldn't be sure what effect it was having upon me. Whatever changes it made to my behavior were probably much easier to observe from the outside. For me, it was simply how I felt. Perhaps in the past my fear of death in a situation like this would have been greater; now it was present but ever so slight. Like a wall or thin layer of fog shielded me from panic. Those emotions were there, but a touch away. I could go to them if I chose, but how long would that be the case for?

Jessica shook her head. "Not coming. Not as far as I can tell."

The relief that ran through me had me wondering about Inner Calm after all. If I was showing calm, I wouldn't have felt it as a tremor as though an earthquake had struck. I shook the useless thoughts out of my head and focused on the ground between us and the incoming mobs. Alan took the front, as did Lucas. Jessica didn't hesitate to put out multiple Quagmire traps. I gave my minions a hard look and realized I might not have any left after this fight.

"Focus!" I said in a raspy voice. "Take them out one at a time, use my minions as shields or whatever you need. They can be re-summoned, but none of us can be revived." No one said a word in response. Every face was as hard as steel, burying their fears deep.

The sound of heavy steps slopping through the swampy ground, splashes of puddles and the ruffling of bush or tall grass grew louder, until they were drowning out everything else. Perhaps it was just my focus, but all I could hear was the approach of the six lizardmen.

We all instinctively backed away just a bit from the tall grass from which they were about to emerge. As far as we could without being right up against the wall: which would put Maria in harm's way. Fear, fear, and excitement coursed through me.

The Children appeared.

Alan, my undead warriors, and Lucas stood side by side to greet them. The moment they came through the tall brush, the first of them caught an arrow through the eye. Blood exploded from its face and guttural roars escaped all their maws.

Alan charged forth and took two by himself immediately, his spear constantly stabbing out from behind his thick shield. Every blow of his opponents' heavy maces sent his knees bending, his feet sinking just a tad deeper into this muddy swamp. Yet my heart filled with warmth for him. Alan was an impenetrable wall they couldn't get past.

Lucas was beside our tank, no care for his own safety in the way he committed himself to holding up one of the mobs. He seemed invigorated even—no doubt a side effect from his passive Ruler. He was getting a huge 60% boost to his stats. In the past, he wouldn't have moved from behind Alan, but now he stood toe to toe with a Child of Sobek, no easy feat.

The remaining three lizardmen were dog piled by my squad of undead, swarmed like intruders to a beehive. I couldn't even see the mobs behind my mass of undead. It was impossible to even tell how my skeletons were faring. I could feel the disconnect when one of them perished though, and they weren't going to last long.

My focus shifted to Lucas, whom I felt was most exposed. Alan was holding his ground beautifully, and Thomas was available to heal him still. What he said hadn't been to placate Jessica—only time would tell how Maria fared from her wound. There was nothing we could do for her but survive this.

I cast Decay over and over. A skill that I hadn't found much use for previously was showing its merit right now. The DoT didn't work on undead, and back in the city, most mobs couldn't hold a candle to Jessica and I so there was no point. The mobs were dead before it ever really made a difference. Now though, every contribution to our total damage counted, and it was imperative we were fast and efficient.

My focus was on the saber-wielding arm of the Child facing Lucas, specifically its shoulder. Under the impact of Decay, its thick, green-and-brown scales started to wilt at a speed visible to the naked eye. Sloughs fell off like a snake shedding skin. Lucas wasn't an expert, but he wasn't blind either.

His Nodachi came down like thunder, and cut across the lizardman's shoulder blade like lightning. Normally it would have left a gash, but its once-thick outer exterior was now soft and rotted like dead wood. One slice: that was all it took to see the entire arm fall, and its weapon with it. The arm had not even landed on the ground when a flash of light appeared on the Child's face, blowing it clean open.

The explosion was something that Jessica had cast, no doubt, but there was no time to ask her. None of us said a word, but Lucas moved like an assassin towards Alan. I cast another Decay without waiting at all, and that flash of light appeared again.

Within a matter of seconds we had dispatched two enemies. I felt elated, but also felt a sickening feeling in my gut as the MP poured out of me. Lightheadedness was overtaking me at the same time as the nausea crawled and slithered up my chest towards my head. Again! I cast another Decay.

I was aware that my MP was basically depleted, but I didn't care. My squad was nearly depleted as well—well, the melee ones—as only the shield wielding skeleton general, one reincarnated Child, and a single melee skeleton had survived the initial onslaught.

My mages continued to pelt spells from a distance, and that feeling of sickness grew stronger. My vision was blurring. Another

Child of Sobek fell and Alan was free to assist my skeleton general. The second reincarnated Child died just then as well, but not before its death roll dispatched another Child.

"Two left…" I mumbled with a stupid grin. The world was toppling around me. Huh? My vision swam, and then turned black.

I heard talking all around me, the sound muffled and distant yet so close. Nothing made sense in my head, and my vision remained black. A throbbing pain came first, right behind my eyes, and I couldn't help but let out a hiss in pain.

The sound came closer, excited and repetitive. A faint shadow cast over my closed eyes. I opened them carefully; a figure drowning out any light that might have blinded me. It was blurry at first, but eventually the face came into focus, the sound made sense.

"Mike, can you hear me? Mike?" It was Jessica just above me, face inches above mine, her expression showing all the concern and worry in the world.

I don't know what came over me, but all I could muster was pure stupidity. "It's you." I half-forced a smile that caused another spike of pain in my head. "How did it go?" I asked. Obviously, the Children of Sobek had been defeated, but at what cost?

"You passed out suddenly and all of your minions despawned. Lucas and Alan had to deal with the remaining two lizardmen alone while I dragged you to safety. Fortunately, they had taken decent damage already, and Lucas got away with a small cut to his forearm, nothing a Bandage and heal couldn't take care of."

I turned my head to the side and saw Maria still lying in the small cranny in the wall. A heavy, dark feeling started to swell up… "Is she…?"

"She's still alive." The face that was just happy to see me turned downcast. "As long as she's breathing, I won't leave her."

"No one is leaving," I promised. "If we have to carry her out of here unconscious, we do so." Jessica gave a firm nod while keeping her eyes locked on Maria. "How long has it been?" I asked while trying to sit up. An involuntary groan escaped my mouth.

Jessica's hands supported me. "Careful," she said. "You've only been out about an hour. Thomas healed you, but it's pretty clear you've not taken any damage. You're physically and mentally exhausted."

I managed to lean up with her support and glance over my party members. Everyone seemed in good shape. Alan was smiling and Thomas didn't have a scratch on him. Lucas had his back against the stone wall and was fighting what was obviously a battle against sleep. "It's probably near sunset now," I took a guess. "I wonder if there's a night-time in the dungeon."

Jessica followed my gaze to Lucas. "He really put up a tough fight after you went down. Alan had to support him so he could even walk over there. We told him it was fine to rest, but he insisted that he sleep when we all do: to keep our schedules as close together as possible."

There was suddenly a loud splash of water nearby, my head jerked without even thinking, causing another groan to escape my mouth. Was it the snake after all? We surely couldn't defeat it without my squad, even if we did have a wall at our backs.

"It's okay," Jessica did her best to calm my shaky nerves. "There's nothing nearby right now. There's also no patrols that come through here, we should be fine to stay the night."

I gave her a nod, "Can you help me get to the wall?" Like Lucas, I wanted to lean back against something solid. I wasn't exactly tired yet, but I'm sure it would be coming in the next few hours.

It was weird to feel Jessica easily lift me—carefully, of course—up off the ground. Somehow, I forgot that she was pumping STR, and was easily several times stronger than me now. A strange development compared to life before the apocalypse, but of course I didn't mind at all. She set me down cautiously, "Thomas got a healing staff as a drop." She gave an embarrassed smile, "I've been wanting to tell you, only now seemed like a good time to bring it up."

"What does it do?" I asked.

"I'm sure he'd happily show you, but off the top of my head…" she thought for a moment. "It gave him some Wisdom and a boost to his healing." Jessica sat down directly next to me as soon as I was safely planted on the wall.

The ground wasn't comfortable, but at least it wasn't wet. The edges along the wall were like hardened clay, dirty yet dry. It was no wonder I didn't wake up with a soaked back. Thinking about how uncomfortable it would be to remain damp sent shivers up my spine.

"Maria will be fine," I thought aloud.

"Yeah, it'll be fine." Jessica said with a yawn.

I was simply staring up into space, into the blackness that was the dungeon 'ceiling'. Whatever it was, it emitted light and yet remained black, an odd phenomenon. Lost in my own thought I suddenly remembered something I had wanted to ask.

"That light—" and before I could finish I felt a weight on my shoulder followed by labored breathing. Jessica had fallen asleep. I was sure it was one of her skills—that explosion in the monsters' faces—but I'd wait till tomorrow to ask.

Alan walked over quietly, "It's good you're okay." He said then glanced at Jessica. "You're lucky to have her. She watched over you like a pup. She's been fighting her exhaustion just as hard as Lucas."

"You're fine as well?" I asked him. Jessica had told me already, but it felt impolite not to show concern. He gave a thumbs up and a smirk that clearly said 'what were you expecting from the best tank known to man?' "Good, let's try to get some rest."

Alan gave a nod and seemed excited to let Lucas know he could finally close his eyes. I closed mine as he started to walk away.

I wasn't that tired, but the drowsiness came quickly. Jessica resting on my shoulder somehow brought me a serenity I'd not experienced in many days. I fell asleep almost as quickly as my eyes closed.

It took two days of camping in this post before Maria opened her eyes. Thomas was the first to notice and he quickly called everyone over.

Maria peered up at us in confusion with dull eyes. "What...happened?" She tried to sit up in her habitual manner, and let out a groan.

"Careful," Thomas leaned down to support her. "Your side is all banged up."

Maria lifted part of her shirt to reveal a huge purplish-green bruise running up from her hip and disappearing just below her chest. It seemed she couldn't remember anything at all that had happened.

"You were stabbed by a surprise attack." Thomas said in the simplest way while helping Maria to lie back down.

Her head tilted without moving her body, "Where is Jessica? Is everyone okay?"

"Jessica's fine." I assured her. "She's been scouting ahead for us, so we can all make it out of here alive."

When Maria hadn't woken up after that first night, Jessica had grown incredibly frustrated. Eventually she decided her best course of action was not to sit and stew over Maria but to find a way out of here. She had been using her scouting abilities to move along this wall and hopefully towards an exit. Her progress had been good so far, and she had drawn a map in the dirt of what we faced ahead, and which direction would best serve us to get the hell out of here.

"She shouldn't be gone much longer," Lucas assured Maria. Originally, Lucas had wanted to travel with Jessica to be safe, but Jessica insisted she go alone, as it was much safer if she only had to worry about herself.

Lucas was right, it was less than an hour later I saw Jessica jogging towards us. Her face was tired and taut. I could tell from a glance she was filled with knowledge she needed to unload upon us, and yet as soon as she saw Maria, her expression of urgency disappeared. I could almost see the mental reset as she rushed to her friend who was now leaning back against the wall much like I did.

"You're awake!" Jessica yelled.

Maria forced a weary smile. "Yahoo!" she said with a dead voice, which got a chuckle out of myself and Alan. It was good to see she had some of her sense of humor remaining. "Where have you been?" Maria asked. She was already over us doting on her and wanted to move the direction away from her condition as fast as possible.

Jessica still forced a hug, which got a groan out of Maria. "I'm so glad you're okay." Jessica's hands raced over the wound on her friend's side, trying to find anything that might be wrong. Maria looked defiant, but didn't voice a word of complaint. At last Jessica turned her attention back to us as a group.

"I've discovered the exit to the next floor." Some of the excitement I'd heard in the past came back into her voice. "I don't know if we have luck on our side or what, but it's around thirty minutes away for me alone. If we move quickly and avoid most packs, I'd say we can reach it in around an hour with all of us together."

Not surprisingly, no one showed much excitement at her comment. Surely it would only be getting more difficult to get out if we went up a level? The mobs here were hard enough. "Good news, I guess." I fumbled out. Nods told me the others agreed, but their faces showed trepidation.

"We can't go anywhere till Maria is able to move on her own," Thomas said.

"Of course, we won't be going anywhere till she is fully functional. We have enough rations for more than a week. If we run low we can start hunting instead of holing up here," I agreed with our healer...

"What about the packs?" Alan asked our scout. "Is there anything we should know about what's coming our way?"

"I didn't look into it too much," Jessica confessed. "I had a distant feeling of more of the same, and then something big. I don't know if it's avoidable or not."

"A boss?" Lucas perked up slightly.

"I'm not sure, I was too worried about pulling it so I didn't try to see what it was." Jessica said.

"That was the safer play. The Children of Sobek don't de-aggro here and maybe that's the same for the boss. If you pulled it, we could have been wiped out," I said. My mind thought back to the fiend we had encountered, and how acute it was even when being sensed. A fight with a strong enemy while unprepared could prove fatal. It was impossible to know for sure, but another night of rest would probably have Maria in a good enough condition to move and shoot. I turned my attention to her, "Do you think you'll be good by tomorrow?"

She looked at Jessica and then to me, "I'll be fine. I can deal with a little pain." She forced a smile through the occasional groan. It seemed even breathing caused her discomfort, which wasn't surprising given the size of the bruise on her side. I was half expecting Jessica to retort, but she didn't say anything.

There was a feeling of urgency prickling the back of my neck and it wasn't any sense of immediate danger for the group but it related to an anxiety for the people back on the farm. Our trip had resulted in a detour, which in hindsight could prove to be a mistake. People were waiting for us to return, an entire farm of low-level people. The farm was out of the way, but anything could happen to them. The situation was constantly changing.

The coming few days journey could turn into weeks if we were unlucky, and who knew how the outside world would change. Would we even receive status messages inside the dungeon? My mind was taking me down a dark spiral of negativity.

"That light you fired into their faces," I suddenly looked at Jessica, "Was it your new skill?" She was always a source of comfort, and just hearing her speak helped lift me out of that mire I was sinking into.

"It was," she smiled. "Pretty good, eh?" There was no doubt she was proud of the choice she made at the shop.

"Have you figured out exactly how it works?"

"Not entirely, but it seems to materialize based on my thought." No doubt I had a stare as curious as the one I saw on Lucas, eyes that said to explain.

"Basically... if I can imagine accurately, then I can materialize the flares anywhere."

"So if you could see through walls…then you could materialize them through solid structures?" Lucas asked.

"I think so." Everyone seemed excited at this thought, which brought on a relatively fun conversation on what might be the limits of this new RPG system. We were stuck here for at least another night, and that extra night of rest was welcomed by everyone.

Chapter 8: Triggering a Boss Fight Takes Courage

The next two days were distinctly gloomy. Everyone was resting and trying to keep their mind in a good place. I couldn't be sure that Maria would ever pull through and nor could anyone else. The two days weren't wasted though, because I used that time to recover fully.

My army of undead were re-summoned, except for my reincarnations. We would need to dispatch a pack of Children of Sobek before I could replenish those. It would be worth pulling a group just for that purpose. According to Jessica, there was a boss fight ahead before we could pass through an exit from this level of the dungeon. A stone island some distance away in the swamp was guarded by an oversize Child of Sobek. We would need every last bit of firepower possible. Still, I remained hopeful. It was unlikely anything would match the Special Shop guardians whom we had managed to defeat.

Judging by the strength of the Children of Sobek, this wasn't a dungeon designed for more than ten people. Not to brag, but I was worth at least three people myself on account of my powerful squad of undead. Without wanting to become complacent, I felt that even a boss fight here would turn in our favor.

That feeling soared during our third day of rest, when Maria said she felt fully recovered and was ready to fight again.

One disadvantage to being the first to explore the dungeon was that there was no information about what lay ahead and no would be no group going ahead of us to give any indication of the boss's abilities. We would fight blind, but Jessica's scouting had revealed that the boss seemed to be just a muscular, thicker and taller version of the normal lizardman—although it did not wield a saber. The boss held a massive pole arm more than six feet in length. The wicked blade was thick enough to lop any of us in two with a direct hit.

The night after Jessica's report was spent strategizing about our upcoming encounter. The ordinary Children of Sobek had been mastered and we understood how best to deal with them. The encounter should be melee, a strong enemy that focused on raw STR and physical prowess. My undead warriors excelled in a situation like that. Alan also had his new shield to bolster our front line.

In the end, a slow and steady approach was chosen. Alan would lead the front line alone while we bombarded the boss with ranged attacks. Lucas and my minions would only move in when we were sure they wouldn't be smashed to bits by a single attack. Losing all of my squad would prove disastrous, especially if some kind of enrage mechanic existed for the boss when it was on low hit points.

After that was decided, speculation about the next floor came next, our conversation turned to potential enemies, and if there would be even more floors after that. The prospect of adventuring deep into a dungeon frightened and excited me. The reality was that we needed to leave as soon as possible—for the sake of Maria and our comrades back at the farm—and this tipped my feelings more towards the fright side of the balance.

"Sleep soundly tonight," I said to everyone while throwing myself down against the wall. "Tomorrow is another day, and we'll all see the next as well...together." No one showed any doubt about my words. We truly had built a remarkable team in such a short time.

I was the first to wake that next morning, my mind grasping at the residual fogginess from a fading dream. I was fishing with my father, and somehow Jessica was there as well... uncharacteristically squealing about how slimy the fish were. Alan made an appearance too, but as soon as I tried to recall what he was saying, it all disappeared into a cloud of smoke.

It was nice to see my father, even if it was only a dream. Admittedly, I hadn't spent much time thinking about my family at all. I was living fully in the present, and all my thinking power was devoted to the here and now. That...didn't make me sad though. Somehow or another I felt...content? The problems of society weren't casting a shadow over me. I didn't need to worry about my future. I only needed to worry about the next day, and the immediate moment.

"Morning," Lucas said from nearby, his hands vigorously rubbing at his eyes. There was a yawn a moment later as Thomas woke up as well.

"Good morning," I replied while pulling a ration from my inventory. I wasn't a morning person. In fact, waking up before 1 PM had been a miracle for me on non-work days. Late night gaming sessions were something I spent years doing. The solitude of night was something I used to love.

I didn't miss it now, though. Strength in numbers. I took comfort in not being alone. I glanced at my team and then Jessica who was still mumbling something in her sleep. I felt happier than I had in a long time. That thought was followed by a hope this happiness wouldn't be short lived.

Breakfast was bland, but it was impossible to deny the Rations did great work at satiating thirst and hunger. It was like eating a buttered biscuit, except without the butter, and if the biscuit was stale and near flavorless. Well, the game world never promised it would be good.

"Did everyone get a good rest?" Jessica asked with a yawn on awakening. Most of everyone else wasn't very talkative in the morning, but it had been her routine to get everyone moving.

"Good enough." Was my reply, the others merely nodded and gave a mumble. No coffee in the morning was rough, truly. Maybe some of that luxury could be regained, but for now everyone would have to accept this grogginess for the foreseeable future.

"Let's go over our plan one more time," Lucas said. "So we're on the same page. We can't afford any mistakes." No one voiced a complaint at his suggestion. In the end, Lucas simply reiterated it without anyone asking a question or voicing a suggestion. We were on the same page, through and through.

"Ten minutes then?" I asked. "Double check yourselves. Make sure you're not forgetting anything important. This would be the time to use any excess stat points." With that in mind I opened my own stats:

Name: Mike Reynolds (27) Class: Necromancer Level: 21 EXP: 47%
HP: 1085/1085 MP: 455/455
STR: 5 Fear Resistance: 5

AGI: 2
DEX: 5
VIT: 29 +14
WIS: 27 +23
Available: 0
Skills: [A] Summon Skeleton LV. 9| [A]
Summon Skeleton Mage LV. 2| [A] Decay
LV. 2| [A] Reanimate Dead LV. 3| [A] Bone
Armor LV. 2 | [A] Vast Shadows | [A]
Temporary Grave LV. 1 | [P] Sixth Sense |
[P] Bravery LV. 2 | [P] Mutated LV. 2| [P]
Pain Resistance LV. 2 | [P] Skeletal
Mastery LV. 4| [P]Intimidate Living |[P]
Inner Calm LV. 2 |[P] Necrotic Vision

I didn't have any excess points to add to stats. Both HP and MP were full from three days of solid rest. I was halfway to level 22; I welcomed that progress. Every Child of Sobek was almost five or six percent EXP. The others must be extremely close to levelling.

"Same formation as before, except Jessica leads the front," I said. She knew the patrols and the direction to the boss, we were dependent on her scouting not to pull a train. I gave her a glance and received a deep stare in return, "Take your time. No need to save a few minutes if it risks our lives." She nodded in return. "No risks." I added softly, not for her but for everyone else to hear.

With that, we moved along the wall in a protect-the-healer formation. My undead squad were currently placed in Vast Shadows just in case they would cause any problems with aggroing. According to Jessica we could avoid all the packs, but I had suggested we dispatch any small patrols for the EXP and to strengthen my undead squad.

I needed two reincarnations, and apparently Lucas, Thomas and Alan were all close to a level. With that in mind, we fought the first

3 packs we encountered. One patrol of three lizardmen, and two duo patrols.

The nervousness I had originally felt on entering this level was gone completely. Four days in this dungeon and a strong familiarity with our enemies had removed it completely. I knew our foes, and I knew they stood no chance against us if we worked properly together.

My reluctance to use all my spells disappeared as well. Decay was a valuable asset in our encounters. Lucas, Maria, or Jessica took great notice when I created an opening for them, and they always capitalized. If that prickling feeling about the people back at the farm wasn't weighing down on me, I'd have wanted to stay and just grind here for as long as possible.

Skirting the outer edge was relatively safe. There was no swamp for enemies to hide in, and Jessica could see every foe well before we aggroed it. There was a smorgasbord of EXP at our fingertips that we couldn't enjoy because we were focused on the upcoming boss fight.

Those three packs were the only mobs we pulled. The remaining thirty minutes of our journey required no effort: I used the time to fully calm my mind and replace the MP I'd used. Unfortunately, no equipment dropped from the three battles, but we did receive some miscellaneous items: three Rations, and two healing potions. These exceptional enemies seemed to have a much higher drop chances for those compared to the mobs outside the dungeon.

"It's here," Jessica said suddenly, with nothing in my view except a tall and thick layering of saw grass. She walked slowly into the growth and gracefully glided between bushes. I followed her with trepidation and excitement. A brief fifteen seconds of slow walking to avoid being torn up by this overgrown plant life brought us to the other side of the thicket.

A clearing appeared in front of us: solid ground splattered with murky water. The terrain didn't look like mud, and instead seemed to be a section of pure stone, much like what we came from originally. Our enemy was there just a hundred feet ahead. An oversized crocodilian humanoid.

The boss's white body was thick and muscular with scales so thick I wondered if our tank could even penetrate them. Its red menacing eyes had no life to them, no end to what felt like soulless depth. A polearm rested across thighs that were thicker than my torso twice over, and it had a tail that twirled to the side, nearly as long as its own body length, topped off by sharp spikes the size of baseball bats. There was no question, this monster had a menacing appearance.

Everyone froze in place: this was a more intimidating opponent than I'd been expecting. Jessica's estimation of the journey here was spot on, but her depiction of this foe was a bit understated. A single hand that grasped the shaft of the polearm could most definitely pick Alan up and toss him a hundred yards.

The thought crossed my mind: Can we go around it? An opening to a region with a white background was visible inside an arch behind the boss, but the gap between the monster and the frame was only a dozen feet. Not only that, its tail covered most of that distance. Nothing short of putting it down would allow us to move on.

"We have to fight," I said aloud. Everyone knew that already, but hopefully my words made the situation a reality. The coming fight wasn't real, even for me, until I heard the words from my own voice.

"We stick with the plan," Lucas said. Everyone gave a nod and spread out carefully as we inched forward.

Alan remained calm, but the dark patches of sweat racing up his back made it clear that he was nervous, and rightfully so. His current weapon was merely for show, no wooden-shafted blade could do any amount of damage to that thick hide. No amount of speed or power would change that, the spear would simply explode into splinters first.

"Focus up," Thomas said from the back. He didn't speak much, but when he did he meant business. His voice seemed to calm Alan slightly who walked on ahead, one step ahead of the other. My heart stuck in my throat, and the only thing drowning out that thrumming was the low splashing sounds of Alan wading through puddles.

I removed my minions from Vast Shadows and spread them carefully in front of the others. They would remain back for now, but could intercept if anything untoward happened at a moment's notice.

Lucas waited off to my left, Thomas just to my right, and Jessica and Maria just past him. We put a few feet between each other to avoid any AE attacks. Appearances could be deceiving, and no mistakes could be made now.

Maria knocked an explosive arrow while Jessica was priming a Quagmire trap. Alan was going to pull with his spear and move back to us: we couldn't risk the enemy going on a rampage in case it simply ignored Alan and went for our ranged DPS.

Alan's feet eventually stopped moving. He was on the precipice of aggroing the enemy. There was no red line that said 'do not cross or fighting will happen', but the feeling was there. An impending doom that grew stronger and stronger, like staring down death's door.

It seemed that Alan felt in his gut that if he walked a few more steps, a life and death battle would ensue. He looked back at us with a hard stare and a questioning eye. Nods, committed expressions, and then a thumbs up from Jessica was our reply back.

Alan let out a shout and then slapped his spear against his shield while moving three steps forward. There was a deep rumbling, like the sound of a distant eruption, as the entire platform shuddered. The portal frame shook like a plucked bowstring and then came perfectly still.

Steam exhaled from the lizardman's nostrils and those red eyes rolled around, producing two black pupils darker than night. A scaly hand grasped the polearm from its thigh and then it stood up in all its glory.

Eight feet was about the height of the boss when sitting, but now standing it must have been about fifteen. A body that had looked slightly loose before was now compact and rock solid, taut and ready to strike. The monster eyed Alan curiously before taking a step forward.

It was at that moment that Jessica sent out her Quagmire trap a dozen feet behind Alan, who was already in the process of retreating. The plan we had all agreed called for this as the first step, and it went without a hitch.

Alan quickly shuffled backwards while the foe in front stalked towards him. Its gigantic size and weight definitely wasn't helping its sluggish mobility, which was a positive discovery right out of the gate. Fleeing from the battle would be possible if needed, but how far could it chase was the question.

Ten seconds passed before the lizardman's burly body moved over the Quagmire trap. As soon as it triggered, that was Alan's cue to charge forward, and charge he did. He rammed his spear directly onto the thigh of the beast and bashed forward with his shield, immediately following up with a Battle Shout that pulled the beast's full attention.

That devastating polearm came down without much speed, but the momentum was incredible. Alan braced himself for impact with shield in both hands, knees half buckled. A groan escaped his mouth on impact, only overshadowed by the massive gong of metal smashing into metal. He took three or four steps back to reduce the damage to his bones and joints.

Jessica must have cast inspect as planned, "Level twenty-seven boss," she yelled while nocking an arrow before letting it loose. Maria let loose the Explosive Arrow she was priming as well and Thomas began to ready a heal.

Alan stepped forward again to take the next blow with a bit of inertia behind him. When it landed, his knees buckled and he still let out that groan of exertion, but he didn't take a step back. While it was shocking to see his HP tick down over 10% from an attack he fully blocked, this wasn't outside our expectations.

I could tell that Jessica was aiming for the eyes, and she was definitely not going to miss a target nearly as large as a basketball. This tactic wasn't going to work though, a thin but incredibly hard film rolled over its eye the instant an attack came. Her arrow simply deflected off its oval shape, not leaving as much as a scratch.

Maria's aim wasn't nearly as good, and she opted to shoot towards its neck. The explosion was impressive, but the damage was non-existent. The extreme heat her arrows produced didn't leave the slightest mark at all. There was no effect at all from either of their attacks.

They both readied their arrows again, and I cast a Decay to aid them this time as well. The skin of the monster withered when the spell landed, but the hide was so thick that even Decay had little effect. It looked like nothing short of three or four casts in the exact spot would provide any opening. That was a possibility, but it would be an extremely costly one.

Maria and Jessica both looked frustrated and even Thomas had a look of uncertainty on his face. It didn't matter how long we could tank this if we couldn't deal any meaningful damage to it. As if Alan had eyes on the back of his head, despite concentrating on blocking and dodging, he called back calmly, "Don't get discouraged, stick to the plan!"

Chapter 9: When You Can't Flee You Must Fight

Sticking to the plan we had made was definitely sound advice; because I was thinking I should send my squad in immediately. Lucas had sent me a couple of glances as if about to suggest the same. As if Alan had been predicting the future, it soon became clear how bad of an idea it would have been to do so.

The gigantic Child of Sobek grasped its polearm firmly with both hands and then started to spin, similar to the move that the normal version of the mob did. This would have been a blender for my skeletons and probably Lucas as well if he had moved in to backstab. Every strike into his shield was vicious and sent Alan hurtling backwards. It was all he could do to hold on as the beast spun like a top.

The special attack didn't stop for over ten seconds, but as soon as it did, I knew this was the development we were waiting for. My squad went in; Lucas went in; the fight truly started now. I didn't know how long of a cool-down that the monster's ability had, but it couldn't be less than thirty seconds. That was the window we gave ourselves to go all out.

I counted in my head from a safe distance while sending out Decay after Decay. My focus was mostly on the right thigh where my warriors were also putting most of their attention. Even with the focused attacks and Decays, the mob's scales were slow to come off, and under the outer layer were even more scales. Only after four casts in the exact same spot and the combined effort of ten undead melee soldiers did I manage to draw blood.

This burst of attacks hadn't even created a big enough wound to require a band-aid in my opinion, which wasn't great news, but any progress at all was better than nothing. "Twenty-five seconds!" I yelled to Lucas, who retreated along with my minions. We had to keep our melee units safe, especially since Alan was putting in his all, and Thomas was doing fine on MP.

I didn't stop counting though, to learn for next time. The spin attack actually didn't come for another 40 seconds after our retreat. The chance it was a minute cooldown or slightly longer was probable, and I made the quick decision to stay in for that long. "Next time, in for a full minute!" I shouted across to Lucas who nodded. This was a calculated risk we would need to take in order to end this fight sooner than later. Allowing the fight to be drawn out risked Thomas running out of MP or some accident letting aggro slip, with disastrous consequences.

The sight of black blood on the white scales of the monster's thigh abated some of my frustrations, and eased my worry. We could slowly chip away at its life while maintaining our own. At least, that was the hope. Hope wasn't always reality, though.

It became clear that the monster's leg, while bloodied, caused no hindrance on its physical prowess. There were no signs of it weakening, or any change in its abilities at all. Even worse, it attacked with more fervor and frenzy than before.

This was what they called a soft-enrage mechanic. We were on a timer, and eventually this beast would be strong enough to swat all of us in a single hit. My minions couldn't reach any higher than the lower thighs, which meant vital damage to organs higher up was left to Jessica and Maria.

This far, though, they hadn't found any opening to work with. We needed to change that and quickly, "Both of you, focus on the eyes! Just keep shooting!" I shouted. My attention completely shifted away from the thigh. During the next lull in the whirling ability, Lucas was doing his best to turn that small wound into a large one. Wind Slashes came in over and over. I turned my attention towards creating a vulnerability in the face of the beast.

Although I was already down twenty percent of my MP just from focusing on a single thigh, I cast Decay again and again as soon as that little rotating lid that covered the eye came forward. Decay rose to Level Three right after my second cast, but I had no time to study any changes the new level brought about.

My entire focus was on that thick film covering its eyes. Maria had no luck with her arrows; she missed the target, but Jessica pelted the left eye with pinpoint accuracy over and over. At first the oval shape acted as the perfect deflective surface, but within seconds that drastically changed.

Targeted by my spell, the crystal-clear film slowly tore open, turning foggy and gray and deflated. Jessica's fourth arrow didn't deflect but struck home; even though its sharp tip went just an inch or so in I felt elation, and the next pierced directly through the eyeball. The boss was so shocked from what must have been a sudden burst of pain that its attacks halted for a moment as it swatted at its eyelid and dislodged the arrow.

This success was enough to know our attacks were working, our strategy was working, and we weren't going to let up. Jessica and I were sufficient to weaken the mob's eyes, "Maria, help Lucas with the thigh!" I yelled. She wasn't getting close enough, and by now Lucas had made a big gash that her little bombs would help expand.

A red aura started to glow around the boss that was visible to the naked eye. Even at the distance we were from the mob, the effect became increasingly noticeable. This was ominous. Some kind of AE effect might be about to trigger from within. Thomas yelled a warning to Alan and only received two words in response. "I'm fine!"

I was so absorbed with the struggle to penetrate the mob's eyes that I hadn't appreciated that Alan hadn't found it necessary to move from his spot in some time. Even with the boss growing stronger he was holding his own. He was learning how to wield his shield properly, and definitely getting a better feel for it no doubt.

The monster's eyes were its most vulnerable organ, and I even instructed my skeletal mages to begin bombarding its face. The attacks weren't dealing real damage, but it made it impossible for the creature to know what to try to block with its membrane covers and what to ignore. Jessica's arrows slipped in repeatedly and by now the film over the left eye was completely useless. It couldn't even flick the film back anymore as an arrow had gone directly through and lodged into its pupil.

The left eye was completely done for, and the right thigh was no better. The gash was so large now that tendon could be seen beneath. Lucas was thick with blood and the white scales were hidden under a slimy layer of black.

Lucas and my undead warriors retreated a moment later as the boss went into death roll, and for the first time in a long while there was a new development in battle. The boss swapped its stance. It's pose changed as it shifted its weight onto its left thigh and moved the right thigh back.

The polearm swapped sides, with the clear signal that anything attacking its thigh would be priority number one for dispatch. That wasn't the only issue either, it used another ability I'd yet to see: a spell that seemed to have no cast time or preliminary animation, or at least I didn't recognize any spell being cast.

Spinning blades appeared all over the arena that swirled like saws of death. Three or four feet across, they rotated about five feet off the ground, high enough to bisect anyone in two or lop off a head in a lapse of judgment. These blades started to move around the area randomly.

The red hue of death swirled and continued to grow more dense around the lizardman's frame. It was impossible to have any accurate information about how much the aura was increasing in strength but there was a change that was visible to the naked eye. The speed and ferocity of the monster's swings left no room for doubt that it was becoming more frenzied, nor did the ever louder clash of metal on metal.

There was nothing any of us could do except to push on. Jessica knew what I was thinking already, and we simultaneous switched to the second eye. Blinding it completely was one of the only things we could do to ease pressure on apart from kill it outright, which wasn't going to happen soon.

Time felt like it was going at a crawl, and yet the ringing metal clap of gongs became more frequent in my ears. The red hue was no longer faint, and I imagined we were nearing the point where tanking it wasn't going to be possible any longer. With that in mind, Jessica and I needed to disable it as quickly as we could. Jessica and I pummeled the second eye with all we could muster, and my MP quickly dropped to below 30%.

The film melted away as arrow after arrow smacked into the creature's eyes. It took only moments to create what resembled the quills of a porcupine's coat. Now the boss was fully blind, but that didn't seem to deter it in the slightest. It lost its accuracy, but still swung that polearm left to right haphazardly hoping to connect with anything.

Lucas was of the mind to move behind it, but the monster's tail started to sway and whip out like lightning. It had previously rested behind motionless except for when it started to spin like a top. If I were to guess, it provided some form of balance or stability to that burly frame and was the reason why it hadn't been used before.

With no sight now, it moved forward like an unstoppable machine. The tail whipped from side to side, completely negating any hope of Lucas or my warriors attacking from behind or the sides. The polearm came across repeatedly in the front, hoping to bisect anything unfortunate enough to remain in its path.

Several of my squad had been taken out by just two attacks and all that remained was my shield-wielding skeleton general and a single reanimated Child of Sobek. My ranged minions continued to pelt at the face to little effect. The two remaining melee minions I had wouldn't last more than another attack.

Alan was barely holding on as he remained in front of the boss. One knee nearly touched the ground for stability while the shield remained firmly grasped in both hands. There was no time to retaliate or even raise it, all he could do was shelter behind it as the boss slowly pushed him around the arena with each attack.

That red hue of death had grown to a full-blown aura, and the initial slowness of the boss had vanished completely. It moved without lethargy or restraint, and even the spinning axes began to move more rapidly around.

For a moment I felt hopelessness. We'd never encountered an enemy with such a strong physical defense, and our party was severely lacking in magical damage. It was all I could do to continue casting Decay on its wounded thigh. The only hope in my head was being able to put the beast to the ground so it couldn't move.

Maria ignored the sweat dripping down her face and into her eyes as she let fly another explosive arrow. It was hard to miss the soft fleshy thigh that was as large as a barn door. The wound was seared black in places and the tendons had been ripped to bits, and yet it only slowed the beast a small amount.

The saws around us were growing faster, and eventually evading them while keeping track of the boss would prove impossible. We were already incredibly lucky that none had pathed towards Alan, who remained like a turtle in his shell.

There was less than a minute remaining before the saws would be moving at a speed hard to dodge even if you saw one coming well in advance. My mind oscillated between calling a retreat or not. I wasn't even sure we could retreat. The boss could perhaps keep up now, or perhaps the saws would chase us down.

If the saws followed us, we had no way out. As a test, I focused on one of them and cast Decay. The blade turned dark as if rusting, but the speed at which it was spinning didn't change, nor did its pathing slow at all. Decay wasn't enough for these.

Almost as if to put us in full despair, the boss ahead started to spin again, and this time the spinning didn't stop. It built up speed and started to swirl like a whirlwind. Alan could no longer sit still and be pummeled any longer. He rushed away in our direction as we grouped together.

"What do we do?" Thomas said in between casting heals. It was the question on everyone's mind. Our avenue of attacks seemed to be gone now. The monster didn't need sight to spin randomly around; eventually we would be forced into a corner and the blades would cut us to pieces.

Not only that, the lizardman's weak points had become hard to target. Only Maria or Jessica could even deal damage without being minced to pieces, with a low chance of hitting the damaged thigh that was now untargetable while it was twirling so quickly.

For the first time since the apocalypse, I couldn't make a decision. Calling for retreat was just as likely to lead us to death as not. Once we ran, there would be no chance of finishing off our enemy, and it would only continue to grow stronger over time. Those blades might find us ten or even fifteen minutes after our retreat, coming so fast that no one would even see their death coming.

We were stuck between a rock and a hard place, and even Lucas struggled for an answer. "Can we retreat?" He asked the question that probably every person was thinking. Oddly enough, they all looked to me for an answer. No one voiced their opinion, and for a moment all that I heard was the heavy breathing of Alan.

"I...don't know," I confessed. I looked at Jessica feeling regretful and sorry for being so useless at this moment, there was also something of a plea in that look. There had to be a way out of this situation, but a Hail Mary was something only Jessica or Maria could produce.

Our breather had felt like it lasted an eternity, but only five or six seconds had passed. "Watch out!" Alan suddenly yelled. He moved as fast as he could and collided with a spinning saw that was going to cut straight through our group. The resulting sound was like a high pitch scream as it grinded to a halt and then deflected off his shield. It then began building up speed again and moved along a different path.

There was no way anyone else could survive a hit like that. It was as strong as the boss's polearm swing, and my fear that they would hunt us down became reality in everyone's mind. "Give me thirty seconds!" Jessica suddenly said. "Thirty seconds and I'll think of something!"

"Keep moving!" Lucas reminded everyone, and we quickly broke apart as another saw came hurdling through the area where we were just standing. I cast Shallow Grave and then quickly re-summoned my melee skeletons. My MP was dangerously low now, and I could do the same just one more time.

My plan wasn't to attack, but instead assist in defending my friends. I sent every skeleton out and around a party member, ready to dive in front of a spinning blade in case someone was too slow to react. My skeletons proved little resistance, but after the saw blade connected with something it always swapped direction, which would provide a moment of relief.

Only the shield-wielding skeleton general could put up any resistance. He was sent flying backwards, with bones nearly cracked, but he didn't perish in one blow. My eyes repeatedly looked around in every direction, hunting for any incoming projectile. My mind was continually racing for where to move so the boss didn't corner me and lop me in two.

Everyone was doing anything they could to avoid being bisected, which was growing more difficult by the second. Thomas had barely managed to evade having his arm cut clean off, a red gash at least an inch thick rested over his bicep. I couldn't wait any longer and summoned my last batch of minions and sent two of my generals to him.

Lucas was having a better time of it and was still swiftly dodging. He had found it necessary to use the Nodachi once to deflect a blade, which seemed to have left his hands numb and shaking. Alan had his shield, and so long as he wasn't in the path of more than one could deflect an attack with minimal injury.

Maria was still recovering from severe injury, and her moves were definitely impacted, but she was quite agile. I sent her a few skeletons as well, which would be life savers in the worst-case scenario. It was when I looked at Jessica that my heart caught in my chest.

She had suddenly stopped moving, and she closed her eyes and nocked her bow. My mind was ringing alarm bells as I sent the remaining warriors beside me directly to her. Without a care for their own existence, they hurried to encircle her.

Even then, that wasn't enough. "Alan! PROTECT JESSICA," I yelled. Everything was happening so fast, and even within those short two seconds did I lose three minions. Two different blades had come right for Jessica, and no doubt would have ended her.

She let loose her bow and nothing shot forth. A sign of frustration covered her face as she opened her eyes and seemed to be experiencing a sense of failure. Another blade connected with a minion and shattered it to pieces before Alan reached her.

I eyed her with quick curiosity before having to dive out of the way of a blade. My stomach rested flat against the floor in hopes that would help in some way, but it truly didn't. I rolled like a madman as one of the blades turned vertical and nearly sliced me in two. A huge slash was cut out the side of my hip, no doubt mitigated greatly by bone armor.

Jessica's eyes closed again, and again she prepared an arrow, this time with more confidence. Alan was deflecting blade after blade and even Lucas had rushed over to assist. I continued to roll along the floor before getting to my feet and making distance for myself.

Three, four, five shots and there was suddenly a change: the boss stopped spinning. It stood upright and then remained motionless for a moment. A thick burly hand rested upon its chest and a gurgle escaped its throat. That gigantic maw opened and then acid and blood poured forth from within.

"Maria! NOW!" Jessica suddenly yelled. And as if they had planned it, Maria shot explosive arrow after explosive arrow into that now opened throat. Explosion followed by explosion echoed out, as tongue and throat and gore flew from the boss. The blades around us stopped spinning, and then clattered to the floor.

The beast shook and wobbled. The firmly grasped polearm loosed and clanged into the floor, loud and hard enough to shake the very ground. The boss didn't remain standing any longer and collapsed forward in a heap, its innards slowly slithering out of its half-opened maw and pooling on the floor below.

Chapter 10: When Your Life Depends on it, Nothing Motivates like Loot

Everyone was silent; I fell on my ass immediately, letting out a loud exhalation of relief. Maria slumped to the ground too and even started to cry, "Ahhhhh, I really thought I was going to die." She shook her head while fighting back the tears.

"Guys…" Alan suddenly said. "I can't feel my arms anymore." And his shield that had been glued to his hands fell forward sending water droplets flying everywhere.

"Is everyone okay?" Thomas asked. Lucas was currently wrapping a bandage around his wounded arm. I groaned while standing up and made my way over to them.

"I need a bandage as well," I peeled my clothing away and examined the wound in my side. The magical blade hadn't gone deep enough to reach my lung, but my skin and the thin layer of fat beneath had been sliced through. Blood started to pour out as soon as the cloth wasn't hugging my skin.

Jessica rushed to bandage me, and then Thomas followed it up with heal right after. Only then did I appreciate that everyone was going to be okay; we had made it out of that fight alive. I sat back down on the slightly moist stone floor and gathered myself. It was still morning, but I felt as tired as if I hadn't slept for days.

My MP was mostly exhausted, but we had succeeded. It was a silent celebration for everyone, and probably we shared an ominous speculation on what was to come. My feelings about this place had changed. Now, I hoped dearly that we would be able to leave this dungeon and make our way home.

More than five minutes passed before anyone even suggested we move. It was Alan who rallied us, expressing an excited curiosity to find out what the boss had dropped. The thought of loot was a good incentive to push down the shock of having been so close to death.

With a groan of pain at having to stand, I took my place behind Alan and our whole party moved forward. Disappointment started to sink in as we approached the boss, and found nothing hovering there or anywhere near the corpse.

"What the hell is this scam?" Alan said in frustration. Even Maria was about to get riled up, but a grimace of pain from where she clapped a hand to her side stopped her from yelling. I had no idea where the loot was, and truthfully, was as discouraged as everyone else seemed to be.

This had been a difficult fight, and no doubt we deserved some form of reward for it. If the creator imagined that our leaving the dungeon was the reward, well that would be a cruel and sick joke. I shook my head in silence.

"We should at least see what's ahead. Entering the arch can wait but we should take a look," Lucas suggested. No one complained and we moved closer to the white portal.

It was only when we were nearly under the stone arch did Jessica notice something, "Isn't that a chest?" she asked.

And there was a chest, an inconspicuous brown box tucked off to the left side of the arch. It was almost hidden behind a thick patch of sawgrass. The bottom of the chest rested on solid mud, and nothing about it looked extraordinary. The metal bindings and rivets were rusted and old, no doubt a side effect of this horrible humidity. There wasn't even a lock on it to secure the contents.

Alan couldn't help himself and raced forward to haul the creaking lid open and reveal the contents within. "Here's our reward ladies and gentleman!" He yelled in excitement while grabbing an arm full of supplies and snuggling them into his bosom. I raced over, ignoring the miscellaneous items he grasped, and eyed the equipment resting within.

There were four pieces of magical gear there packed tight in the wooden box: two with a green hue and two with a blue hue. A breastplate; a long tooth-like dagger, or maybe a sword; a pair of gauntlets or gloves; and the fourth was some sort of rod or staff? I took them out one at a time to look and pass around.

Sobek's Gnarled Tooth: The tooth of an ancient God. Its serrated edge and sharp tip allow for great versatility in close-range combat.
STR +4, DEX +2
Grants the user Rend.

This was the first blue item in the chest, a long tooth that would work perfectly as a sword, more for hacking than slashing though, and it could double as a piercing weapon. Although Alan had just gotten a new shield, it was obvious this should go to him.

"Looks like you got a new weapon," Lucas said while patting our tank on the shoulder.

Alan let out a wince of pain and couldn't help but drop some of the miscellaneous items that were hugged against his chest, still, the pain didn't stop him from nearly falling over to get his hands on the tooth.

He took the weapon in one hand and marveled at the lack of weight, and the fact it was entirely made of ivory. The blade and tip were sleek and smooth, with saw-like chips along the blades edge that would clearly do incredible damage if dragged over flesh.

Not only that, the weapon looked stylish as well. The handle was less sleek and more rugged, like fossilized bone. The grip had been gentle to my touch, but the ridges meant I had been able to hold it tight: it wouldn't slip even if your hand was sweating. Then there was the passive, Rend, and all of us wanted to know what that did.

"It's an active skill," Alan said after taking up some poses. "It's an attack that always applies the Bleeding ailment. Cheap MP cost, too," he added. He couldn't help but swing Sobek's Tooth around in the air a bit more before slamming it into the nearby stone arch, which gave everyone a shock from the noise.

Maria was having none of it, "Did your brain melt in that last fight?" She let him have it, "You could have brought our way out crashing down. Save it for the monsters, please!" And then she continued to mumble under her breath until even a sound was inaudible. We were still on edge, especially Maria.

I pulled out the gloves:

Chain Steel Gauntlets: A sturdy pair of gauntlets that have surprising flexibility given their unique material.
STR +1, DEX +3
Grants the user Sturdy Grasp.

This was another item that could have gone directly to Alan, unfortunately for him Lucas was also eyeing the gloves with interest, especially after taking them from me and reading the skill.

"Passive: Sturdy Grasp increases resistance to disarming affects by ninety percent," Lucas said.

There was a moment of hesitation while Lucas and Alan eyed each other up. Neither wanted to come out and say they wanted these gloves, but it was clear they both did. The effect was potentially life-saving for both of them. For our tank to not lose his shield or sword was huge, but then it was just as big a deal for Lucas.

I had no idea how common a disarm attack was, as we hadn't encountered it yet. I was going to suggest they pick a number to decide, but didn't get to that point when Alan spoke up. "It's fine, I've already gotten a new shield and sword already. You take it Lucas." I was happy to see Alan didn't begrudge the gauntlets going to Lucas, even though it might not have been the best decision as a group.

Fighting over loot was something that happened in games all the time. Greed was a powerful motivator, and even more so when your life could be on the line at any time. Despite that, Alan wasn't fazed at all, and simply gawked at his new weapon and shield as though they were candy on Halloween.

"Thank you!" Lucas said and immediately put on the gloves. It wasn't like they were bound, so if we had a situational encounter with a disarming opponent we might have a chance to swap them around according to our needs. These two items had already restored my morale. And there would be more to come. We were only heading up from here.

Despite his generosity over the gloves, I could see Maria was still a bit peeved at Alan; her yelling at him seemed to be a common occurrence. She was always jumping at him, and yet Alan ignored her reprimands almost like he was oblivious. Honestly, I thought that obliviousness annoyed Maria even more, which created an unhelpful loop. Still, her temper was diminishing as she gave hopeful glances towards the breastplate in the chest.

I took out the armor, which was made from some type of leather or hide material, and passed it to Jessica who held it up while inspecting it.

Sobek's Cuirass: A cuirass made from an unknown material. Its light weight and flexibility make it extremely good for fast maneuvers.
DEX +3, AGI +3

This was the only item of the three without an active or passive ability on it, but it boasted impressive stats for either Maria or Jessica. Not only that, it was extremely light weight and the material—which looked glossy and hard, but had amazing flexibility—was actually soft and comfortable to the touch.

It was perfect for either of them, clearly. There wasn't even time for me to express my opinion before Jessica handed the armor to Maria. The annoyance on Maria's face disappeared instantly. We watched as a group as she morphed from annoyed, to surprised, to happy, and then to tears. She buried her face into Jessica's shoulder and sobbed like a baby.

I couldn't blame her for it though. It had been a rollercoaster ride for everyone, and especially for her. If she had this armor just a few days prior, her life would have never been in danger. I suspected that was half the reason Jessica gave it to her. The other half was her kind soul and that bit of older-sister doting she felt for Maria.

All that was left was the staff resting within. It had a blue hue covering it, similar to Sobek's Gnarled Tooth, which I suspected indicated the item's rarity. The staff was three or four feet long and perfectly sleek with an impeccable sheen. It looked as if it was freshly polished, and yet it had sat in this dirty and decrepit chest for some time.

The blue shaft didn't have a single nick or indentation, as if it was carved with the most precise measurements and tools. Its top tapered off into a cluster of sapphires encased in golden prongs shaped like the claws of a lion. Holding it in my hand caused a slight chill to race up my hand and through my spine.

**Staff of Piercing Ice: INT +5, Damage with cold abilities +25%
A staff imbued with the power of ice. Its magical properties enhance any capable of wielding ice magic.**

This was the first caster weapon I'd seen besides my own, but this one was clearly specialized towards elemental magic. It was a bummer that no one could make good use of it. The last fight showed a gaping hole in our offense. Besides my Decay, we didn't have anyone skilled in magical attacks. I passed it around for everyone to see and feel, as the cooling effect it provided was quite interesting. Then I placed the staff into my inventory. Could one of my summoned mages use it? But then it would be wasted if one of us got an ice magic attack.

"Let's take a look through the portal now, shall we?" I asked.

"Wait, we didn't go over the miscellaneous items," Thomas said.

"Oh, right," I felt foolish. I had been bit sidetracked in my own thoughts.

"That's because Alan snagged them all already," Maria teased from beside me. She was cheerful now and winked at Alan when he glanced in her direction, to which gesture he showed no response. Oddly enough, she then adopted the face of someone who had been wronged and crossed her arms with a harrumph.

"Anything interesting?" Jessica asked.

"Uh, just the regular potions, some Rations, and then this." He held out an orb of solid glass or crystal. It was slightly smaller than a tennis ball in size, and perfectly see-through.

"What is it?" I asked. He didn't respond and simply passed it to me instead.

Spawn Protection Stone: A mystical stone that prevents monsters from spawning within the radius of its placement. Up to nine stones can be stacked together at one time. The stone can be placed a maximum of three times.
Duration: Indefinite
Distance: 20 Meters

I read it to myself before reading it aloud for everyone else, still slightly in shock from what I read.

"Isn't...this the answer to our problems?" Jessica was all smiles, the excitement clearly audible in her voice.

"Does this mean if we place it at the farm, monsters cannot spawn there?" Maria asked.

"I think so. They weren't spawning there before anyway, but it would be a layer of protection for the future," Lucas said.

There was more potential to the item than that, though. "We could place this deep in one of the cities, couldn't we?" I asked. Reclaiming the city wasn't going to be our primary use for this magic, the farm was the priority, but it was possible. With three uses, we might have one for the farm and two for the worst spots in the city. The duration was indefinite, so long as we didn't relocate it would make sense to use the magic rather than save it.

"Nine can be stacked together, so if we can find more, that would give us a hundred and eighty meters of protection?" Thomas said. "That's enough for a small estate with dozens of homes." It was a fantastic discovery. Was there an implication that spawns might become more evenly distributed in the future? If enough of these stones were dropping, humanity could control the most intense spawn centers and surely the game creators couldn't allow that?

"Does that mean spawns will become randomly distributed?" I wondered aloud. As of right now, most monsters spawned within a city hub and then spread outward. There were random spawns between that, but few and far between, definitely not enough of them to warrant these stones if you lived outside of a city.

"Never mind," I said when everyone looked at me blankly. This was purely speculation on my part. If monster spawns became more random, then nowhere would be safe, not unless you had these stones. In any case, this was a fascinating and important find.

I pocketed the stone away and then made for the arch. It was time to see what was lying in wait on the other side, and my heart slowly crept up my throat. We needed to get out of here, and the thought of traversing dozens of levels of dungeon sounded fun, but people were relying on us. Without our Rations, there was only enough food for so long at the farm.

They should be able to make do on their own, but things could flip on their head in an instant. Long term survival was the issue, and our being trapped down here threatened their survival chances greatly. Every day we were away stacked the odds against them.

Chapter 11: The First Post-Apocalypse Dungeon to be Cleared.

I dug my nails into my palm as we approached the gateway. It was only possible to appreciate the sheer size of it as we stood directly underneath the stone arches. It was gigantic, and even had two of the bosses we had just fought stood on one another's shoulders, they would not had reached the top. I couldn't imagine why such a big construction was needed, but had no intention of speculating aloud. It was an odd feeling, thinking that asking what everyone thought might jinx us, even though I was far from superstitious.

Alan led the way, disappearing through the portal and I followed, anxious about what I would see on the other side. I caught Alan's eye and we both let out relieved sighs at the same time. There was no giant monster, nor was there another large environment to explore. We were in a simple room with a spiraling staircase that ascended upwards. Atop that was a small doorway, whether this was to the second floor of the dungeon, or an exit, we couldn't know.

Once everyone was through the gate, the walk to the top of the stairs took nearly ten minutes, as everyone was thoroughly exhausted. My mouth remained shut, and apart from the trudging steps on the stairs, the only sound was a barely audible mumbling that came occasionally from Maria. I wanted out, and probably everyone else did too. It seemed to be quite likely that we were coming back up from the dungeon to the surface, but I didn't want to voice this opinion: to excite everyone and then send us crashing into an emotional abyss if I was wrong.

"It's…an exit." Alan said from ahead of me as he tentatively opened the door and looked out. "This isn't to floor two, if there even is a floor two. It's the rainforest world again."

Behind me came cheers and laughter. I turned and I couldn't stop myself from squeezing Jessica in a hug. I was so caught up with myself that it took a moment to appreciate that she was hugging me back with equal enthusiasm.

"We made it." I said aloud to everyone. "Let's get out of here." No one hesitated at all as we pushed through the doorway into the humid atmosphere of the rainforest we had arrived at via the teleport spell. Sickeningly though just as I was feeling a sense of freedom, my surroundings morphed again, and I found myself back in the main room. The hieroglyph type drawings were still there, the opening of our chosen path was still there.

It was like we hadn't been gone at all. Even the purple and eerie lights that raced through the hallway and up the stairs to that closed door—the door that had locked us in this tomb—remained on and there, haunting us. A premonition of disaster welled up inside of me as I looked around at the others.

Their faces fell from happiness, to confusion, to distress. "Are we…trapped?" I asked. I was afraid of the answer I might receive, and before anyone could even respond, the entire place began to shake.

Maria let out a squeal of fright and Alan gestured for everyone to move towards him, "To me, come to me!" he yelled while hoisting his shield up. He was doing his best to block some of the small stones and sand that had begun to fall from the ceiling.

Was the whole place coming down? My mind was racing; I didn't have any of my squad to protect us. There had been no corpses to use to recreate them and my MP was basically shot already.

The rumbling and shaking continued until the entire chamber was a dusty mess, and then it stopped.

The dust caused me to cough and gag, and visibility was awful. It took moments for me to orient myself, and before I had done so Thomas shouted, "The entranceway is open!" He was right, the purple lights were off and yet we could see.

There was a glaring light from above, piercing through the dust and debris, guiding our way out. No one spoke as we rushed up the steps while trying to not slip and fall. In the moment I staggered clear, I exhaled more deeply than I ever had before. Fresh air in my lungs had never felt so good.

We had returned—we were back where we started, out in one piece and almost as good as new. "My god," Alan panted, "can we have a single moment without excitement?"

For once, Maria agreed with him. "Seriously, this isn't good for my heart."

Everyone agreed with both of them. The constant swapping from jubilation to despair was enough to stop any healthy person's heart. It was a cruel joke, it seemed. Someone was getting a laugh out of it, and it wasn't us.

There was suddenly more rumbling as the stone doorway behind us slid to a shut, causing the earth to quake. This time, however, we were ready for such a development. No one lost their cool and in fact, when I thought about the potential loot and levels down there I even backtracked on my relief to be out and felt a touch of melancholy. "Let's go home," I said.

Where was the way back home? Well, I didn't know exactly, but I felt that if we kept walking directly towards the red dot on our map we would come upon a road soon enough. The random teleport was limited in terms of distance, and if luck would have it our destination was our own secret shop. Even if it wasn't, we were strong enough to deal with any random spawns, find a vehicle and make it back to the farm.

The first dungeon in this region has been cleared. New dungeons will now spawn periodically. Monsters will continue to escape uncleared dungeons and enter the world.

A message was broadcast and I could see that everyone had got it.

"So we were in a dungeon then," said Jessica. To me, that had been clear for some time, but it was good to know that the system deemed that event a dungeon. I wondered if this broadcast was seen by all of humanity's survivors? Given them hope perhaps, that there was at least one high level group in action. Or was it seen just by nearby people? Or even just our group.

The message about uncleared dungeons didn't seem like a good one, and another way to look at it was that we had potentially sped up the process towards world destruction. Monsters as strong as the ones we had fought leaking out into the world would prove fatal for anyone struggling to fight goblins and zombies and the plethora of starter monsters. I expressed this concern aloud.

"Let's…worry about it a different time," Jessica said. And no one had a single complaint. We were exhausted physically and mentally, and the sooner we could find a road and then a vehicle, the better.

I couldn't be sure what time it was, but judging by the sun glaring from above, it was sometime midafternoon. I didn't want to camp the night in a swamp, especially with the myriad of insects that would crawl out in the darkness. Nor did anyone else and despite our tiredness we pushed on with determination.

Alan led the front with confidence, and his mood was a dozen times better than it had been on the way in. Even though I was being eaten alive by mosquitoes, I was also cheerful. Itchiness was better than being trapped underground.

Ours was an uneventful journey, and there was no need to summon my undead, nor anything to summon them from even had I wanted to. We didn't encounter a single enemy despite hours of steady walking. The only change was the buzzing of insects and the ground beneath our feet.

The number of insects subsided, the general mugginess of the atmosphere transformed into that of a forest, and even the ground was no longer covered in peat, but instead was solid grass and decaying leaves and pine.

We walked on for what felt like an eternity, until my legs hurt so bad they felt like jelly, and then Alan cried out: "There's a break in the trees! I think I see a road!" Suddenly my legs moved like I hadn't been walking for hours.

A light coming through the trees almost horizontally is what I noticed first, and then I saw through the gap in the trees. Ahead was a single two-lane road, and on the other side was just open field. I imagined it would have been where cows and cattle would have grazed, but now there was nothing.

Along the road was nothing but decaying hay bales and the remnants of a rickety barbed fence that stretched into the distance. There was no clue as to where we were; all I could guess was that to judge by the sun, we were vaguely heading northwards.

The only definite orientation we had was to aim at the red dot in the distance on our map, which marked the existence of the secret shop. I recommended taking the road, which was only a little out of line with a direct route to the red dot, "It's better than walking across fields and perhaps we'll find people or houses." The rest of the group agreed with that decision, and so we walked the road like hitch hikers.

Again, the journey was uneventful, just more arduous walking as the sun slowly crept downward. Alan remained at the front and we separated ourselves from the forest edge, walking in a close group directly down the middle of the road. Any zombies and goblins that meandered along our path were dispatched by Alan in a single slash.

Our tank spent most of his time holding his new sword and slashing it in the air. Alan had the biggest raise in power of anyone, going from wielding a wooden spear stolen away from a level 1 goblin all the way to having a rare weapon from a dungeon boss.

I wasn't jealous though. Instead, it made me feel jubilant that he was in high spirits. Alan was arguably the person who was in the most danger during the difficult encounters, and I'd imagine the mental stress of being in that position was demanding. If he decided he didn't want to tank anymore, I wouldn't be able to blame him.

"What's the plan for when it gets dark?" Lucas asked from my left-hand side.

"Jump the fence and make camp in the field?" I wondered aloud. "Safer than the forest." I was hoping it didn't come to that, though, and we'd find an abandoned house or at least a barn.

"Not much of a choice, really." Thomas said from behind me, "I can get a campfire going if we need." Thomas and Alan were both the outdoorsy type.

"Yes please. We'll need the light," Maria said and I sympathized with the urgent tone in her voice. Darkness was eerie enough at the best of times and it was even worse when there were monsters lurking in the darkness.

I opened my pack to check our rations, we were good for at least a week, maybe a few days longer. Things would be okay. "How much longer can we go on today?" I asked.

It was actually Alan who responded from the front, still twirling and slashing at the air, "Let's do another thirty minutes."

Maybe fate did exist, or at least I thought so about fifteen minutes later. There was a gas station up ahead, digging its own little cove out of the forest. Even better was the vehicle there fueling up.

"Two people," Alan called back. His cheerful demeanor had transformed into total seriousness. We knew well enough that other people were just as dangerous as any monster, maybe even more so. "They just went inside."

Good. This gave us some time to advance unnoticed. "Let's move quickly," I said. "We aren't fighting if we can avoid it." I still didn't have any of my undead squad; hopefully, even if things went south we wouldn't need them against just two opponents.

Chapter 12: Two More Survivors of the MMRPG Apocalypse

It took us two minutes of heavy running to get within a hundred yards of the vehicle, a big four-wheel drive truck. I could tell from a glance it was nearly antique, so old the sun had left it a rusty grey, the previous color being completely indiscernible. "Slow our pace. We aren't here to intimidate them, stay visible and in the open," I said.

We came to a stop in plain sight about ten yards from the truck. Being out in the open like this was risky, but I just didn't want whoever it was in the garage to take off or treat us as a threat the moment they saw us. If they had firearms this could prove dangerous, but I made sure to put myself at the front alongside Alan. I had no doubt his shield could deflect bullets, and my bone armor wasn't bad either.

We waited patiently for thirty or forty seconds before a tall man appeared through the now dusty glass doors. He spotted us when the door was half-cracked on his way out and stopped like a deer in headlights.

With my skull mask on I knew I wasn't the most inviting looking, but protecting my face and head was a priority. I waved my hand at him and shouted, "Friendly." Not too loud, but loud enough that he could hear me clearly. I could see him turn to some-one still in the shop and there was a short moment of bickering before the man turned to face us again. My nerves were on edge.

Judging by his body language, the man wanted to avoid us all together, and I feared things could turn violent in a moment. We were an obstacle in between him and his escape—the truck was no doubt theirs. I couldn't see who he was bickering with either, or if they were even bickering. He could be whispering for the other person to "Get the weapons" For all any of us knew. I realized I hadn't taken a breath for over fifteen seconds.

It was a woman that appeared in the door and urged him for-ward, presumably demanding he see what the situation was. The man was cautious, and for good reason. We weren't any danger to them, but there was no doubt we could be. His caution calmed my nerves. Those that lacked fear were dangerous, maybe the most dan-gerous.

He resisted her for a dozen seconds until, in a similar fashion to how my father always lost out to my mother, he opened the door halfway and spoke without leaving the store. There was a neutral tone to his voice, not hostile, not friendly: he was on guard. "What do you want?"

I had already thought about what I wanted to say. There was no doubt they had leveled, knew about the system, and definitely knew about monsters parading Earth. That much was evident from their vehicle, which was banged up terribly. Dried blood and even some flesh from goblins and zombies splattered the grill of their pickup.

"We're friendly and mean no harm," I started. "We were trans-ported nearby due to some teleport mechanic and have found our-selves lost." He looked back at me without a hint of concern. His brown eyes didn't convey any clue to his thoughts, nor did the

106

expression on his slim but steadfast face change in the slightest. "We were hoping to get some directions, maybe even a ride if possible," I finished.

They both eyed us all from the doorway in silence for a good five or six seconds before his expression finally broke. I could see reluctance mixed with a bit of fear as he turned his head, "Hold on a minute." He disappeared back inside. The two argued again, but this time their discussion was definitely more heated. The woman caught the man by the elbow as he looked to walk past her towards the back of the store, and eventually she must have convinced him to give it a chance.

The door opened again, but this time it was both of them. "I'm Anna, this is Richard," the women said. Her voice was surprisingly gentle and kind for the environment we now found ourselves in. It would be easy to imagine she hadn't seen any combat yet, but her frizzled brown hair and the bloody stains upon her sweater told a different story.

"I'm Mike, these are my party members Lucas, Samantha, Alan, Thomas and Maria." To which everyone gave a simple nod and wave. "As I just said, we're lost and are simply trying to find a landmark we know, or even a ride. I promise we won't inconvenience you. We can hold our own against monsters, and even have a safe farm you would be welcome to stay in at the end of the journey." I felt cheesy alluding to our power in such a way, but I worried that demonstrating our strength too quickly would have the opposite effect.

"I'm a Necromancer, Lucas is a Shogun, Alan is a Knight, Samantha is a Trapper, Thomas is a Bishop and Maria is a Sniper." I listed them out and by telling the couple our classes, was hoping to extend an olive branch. I was giving away a lot of tactical information, but I wasn't worried. The pair wasn't hostile or interested in trying to attack us for our gear.

"I'm a Wizard, Richard is a Paladin," Anna said in return.

For a moment my eagerness took over, "A Wizard? So you cast spells?"

"Right."

"And you?" I looked to Richard. "What role does a Paladin play?"

He took longer than I expected to respond, "I guess I haven't really thought on what role I'd fill in a group. It's just been the two of us." He thought aloud. "Half tank, half support I guess?"

Suddenly, I changed my goals. Yes, we had found a vehicle, which had been my main concern. But now I was interested in the couple as two potential party members. They both had classes we could absolutely benefit from having in our group. We desperately needed a magic damage dealer, and a second tank would make harder encounters much easier on Alan.

"What level are you?" I asked. Unfortunately, my question put them on guard instantly. Your level was a direct indication of your power. Right now, we were still enigmas to each other, which was conducive to peace: but if either side significantly out-levelled the other, then the balance was gone. "Sorry, I'll clarify—I was only intending to ask for a ride in your truck, but after hearing you're a Wizard and he's a tank, I'm interested in recruiting you two. Our party desperately needs magic damage, and a second tank will always find use."

There was a long pause as they contemplated, "We're decently leveled," I added, "We're all around level twenty." I said without going into too much detail, hoping that the advantages of being in a strong party would tempt them to join us.

Richard hid his reaction well, but Anna couldn't. She realized a moment too late that her eyes must have betrayed her attempt to present a calm outer demeanor, "We are level thirteen." Anna said at last and then glanced at Richard who was looking a bit uneasy.

"We can level you," I said. "It won't be an issue at all." I had forgotten myself in the moment—this was something I should have run by the group first—and I quickly turned back to gauge their reactions. No one had the slightest hint of disapproval on their face. "Is this fine?" I whispered back to them. Jessica flashed an okay sign and the others nodded in agreement.

"In fact, we just recently cleared a dungeon." I continued. This was a match made in heaven for us; I needed to seal the deal. "Is there any chance you use frost type magic?" I pulled out the Staff of Piercing Ice and held it in my hand. The cold chill started to quickly penetrate my bones.

Anna's eyes lit up like Christmas lights as she looked from the staff to Richard. She coughed hard and then put on the most fake neutral expression possible, "I have two cold spells." The look in her eyes and the smile that constantly tickled her lips betrayed any feigned indifference she had for the rod resting in my hands.

"Perfect then," I said, "This can be yours if you join us."

Anna nearly rushed forward to grab it when Richard stopped her, "Wait. That offer sounds nice, but what if our goals don't align?"

"What are your goals?" I asked. It was a valid point. "I have some personal ones, but right now we are working as a group to survive. We want to create somewhere where a large community can cope with whatever this world throws at us. After that, well, I want to search for missing people." Specifically, I wanted to find my parents, but driving six hours across state wasn't exactly on the menu right now. "We haven't really planned for the future other than getting ahead of the curve," I added, "but surely survival is your number one goal as well? You can't save anyone else if you can't save yourself." I could see that my words had caused the two of them to pause and really think.

"I will join on the condition that if one day I wish to go my own way, you will let me." Richard said after a good half a minute contemplation.

"That's fine. You'll always be your own person. I simply ask that while we are in a party you follow the will of the group, for everyone's benefit and safety." I looked to Anna next, "And you? What do you want?"

"I…" she paused. "I will ask the same then."

Jessica called over, "Not a problem. Hopefully, there will be a time when the immediate danger is past, and we can all stay or go as we want."

As soon as the woman nodded, I sent them both a group invite, which they accepted. "Do you know where Sangeal is?" I asked. Waiting for an answer, my heart was in my throat, as I worried we were much farther than we expected from my home city.

"It's about five hundred miles to the northwest. Is that where you're headed?" Richard asked.

"Around there," Thomas said. "You're familiar with the special shop? We were ported away from there."

"There's a special shop a good six or seven hours south," Richard said, "We've been there twice but no one has been able to get past the entrance."

"That's where we were headed," Lucas said while shaking his head. "The secret shop in that direction can't be the same one we went to then." We had been walking in the wrong direction, and it seemed I was going to be driving more than six or seven hours after all. Getting back to the farm was the priority right now though.

"You got into the shop?" Richard was impressed and when he looked to Anna she raised her eyebrows. "No one at our shop was even close to being able to defeat the guards." The tense atmosphere disappeared as Richard started talking more casually. Everyone who had been standing safely behind Alan and I now came forward and we gathered as a group.

Although I'd named everyone, Richard and Anna went around giving a firm handshake and a proper introduction to each of us. Anna found herself comparing experiences with Jessica and Maria and it seemed she was going to fit right in given the laughs arising from their conversation.

"So what exactly is the safe place you're returning to?" Richard asked.

"We're working on fortifying a farm," I said. "The plans are in place, and we have about thirty people on site now, maybe more since we left."

"Thirty? As powerful as you?" He was surprised.

"Oh, no." I made to correct his misunderstanding, "mostly normal people and a few that are interested in leveling up. Those that have leveled up to your strength are few and far between—at least from what we've seen."

"What's your plan for after we arrive at the farm then?" Richard continued his questioning, "and for levelling up quickly?"

"Well—" I started before Lucas swooped in and cut me off.

"If you don't mind, we should set up camp in the garage and I'll be happy to explain everything in detail to you then." Honestly, I was more than happy to let Lucas take on that task. He was invested as I was in the farm, and arguably knew more about our plans for going forward than me. I was tired.

"That's a good idea." I said while looking off towards the sunset, "It's going to be dark within the hour. We should sleep soon and then leave early in the morning." I looked towards the truck, "Did you manage to fill up?"

"Not only have we filled up the tank, but we also got hold of two full gas cans," Richard replied before Lucas guided him away. That was more than enough gas to travel six hundred miles—amazing news.

"Well everyone, the gas station is probably our best bet tonight for protection. First come first serve on the spots, I'd guess." This triggered a good-natured rush towards the door, while bumping into each other trying to be first in, to get the best real estate on the floor for sleeping.

Once inside, my attention shifted over to where Jessica and Maria had found some space near a coffee machine, and they were bombarding Anna with questions. Just walking over proved hard to do, as it felt like my presence altered the atmosphere, making it more tense. Their aura said, 'NO MEN ALLOWED'. A nervous cough escaped my mouth, "Excuse me ladies."

Three heads turned, three hard stares, a collective desire not to be interrupted was clear on every face.

"Tomorrow morning we leave for the farm. Can you two fill Anna in about what we are doing there."

"We already have," said Maria.

I didn't stay a moment longer than needed.

The main aisle was taken by Alan and Thomas, who had more than enough space to sleep. My fault honestly, that I put the idea of a race in their head. All the same, when I walked around the garage I could see there would be enough space for everyone in the end anyway. Most of the store had been ransacked, and the middle shelves that held food had been pushed over to on their side already. We weren't the first group to spend the night here, clearly.

I made a circuit around the store and into the back, just to know the layout in case of an emergency. Ever since that crisis night in my own workplace, I had never felt safe inside a building if I didn't know exactly where my points of escape were. The idea that Richard and Anna might try something tickled my thoughts, too.

"I'm gonna sleep early," I said to Alan and Thomas. "I'll be in the backroom if anyone needs me." The backroom wasn't much different to that in my gas station, with just a shitty plastic chair behind a wooden desk. It contained a lot of garbage, probably left by customers and the former owner had never ended up throwing it out. A single shelf of binders was filled with transaction histories that badly needed dusting. Somehow, it all felt comfortable, and normal. Funnily enough, I'd never slept in my old workplace even once, and yet sleep came quickly.

Chapter 13: A Wall of Fog Confronts You: Do You Step In?

It was still dark out when I woke. My back ached something terrible and a wet patch of drool coated my forearm. A memory of sleeping during class in high school floated by as I raised my head off the desk and stood. Simpler times, and no doubt my body was better suited for such a terrible position back then.

Stretching helped ease the aching in my spine. My eyes were partially acclimatized to the darkness already and my vision improved rapidly as I made for the door to the main room. I hated the smell of this gas station, hated the smell of every single one I'd ever stepped in: cheap cleaning products and some scent of lemon or fruit that never quite smelled of anything other than chemicals.

No one else was awake; they had all found various spots on the floor to sleep on. I nearly couldn't stop myself from giggling to see that Alan and Thomas had been evicted from their wide space, which now was the place that Jessica, Maria and Anna were sleeping in. Alan and Thomas were now clumped in a corner nearly leaning against each other for support.

Seeing Anna laying there caused a wave of relief to wash over me. The fear that Anna and Richard would flee in the night had been there, clawing at the back of my mind. We'd locked the doors and I'd been tempted to take the keys, but I couldn't have done that and then expect them to believe we wanted a friendship based on trust. So whether they ran out on us had been left up to fate. It appeared that Maria and Jessica had hit it off with Anna quite well, though.

After unlocking the door and leaving the building, I found the pre-dawn air so humid it smelled more of moisture than grass, which spread as far as the eye could see just across the highway. Our ticket out was untouched, and I'd not heard a vehicle drive by through the entire night. Encounters with other people were few and far between these days.

It was such a surreal feeling. Nothing but nature around me and a serene atmosphere that most definitely wouldn't have existed at this time in the morning even before the apocalypse. The stars in the sky were denser and brighter than I'd ever seen. Light pollution would have obscured most of them in the past.

I'd always understood that life could never go back to normal, but this moment really solidified that thought. Humanity was experiencing a slow and steady destruction through death, a death that I hoped to evade for as long as possible. I don't know how long I sat in silence, but it was quite some time and the first hint of light grew in the east.

Some time later, I got up with a groan, my ass aching from sitting so long.

Richard was there, leaning against the building wall. "It's something to see, isn't it?" He was looking at the orange hue slowly pervading over the land. "Shame the circumstances invoke melancholy instead of happiness, though."

He wasn't wrong. Dawn was a bittersweet sight now no doubt. How many more of these sunrises would I live to see? "Do you and Anna have rations? I have extra if you've been going hungry." I didn't want to talk about the potentially bleak future ahead. The here and now, that's what I wanted to live in.

"We have some rations, not many left though, just a few days' worth, that's why we took the risk to stop here. That and the gas."

"We have enough for about a week, a little less than if we're feeding you two. But if it's a seven-hour drive, we'll be home before nightfall."

"The road has been good to us so far," Richard said while looking at the battered vehicle. There were bits and pieces of zombie and goblin mess inside the front grate. "Let's hope it stays that way."

I gave a nod in response and the bell from the gas station door chimed almost at the same time. Maria, Jessica and Anna were all coming out. I could see Alan, Thomas and Lucas in the back stretching and rubbing their faces. It was an early start, and sleeping without being totally exhausted proved difficult these days.

"We shouldn't dally for very long." It was all very well saying this, but the reality was that we were slow to get going. Being able to use a toilet was a luxury these days, which meant there was a good twenty-minute line while everyone did their business.

Richard couldn't be bothered to wait and didn't mind going out back. And there he found a well pump that produced clean running water. How long had it been since I had a proper shower?

That twenty-minute wait took over an hour and a half, but everyone got to wash themselves off with clean water and scrub some of the grime out of their hair. I never realized just how much of a morale boost being clean was, and the annoyance I felt having to wait vanished after I got my turn.

"There's room for another with Anna in the front, but it's kind of a squish," Richard said. "The rest should be able to sit comfy in the bed." The men looked towards the girls, who were the smallest of us. In the end, it was Maria who volunteered for the front. Jessica loved the idea of wind blowing in her hair, and joined the rest of us in the truck bed.

"It's only been a few days away from the farm, but it feels like such a long time," Alan observed. The engine came to a start and the bed shook with the shift of a gear.

"Yeah, but our lives were nearly forfeit," Thomas responded, "that changes how we feel about time passing."

"It feels like I've aged ten years," Jessica said.

I couldn't help but look at her, "Doesn't look it though." I didn't mean much by it, but somehow, I could see a tinge of red appear on her cheeks.

"I don't know about you guys but I fe—" Lucas couldn't even finish his words when the entire bed rattled as we pulled over a bump. He grabbed his mouth so fast that I thought he might have bit his tongue off by accident. "God damn thathhurth," he said with a lisp. "Don't feelththo good anymore." And that got a light-hearted laugh out of Alan.

The ride was completely different to how I had thought it would be. We were shaking and bumping all over the place, and not on account of Richards' driving. This truck was on its last legs, and if it made it the seven-hour trip I might find myself believing in a god. Having seen Lucas' mishap, I kept my mouth closed to avoid biting my tongue.

At first the bumping and rattling was unbearable, but after getting up to a decent speed the droning and rhythmic bouncing was almost sort of relaxing. We occasionally got jerked around when Richard needed to avoid a zombie or goblin in the road, but besides that it wasn't that bad.

117

Time didn't drag on even though I wasn't doing anything other than sitting in the truck bed. In fact, it felt like time was moving too quickly and after several hours, I realized I was going to miss this feeling. I felt carefree for the first time in such a long time. There was nothing I had to worry about, no plans to make. I slouched down a bit and closed my eyes.

I wasn't sure how long they were closed for, and I was on the cusp of falling asleep even, when we came to an abrupt halt. The sudden change caused us all to slide into the back window of the truck in a bundle.

I collided into metal with a hard smack as did everyone else. Alan ended up beneath us nearly smothered by our falling bodies, "What's happening?" he yelled.

None of us could find the time to answer in that moment. We were all off balance and it was all I could do to avoid toppling over only after I'd caught myself one-handed from landing on the pile of bodies did I yell, "I don't know."

"Is everyone okay back there?" This was Maria's voice coming through the plastic partition from the front. I could only let out a groan in response.

"We're okay!" Lucas said while grabbing my loose hand and helping me balance. "What's going on?"

I could hear Richard's voice now, "Look ahead." And we all stood up and then peered over the top of the vehicle, "What do you make of that?" he asked with sadness evident in his voice.

It looked like the sky was now vertical in front of us. A wall of fog stretched from left to right as far as I could see and disappeared into the sky above with no end in sight. The look of it made me think that we should be entering a roaring a storm, and yet the area was silent. Just an eerie and uninviting choice lay ahead of us.

"What's the call, boss?" Richard said jokingly. "Do we go into that?"

This was definitely a choice for all of us to decide.

"How far away are we from the farm?" I asked. It was impossible to know if this was a short film of mist in front of us, or an endless abyss of murk and danger that covered a vast amount of land, including our base.

"About two hours left," Richard said.

"Is it possible to drive in that fog?" I asked.

"Well, I know the road and it's mostly a straight shot. Problem would be if we run into something along the way," Richard replied. "That something would either be monsters or humans, and either way if they were on the road it might be hard to stop before hitting them."

"What does everyone think?" I looked around. I saw faces that were still uneasy and recovering from the near accident moments earlier.

"Well, it doesn't look like there's any way around it," Jessica said.

"True, but is everyone okay with going in?" I asked. For me this wasn't so simple. This was some sort of event or new worldly phenomena. No one could know what it entailed. Hell, it could be a fog of death that instantly killed us when we went inside.

Maria looked upset. "We have to get back to our friends at the farm."

Despite my worries, which must have been shared by everyone, no one disagreed. As I looked around and saw nods, it was clear everyone was ready to traverse through the wall of fog. My next question was this though, "Do we drive through or go on foot?"

"The faster we're through the better." Alan said. No one disagreed with that sentiment, and it was settled. We braced ourselves and Richard drove slowly towards this unknown fog wall.

I was expecting some development as we approached, but there was nothing. It was simply a menacing grey wall that obscured our vision completely. Not a single sound came from within, and nothing could be discerned from outside.

The truck drove at a snail's pace as we passed through, and even as the front of the truck went in, we in the bed couldn't see even a few inches from our face. There was no feeling, no scents. It was as if we had passed through nothing at all.

Richard put the pickup in park as soon as we had gone about ten feet deep. We stopped and waited: waited for anything that might come at us, any development, and yet nothing happened. It was just a dark and gloomy atmosphere on all sides. The visibility to the front was low, anything beyond three or four feet in front of us was obscured completely. Even the tips of my hands when fully outstretched were hard to pick out.

"It will be absolutely impossible to see where you're going," Maria said. She was nervous as could be, and I didn't blame her.

"The road's still there," Richard replied. That was true, and it seemed that answer was good enough for all of us. He turned on the high beams, which helped slightly, and eased forward.

I couldn't tell how fast we were going at all, but I knew we were moving. The truck still rattled and shook, and we were tossed like clothes in a dryer. There was no wind in this place, the fog around us didn't displace as we drove. My hand just passed through the fog as if it was some ghastly vapor all around us.

"This doesn't feel right," Alan said what I was thinking, but what choice did we have? Well, we always had a choice, but we needed

120

to get to the farm and fast. That feeling prickling on the back of my neck was growing stronger. Was it for the farm? Or was it this fog we currently found ourselves inside.

"We'll be fine," I said. I didn't know for certain, but I said it anyway. We had to keep moving, and moving we did, for about thirty minutes. At least I think it was thirty minutes? I couldn't tell how long I had been rattling there in the bed.

There was a loud sputter and then a pop. Something happened with the engine, and in moments we came to a slow crawl—something I could only tell based on the shaking we were no longer experiencing.

"It finally gave out!" Richard yelled to us. He had to yell, everything was muffled here. Sound just didn't travel normally. Nothing about this place felt right. The doors on the truck opened and the three in front jumped out from within the cabin.

Those of us in the back leaped out too and then we all gathered together. "Is this something you can fix?" Thomas asked. Repairing the vehicle was worth a shot, at least. It was hard to know how far we had gone given that judging speed and movement was terrible here. Only Richard could really know based on the speedometer, assuming that was working as normal.

The air was stagnant. I hadn't felt even the slightest bit of airflow even when driving being fully exposed in the back. The prickling on the back of my neck grew even worse. "I can look, but it's likely we'll be walking," Richard said. "We made good progress though. I'd guess about two or three hours left on foot." His estimate was so wildly off the distance I thought we had traveled I was shocked.

"Walking…in this?" Jessica was thinking the same thing as me. We didn't have a choice though. It was either sit here and hope something changed, or start walking and get out. Plus, we didn't know if the fog even extended as far as the farm. Maybe it was merely thirty more minutes of this nightmare?

I was about to open my mouth and try and boost our morale when I realized the words wouldn't come out. I couldn't speak and my thoughts started to muddle. Fear was visible on my comrades' faces—I wasn't the only one experiencing it. Fear and adrenaline coursed through me, keeping me standing long enough to see Maria fall to the floor.

Chapter 14: The Fog of Illusions

A hand gripped the side of the truck as I curled like a shrimp. It was all blurry, and then I felt nothing, heard nothing. I could only see the others fall over like dominoes in the periphery of my blurred vision.

"Can you wake up and turn that shit off?" A voice came from across my dreams.

I jerked out of bed to the sound of an alarm blaring over and over. My left hand grasped my head as a sharp pain raced behind my eyes; my right jerked outwards, feeling for the alarm clock.

The sunlight coming through my curtains was bright enough to blind me, and in my haste I knocked the alarm clock off the dresser. It smashed into the ground with a bang and ceased making noise. With any luck it was broken and I'd not have to deal with it again.

"Thank God." I let out an exasperated sigh while falling back into my pillow. The alarm clock could wait, broken or not. My eyes burned; my head pounded. I'd never felt such unbelievable pain after waking up.

"You're late!" The voice came again. His name eluded me for a moment—my roommate, and once friend—that was it, Alexander. We got along great as friends, but living together was something else entirely, and we were now strictly roommates.

I forced my eyes open a crack and leaned over, my hand scraping along the floor to find the alarm clock. It was 4:30 in the afternoon.

Why didn't that mean anything to me? I opened my phone to check, and sure enough on my calendar, I was scheduled for a shift at 4. The panic hit me instantly and then subsided like I'd never felt before.

I dialed work and a voice I'd learned to love to hate came through, "Where are you? You're already thirty minutes late." Decrepit, uncaring, judging.

"Sorry, someone parked me in and they just left now. I had to call a towing company. I'll be there as soon as possible." It was a blatant lie, but it was out there and specific enough that maybe I could slide by this time.

There was a pause on the other side, and I was expecting some scolding, but all I got was "Don't let it happen again."

"Got it," I said while jumping out of bed. My lethargy was quickly gone, but the headache remained, stabbing me behind the eyes. Headaches weren't uncommon with my lack of proper sleep, but a migraine this bad wasn't normal.

I moved to the kitchen while half dressed and found the ibuprofen, popped three in my mouth, and then opened the fridge and chugged straight from the container of orange juice. Alexander was eyeing me, and normally I'd have muttered an apology, but honestly, I didn't care in this moment.

My vest was half on, and I could only shrug one half of my body, and that would have to do. He walked away without a word, typical of our interactions lately. I didn't remember exactly what started this mess but it was my current life. Every day I expected him to let me know he was moving out and weirdly enough, that feeling didn't illicit any emotion on my end: a scary thought.

Life was like that these days. I merely existed without much thought. My closest friends were all acquaintances I made online, and Alexander, the one whom wasn't strictly online, wouldn't call himself my friend if asked, at least not anymore. Most of my enjoyment came from not living in the real world, and my relationships suffered greatly for it.

Prospects weren't great, really. My parents tried their best to be supportive, but somehow I found a way to fuck that up, too. I just didn't try enough with them, which was crazy in comparison to my efforts with video games. With the games you'd think that losing was the end of the world.

A day wouldn't be enough time to bitch all about my life. Unfortunately, it was me who had fucked it up in the first place. I told myself that made it okay, but obviously it wasn't. Things were crumbling around me and I still spent most of my time gaming—addiction or coping mechanism, who knew?—or at least that's what my parents liked to throw at me lately.

The drive to work was a blur. I found myself a bit more excited than usual. Eventually I grasped why: the late shifts were way better than the morning shifts. Less foot traffic, and that let me get my work done in peace. I always got an earful when I clocked out in the afternoon and things weren't tidied up.

No amount of explaining that I had customers nonstop for the entire shift would get me out of that earful. A slow night tonight, I hoped. Plenty of time to browse my phone and then get the shop ready for the morning. A feeling of happiness crept up without me even realizing it. Why was I so pleased about this?

The scolding I expected to get in person didn't come either. I figured on the drive over may manager must have had a customer she was dealing with, else I'd have got a good licking over the phone. Things felt…off.

As I entered the shop, a fake lemon scent struck me like a hammer and the aching behind my eyes grew so strong I almost keeled over. "Don't try and pretend sick, boy," my manager said. She? Why couldn't I even remember her name?

"Sorry, I'm not. I just need a moment," I groaned while racing to the bathroom. The pain became so extreme I felt nauseous. The thought of throwing up hadn't even hit me before I was emptying the contents of my stomach. The burning sensation in my throat and mouth was the only other thing I could feel besides the stabbing behind my eyes.

I turned on the faucet and splashed my face, pushing my fingers hard into the crevice of my eyes as if trying to pry them out, as if that pressure might relieve this pounding. Somehow or another it did—it helped for a moment. I stood in front of the mirror massaging and rubbing my eyes.

"Mike, let's go!" A knock came abruptly and the headache that I had alleviated spiked back up for a moment.

"Coming." I flushed the toilet as a cover and then wiped my face hard before drying my hands and face and walking out. The hammering that made it hard to function abated slowly and the nausea dissipated.

"Just do your best. It will be a slow night," she said. Words of encouragement? This wasn't normal. Everything felt off. I fumbled behind the counter and locked the door behind me. It was almost 5 PM, the time everyone was getting off work, and yet it was slow.

It was as though her words held some weight here, that they morphed reality. Nothing felt right. A ding at the entrance pulled my attention outward. A regular, his name traced the tip of my tongue. "Hey Mike, I'll take the usual."

His voice put a name to his face, "Hey Rick, how's it been?" I asked as if it had been the thousandth time. My hand searched beneath the register for the scratch offs. I pulled out the ones with the ladies on 'em. "Two?" I asked.

"Two," he said back. I placed them on the counter and his face looked off, "You know I get the ones with the cowboys on 'em." And it was like a bomb had gone off in my head. This isn't real—nothing that's happening is real.

My head started to pound like nothing before. I could only barely hear Rick in the background, "I didn't mean to upset you Mike. I'll take the ladies." He spoke as if he was trying to appease me, to keep me trapped here.

This isn't real. The images in front of my face started to wave like a blur, and for a moment I hesitated. Lightheadedness—I was going to black out. This isn't real.

I opened my eyes. The pain was gone, but my thoughts... they moved like dried clay—slow, lethargic—I was confused. Where am I? The ground beneath me dug in sharp. A hand traced the floor. It was concrete, dirty and old like a country road.

I sat up as best as I could, my thoughts grasping at anything that would fix me to a particular place. A truck was there to lean on and supported me. Wait, a truck? I scurried up and things started to come back to me. "Jessica!" I yelled.

My feet moved and before I could finish that first step I stumbled into something. It was impossible to see a damned thing, even the bottom of my feet. I knew what it was and my heart stopped instantly. A body.

I leaned down low, it was Alan. My hands raced up to his face—felt his cold cheek. My heart was in my throat. I leaned in close and put my cheek so I was nearly touching his lips. Felt a warm exhalation. He's breathing!

Alarm bells started ringing in my head. The others were all here around the truck, hidden by the fog. Alan was alive, they were all hopefully alive. His breathing was so shallow though, and checking the party window I could see his HP was slowly draining.

They were all there in the party window—alive and barely hanging on. I didn't know how long I was out, or why I was even awake at this moment. It felt like the illusion—or whatever that was—was trying to appease me, to let me live my old life. My old life though…it wasn't great.

I buried that thought as I leaned down and grabbed hold of Alan. It was a struggle to get him up. Moving someone that was as lifeless as a doll and weighed over one-hundred-eighty pounds was not easy at all. I was huffing by the time I had him pinned up against the truck. I couldn't carry everyone, and so I'd have to find a way. I'd also proven to myself that I couldn't wake Alan by slapping or shaking him.

The truck bed came down and I forced him inside, dragging him in like a bag of grain. There was no time to stop or catch my breath. My sweat was clinging to my body and there wasn't the slightest movement of air to provide any cooling sensation. I was sweltering.

I found them all one by one, each as unconscious as Alan, each as cold as Alan was, lips purple and skin slightly dark. Their life force was being slowly drained away by whatever visions they were seeing.

It took me dozens of minutes to load them into the truck, and by then I was so exhausted I could barely move. The only thing I knew for certain was this fog was the cause. Judging by how their life was being drained, I had a few hours max to get them out.

Panic started to set in, and then inner calm fought that panic back. The vehicle wouldn't move on its own, and so I opted for the next best thing. I put the vehicle in neutral and then cast Shallow Grave. I needed to repopulate my skeletons. There were no reincarnations available so basic skeletons would have to do.

There was a road beneath us and I could at least follow this wherever it went. I instructed my minions to push, and the lot of them moved behind the vehicle and started pushing. It wasn't fast, but it was better than nothing.

The murmuring of my friends from inside the truck scared me. I could hear a mixture of sounds of pleasure and excitement and the occasional laugh: it seemed most of them weren't exactly unhappy with their previous life. They were enjoying whatever they were being visually fed.

Richard had said the farm was a few hours on foot, but would this hellscape end before then? Before anyone died and I could have them out safely? That was now my goal, and the best-case scenario was that the cursed fog would end soon. I didn't want to think about the alternative.

I watched the party window like a hawk and counted in my head. They were losing around one percent of their HP every three minutes, and, as far as I could tell, the effect didn't harm any one person more than another. Currently, they were all somewhere around forty-percent HP, which gave me roughly two hours of time.

My HP wasn't going down at all anymore, which helped calm my rattled nerves slightly. If they woke up on their own as I did, they would be safe, albeit a little out of it. For now though I needed to get the vehicle moving.

I could hear my minion's bones quivering and clacking as they pushed into the truck. It was no easy feat to keep the wheels rolling, especially when we went up an incline. My minions' skinless feet didn't have the best traction on solid ground and they toppled over constantly.

The two abominations I had previously would have made easy work of this, and even the reanimated Children of Sobek could have helped tremendously. I had no choice but to buck up and join them at the back.

I was already at the end of my rope on stamina, and the lack of airflow made me wonder if I would get heat stroke if I kept overexerting myself. It took over a minute of breaking my back before the vehicle started cresting a rise and began to move forward.

The truck built up momentum slowly, and only after thirty seconds of steady rolling did I dare stop putting all my weight into it. The skeletons had an easier time of it now too that it was already moving, and they kept it going.

This was the kind of pace we would make if we took our time walking at a leisurely pace, and it made me nervous to no end, but instructing my skeletons to push harder didn't do anything but make them tumble and fall over.

The wheels of the vehicle clearly hadn't been aligned anytime recently, as the truck constantly tried to veer off course and take a right turn directly into a barbed wired fence—one that I couldn't see but assumed was there. I had to sit in the driver's seat and fight the vehicle's urge to turn, which made it even harder to see the path. Crashing into a fence or pit would mean the death of my comrades, most if not all of them.

That dark thought raced through my head, and somehow or another I found myself picking who I would save if the time came to abandon the truck and move faster on foot. Jessica was a given, and if necessary I'd carry her on my back no matter what. It was the others that left me conflicted. I could maybe take one to two more people with my minions bearing their weight.

It was hard to shake that scenario from my head. Without the high beams guiding the way, I really couldn't see where I was going or if we were leaving the road. Fortunately, there was a different feeling when the tires touched grass, and I used that to stop from losing the road.

I could feel the bubbling anxiety inside my gut. Inner Calm was the only thing keeping me together, and no doubt the only thing keeping me from losing the little food I did have inside my stomach. It was a building tension though, one that I feared would burst forth.

Every minute that passed without exiting this miasma made the anxiety worse. Even Inner Calm only worked so well and I started to feel a growing dizziness: a feeling of impending doom weighing me down.

Chapter 15: Trying to Escape the Miasma of Doom

Time dragged on and on. Every minute inside this miasma felt like five, and my mind started to play tricks on me. I would reach a panic thinking twenty or thirty minutes had passed only to check my party window and see that it had been just a few minutes. I was too far to turn back now, and no direction was the right one.

I was near my breaking point after an hour—a real hour of time. Even holding the steering wheel proved difficult as patches of black fluttered over my vision. I was ready to close my eyes and a thought raced through my head over and over. Going out like this wouldn't be so bad.

Eternal sleep would hardly be the worst way to die given the current state of the world. It took seconds to think of many more ways to go out that caused chills to race up my spine. I wasn't in my right mind, and even knowing that didn't change anything.

I let go one hand at a time. My eyes locked to the steering wheel as it turned on its own to the right—emotionally I felt nothing. The feeling of tires rolling over grass came through the seat and then my body jerked abruptly as we came to a stop.

Even the collision sounded muffled, or maybe we just hadn't hit that hard. In that moment I didn't give a shit which it was. I was mentally exhausted and only wanted to close my eyes for a moment. The silence of this place didn't bother me right now, it was peaceful.

The longer I focused on that silence, the more I could hear a muttering coming from the truck bed. It took a moment to realize it wasn't normal. The laughter, the cheerfulness, the excitement was something I had to hear the entire trip, I had learned to zone it out. This, this was different—muddled confusion from someone talking to themselves.

The voice was feminine and an image of Jessica flashed through my head instantly. An electric shock raced through me as all the lethargy left my body. I whipped around as I opened the window from the truck cabin and peered out.

It was Anna struggling to get upright in the truck bed. The sight caused my stomach to churn, like a body resurrecting out of a pile of corpses. None of them are dead! That thought crossed my mind instantly.

I opened the truck door and jumped out. The incline I expected to see wasn't that steep, but we had hit the barbed wire fence as I had anticipated. Relief washed over me as I realized this situation was probably salvageable. My focus shifted to Anna as I came around the back and helped get her out of the truck.

The confusion in her eyes slowly faded as she came to realize where she was and who I was. That confusion morphed to fear as I explained what was happening, "What do we do?" were the only words that came out of her mouth.

Guilt washed over me and my mouth struggled to open as I wondered whether I was even fit to answer that question. I wanted to answer, "I don't know." But there was only Anna and I. It was only us that could answer that question, "We have to get the truck back on the road. The incline isn't that steep so we just need to push it out with the help of my undead."

She gave a nod and then came with me to the front of the vehicle as we both assessed the situation. The ditch off the road really wasn't steep at all. The front of the vehicle was merely three feet down on an incline, maybe less, with the truck bed still resting on road level.

I tasked my undead to start pushing as hard as they could from anywhere they could find some leverage in the right direction. Some even went over the barbed wire fence and started to push from that side. The vehicle shook with each push, but wouldn't budge.

"The fence is caught in the truck grill," Anna called out frantically. The grill had been bent and broken from collisions, which left plenty of openings for the barbed wire to slip in and get stuck. Visibility was terrible so I leaned in close to take a look. It was a tangled mess, and her simple observation was the biggest understatement. It would have been more accurate to say the fence and the truck were now one entity.

A nauseous dizzying feeling raced through my gut and I nearly threw up on the spot. Nothing short of pulling out this entire fence would get the vehicle back on the road. My mind raced for answers as I called my skeleton generals forward to hack away at the fence.

The Zweihander came down repeatedly, but merely acted as a bludgeoning weapon. It was sharp, but that sharpness was measured by how well it cut flesh, not metal. We might as well have been smashing into the barbed wire with a hammer. There was no tool in the truck that could get us out of this either.

Even worse was the fact this barbed wire was nearly new. I had seen the rickety barbed fence hours ago, nearly rusted to nothing. That would have probably been easy to cut in just a few slashes.

Decay…

"Move back for a second," I said to Anna. An idea had come to me. Anna removed her hands from within the grate and stepped back. Her mouth moved to open but I started to cast Decay before she could even ask what I was doing.

At first there was no indication anything was happening, but after the third cast the sheen on the metal started to fade.

"Whatever you are doing is working!" Anna said in excitement. By the fifth cast, the steel was turning a reddish hue that indicated rust. When my MP was nearly exhausted, the truck grate and the steel wire were chipped and rusted almost completely through. The barbs had fallen off and it was simply a metal string on its last legs.

My skeleton general came forward with his Zweihander, hooked the blade inside the links and pulled outward instead of smashing in. Like broken kite strings each piece of metal began to bend and snap in sequence. The flexibility they once had was gone, and even the slightest tug at an angle caused them to snap, sending rust flakes and dust flying into the air.

Anna rushed forward and grabbed the entire bundle before pulling any loose threads of metal free and tossing them to the ground. Red dust caked her hands, but a smile of excitement covered her face. "Whatever you just did, was so cool."

I wanted to smile, but I almost keeled over right there and then. My breathing was labored and the heat I was feeling overwhelmed me. The lack of airflow here came back again and again to haunt me. I just couldn't cool myself off.

"Let's try it again." I said to Anna through labored breaths.

"Will you be okay?" she asked.

"I will be if we can get out of here." She gave a nod and we positioned ourselves in the front of the truck to push. "Three, two, one." I counted down and then we shoved with all our might. The vehicle rocked and moved several feet back up the ditch onto the road and then came to an abrupt halt before moving back down at us. "Watch out!" I yelled. Anna and I jumped to the side in a hurry as the vehicle crashed back into the wooden stake the barbed wire was originally attached to.

There was a small hump that the front wheels had gotten stuck on—the final hurdle to get the entire vehicle back on even ground. The front tires just couldn't make it over that little lip off the road. "Would ice help?" Anna suddenly asked. I looked at her with a face that probably said explain more. "To like, maybe make it easier to slide up the hill?" she asked.

"It...could work," I spoke slowly, trying to imagine it in my mind where ice might be effective. "Can you put it only under the truck's tires? Or even right here." I pointed to the little section we had gotten stuck on. If the entire ground was ice, we'd lose all traction for pushing at the truck.

"I can." Anna spoke with confidence. The Staff of Piercing Ice she had received from us entered her hand from thin air and began to grow a brilliant blue hue. It was the most dazzling and beautiful blue I'd ever seen, even in this grey world that sucked the life out of everything.

Her lips moved eloquently as I struggled to hear the words coming from her mouth. I doubted I could even understand them if I could hear them, anyway. A blue aura surged and then her eyes became laser focused. Her hand pointed outward as ice began to rapidly form under the vehicle. It took mere seconds before the bottom of the wheels and the ground under the truck was a solid layer of ice.

For the first time in hours I felt a chill rush up my spine that was pleasant. The area around me was cool, and even my rattled nerves calmed rapidly. "Let's try again!" I said with excitement.

This time the pushing was easy. There was no friction at all, and the only thing that kept the truck from spinning wildly was the fact the back two wheels were resting on non-frozen ground. One solid shove and we were back on the road.

With that success filling my mind, I asked Anna to freeze the entire pathway ahead so we could glide along like a vehicle on ice skates, but she assured me that was a terrible idea. It didn't need to take any extensive thinking to realize that, and, truthfully, I told myself I wasn't an idiot, I just liked the feeling of being cooled off.

It felt like an eternity had passed, and the thought of opening the party window left me nervous to no end. Even Anna had been skirting around the topic of how everyone else was doing. She was probably scared to find out the answer, and for good reason: they were piled in the back like we were headed straight for the morgue.

"They're alive, just barely," I said, "But we don't have long." The little detour I had caused was merely ten minutes of time, but that was ten less minutes we had to get out of this place. Another fear gripped me as well: what if they didn't wake up even after we left the miasma?

I was going to spiral in a negative way thinking about it, "You steer," I said to Anna, "I'll push." I didn't want to think about it. I joined my skeleton warriors at the back and shoved as hard as I could, shutting my brain off and fighting off the dizziness.

There was no reason to even look ahead anymore. My eyes looked down at the miasma blocking my feet from view. They were there of course, moving one step at a time. I was in a rhythm, so much so that when the miasma no longer blocked my feet from view, it didn't register in my brain.

It was Anna's excited yell that shook me from my labored stupor, "We're out! We're OUT!" She yelled from the truck. Her voice was so loud now that it carried quite a distance. Her hands came over her mouth in shock, "Sorry!" she whispered between fingers. Shouting was bad, it drew attention from monsters, but I didn't care at this moment.

How long had I been pushing that vehicle from behind? I couldn't even guess. My stomach churned as I gained the courage to open the party window and check my friends' status. The relief put me on my ass. They were all alive, with merely a few percent of their life left each.

We weren't out of it yet though, and the next thought nearly put me out cold. There was a chance their HP would continue to drop even after leaving the miasma. They hadn't instantly woken up yet after all.

I watched their HP bars like a hawk for several minutes. It felt hard to breathe that entire time, and Anna must have felt the same as she did not break my concentration. After several minutes, their HP ticked upwards instead of downwards.

Everything I had been feeling came out at once in the loudest scream I'd ever let out in my life, "AHH!" I screamed till my voice cracked, and Anna, who was keeping her distance, ran over to cover my mouth.

"Are you crazy?" she yelled back.

"I am crazy," I said. "But I'm also happier than I've ever been." I let myself fall back till I was lying on the road. The free gravel and rocks dug into my back. It was as painful, maybe even more so, as stepping on dozens of Legos. Yet I knew in this moment I was alive, as sure as the sky was blue and grass was green. So were my friends.

"Should we wake them up?" Suddenly Anna was looking down on me from above.

"Let's wait a little bit and see if they wake on their own." I was a bit worried forcefully waking them after everything would cause problems. Something else also tickled my curiosity, "How come you woke up?" I asked. There was also the fact I had woken up as well.

I opened my stat page in the hopes I'd find the answer there.

Name: Mike Class: Necromancer Level: 21
EXP: 93%
HP: 434/1085 **MP:** 35/455
STR: 5 **Fear Resistance:** 5
AGI: 2
DEX: 5
VIT: 29 +14
WIS: 27 +23
Available: 0
Skills: [A] **Summon Skeleton LV.** 9| [A]
Summon Skeleton Mage LV. 2| [A] **Decay**
LV. 3| [A] **Reanimate Dead LV.** 3| [A] **Bone**
Armor LV. 2 | [A] **Vast Shadows** | [A]
Temporary Grave LV. 1 | [P] **Sixth Sense** |
[P] **Bravery LV.** 2 | [P] **Mutated LV.** 3| [P]
Pain Resistance LV. 2 | [P] **Skeletal**
Mastery LV. 4| [P]**Intimidate Living** |[P]
Inner Calm LV. 2 |[P] **Necrotic Vision**

It had only been two days, but it felt like an eternity since the last time I had checked my stats. We hadn't encountered anything of note on the way to meeting Richard and Anna.

Surprisingly, Decay had reached level three while in the miasma. I didn't realize that using it on an inanimate object worked to gain

EXP, but it had seemed to increase my mastery none the less. The cast-time had vanished, and it gained an enormous range increase, up to six meters. Did that mean it was instant?

Mutated had leveled to 3 as well, yet there was still no indication of what effect resulted from it. It was possibly an all-or-nothing passive ability, but what would the max level be then? Five? Maybe Ten? Could it have been the reason for my waking up? Perhaps the deathly properties of the miasma just didn't affect me as much because I was mutated in some way.

There was no point in speculating about this, so I turned my attention to Anna. She began to read out her passives to me, and after exhausting every option, there was only one that I thought might have been relevant. She had a passive called Clear Mind. This was something she had gained when becoming a Wizard, which helped her focus and improve her casting ability, and also seemed to have a benefit towards seeing through or breaking illusions.

"I didn't mind the dream I was having," she said. "In fact, a part of me wishes that I'd not woken up. It was so pleasant." I could see the longing in her eyes as she said that. One thing I'd noticed about Anna from the beginning is how easy she was to read. Her emotions were always visible on her face, something I appreciated. "What about you?" she asked.

"Uhh, it was okay." I fumbled out. "Nothing special." I honestly didn't like talking about myself that much. My situation felt shameful, and I realized in that moment that I was actually ashamed of who I was before the apocalypse. It suddenly got a whole lot harder to even talk about what I saw in my illusion or about myself. "How do you know Richard?" I asked instead.

"I didn't know him before all this," Anna replied. "There were five us originally, but now it's just us two." I didn't ask her

140

specifically, but she started to talk about her past—Twenty-three years old, swam in high school competitively at state level. Didn't make the cut for college, and couldn't decide on what she wanted to do that wasn't swimming.

"Then after that, I decided that I should take a break from school because I couldn't make a decision. Long story short my parents didn't like that, and my relationship with them turned sour. That was three years ago, they live several states away now and we talk once or twice a year. I wait tables on the weekend and am a swim instructor during the week to make ends meet." She paused in thought, "The dream…was honestly a struggle, but it was better than this."

I could see in her eyes all she wanted was some assurance. Someone to tell her it would be okay. Lying wasn't bad all the time. "It's gonna be alright. We'll make our way to the farm and start fresh," I said.

Chapter 16: Just Who Are My Group Members?

"And them? Did you know them before?" she asked while looking at the truck with the bodies of my friends in it. "What's their story?"

"I didn't know them before…and uhhh." I paused awkwardly. I really didn't know much about any of them. In fact, Anna had shared more information about herself in these brief five minutes than any of the others had since we met. "I think it would be a good bonding exercise if we talked about it as a group." I suggested.

After Anna told me her story, it really felt like something was missing. These were people that I wanted to remember, and yet I knew nothing about them past their name and how they acted.

How would I even describe them in the future if something happened to them. Yeah, I used to adventure with some guy named Alan and… that's about all I know of him. I was joking with myself, but deep down it bothered me that I hadn't made more of an effort.

"So what do you make of this?" she asked. "This…situation?"

"The monsters, the leveling?" I asked to clarify.

"Yeah, what do you make of it? Is it some random event or is there something behind it?"

"I…haven't thought about it that much," I admitted, "but something must be behind it, right? There's an intelligence behind the design."

"I bet its aliens," Anna said suddenly. Her expression was so determined it was almost like she had the answer already. "Definitely." She crossed her arms right after and then looked at me for approval.

"It might be, yeah…" I scratched my head. "Maybe God was bored?" I threw that out there.

"Nah, if it isn't aliens then it's probably sentient AI from a distant galaxy." I felt my eyes nearly popping out of my skull. She crossed her arms triumphantly and then kept stealing glances, no doubt for more approval.

"You know…you might be on to something." I was struggling to find words that didn't reveal my incredulity when I saw Thomas sit up in the truck with a most confused expression on his face. "Thomas!" I yelled out to him.

His face showed surprise as he looked at me there was no sign of recognition in his eyes: my heart almost stopped right then.

"Mike!" Thomas suddenly yelled after about ten seconds of gathering himself. God damn, this was a roller coaster of emotions. I had been worried that he had lost his memories.

Like clockwork everyone started to wake up, and in every case, found themselves slightly muddle-headed for a short while. After about fifteen minutes the whole party was fully coherent and grouped up once more. There didn't seem to be any long-lasting effects from the mist, and besides being low on HP, everyone was fine. They all did report feeling extremely lethargic though.

It made sense that losing so much HP would cause fatigue, and even after being healed by Thomas, they remained exhausted. The good news though was how close we were to Sangeal. "Two hours of steady walking and we'll be able to see the city," Richard said.

It was only midday and I didn't want to lose an entire day to resting. That prickling on the back of my neck was still there. My intuition was that we needed to hurry and so I pushed the group to continue onwards, "I'm good to walk," I said. That got the ball rolling.

"Me too, we can go around Sangeal while we recover," Lucas suggested.

"I know everyone is tired, but we aren't exactly nocturnal," I added. "Sleeping during the day can mess up our schedule in a bad way." And if anyone was still on the fence about resting up they must have decided I was speaking sense as we all got underway at a decent pace.

The countryside looked beautiful and I felt like we were walking through an area untouched by the world's current blight. If I had woken up here with no memories of the apocalypse, I wouldn't have been able to imagine a single thing was wrong. Just a few moments after having that thought, it was shattered by a ghoul rushing out of the forest in our direction.

"Even the most uninhabited places will probably be over-run soon," Richard said suddenly. He took the words right out of my mouth and then smashed the ghoul's skull in with a mace.

"Were you two in any of the bigger cities?" Jessica asked.

"Thankfully not," Richard said. "I heard it was really bad." This was an opportunity for me to redress the feeling I should take more of an interest in my companions—to learn about their past and what they experienced before this event, but Richard did so on his own volition.

After he'd talked about his experiences in a small town, Richard seemed very intent on knowing as much about us as possible and one after the other, asked questions of us. "Sorry, I just have a hard time trusting someone if all I know is a face and name." Somehow, that was enough for everyone to start talking.

We talked as we walked, each person took a turn at explaining their lifestyle before the apocalypse. I didn't know what I was expecting, and the ages I had in my mind were actually quite off.

Alan was only nineteen years old, yet he looked like he was at least twenty-five. Loved the outdoors: fishing, hunting, bush craft. Graduated high school and started working in a bait and tackle shop with no intent of going to college. Bad upbringing, no mother in his life and his father was an alcoholic. The non-violent kind, he specified.

Thomas was his cousin, twenty-two years old. Outdoors type like Alan but not nearly as much. Went to high school with Alan, decided the small-town life wasn't for him and went to college studying Psychology and was in his third year. Was planning to graduate and move away.

Lucas was twenty-seven. He had lost his girlfriend at the start of the apocalypse, which Jessica and I knew about already. Parents died when he was much younger and his grandparents took care of him. At eighteen he had moved to Sangeal with the inheritance money and tried to make it as a game designer: hadn't been going as planned.

Jessica was the person I was most interested in finding out about, and her story made my heart hurt. Two years older than me, her parents passed away just two months prior to the apocalyptic event. She had no siblings, and the only family in her life was her grandfather on her mother's side. He lived several states away in a retirement home, so there was no hope in checking up on him anytime soon.

Having gone to school for nursing, Jessica decided it wasn't for her, that she enjoyed working with numbers more. She restarted her degree in business, focusing mostly on accounting. Went to school and was working part-time at a bank when the apocalypse hit.

Maria was only seventeen, which was right around my guess. She was a junior in high school and according to her, a first-generation immigrant. Both of her parents were killed when the apocalypse began and even if the remainder of her family were alive, they were on a different continent. When she finished her account, there were tears on her cheeks and both Jessica and Anna ended up squeezing Maria till her face turned blue. They assured her that she was going to be well taken care of.

I told my story honestly, even though I felt embarrassed the entire time about it. I wasn't wrong that it sounded shameful. Maria revealed that when she came right out and stabbed a dagger through my heart, "Really? You did that dead-end job and had no plans, not even to manage the garage?" she added. "But you're so much more…impressive now." I could only cough at her remark and quickly gestured towards both Anna and Richard.

Anna I had already heard about and Richard went last. Thirty-three years old, high school education, he worked part-time as a guard for a storage facility on the night shift. Parents lived in a different state, his brother lived about five or six hours away in one of the larger cities.

When I thought the story time was over, he threw another curveball. "Have you killed anyone? People I mean, not monsters." It was like a bomb had been dropped on the group. As far as I knew,

Jessica and I were the only people to kill anyone. I had taken out the two brothers, and Jessica had put an arrow in Thomas's and Alan's cousin when he pulled the shotgun on me. There was Ghost Hand too, and I really wasn't sure about the others and what they did then. Everything had happened so fast.

One after the other, the group members said 'no' to Richard's question until it got to us. Lucas and the rest knew about Jessica, but none of them heard the story of the fight at my workplace. I brushed over the gruesome details and told the gist of it: we were facing bad people, and I had to choose between Jessica and myself, or them. I added the caveat about Ghost Hand, with Lucas and Alan chipping in as well for that story.

With hindsight, the choices involved were simple, even though they were a matter of life or death. No one showed any reservation or surprise when I finished explaining the incidents. Richard actually seemed relieved to hear them. It turned out too, that he had killed one person as well. It wasn't something out of the ordinary I suspected.

A man had attempted to rob them of their truck. This was when everything started, and they had about five people in their group. Losing the vehicle was most definitely a death sentence for them, and Richard made the call. One life versus five, it wasn't a hard decision to make, but definitely one to carry out.

"I was worried I'd be the only one," Richard said. "If I'm going to be following someone, I need to know they are ready to make decisions at a moment's notice and prioritize our lives above all else."

"We've been in some shitty situations and have pulled through every time so far," Alan suddenly said to Richard. "I trust everyone here, and I hope to learn to trust you, too."

"Good!" Richard suddenly laughed hard. "I hope to be able to trust each and every single one of you as well." His face was all smiles, and it seemed most everyone else felt the same. It was good to lay everything on the table.

We kept walking for at least another hour and the conversations fragmented. Richard and Alan both took to the front discussing who knows what. They were both tanks now, and would be working together. It almost felt like Alan might get that father figure he was missing.

Maria was in the back nearly hissing. No matter how many times she repeated the phrase "I'm fine. It's okay," Jessica and Anna continued to pelt her with love. I heard a few promises thrown in that I wasn't sure either of them could keep, but they put a smile on Maria's face regardless. It was good to have hope.

"Do you guys smell that?" This was Thomas who was on the road bank. He hadn't wanted to keep walking on the concrete and had opted to move on the road bank's half-dead grass—something about being easier on the feet. "Smells like someone lit a bonfire."

I inhaled a scent that was smoky without being unpleasant; it was a bit like the petrol fumes you got around the garage. The smell became stronger as we moved closer towards Sangeal. We walked for what felt like couple more hours before we crested a rise in the road and saw the city.

Technically a city, Sangeal was really just a small town. The tallest buildings were no larger than twenty floors, nothing like you'd see in New York or Los Angeles or even Miami. Modest was the right word for it. A town that had once had around thirty thousand total people.

Our journey had taken longer than I expected, but I was baffled to see changes from this distance. Nature was already well on its way to reclaiming what remained. Vines and plant life crawled through the streets like an unstoppable plague. Buildings facing the sun had moss growing up their sides and disappearing into shattered windows. The once colorful and bright shades were now darker and dirtier.

It felt like years had passed in just a few weeks. Melancholy hit me hard, the realization that humans just weren't going to be missed by this planet when we were gone. Extinction seemed likely, as everything pointed to an increasing difficulty in the RPG system that had been imposed on us, tougher challenges that would eventually kill us all.

I wanted to walk through the city, just to see what remained. To look at the broken shop fronts and downed power line poles. The torched vehicles and the wild animals and rodents that now called Sangeal their home. There was no real need to go there, though. It had to be a bad idea. "Let's go around as planned."

We did get closer before taking a side road, close enough to see that it wasn't just plants that had surged up through the city. The monster spawns that had originally rested near the center had already pushed their way to the outskirts. Snake-men, abominations, goblins, ghouls and those weird alien creatures were crowded together in a mess of monsters.

"How long till those just freely wander the land?" Richard was only thinking out loud, but it was a good question none the less. How long did we have before nowhere was safe? Until we woke up fighting and went to bed on the brink of death just to do it again?

"I hope never." Lucas responded. "But that's probably not going to be the case."

The pulsing beam of light sometimes fluttered at the center. It was hard to see during the day, and it was a rare occurrence, but it was still happening. It was a reminder that monsters were growing stronger, taking a hold on the land and expanding their territory.

The thought, and the sight, put a damper on our mood. Time was ticking and we didn't have the answers. That prickling on the back of my neck was an incessant scratching that wouldn't go away.

Chapter 17: When a Plan Falls Apart, it Really Falls Apart

We made a wide detour around Sangeal, yet the smell of smoke only grew stronger. We were walking towards the source of that smell, surely? It was only when we were on a bridge crossing the main western highway out of Sangeal did I see a plume of smoke rising into the sky.

"Isn't that where yer headed?" Richard asked. My heart stopped and I couldn't speak.

"That is the direction of the farm," Jessica confirmed.

"I have a bad feeling, let's hurry!" Alan started jogging out in front of us. The smoke was coming from the direction of the farm, and judging by the low billowing smoke, the height of the fire had passed. Whatever was burning had burned for quite some time already.

We rushed ahead as fast as we could move our bodies. I ran until my legs screamed and my throat was as dry as sandpaper. My saliva was thick by the time we stopped running. The smell of smoke faded gradually as we walked the gravel road off the highway.

Slowly but surely a scent of death replaced that of burning wood. A cloying, acrid smoke remained that seared the throat and nostrils. Buzzards flew above and their squawking was only matched by the crunch of rocks beneath our feet.

We hadn't even made it to the farm when Jessica approached my side. She grasped my arm tightly, "This isn't your fault," she said in a low whisper. "You're not the person you were before." And those words hit like a ton of bricks. I wasn't ready to see whatever had prompted her to speak this way.

We walked for another five minutes until reaching the gate of the farm, what was left of the gate at least. The entire thing had been bent and thrown off the hinges, and, from the looks of it, was the result of a large vehicle slamming into it at full speed.

There were no cars or trucks or any transportation remaining anywhere. The main farmhouse was mostly gone, a mixture of black and grey coal with the support beams standing barely on one side. A low smoke wafted from within.

"IS ANYONE ALIVE?" Lucas yelled out while walking forward. The nauseating smoke billowed thick in our direction and I pulled up my shirt to breathe through it. There were bodies around, some badly burned and others that had looked like they had lain in the sun for a day or two. There were no savage wounds, missing limbs, or signs of bites: this wasn't the work of monsters.

"WE'RE HERE TO HELP YOU!" Lucas yelled again. The rest of us started joining in the shouting, but no one responded.

"Those are bullet wounds." Richard said while pointing at one of the corpses. I fought the urge to vomit as I recognized the face immediately. It was Will, the man who had driven us to the steel mill. Things changed so quickly...

I kept going as best I could. My eyes were starting to water, but not from the smoke. This was eating me up inside, and the thought that if I had turned down the dungeon idea from the get go these people would be alive, haunted me. A glance towards Jessica helped, I saw the sympathy in her eyes.

"Doesn't look like this was more than two or three days ago," Thomas said. That thought stabbed me further. I should have prioritized the most important task: keeping those dependent on us safe!

"Let's keep looking," I fumbled out. "Maybe we can find some survivors." But as much as we looked and called out, all we found were more bodies. As far as I could see… no one was missing. It was a wanton slaughter, and for what reason? Nobody could know for certain.

Everything was burned, even the things that had no business being burned, which suggested that this was just someone being evil—like a mob of demons had been let loose to have fun.

We rummaged through the ruins for over an hour before acknowledging it was futile to keep searching. There really was nothing left but corpses and burnt wood, and each new body was just more weight on my shoulders. The scratching on my neck was gone, and was replaced by regret and a feeling of impending doom.

This felt like a complete reset. Everything we had worked for was all for nothing. The farm was supposed to be the beginning of a rebuild, a way of regaining a life that resembled some normalcy. That was the goal, and seeing it all up in smoke like this was more than a punch in the gut.

No one knew what to say once we stopped searching. What positive spin could even be put on this situation? I was overwhelmed by the doom and gloom. Crouching behind a charred wall, I took a moment to myself before rejoining the others near the battered gate.

"What now?" I asked everyone. I didn't even know what my plan was. My goal had been to thrive, and for that to happen I felt I needed a place to call home and people around me I cared about.

That seemed to have been shattered just now. My only motivation for living right now… was to keep living.

"The goal I had for us has been destroyed," I admitted. I was in utter shock, and had gone past the point of expressing emotions or planning my statements. "I'd understand if anyone wanted to go their separate way." I could hear in my own voice how cold I sounded.

The response to my words was shocked faces, and a swift rebuttal from Jessica. "What are you even saying?" she asked. "Do you think this farm was the only reason we stuck together?" Her tone was definitely growing heated, and in that moment I realized…I had fucked up.

"I…shit." That was all I could fumble out.

"You would be truly stupid to think so," she said. "and I know you're not. So don't act like you are." She finished that off with a hmph that made everyone go silent.

It was Alan that broke the silence first, "I have no plans of going anywhere without you all." He looked around at everyone else.

It seemed I had really overestimated the value of the farm in everyone's mind. One at a time they all reaffirmed exactly what Jessica had said, except in their own words. Before anything else, we were a team. And as a team we would survive the apocalypse, base or no base.

"I love the team building," Richard said suddenly. "But I'll be honest…this kind of throws a wrench in my plans."

"How so?" Lucas asked.

"Well, I was planning to make this farm a place to recuperate for a while, grow a bit stronger, and then go searching for my brother. Obviously, the goal was to come back after…but now there's nothing to come back to." He sighed.

"That doesn't mean I don't want to be a part of this group, or was planning to run off… but it will be hard to be able to branch out and meet up again without a home base. Saving my brother has been my priority, and matters to me just as much as surviving."

He had only previously mentioned his brother in passing when he had talked about himself, so learning of this strong determination to find him was very surprising.

"Was he captured? What's the situation?" I asked. Richard made it sound like his brother had been kidnapped.

"No, he lives in Rotterdam." Rotterdam was one of the biggest cities in the entire state, with a population before the apocalypse of millions. It was also the place my parents lived. I suddenly had a new goal.

"That…" Alan paused, "that's gonna be dangerous, right?" He looked around at everyone.

"Very…I think," I said. "Don't take this the wrong way, but are you sure your brother is still alive?"

"My brother is a smart guy. He would adapt," Richard said. "Besides, even if not, he's all I got. Dead or alive I'm gonna find him."

"My parents…live there too." I added.

"Thomas and I have an uncle that lives there. He's an engineer, with a real talent for figuring things out," Alan added. "If he's still alive he'd be a big help."

"My grandparents were living there too." Lucas added. It was starting to look like we had plenty of reasons to go to Rotterdam. The problem was how dangerous it was going to be as a trip.

"So, the question is: are you all willing to join me on my search?" Richard asked. "Regardless, I'll be going."

I knew deep down I wanted to go. If I could see my parents now, I could make amends for the shitty person I had been. That thought brought joy. The darkness that had shrouded me started to recede as that daydream grew. "What does everyone think?" I asked. "I want to go."

"Let's do it," Lucas said.

"I'm all for it," Alan said.

"Me too," Thomas said.

Everyone who had stakes in exploring Rotterdam immediately agreed. I looked at Jessica, and then Maria and Anna, none of whom had relatives living in the city. "I'll follow you anywhere," Jessica suddenly said.

I suddenly understood that Jessica was more vulnerable than she appeared, that when I had voiced the idea of people separating, it had really struck her hard. Right now, we only had each other. As capable as she was, without us...she would truly be alone. This was the moment that I realized she was someone I couldn't replace.

"And I you." I said, I raised my arms and she was there, the two of us hugging tight, becoming one. The two of us against the cruelty of the world we found ourselves in.

"I need a break," Maria brought me back to myself. "This conversation is all over the place." This got a chuckle out of Lucas. She walked off a bit to be by herself, and when she returned her eyes and cheeks were puffy and red.

I realized I'd made another mistake. Although none of us had any real connection to the dead here, plenty of people on this farm had treated Maria like a daughter. All the women she was with had doted on her and tried to shield her from Ghost Hand.

"Should we...say something for the dead. Some kind of service?" I asked Maria. I wasn't religious and didn't believe in any afterlife, but respect for the dead was a given.

Maria wiped her nose and sniffled, "No, it's okay. I'm just gonna miss them is all."

"Live on for their sake, then," Anna said. "They were there for you because they wanted you to survive; so don't let them down."

"You're rig—" and before she could finish the words coming from her mouth she started to bawl like a baby. Orphaned at seventeen and not a relative she could turn to. Life wasn't fair. Jessica and Anna came close and embraced her.

"It's already mid-day. It might be best we camp near here tonight then work out our next move tomorrow?" I asked. "We can discuss it over a fire."

"I think that's a good idea," Lucas chipped in.

Maria pestered Alan to help her find firewood once she came back, even though it was readily available all over. The two of them disappeared off into the forest while the rest of us found a reasonable place to sleep. Although the best security was offered within the walls, no one wanted to be that close to the dead, so we ended up at the back of the farm, the building between us and the disaster.

When Alan and Maria returned, I saw the three women go have their girl talk. Somehow or another I could feel them staring daggers at Alan and myself. I couldn't read lips, but I swear Jessica said, "let's hope he isn't as oblivious as a certain someone." Nah... it couldn't be.

We found some old hay bales that had managed to avoid being torched, and after ripping those up we had decent bedding for the night. Thomas could have gotten the fire lit if we needed him to, but there was smoldering remains all around us. Dinner was more rations, which we were running dangerously low on.

"The goal is Rotterdam," I said when we'd finished eating. "That's hundreds of miles east, we have no vehicle and our supplies are low. Let's put everything on the table and figure out our best course of action." I had some ideas of my own, but wanted to let the others speak their mind freely first.

"We should focus on transportation," Lucas said, "find a vehicle or multiple vehicles so we can make the journey faster and safer." Multiple people agreed instantly, it seemed no one wanted to spend days walking.

"Alright, vehicle's the number one priority," I reiterated. "What else?"

"Supplies are a given, but from where?" Jessica asked. "Sangeal is the opposite direction, and Withersburg is on the way, although it might be a bit more dangerous." We knew there was the blood lich at Withersburg, which definitely was an above-average opponent.

"I'd rather not backtrack to Sangeal," Alan said. "We've seen enough of that place, and we took a bunch of vehicles from the outskirts already."

Lucas nodded. "True, it might be harder to find anything worthwhile without venturing deep inside the city, which would prove dangerous."

"Any thoughts on hitting a second secret shop?" I asked. There hadn't been any notifications about only being able to conquer one and we were a lot stronger both in level and by having Richard and Anna with us. The payout could be enormous.

"As fun as that sounds..." Richard said. "I'll have to pass on that. That will take a while, and the danger is gonna be through the roof. Even if we manage to conquer it, we'll become a target in a heartbeat. We'll have to do your random who-knows-what scroll again and probably won't even be able to find Rotterdam afterwards."

"Alright, I didn't think about it that deeply, but you're definitely right," I said. "No one has mentioned this yet, but I want to level both you and Anna and—"

"I don't need levels, I just need to find my brother." Richard cut me off.

"I understand that, but this is going to be dangerous. You can't help your brother if you die before you make it there." My words seemed to get him listening. "We need vehicles, we need supplies, and you and Anna need levels. We ALL need levels," I said.

"Yes please," Anna suddenly said, "I'm all for being leveled." I was happy to hear she was a go for the plan, because she'd been mostly silent when we discussed Rotterdam. I was worried she was going along because she felt she had no choice.

"So this is what I propose…" I started to explain what I was thinking. "First thing tomorrow we make our way to Withersburg on foot. Once there, Jessica and I will secure an area for you and Anna to farm safely. We'll get you started on some quick levels with my minions and her CC abilities. Lucas, Alan, Thomas and Maria—I want you four to venture a bit deeper, level up, but also scout.

"Take note of any vehicles you see that are in decent shape that we can salvage. Focus on trucks, SUVs, sturdy vehicles that we can load multiple people into with ease." I paused. "As we level up, everyone will be finding rations, bandages, and potions—that should be even more common for Richard and Anna as they're low level.

"We'll stick around for a day or two, more depending on how quickly we make progress, and then head for Rotterdam. Thoughts?"

Richard seemed conflicted, so I gave him a bit of a reminder, "If this farm was intact you would have stayed here for a bit anyway, no time lost," I added.

"Fair enough," replied. "But why would Anna and I be finding more Rations and supplies?"

"I'm not certain, but I have a suspicion that the more difficult the opponent is for you, the better the drops. The monsters in Withersburg are up to six levels above you. If you defeat one, the game world rewards you with better and or more drops."

No one else seemed to voice an opinion on my suggestion, which I took for tacit agreement. Still, I made sure to include everyone, "Is this good for everyone then? Anything I've missed?" I received nods and affirmations all around. We had our plan.

Chapter 18: In the Aftermath of the Burned Base

"We take any problems as they come. I'm calling it a night," I stood up from the campfire and moved a dozen feet or so away where I had laid some hay for myself. It wasn't much for comfort, but it felt better than the cold dirt I'd have slept on otherwise.

It was a chilly night, and I missed the warmth of the fire almost immediately. Sleeping on dry hay near a fire wouldn't have been the brightest, so I sucked it up and crossed my arms across my chest. The hay would grow warm from my heat, and I'd grow comfortable staring at the stars.

It was a beautiful sight, the night sky, and a terrifying one. The thought came that something or someone was trying to kill us all: erase us from existence. We wouldn't be missed at all. Not by anything that wasn't human, at least.

Life would go on, and even now that much was clear by the insects chirping into the night. The occasional hoots of an owl, the shaking of nearby shrubs as some rodent or feline or predator lurked within. How long could I survive?

"Mike, are you still awake?" A whisper came from the side that turned my eye. Jessica walked in my direction, her features dark in the night, a shadow wrapping around her from the fire at her back.

I leaned up on my elbow, "I'm still awake. I probably won't be sleeping soon," I confessed. There was a lot on my mind and shutting my brain off before bed was never something I was good at.

"Do you mind if I join you then?" she asked. Even as a silhouette she really did look beautiful.

"Feel free, although there's not much space." I said jokingly.

I was expecting her to bring some hay for her own spot near mine, but instead she just plopped down right next to me. "Scoot over a bit," she said and nearly pushed me off my own bed.

I was at a loss for words in that moment, and the thoughts of danger and the end of humanity left my head. We laid in silence for a dozen seconds before she spoke, "I'm sorry about earlier. I lost my cool."

"Ah. It's fine, it's fine," I fumbled out, "I was being an idiot and wasn't acting myself. I don't want anyone to leave, but it's not my choice. I felt... lost," I admitted. "It was a moment of vulnerability. I felt utterly defeated seeing the farm in that state. I hadn't appreciated that the farm was only one part of what we have built. Our party, these friendships, might prove much more important than trying to build up a base. And creating a group like ours is more difficult to forge than putting up buildings."

"That's good." Her voice grew a bit more cheerful. "I was... surprised when you squeezed me like that earlier. I didn't think you would do it in front of everyone."

"Ah, was that the wrong move?" I said in a hurry. "I was scared."

"Scared of what?" she asked.

"Of losing you," I said. She looked back at me in that moment with soft eyes I'd not seen before, "We're a team," I added. And like I had ruined everything, her eyes changed.

"You really are oblivious, aren't you?" she said.

"I…what do you—" and before I could finish my sentence her lips were touching mine. An electric shock raced through my entire body as I was frozen in place. My mind was filled entirely with the presence of Jessica and the kiss that made me feel like molten gold.

"Don't think about it too much," she broke the kiss before turning around. "Now go to sleep."

I couldn't even retort. I was stunned. My experience with women was not great, that was for sure. I felt wooden as I lay back on my side. Then I felt her hand grab mine and place it over her stomach. "I'm cold, so be useful," she said while wriggling back into my embrace.

All the problems, all the worry vanished. I knew it in my heart that as long as I had Jessica here, things wouldn't be so bad. Although it took a while for my beating heart to settle, the rest I gained that night was one of the best I'd ever gotten, including the nights before the apocalypse.

Morning came too soon, and Jessica wasn't in my embrace when I woke. The smoldering had mostly stopped last night it seemed, and the burning smell of wood had mostly dissipated; only death remained.

A low fog covered the ground and the humidity was awful. Every surface was covered with a layer of dark grime. The well on the property had been ruined, which you'd think would be hard to do, but throwing a few bodies into it really did wonders to deter people from using it.

Breakfast was another Ration, a type of food which I was starting to detest. Not being hungry after eating a single biscuit, not being thirsty, it truly removed one of the joys of living. I was complaining about a good thing, but the feeling of thirst and hunger was a part of being alive, and instead I sometimes felt I was existing without purpose.

Jessica, Richard and Alan were already up at the crack of dawn. The fire from last night was low enough to provide some heat as they ate their breakfast around it. I sat down just in time to realize I wasn't the only one missing real food, "I would kill for some scrambled eggs right now," Alan said.

"Just scrambled eggs?" Richard scoffed, "how about ten pancakes, five sausages, five pieces of bacon, some grits, some hash browns and then a side of corned beef hash." Richard was already licking his lips by the time he finished his sentence.

"Sounds good, except for the corned beef hash," Jessica said.

"Never liked that stuff," Alan said. "Looks like dogfood." He spat into the fire to show his disgust.

"Well, even dogs are eating better than us right now," Richard said, and then he also spat into the fire.

Am I sensing a rivalry here? I wondered. I let out a light chuckle, "Good to see you two so energized in the morning." I looked at Richard, "Can you detail your skills for me? Do you have any offensive abilities or are you purely defensive?"

"I have one offensive ability, one defensive ability, and an instant cast heal," he replied after looking over at me. "The defensive ability increases my block and makes me take less damage from attacks, bonus if it's undead, undead also takes damage when they strike me." I gestured to him to continue. "The offensive ability is a single target hard-hitting attack, also bonus if they are undead. The heal is a small heal on a high cooldown with no cast time, don't use it much cause it's quite expensive."

My conclusion was that Richard basically was a support tank to Alan. He must have been aware of that, which might be affecting his relationship with Alan. "Do you know Anna's abilities?" I asked. "I'd prefer not to wake her but it would be useful to know."

"I don't know what they're called, but she has three offensive abilities. Two of them are single target abilities and one of them is an AoE." Hearing this was a relief. If her AoE ability was strong enough, Anna and Richard could level incredibly fast with the help of my undead squad mobbing for them.

"Alright, that's good to know," I said. "We'll depart from here once everyone has woken and eaten." I said 'eat', but God, it didn't feel like eating. A small biscuit that you ate in two bites, it was like taking a pill.

It didn't take more than thirty minutes for everyone to get up. Nerves were always high sleeping in the open, and just the shuffling of our feet and the low talking was enough to eventually get the rest from their hay beds.

"Let's move before the sun is high, at least it's still cool in the morning," Lucas suggested and no one complained. We weren't dehydrated, but having the sun above your head and no cold water to drink always sucked. I found myself daydreaming about a nice hot shower to wash the smell of smoke off my skin.

We walked to the broken fence as a group, and Maria was the last one out. She paused for a good thirty seconds and looked back at the now-destroyed farm. It hadn't been a great home to her. She probably didn't even have positive memories of the place, but it was where she met some amazing people in a truly dire time and no doubt she was thinking of them.

"Let's go. Become someone they'll be proud of," Jessica called back to her, evidently having the same take as me. Maria wiped the smallest tear from her cheek and then hurried to catch up with the rest of us. We had a good walk ahead of us, and no one knew exactly what Withersburg had become.

I noticed so much more as we moved on foot. The last time I made this trip was with Jessica, and admittedly I spent more time looking at her hanging out the jeep like a madwoman than the surroundings, but hadn't been so oblivious that the changes I could not see were lost on me.

"Did someone torch the fields?" Richard asked. The farmland and even all the trees had been deliberately burned. There were at least two tractors within a mile of each other that had been torched. The remnants of burnt wood remained against their frames, no doubt timber that had been used to get them burning.

It was more of the same as continued to walk: random acts of destruction for no apparent reason. Even the gas station that was about halfway to town had been burned to the ground. Three vehicles along the road were burnt to the frames, too.

"This is...ominous." I said as we walked past the third. No one knew what to expect when we got to Withersburg. I suspected some destruction, but what if the whole city was torched? How big of an organization would it have taken to subjugate a city of monsters and then torch it to the ground?

The weird sightings continued all the way till Withersburg was in view, but from a distance I couldn't see any signs of wanton destruction. "What does that sign say?" Anna pointed to a piece of wood that had spray-painted letters on it. "My vision isn't that great without my glasses." To be fair though, it wasn't the most eligible writing.

"The wrapped is upon us?" Alan asked.

"HAHAHAHAH, can you not read, stupid?" Maria asked. "It clearly says 'The RAPTOR is upon us," she snickered triumphantly.

"The RAPTOR?" Now Lucas couldn't hold back his laughter, "it says The Rapture is upon us."

Maria's face turned beet red. "Hmph, it isn't my fault the writing sucks. What's a rapture anyway?"

"It's a religious belief," Thomas said. "With the second coming of Christ, all true believers will be transported to Heaven."

"Why do you think it's here though? The sign?" I asked. Whoever placed it here, did so for a reason. But there didn't seem any particular place of interest nearby.

"I don't know," Richard said. "But that paired with everything we've seen so far…gives me a bad feeling. There's only one thing I'm more scared of than crazy people, and that's crazy religious people."

"We'll take it as it comes," I said. "We only have about fifteen minutes of walking left before we reach the intersection we've been aiming for. Then Anna and Richard will go with Jessica and I for some level grinding. Everyone else can do some exploring nearby for gear and grinding if it's safe and the mobs are easy."

The idle chit chat ended as everyone gathered themselves for a resumption of battle. The buildings of Withersburg became clearer, and, like with Sangeal, they had started to see some physical decay. Plant life was already reclaiming the land as fast as the rain and sun would let it grow.

Still, my worst fears, regardless of how improbable it was, had been that Withersburg would be barely standing. In hindsight it was a foolish thought, but this new world threw curveballs all the time, nothing was out of the realm of possibility.

"Seems the same as before." Jessica remarked. "At least from here the buildings don't look burned or even vandalized."

"Stay close until we've entered," Alan said. "Let's make sure of no surprises before you start your grind." And since we all agreed with this, we huddled up with Thomas and Anna staying in the middle of the group.

The one person to move freely around the group was Jessica who was constantly tracking and scouting the area, "Nothing but monsters so far." And we started to see them, those demonic goats with their giant maces, the occasional blood lich, and even those disgusting eyeballs that shot lasers. This city was a lot more difficult than Sangeal.

"This looks like as good a place as any," Jessica finally stopped us when we were about a block in. The terrain here was good. Behind us, the street was open for us to run away if need be, and three streets lay ahead of us from which we could pull. There were downed power poles and multiple burned vehicles here as well to obstruct monsters.

"These weren't here before, no?" I asked while pointing to the torched cars.

"Not that I recall," Jessica said.

"Lucas, prioritize your leveling but keep track of anything of use. If you find survivors and they seemed armed or leveled in anyway, retreat." People were the most dangerous right now. Monsters were predictable, even the roaming ones. You could usually choose when and where to fight them. But humans could hunt you and ambush you. That was my feeling about the farm. It didn't look like monsters had somehow formed an army and invaded. Instead, I feared some raid part of levelled up humans was doing all the burning, perhaps in a spirit of religious zeal.

Chapter 19: Power Leveling with an AoE Spell

"Right, we'll be going left and a bit deeper in. I think there's a children's park about three blocks that way; it should make as a good hunting ground to start.

"If something happens, we'll come get you," I said. "Richard, Anna: you're with Jessica and me."

The two walked over curiously, and I could see a certain amount of trepidation. They had gained their levels on the run out of necessity; I doubted they had hunted monsters for EXP out of their own volition so far. "Take these." I handed over my two remaining EXP potions, one each. Jessica and I never got the chance to use them in the dungeon exploration.

"Anna, can you demonstrate your AOE ability for me?" I asked. "If it's a lot of MP consumption, you can just explain how it works."

Anna gave a nod and then removed the Staff of Piercing Ice once again. Her eyes closed a moment as a runic circle appeared beneath her feet. Her lips moved quickly, each word coming out faster than the last.

Suddenly, the air went still, and then as if exploding, cool air howled and rushed past us. My clothes and hair fluttered in the icy wind as a storm kicked up a dozen feet away from us. Howling wind that froze the air instantly, creating sharp shards of ice that swirled like a blender.

It moved slowly over a torched vehicle and caused it to rattle and shake. Metallic sounds rang out from the vehicle over and over again, as ice bit out chunks of metal from its frame and added them to the spinning chaos. The whole effect lasted a dozen seconds before it dissipated, and the aftermath could be seen.

The frame of the car, what was left of it, was riddled with holes like cheese. Inches of metal tore out and cut by the freezing ice. "That…was way cooler than I expected," Jessica exclaimed. "How many times can you cast that?"

"Maybe eleven more times?" Anna replied.

"Alright, perfect," I said, "follow Jessica and I from a distance to start, I want you to see the mob's abilities before you do anything."

Jessica and I walked straight ahead down the main street. I hadn't forgotten how close I was to leveling either, and the itch was there again, the itch to grow stronger. "How close are you to leveling?" I looked at Jessica.

"Ninety percent," she said.

"I'm at ninety-three. We can probably get that in a few minutes if we try: that will clear out a bigger area for us to work with, and allow me to get some reincarnations. After that we can concentrate on levelling Richard and Anna." The goal was to get them as close to twenty as possible in two or three days.

If the rest of us were anything to go by, there would be an exponential jump in their abilities if we could get them another skill to learn. Without the secret shop though, a good skill was hard to come by. Maybe in the future if another shop remained unconquered we could give it a second shot.

Jessica continued to lead us from the front while taking note of the mobs around us. They were the same as we remembered: the levitating eye; the sickleman; the demonic goat; and the blood lich. There was a difference though...

The monsters had all gained levels from our previous battles with them. The levitating eye and sickleman used to be level 10; now they were both level 13. The demonic goat was now level 19 and the blood lich was 20.

"So the weaker mobs got a lot more levels compared to the stronger mobs?" Richard asked.

"Seems that way," I answered. "Maybe it's not that there's a steady increase in levels...but an EXP gain over time?" I carried on, thinking aloud. "If that were the case, the low base level monsters would rise quickly while the higher-level monsters would only gain strength slowly..."

"That makes sense to me," Jessica said. "If these mobs all gained even one level per week, it wouldn't be long till we were completely outpaced."

"It only makes sense if the game world isn't trying to kill us," I said. As far as I could tell it was trying to kill us...but maybe there was still hope.

"Let's start with that blood lich." Jessica pointed, before laying a trap directly in its path. "We should focus on ranged mobs and leave the melee for Richard and Anna."

"I was thinking the same," I said, "that way I can mob them up with some minions and we can see how Anna's AOE fairs." Jessica gave a nod and nocked an arrow. We had only gained a few levels since our last time being here, but the experience we had in fighting together made the difference with the past like night and day.

Jessica was now a seasoned archer, and the way she worked the bow and arrow was a sight to behold. Her focus was unshakeable and her shots were pinpoint. I lost the ability to follow the path of her arrows long ago, and now I could only go off the twang of her bow.

The strength and speed of her shots was so powerful that new phenomena appeared in the air with each shot. There was a mini sonic boom when an arrow was released, and the displaced air caused her hair to lift off her shoulders. "Incoming!" she called as the first arrow was loosed.

My minions had been put in position already, but the ghastly wail and those deep, penetrating eyes of the blood lich still caused me to shiver. It had deathly AoE abilities, and if not for the fact my minions were undead, would have been a nightmare to deal with. The blood lich floated towards us like a ghost immediately after the arrow hit, and then landed in the quagmire trap as planned.

The trap didn't physically touch the monster, seeing as it hovered over the ground, but fortunately it still activated and the blood lich took the full effect of Quagmire. After several seconds, the howling coming from its mouth had slowed to an almost reverb-like sound, and that was my cue to send in my army of undead.

They rushed forward like an unstoppable wave, but this time I also had my skeletal mages as well to back me up, and within seconds of arriving in the Quagmire, my squad were pelting the blood lich with varying elements of magic. I was the bane of its existence, and all of my minions were fully immune to its attacks. If I had no other responsibilities, I would have just farmed this monster repeatedly with Jessica.

Arrow after arrow twanged while my minions hacked and slashed. The damage they could deal now was considerably more than before. The black garb of the blood lich took slice after slice until it was mostly in tatters. The magic that protected its boney frame was no match for a dozen monsters plowing into it unhindered.

There was no recourse for the blood lich in this fight, and it put up no real resistance. Soon the staff and bones fell to the floor like a puppet with no strings. A ghastly wail akin to screaming down a tunnel chilled the air as it despawned. Strangely though, the fight hadn't gone much faster than last time. Maybe it had high magic resistance?

"No loot? For that thing?" Anna asked. She was still shivering from the fight, and she hadn't even been a part of it.

I turned to her. "It's expected. We are at a higher level than it, and that means few drops. As far as I can tell, monsters the same level as you and above give decent loot."

"Should we leave the demonic goats?" Jessica asked. "They are sort of melee." When I looked at the morning star that was nearly six-foot long in the hands of the monster she was looking at, I questioned myself whether it was melee. Not only did it have a huge reach, these types were level nineteen and would not be very easy to kill for Anna and Richard.

"I think the ones you call a sickleman should be the only type we fight," suggested Anna. These were average-sized skeletons that dual-wielded sickles; she was right, they were just so-so in terms of their physical ability. Outrunning them wouldn't be an issue if it came down to it, and as far as Jessica and I had seen, they had no spells.

I made my way over to the body of the blood lich and summoned it as a new minion for me. For now, it would have to do until I could get something bulkier. I liked the idea of having two tanky reincarnations, and even more so with the thought that Anna would eventually be in our level range. Multiple pulls would be on the menu again.

"Ready for next," I said.

"Pulling." And Jessica let another arrow crack the air. We ended up getting our level in around ten minutes after killing all the levitating eyes, demonic goats, and blood lich in the area. The only type of mob left was purely sickleman, and there were plenty of them: they were the most common spawns here.

I opted to reanimate two demonic goats rather than blood lich. I wanted something that could melee and was durable. It would make the sickleman pulls much easier, and we'd have a beefier frontline if things went awry and we needed to run.

"Let's do this at the entrance where we came in," Jessica suggested. It was a good place to fall back from, and the vehicles provided great cover. There was the added bonus of the metal from their frames being tossed into the storm and essentially acting like a blender.

"I agree. We can retreat easily from there if we have to," I said.

"I'll set a trap here and one between the buildings there," Jessica announced before laying Quagmire traps.

I voiced the biggest question, "how many should we pull? Do you think it will be fine if I get the whole lot of them?"

"Suit yourself," Richard said. Somehow, he seemed completely nonchalant about the whole thing, and my curious stare seemed to make him realize that. "Hey, I'm not the one pulling nor killing, so suit yourself," he explained further.

"Sounds good to me, I'll get them all then." I opened the party window and removed the two of them from party. "Make a party between you two," I said.

"Wait, wait!" Anna interjected. "Don't I get a say in this?"

Jessica reassured her, "It should be fine. This isn't the first time we've done big pulls." And that wasn't a lie. When I first got my reanimated abominations, I used their bile ability to kill the fodder in Sangeal.

Anna still looked uneasy.

"It'll be fine. I'll keep my summoned undead in front to stop any pushing through your AoE. If that doesn't work, we have traps to fall back on and as a last resort we can outrun them on foot," I said. Anna gave a timid nod and then prepared herself to cast.

"Did you make the party?" I asked Richard who gave a nod in response. "Alright, I'm going." I had to move to keep up with my undead squad or they would lose the ability to function. It just wasn't possible to send them out as far as I wanted. I imagined them like a remote-control car, eventually they wouldn't be in range of my signal if I didn't go with them.

Once I ordered the attack, the lot of them rushed around pulling every sickleman they could. It was impossible to count in the mayhem, but if I was a guessing man I'd say there were almost thirty mobs running along behind my undead as I pulled back towards Anna.

The sicklemen were the same speed as my summoned warriors, so after only using one attack, they fell behind the withdrawing undead and couldn't catch up. In a little over forty seconds, I had brought a train of sicklemen behind my own. The sound of the bones clacking on asphalt was an eerie one, and when seeing that mob facing me down, I wondered if I had pulled too many.

"INCOMING!" I said while rushing between two vehicles. The first Quagmire was triggered a moment later, which allowed my squad and I to make the distance we needed to avoid being inside of Anna's AoE.

The pack of mobs following me slowly compacted into something much more manageable. The front ones, slowed by Quagmire and funneled by the two vehicles in their path, reached a bottleneck. It allowed every straggling sickleman to catch up, until they were all just one nice big ball of EXP.

As soon as the first sickleman made it through the corridor between the vehicles, the second Quagmire trap was triggered, and that was the signal to go. "Now!" shouted Jessica.

Anna had already been casting, and that storm of ice and wind appeared in the air just moments after I managed to clear the obstacles. Shards of ice and snow swirled with God's fury as the sickleman were nearly frozen in place.

Between the Quagmire and the bone-freezing cold, the mobs couldn't move another foot forward. Their bones rattled as every shard of ice smashed against them. In moments, those shards were removing chunks of bone from their frame, and sending those hurling around as well. The AoE had become a literal blender, with bone and ice and steel swirling endlessly, like a symphony of death.

Each impact caused a snap in the air, and even the metal frames of the vehicles rang out like a gong with each collision. Vision of what was happening grew worse as each piece of bone was ground to almost powder, that in turn eroded more sickleman into dust. The spell started to sound like a sandstorm as the bone powder was driven into the vehicles and buildings nearby.

I couldn't stop watching the spectacle, and my minions that had blocked the path in front of us were not needed. "Wizards... are strong," was all I could mumble. Soon, every sickleman was dead

176

without even a body remaining. I wasn't sure if it was because Anna was strong, or if the sickleman were weak.

Thinking about it logically, a monster with sufficient defense would probably be impervious or at least affected minimally by the impacts. The sickleman were simply too weak defensively, they were under the threshold to resist the effects of the spells, which made them the perfect target for Anna's AoE.

"It's...beautiful," Anna suddenly said. "GIMMIE!" She rushed ahead and towards the pile of loot now floating there. From a single glance I could see the Rations and Bandages, the multiple skill books, and the pieces of gear waiting to be looted.

There were so many supplies that some of them were behind the vehicles as there just wasn't enough room for it all. Anna started to scoop it all up like a madwoman. As I walked closer, it almost seemed like she hissed at me to stay back.

When all was said and done, I got the tally. "Seven rations, five bandages, two HP potions and one DEX potion," she said. "Besides that, there was some miscellaneous gear, and two skill books. The skill books were pretty low level, though."

"How much EXP did you get?" I looked from one to the other.

"One-and-half-levels," said Richard and Anna nodded. That was way above my expectations. It would be possible to make a pull like that happen within another hour, too. If we kept going like this for the remainder of the day we could hope to get them to level seventeen or eighteen, which would be close enough in level to really grind as a group.

Chapter 20: A New Elite and a New Scar

"Let's set up for another pull," I said. We needed to clear another area, one which would mean EXP for Jessica and I as well. We moved through the funnel we'd created between abandoned cars and then continued walking the streets, exploring to the sides rather than go towards the center of the city.

"Something strong is coming," Jessica said while we were picking out our next group of targets.

A bad feeling prickled my neck, and for a moment the memory of the Fiend popped into my head, "Do we run?" If so, we had to leave right now.

"It isn't a Fiend," Jessica said, as if she could read my mind. "Definitely an elite though. I'll know more once I can inspect it. It's coming right for us, one block more inward," her eyes flashed towards the area she meant.

"You two should find somewhere safe to hide," I looked at Anna and Richard. "Elites can have nasty skills that aren't as simple as targeting you with an ability." The banshee from Sangeal was an enemy like that. Its Fear was a dangerous ability that could send Anna or Richard directly into more monsters.

"We'll watch from a safe distance," Richard replied. I could see that Anna wanted to stay, as she was constantly turning her head as

178

Richard scooted her along and into an alley. They were watching from behind a skip and I estimated that they were out of the way of any AoE attacks.

I waited a long twenty seconds with bated breath for the Elite to show itself.

"That's it," at last Jessica pointed at an inconspicuous figure that could have passed as simple EXP fodder. "Ghastly Miscreation: Level Twenty-One. Elite."

The Elite was a female figure with sickly, pale skin. Her facial features were hidden behind sleek, pitch-black hair that went down to her knees. Instead of arms, tentacle-like suckers extended from her ribs, one from each side. Her chest cavity was torn open as if something had burst from within. A small spike rhythmically protruded from each tentacle as if they were breathing.

Jessica and I were used to these city battles. In mere seconds, we had scanned the surroundings and called out the positions of possible adds. I didn't even need to give her any instruction as she placed a Quagmire trap in the perfect location for a safe pull, then moved to cover behind an overturned car from where she could hope to keep her aggro down as she fired. I found a jeep for my own cover and then lined up my undead squad between me and the Elite. "Ready," I called over to her and she gave me a nod.

I watched Jessica nock her arrow. There was something different about her look. The usual fierceness in her eyes wasn't there, instead, she closed them. Her face showed pure serenity, and then the arrow loosed.

There was no sound, the arrow simply disappeared. I was incapable of following her arrows, but I was convinced that nothing had moved from that bow. Nothing material, at least, as fractions of a second later a bright light flashed in my peripheral vision. A hole had been blasted clean through the shoulder of the Ghastly Miscreation.

Its attention shifted to Jessica who nocked a conventional arrow and let it loose. To my surprise and no doubt Jessica's, that arrow didn't connect. The Miscreation instead swatted the arrow away with one those disgusting tentacles that slithered and danced like snakes. It hobbled clumsily, but obviously had incredibly high agility.

Once Jessica had taken the second shot she rushed back further to new cover in a shop doorway and allowed the Elite to pass over the Quagmire trap. As soon as the Miscreation triggered it, I sent my skeleton warriors forward to intercept it. It wasn't fast on its feet, but those tentacles were like bolts of lightning. Half the attacks of my summoned undead were being deflected, and that was with a massive slow affecting it.

Even worse was the protruding spike from within each tentacle. Closer now, I could see it was made of either bone or tooth. Each spike stabbed out repeatedly and the Miscreation returned at least two attacks for every one that it received, even with twelve minions attacking it.

The clacking of bones being cracked and broken sounded out constantly. My regular undead troops were being shredded every few seconds, and only my generals and two abominations could hold their own in melee.

My skeletal mages were having an easy time of it, and it seemed the Miscreation didn't have any ability to block spells. Bolts of every element constantly pounded into her pale flesh and caused elemental blasts to race along her skin. Jessica had an easy time of it too. The Elite didn't have the ability to deal with this barrage of attacks.

Purple blood as thick as jelly gurgled from each wound on the Miscreation's body as it dribbled down her flesh. Her sickly white skin was slowly being carved to shreds as chunk of flesh flew through the air.

Just when I thought the fight would end easily, the Quagmire trap expired. Those tentacles became blurs in the air as my skeletal warriors were minced to shreds. Within just a few seconds there were only my two abominations and one skeleton general remaining. The rest had been torn to fragments.

Untroubled, I went to replenish the warriors by using Shallow Grave when I was stopped in my tracks by the fact the skill was still on cooldown. It hadn't been 24 hours since I used it last.

"I can't get any more undead warriors!" I yelled to Jessica. "You have to finish it!" Almost immediately after that shout, my final skeleton warrior died: the Zweihander-wielding general. The Demonic Goats made for formidable reanimations but even they wouldn't last much longer.

The prickling on the back of my neck spiked through the roof. My eyes turned from Jessica to the Miscreation as I raised my hand to cast Decay. The Miscreation raised a tentacle and pointed it directly at me. A moment of confusion for me almost proved deadly. There wasn't even time to think, let alone cast, as I jumped to the side.

The tusklike spike shot out like a missile in my direction. I could feel my life flashing before my eyes as my right ear started to burn. The bone armor around my face had been ripped through like paper: it might as well not have existed at all.

With my hand placed against my ear, I dashed across the concrete and ducked behind a torched pickup truck. "Mike! Are you okay?" Jessica yelled while twanging another arrow. I could see the impatience in her body language; she was about ready to rush out from behind her cover to me.

"I'M FINE DON'T COME!" I yelled. The last thing I needed was her rushing into the open and getting pierced through by another of those missiles. Despite our high level, neither of us could survive a direct hit to the body.

The gloves on my hands made feeling my ear impossible, and so I removed one quickly. My hand was slick with blood. Something was dangling off the side of my head, and it took me a moment to understand that it was a part of my own ear. The spike had torn my right ear nearly off and I didn't want to know how badly it looked dangling there. Adrenaline and pain resistance were a remarkable combo, because I honestly didn't feel shit in this moment.

"Finish it off!" I yelled to Jessica, "I need bandaging after." I concealed the panic in my voice as best I could. A part of me didn't want to lose my ear so I needed her to be in peak condition to finish this fight cleanly and quickly. I sat up and peered over the truck just in time to see my first Demonic Goat perish.

I made the call at that moment to send my Skeletal Mages closer in so they would be the next targets. Jessica continued to pelt the Miscreation from a safe distance. I now managed to cast Decay, only to see it had minimal effect. This was an undead creature of some sort.

There was a loud gurgle as Jessica put another Godless Arrow through the Miscreation's throat. A hole the size of a tennis ball appeared that dripped purple blood and bits of organ fell to the floor on either side of the Elite.

The tentacles suddenly stopped moving and for a moment I thought the fight was over. My senses started firing like crazy as danger bells rang in my head. The pitch-black hair of the

Miscreation began floating as if there was no gravity, and the dangling tentacles rose abruptly. They didn't sway or slither in the air, just remained perfectly still and then they suddenly exploded.

"DODGE!" both Jessica and I yelled at the same time while taking cover behind our respective vehicle frames. Those spikes shot with explosive force in every direction like shrapnel. The sounds of metal dinging and bricks breaking off building edges in an orchestra of destruction rang out all around me. A burning feeling raced through my leg as well. I had been hit in the right thigh.

"That was no joke!" Richard said behind us. He was crouched behind a shield that held a cross on it. Anna was sitting behind him looking like she'd seen a ghost. That had to be his defensive ability, because as far as I could tell he didn't have a physical shield.

I peered over the vehicle to see the Miscreation still standing there like a statue. None of us moved from behind our cover: if there was even a 0.1 percent chance it could still attack in some way, it wasn't worth it. Jessica closed her eyes instead and then used Godless Arrow for a third time. The remainder of the neck blew open after a dozen seconds of concentration and the Miscreation plopped forward to the floor and despawned.

As soon as it was clear there was no danger, Jessica rushed over to my side like a doting mother ready to put a Band-Aid on her kid's knee. "Show me," she said without the slightest room for argument. I pulled my hand off my dangling ear and revealed the mess to her.

"I think I got hit near my ass, too," I tried to joke.

My comment wasn't really a joke though, as I had been hit on my upper right thigh, I couldn't tell the exact location as the entire area felt on fire and I feared it might have some sort of poisonous aspect. Elites were no joke, two attacks and I had lost half my health, one of them merely grazed me as well.

Jessica raised a bandage to my ear as she struggled to hold it in place while wrapping it. I hoped as it healed that it wasn't mangled or dangling too weirdly. I would be fine with a badass scar there, too.

As soon as my ear was bandaged, she forced a HP potion down my throat and then sat me up. "Off with them," she said. I felt like a child being scolded as I removed my pants. This was perfect timing, as Richard and Anna ran over.

"Heal him please," Jessica said to Richard who obliged with no complaints. A warm feeling washed over me and some of the burning instantly subsided. "This is gonna hurt real bad," Jessica warned me. I couldn't even react at all before a dizzying pain that nearly put me on my knees ran up my body.

Richard raced over to me and I could feel him supporting my weight, "Careful." He held me long enough for me to regain my balance as the pain subsided quickly. I looked to Jessica who now had blood covering both of her hands. She held a spike of bone in her hand about four inches long.

"I just pulled that out of you," she said. "I just need to wrap you up and we'll get to Thomas just in case." A feeling of relief washed over me in moments as the bandage went around and around my thigh. Thirty seconds later and my pants were up and I was no longer bleeding to death.

"Are you both good?" I asked. My face was covered in sweat, and no doubt I looked like hell.

"I'm fine, just barely," Richard said while flashing his arm. There was a thin gash along his bicep that was barely bleeding, not enough to even warrant a bandage. Anna gave a guilty nod and apologized aloud for using Richard as a human shield. He laughed, "That's my job, get used to it."

"Let's get our loot," I said. After being bandaged I felt strong enough to move around, albeit with some soreness in my thigh. There were three items floating there waiting for us: one skill book; one ration; and a weapon.

Anna's eyes were sparkling as I hobbled fast to overtake her. I could be protective of my loot, too. It was Jessica who reached the loot first though and picked up the Ration and Skill book. I grabbed the weapon and gave it a look.

Berserker's Axe: AGI +3 STR +3 Attack Speed +10%
The unique shape of this axe makes swinging it repeatedly easier with every attack.

It was definitely a high-level weapon. I shared the info with everyone and glanced at Richard, the only other person who could make use of the axe. He shook his head, "My skill requires a blunt weapon." I held on to it; the axe might be useful for my next skeleton general, but I didn't know when that would be.

Chapter 21: The Most Dangerous Post-Apocalypse Encounters are with Fellow Humans

"People are coming fast!" Jessica suddenly said.

"How many? Which direction?" I asked.

"Five, wait, more! Directly in front of us three blocks." She pointed at the direction we had been clearing towards when we encountered the Ghastly Miscreation. "We have fifteen seconds, twenty maximum. They know we're here," Jessica added.

I wasted no time at all in summoning my skeleton warriors from the corpse of the Ghastly Miscreation. The berserker axe I was saving for a general was equipped onto a skeleton warrior and then everything was recalled with Vast Shadows. If they were enemies, I didn't want them to have an idea of what kind of abilities I could use until a fight broke out.

"We're friendly until we can't be." I looked at Richard and Anna. They weren't aware of how we did things yet, and Jessica needed no reminder. I did my best to clean myself up and recovered my defenses with a fresh coating of Bone Armor. "Anna, stay towards the back behind us." As a wizard she was especially susceptible to surprise attacks.

Within ten seconds, the first of the newcomers appeared around a block away. It was a man crouching behind a car and eyeing us suspiciously. As soon as he realized we knew they were there, he waved to someone out of sight and they came out in a group. "Five in front of us, three more scattered to the left and right of them, watching," Jessica said.

I put my hands up "Friendly!" I yelled out. The people coming at us looked odd. As they got closer I realized they had wiped charcoal or ash on their faces, almost like battle paint. Even weirder was the clothing they all wore: pure white, well as white as you'd expect. Not only that, some of it wasn't even clothing but instead was clearly white bed sheets they had wrapped around themselves.

As they moved towards us fearlessly, a prickling on the back of my neck grew. These people were bad news, the question was whether they had bad intentions, too.

"I'm getting freaky religious crazy vibes," Richard whispered from behind me.

I almost lost my cool in that moment. It was careless to say something so stupid when you didn't know if the person in front of you was friend or foe. There was no end to the rare and unusual skills people could have, super hearing could be one too. My mouth almost opened in frustration, but instead I snapped my finger behind my back.

As they got closer, I expected them to stop, but instead they kept walking. A few seconds more would be uncomfortably close and even Jessica had enough of it. She nocked an arrow and pointed it directly at the person closest to us, "You've come close enough. We're friendly, but not naïve."

They did stop, but remained uncomfortably silent. Their eyes looked us over in an almost deranged way. Finally, the frontrunner, wrapped gloriously in a white bed sheet, spoke. "Do you believe in God?" he asked.

The atmosphere was stifling. I was confident in our abilities, but I truly didn't want to fight someone for no reason. It was too easy to lose your life at a low level. "What can we help you with?" I asked instead. I didn't want to answer such a nonsensical question.

"You can't help me. It is I who has come to help you." The man said. "I take your non-answer as a no."

"I appreciate the offer, but we are fine on our own," I said. "We mean no harm and just want to be on our way." I was conscious that the rest of our party was merely three blocks away or so. This timing was terrible.

"We belong to the true believers," their spokesperson said. "It is us who will be saved when the Rapture comes." I was at a loss on how to respond, but it seemed he didn't want an answer. "Any who don't join us will not be saved, and those who aren't saved are simply demons."

"We aren't demons." Anna said from the back, "we don't want any trouble." The way they were acting was so insane that I feared trying to reason with them would get us nowhere. He hadn't come out and said it outright, but we were demons in his eyes: enemies.

"You're right, you're not demons yet." I felt a sigh of relief for a mere moment, "but you will become one in time. That is why you will come with us, you can still be saved."

"No one is going with you," Jessica said firmly and aimed at his heart. I was ready to summon my undead squad at a moment's notice if I needed to. If they pushed the issue, blood would spill, and it would be more theirs than ours.

"Don't hold back if any of them start casting," I said to Jessica loudly enough for them all to hear.

"Oh, I won't," she responded in kind.

He paused in thought for a moment, "You won't come with us?" The four behind him started to fidget with impatience, placing their hands on weapon hilts. This was going to end in a bad way. "We don't want to hurt you, but you leave us no choice." His voice was filled with fake sincerity that made me sick. "Take them!" The four beside him rushed past to grab us.

It had become us or them, and Jessica didn't hesitate or aim to wound only. An arrow went directly through the head of the foremost and dropped her to the ground: a causality on their side in under a second.

The other three paused for a moment, and it almost seemed like they would retreat. It was natural to fear death. "Don't stop!" cried their leader. "Death in his word will only allow you to see God sooner." And as if a spell had been cast, the remaining three started running in our direction again.

Jessica exhaled through her teeth as she nocked another arrow and drew back the string of her bow. I let my undead warriors run loose and sent them forward. "There's a lot more on the way now!" Jessica said. "We have to run." She didn't hesitate to let loose another arrow, which found itself embedded deeply into a thigh, before turning tail.

The unease in my mind confirmed that that this was dangerous, and even if we took only one casualty in thwarting them, that would too much to bear. I wouldn't make the same mistake again. "Run!" I yelled to Richard and Ana. My undead were a wall of death in front of these cultists and I wasn't pulling any punches. My orders were clear: kill all enemies attempting to pass them.

Jessica dropped a Quagmire trap after ten feet or so and then sprinted ahead of us, "Follow me." She had radar, and was taking us directly to Maria, Alan, Thomas and Lucas. I hobbled as best I could with my leg in bad shape, but even at my slow speed, we were buying time for ourselves thanks to the Quagmire. The wall of skeleton warriors threatening to chop them to pieces helped as well.

We moved three blocks over in a flash and rushed for the park the others were fighting in. There we spotted them striking the finishing blow on a Blood Lich. "We gotta go!" I yelled. They looked at me like four deer in headlights, completely lost as to what was happening.

Jessica reached them before I could, "Enemies coming, we have to go," she said urgently.

Alan paused, "Can't we just fight them?" he asked.

"Human enemies, and more than ten." Jessica didn't wait for a second response and simply ran right by them.

Somehow, they were still standing there in a stupor, "What are you waiting for? GO!" I shouted as I reached Alan. I cast Vast Shadows and pulled my undead back, only to find that half had already been dispatched.

"Just make it a few blocks!" I said. Once out of the city we could move through open grassland and into rural neighborhoods.

Alan grabbed all the loot on the floor and then started to rush after us. "Where are we going?" he shouted.

"I don't know yet, just follow Jessica!" I called back.

Her speed was remarkable, and the gap between someone that had put stats in physical attributes and one that hadn't was becoming very clear. I almost couldn't keep up, and my hobbling wasn't helping either. "Are you hurt?" Thomas came to my side after taking notice of my slow pace.

"Just a small wound," I replied. "Let's deal with it when we're out of this mess." The problem with putting our heads down and running as fast as we could is that we ended up aggroing monsters. But Jessica didn't hesitate at all. Instead, she kept going through dangerous sections of mobs, much farther than among them, in fact, than I thought was necessary.

Fortunately, outside of dungeons, mobs had a certain radius on their aggro. An invisible tether or leash if you will, that they eventually reached the limit of. So although our charging through clusters of monsters built up quite a train of them in our wake, they eventually lost interest and drifted back to their original places. Far from being a crazy strategy, triggering mobs was creating concentrations of monsters, including one group with over twelve members. And it was possible that having to wade through these trains would deter our new adversaries from chasing us.

After rushing six blocks towards the outskirts of the city Jessica turned abruptly down an alley, waving for us to follow her. By then, my leg was screaming for me to stop and I felt dizzy. I had lost a good amount of blood already, enough to make physical activity rough.

I felt like I was going to fall at any moment, and as I almost stumbled over myself an arm came under mine. In fact, it was both Alan and Lucas on either side of me. "No, you don't," Alan joked. "Just a bit further."

We cut through the alleyway and Alan and Lucas hoisted me up atop a dumpster that was pushed up against a stone wall. Jessica was already waiting on the other side of the wall and behind her were open fields with farm houses in the distance. I felt oddly about letting Jessica catch me like a princess as I hung down the far side of the wall, but I couldn't land on my own feet without howling in pain.

"Hurry, I'll catch you," she said. There was nothing for it but to let go and fall into her arms. Alan and the rest tumbled over the wall with nowhere near as much grace as me a moment later. "They're still coming," Jessica said with a distant expression. "Less of them now though."

It seemed like our crazy sprint had caused a bunch of the pursuers to fall behind, but they were still on our trail. "One of them can clearly track and it has to be someone close," Jessica added. "Unless they have a special skill that isn't tracking, but something else."

"Move to open field." I suggested. "The person tracking us won't have cover from your arrows, and they may choose to not follow."

"You can barely support yourself." Thomas was on my side poking and prodding at my thigh. "Heal probably won't stop you doing permanent damage to yourself."

I knew he was right, as I could feel the sharp stabs of pain. The bandage was slowly trying to heal my broken muscle and tissue, and at the same time I was breaking and tearing it with my haphazard running, "Just a little further," I forced through gritted teeth.

No one moved, not because they wanted to disobey, but because they were worried about my well-being. "Let's move to where Jessica can pick some of them off before they reach us, or we fight to the death here. Will my leg be of any use if we're all dead?" I asked sarcastically.

That got them going, and Lucas and Alan continued to support me as I hobbled through the grassy field. It hadn't been grazed or maintained in some time, and the grass came all the way up to my knees. Moving through wasn't easy, and I instinctually scanned for snakes or predators as we ran.

We made good distance, at least a hundred yards from the city wall we had jumped, and there we set up and turned to wait. I pulled my minions from Vast Shadow and spread them around us, while Jessica nocked an arrow. It took ten or fifteen seconds for us to spot the first of the cultists peering over the wall. He acted as though fearless, but I'd never met someone not scared of death.

Jessica released as soon as that man slid down our side of the wall: she closed her eyes in concentration and then the bow twanged. There was a flash of light on the person's chest, bright and blinding. An explosion of red gore tore through a white shirt and they collapsed with a hole where their heart was. That was all it took for the remaining pursuers to lower themselves back to the far side of the wall, rather than come on to us.

They were oblivious to the fact that Jessica could hit them there too, so long as she could imagine where her arrow would materialize. She'd seen their faces, their clothes; she knew the wall and the dumpster. It might not be easy, but that was enough for her to materialize an arrow and do serious damage, if not kill.

"Does anyone want to explain what the hell that was just now?" Alan asked. It seemed for now we were safe from their pursuit.

"Religious sycophants," Richard answered. "I'd bet my left nut they were responsible for all this arson and vandalism too."

"They attacked you?" Lucas asked.

"They were going to kidnap us," I said. "We avoided fighting until it was clear that's what was going to happen. No one here is at fault for this." That got some skeptical stares and a nod. It was hard to believe someone would chase us for no reason, but here we were.

Chapter 22: Watchers in the Night

Once it was clear we were not going to be attacked, we continued to walk slowly away from the city and as we did, we talked over the situation. I was hopeful the cultists would leave us alone, but the fact they continued to watch us from the city worried me to no end. This probably wasn't going to be the end of our encounters with them.

I left the others whom were talking about the True Believers and moved to Jessica who was scouting at the front alone. She reached out an arm to support me as we walked side by side silently. It was an uncomfortable silence, and eventually I cracked. "Are you okay?" I asked.

"I don't like this," she said.

"Are we being followed?"

"That too," she said, "but I meant the killing; the hurting people." I didn't really know how to respond to that. Were there any comforting words to say in this situation? I still had random moments when I remembered having to kill those two brothers, but I always tried to push those memories away, and if I did think about that fight... well I always justified it in my head. It was the only way to accept these actions: to remove emotion and rationalize.

"It was us or them," I said. That was the only reality I could put forth. "Not fighting, not killing…would be the same as killing ourselves."

She thought on my words for a moment, "I know, but I'm not sure I can get used to it."

"I hope none of us get used to it." Even as I said this, I had almost the opposite thought. It was scary the things humans could become used to doing, and killing wasn't even the worst of them. "Can you still feel the cultists?" I changed the subject.

"They're staying really far back so I can't see how many, but there are definitely some people coming after us," she revealed. "One of them can surely track or follow our positions in some way." I turned my head and sure enough, hundreds of yards back, making no effort to conceal himself, a male figure in white clothing was on the road. We were still visible: only after getting out of sight would we know for sure if they would pursue further.

I would have loved to just tell Jessica to not worry and everything would be fine, but I really didn't know that. We were being hunted like prey, and I couldn't fight back at the moment. I had no abominations and just five skeleton warriors at my disposal. Not only that, my summoned undead didn't function as efficiently versus other people as they did monsters.

"There are some houses ahead that we can use as cover. It should be obvious enough if they can continue to track us after we get off the highway," I said. Once out of sight, they would need to close the distance quickly in order to not lose our trail.

I also just needed to lie down. The dizziness was growing overwhelming. My leg was burning and even through the healing of the Bandage there was no doubt I'd ripped the wound open. I could feel a moisture in my shoes, which soon revealed itself to be fresh blood leaking down my leg. This would leave a trail anyone could follow.

"Don't move." Jessica had followed my gaze and noticed the blood drenching my sock. She rushed to the others. I could barely hear what she was saying, but I could make out a few words, something about getting me to a bed. Alan and Lucas were on my side a moment later, basically dragging me through the field.

We stopped four houses in, which was a fair distance from the highway, given that each was separated by acres of land. The house we entered was abandoned, but still intact and in good shape. There were zombies roaming the far side of the field, but overall the density of monsters in this place was low. We would be safe from mobs for now, it was the humans we had to worry about.

I almost couldn't react to being helped off my feet when we walked inside and slumped onto a couch. The sudden change in my positioning caused blood to rush to my head. My eyes could only focus on the ceiling as I landed. Thomas fumbled with my pants to pull them off as I grew more incoherent, "Wash it poishon?" I asked in a stupor.

"Turn him on his side." Thomas' voice was distant and distorted in my head. I was forced to close my eyes as dizziness assaulted me. I felt like I was on the ocean in rough seas, bobbing up and down as the nausea washed over me. My world was spinning, even my thoughts were spinning, and I felt that opening my eyes now would cause me to hurl.

My leg was numb, but I could feel the pressure of their touch, their grasping. A burning sensation had crawled even lower down now to my ankle. "There's another wound," Jessica said. I could feel them wiping my thigh with something, and then feeling returned to my leg for a brief moment.

An intense stabbing in my lower calf shocked the dizziness out of me, "AHH!" I yelled while involuntarily struggling to get away from the source of the pain.

"Hold him down!" Thomas yelled. I opened my eyes in time to see Alan and Richard pressing me into the couch. "It'll be quick just hold him." The pain rose and rose till it felt like someone was jabbing molten metal into my skin, and then it subsided as fast as it came.

I stared at the ceiling in relief, no doubt the result of a Bandage and some healing by Thomas. Richard and Alan backed away as Jessica sat down beside me. I felt her hand grasp mine, warm and alive. "You had another spike in your calf," she explained, "Thomas had to pry it out of you." I laid my head directly back and sighed. "That's what you get for being shy and not taking your pants all the way off," Jessica joked.

Her laughter put me at ease. "I didn't think it was the right time to take it all off."

"Behave yourself and rest," she leaned over me with a smile. "We're going to take turns on watch. Lucas and I will be first. You should try to sleep a bit. Don't worry about anything—if anyone approaches I'll tell you."

Jessica was the person I trusted most in this world, and her assurance was all I needed. I was exhausted and my eyelids felt heavy.

When I opened my eyes again it was dark, and truthfully, I couldn't even remember falling asleep. My gums were pasty and my tongue was stuck to the roof of my mouth. Even my lips were dry and cracked. I had lost a lot of blood and not eaten anything since then, no doubt leaving me hungry and dehydrated.

I leaned up in bed and let my vision correct itself. There was no electricity, and the only source of light was moonlight flickering through the half-opened shades. I opened my inventory and pulled a ration before stuffing it into my mouth.

We didn't usually move at night as it was much more dangerous than travel during daylight hours. Monsters didn't seem to have any issue seeing in the dark, which wasn't the same for us. With that thought, I did recall having an ability that I had never fully experimented with.

Necrotic Vision allowed me to see a creature's life force, and that included other people. Lucas was sleeping in the corner, completely engulfed in darkness, and yet an orange hue swirled around his frame. It was almost like he glowed in the dark. I could see him clearly as if it were daytime.

As far as seeing enemies that were living, I'd not be ambushed in the dark. Traps and obstacles and pitfalls and anything that was inanimate...they were still threats. They meant it was still a risk to move at night, which was why I didn't want to end up in a situation where we swapped our schedules. This was the exact issue I wanted to avoid after the miasma incident.

I could hear low talking upstairs. Judging by the fact that Lucas was sleeping, Jessica would be asleep too, with the others keeping watch. A few seconds later Richard stumbled down the steps and nearly broke his neck. It was hard to not fall over yourself in this darkness.

He walked to the blinds slowly and then tilted them lightly with his fingers. His eyes were focused as he scanned the outside and then he moved back a moment before exhaling loudly.

"Is everything alright?" I asked.

"Jesus!" Richard said, "you almost gave me a heart attack." Via Necrotic Vision I could see him raise his hand to his chest and catch his breath. He calmed himself and continued, "Alan thinks he saw someone outside."

"They followed us?" I asked.

"If Alan wasn't seeing a ghost, then someone is out there."

"What did Jessica say?"

"She went to sleep about an hour ago. We didn't want to wake her." I turned and dangled my legs off the bed. My right thigh was sore, but I reckoned that I could at least move on it for the time being. Running hard was probably not a good idea for recovery, though.

Richard came over as soon as he saw me starting to move, "Jessica warned me you would try something. She told me to tell you: 'stay put or I'm gonna pull what's left of your ear off.'"

I winced at the thought, she might just do it if I pushed her far enough. "Just help me upstairs," I said, "I can move alright, just nothing strenuous." He gave me a questioning look as if he should even bother listening to me.

"You know, she also said she'd pierce both my ears if I let you convince me."

I couldn't help but sigh in annoyance, "This isn't the same. We could be in danger right now. If the cabin started to burn, you wouldn't insist on keeping me in bed then, right?" I asked.

"Of course not."

"Well, imagine the cabin is burning, because it very well could start soon if a pack of Religious arsonists are waiting outside." It seemed he got the point pretty quickly; not that he was stupid, but it seemed Richard was good at taking orders. He did what he was told, but had the independence to decide when not listening was good.

He helped me to my feet and then I caught him feeling both of his ears in the darkness, "It's gonna be fine," I said. He didn't respond, but his hands went to his side pretty quickly. He walked behind me while helping me to not fall on the staircase. I could see why he had tumbled earlier, there was barely enough space to put half your foot on each step, an absolute nightmare in the pitch dark.

Jessica, Thomas, Maria and Anna were each sleeping in a different corner of the room. Moonlight beamed through the only window and illuminated all but the corners, leaving them fully in the dark. Alan and Lucas were sitting on low chairs on either side of the window, just out of view from outside.

As soon as they saw me, both of them suddenly grabbed at their ears. I almost wanted to smack both of them for being silly, but Jessica could be convincing when she was mad. I brushed over their unusual behavior, "Where did you see them?" I asked Alan.

Unaided, I walked over until I could see out, without going into the patch of moonlight and Alan stood beside me. "Past the two buildings that way, right in between those three trees." He pointed at an inconspicuous spot barely illuminated by the silver light.

My eyes scanned the area for at least a dozen seconds without coming up with anything. Then, about a dozen feet behind the trees, I saw the orange hue of life energy, picked out by Necrotic Vision. There were a series of low bushes, and the hue would occasionally show every time the wind howled. "Someone is watching us."

"Wait, how can you be sure?" Lucas was skeptical as he had been when Alan had first claimed to have seen someone.

I explained Necrotic Vision, and then to further prove my point I gestured to each corner of the room: "Jessica. Maria. Thomas. Anna." I picked out who was sleeping where.

"The watcher is ten feet back from where you showed me, among those bushes," I pointed, but no one else could see what I was pointing at. The person in the dark was looking through the gaps in the bushes, essentially watching us from the darkness.

"Should we wake everyone else?" Lucas asked.

"What time is it?" I wasn't expecting an accurate time, but it would be helpful to know if it had only recently got dark or if our group had slept for several hours.

"Probably eleven or twelve," Alan replied.

"I don't think they are in range of Jessica's tracking ability, so waking her won't change anything. Let the others sleep a bit more and we'll leave in a few hours." My idea was to time our move so that it would still be dark enough to escape, but then the sun would come up soon after we left: the best of both worlds. "Did either of you sleep yet?"

"I haven't," said Alan.

"You should try to get a few hours at least," I said. He was the tank, and we couldn't afford for him to be exhausted for the coming day. No one could afford to be exhausted in the face of deranged humans or vicious mobs. "Lucas and I should be enough up here; we have Richard downstairs too," I added.

Alan was reluctant but eventually went downstairs and slept on the couch I had rested on earlier. "I said that to encourage him to sleep; but we need to be prepared to go at any moment." I warned Lucas. It wasn't out of the realm of possibility that our enemies attacked or burned the cabin to the ground to get us out. "If anything happens. I trust you to stay calm."

He gave a firm nod and then focused his attention back outside.

Chapter 23: Killing to Survive

I spent the next hour constantly scanning the tree line as well as any uneven ground or dark spots where someone could be sitting and watching carefully. In the end, I spotted two more people. Three in total were watching us.

Once I had sight of them, it was easy to figure out what exactly they were doing. Two of them were actually resting while a third was keeping watch. While that one was often moving a little, the other two were still as boards, and no one could sit so long without moving about to stretch their legs unless they were asleep.

"There's a way out of this safely," I looked at Lucas, "but I'll probably have to kill some people." If Jessica didn't want to do it, then I wouldn't share that burden with her. If I had to become something less-than-human in order to keep my people alive, then so be it.

I explained how my summoned warriors worked to Lucas, and then added the fact they were truly not living. That was the most important part, and Jessica had told me before that my skeletal squad did not show up on her radar. I found that odd, because while zombies were also not alive, and they did. Presumably, the difference was that zombies were a game-world monster but my summoned troops were an extension of me...or something like that.

It was impossible to be sure about the reason, but after testing in party and out of party, we had confirmed that Jessica couldn't see my summoned undead. That meant it was possible to sneak them out undetected, especially if the person tracking us was among the three outside.

This was similar to the situation at my old workplace. I could maneuver my squad in the darkness and take care of these three. If the true tracker was asleep, they wouldn't notice one of their comrades going missing. If it was the person that was awake... well that would be my first target.

The challenge lay in my ability to take out the watcher before he did something to wake the others. It was imperative that the other two remain asleep or this would turn into a fight and not the assassination I had in mind.

"Why do you think they're waiting?" Lucas asked.

"Probably the same reason we are." The moon only illuminated so much when darkness was everywhere. Fighting, running, or chasing in the dark was a nightmare. "The darkness is as dangerous an enemy as we are."

I pointed out the window for Lucas, "See that building down there, right next to the patio steps? That's where they are."

"The awake guard?" he asked.

"Yeah." It was a good place to hide. Completely engulfed in darkness and in such an odd position that even with more light, he would look like a trash bag or some patio decoration.

"Their back is to something solid and there are stairs to their left," Lucas observed.

"Right, which means I can't get behind him. He is mostly protected on the left side and anything going in from the right will be seen." Beyond the edge of the house on that side was an open plot fully illuminated by the moon. For my skeletons to approach from there undetected was impossible.

"So the left is the only option then."

"Yeah, taking advantage of the cover of the stairs, but the slightest movement in their peripheral vision is going to set him off, and my skeleton general isn't exactly small."

"So we need to keep their attention here then," Lucas thought. "Why don't I open the door? Take a walk outside?"

"That's good, but I'm slightly worried that would make them think we're making a run for it and they'll wake the others."

"Okay, so give them a good reason we went outside. Let's just have Richard walk out and take a piss on the tree just off the patio. It will be enough to hold their attention and also understand Richard isn't trying to escape."

I ran the thought through my head a few times, and I couldn't think of something more appropriate. If the guard woke up their sleeping comrades because one of us went outside to use the bathroom, they would probably get an earful.

"Let's try that."

"No, let's not try that." I heard Richard's muffled voice from downstairs, "I heard my name, what are you conspiring about up there?" The voice grew louder as he came up the stairs. Lucas took the time to explain the situation to him. "So they're out there then." He grabbed his head. "Fucking religious crazy people man, this is not how humanity should respond to an apocalypse."

"I didn't bring up your name at random. They may attack, and your ability allows you to summon a shield on use out of thin air. No one else can go outside and act nonchalant while still being safe." Lucas explained.

Richard inhaled loudly through grit teeth, "…Fucccking hell." He groaned. "I'll do it, how soon?"

"We wait one more hour," I said, "Everyone but Alan should have a decent amount of sleep. After that we'll double check with Jessica. This could all come crumbling down if they have more than what I've seen." There were only so many windows, and the possibility I missed someone existed.

It wasn't that unlikely that both exits were being watched; it was also possible there were people further back who hadn't wanted to get too close: they couldn't know for sure Jessica could track. There was also no denying that sneaking out eight people without being heard or seen was no easy feat, especially with how close that guard was.

I kept track of the three I could see for the next hour, and nothing untoward happened. The two remained sleeping while the patio guard remained awake. His fidgeting got less and less as he was clearly getting tired. Waiting had worked in our favor.

We woke Jessica up first, who definitely wasn't happy about having her sleep interrupted. Even less so about my being up and about, "Mike… why are you out of bed?" Lucas and Richard immediately backed out of the room and I didn't think it was out of fear of what they might hear.

"I promise I'm okay, but what I'm about to tell you is more important." I reported what we knew about being followed and our plan for getting out of this mess for good.

"I can feel one person in range of my detection," Jessica said, confirming that what I had seen with Necrotic Vision was a person. "Besides that…didn't I talk about this earlier? Is there no other way?"

I couldn't think of any other way. "Detaining him leaves the chance for him to yell out. If that scenario comes about, we will have more than we can handle on us. It might not just be these three. And every player brings something unknown to the battle. What if one of them can use telepathy and instantly alerts everyone else of our escape?" I didn't know if telepathy was a skill, but it served as a solid example for my reasoning.

"Just that one then," she said, "just the one in range and actually awake."

I didn't like it, but after a pause I agreed. "Okay." I had planned to kill all three to be absolutely safe. Killing less people was my preferred choice too, but I just didn't want our mercy to bite us in the ass in the future. "Just the one." I promised. "Are you about ready Richard?"

"Ready when needed," he replied.

I made for the stairs and found Jessica right on my tail. She placed her arm under mine. "Careful. We can't escape if you break your neck, so don't complain." I made a face, but secretly enjoyed the considerate attention. That, and the steps truly were treacherous.

When we reached the ground floor I walked to the center of the room, stepping into a ray of moonlight that granted me a shadow. Without one, I couldn't cast Vast Shadow to bring my undead squad into the world. I pulled them forth and my squad of skeletons appeared in the living room, nearly filling it. Lucas and Jessica moved to the staircase just to have some room.

Fortunately, the Demonic Goats had perished earlier or we might have made a large commotion. The other positive was none of my warriors had stepped on Alan who was still sound asleep, completely oblivious to what was happening.

I picked out my most trusted aide, the Zweihander-wielding general, and made the remaining skeletons open a path to the backdoor. The timing of this needed to be somewhat accurate.

Richard could only pee for so long, and in that time frame I needed to cross and approach from out of sight, and then initiate the execution. I reached the backdoor just behind my skeleton general and turned the knob. If there was a god on my side, he would surely make this door not squeaky or loud.

The back door opened without any issues, but the screen door was something straight out of hell. The hinges holding the frame were wobbly and barely screwed into the wood. I could tell from a glance it was going to squeal like a pig. Not only that, the pump was going to rip this thing back so fast you'd think Jessica would have shot it out of her bow.

"We might have a little problem," I said. How could I tell them a screen door may have defeated us? Lucas and Jessica squeezed past my undead and examined the situation curiously. I grabbed the plastic handle and pushed the button and moved the door just an inch. The noise it made in that short movement was enough to put the crickets outside to shame. "Well, maybe I have a solution. Come hold it."

Lucas and Jessica scooted forward and grabbed the door frame, both looking at me in confusion. "I just don't want it to fall." I said while raising my hand. I hadn't cast Decay since it had reached level three; I had tried during the Miscreation fight and nearly been impaled.

The lack of cast time it had in the skill description was something I wanted to test. How would that work? Was it just instant cast now? I aimed at the top hinge and cast. In that moment I felt

Decay flow from me and then stop, but the feeling it gave me was odd. It felt nothing like it had when using the spell before.

I cast again, and this time I held the thought. To my surprise, Decay didn't stop. Instead, it was as if I was channeling an ability. The wooden frame began to age and peel and crack until it was splitting off the frame, even the screw that was originally half-in started to rust and break apart. Eventually, the screw melted out of the decayed frame and clacked into the wooden back steps.

Everyone froze, and didn't even dare to breathe. The ageing of the screen hadn't been that loud, but sound traveled on such a quiet night. "Did he move?" I asked Jessica.

"No, he hasn't," she said.

I let out a sigh of relief and then marveled at how much faster Decay worked now. Even better was that the MP consumption was half the cast if I just kept channeling it. It cost less and worked faster: an amazing upgrade.

Before, casting Decay created a gradual change that you could only see from one cast to the next. Now it was just a constant withering of whatever substance it touched. The wood deteriorated in real time and the frame and screw rusted as if aging dozens of years in a few seconds.

It was now easy to take the screen off its hinges. Lucas caught it before any noise was made and lowered it quietly to the side. I took that opportunity to look out the backdoor and move to where I could see the building against which the enemy scout was sitting. It was just fifteen or twenty feet away and there were no obstacles that my skeleton general needed to go through to get there.

He needed to cross the open ground unseen, and then approach as far as the stairs under cover. Ideally, he would then inflict a swift and painless death. I instructed him to walk down the porch steps, which was awkward for him. The ground outside was a mixture of dirt and grass, and his boney feet made no noticeable noise.

I walked him slowly to the edge of the building and had him wait. "Whenever Richard's ready." I whispered back over my shoulder, "he can be flashy about it, too."

Lucas nodded and moved through the rows of skeletons to the front room. I could hear their mumbling.

A moment later, the front door opened violently as Richard fumbled out. He burped so loudly, that I wondered if this was practiced or if he was just showing his true colors. He walked two steps onto the patio and gazed into the distance—nothing out of the ordinary, just having a look.

As soon as he stopped moving, I urged my skeleton general to cross the short gap between buildings and position himself against the wall, out of sight. This wasn't supposed to be the most difficult part, so when my skeleton general suddenly tripped on a root and tumbled to the floor, I wanted to scream.

Don't get up! That thought boomed in my mind, and no doubt my Skeleton General received it loud and clear. His instinct when falling to the ground was always to instantly get back up and fight, but lying on the floor there would probably save us from having to start a blood bath. He was large and had no doubt made some noise, but to see him the guard would have to fully stand up and look over the stairs he was perched behind.

I prayed for his drowsiness in that moment. Please be so tired and lazy you don't care enough to stand up and look. My heart was in my throat as I expected any second for the guard to yell out. Ten seconds passed in pure silence and then I gave Jessica a look that said 'go tell Richard to do something.'

She raced back through the house as quietly as she could, and then I heard Richard mumble something and then tumble on the floor. His acting was impressive, and I used that moment to stand the general up slowly and cross the gap. After that, Richard started to relieve himself as planned.

I rushed to the second floor as fast as my bad leg would let me, and glided up the treacherous stairs. From here I could see the watcher clearly and would be able to tell if they were doing anything fishy. My skeleton general now had a target and was instructed to move slowly towards him.

Against the building, my general was fully engulfed in its shadow, barely noticeable: he could only be seen if the guard fully stood and turned around. Being so low and right next to the patio was a double-edged sword. They were hard to spot, but it made watching to their left impossible.

My general was just a few feet away when the watcher suddenly stood up. It didn't seem like they turned around or heard anything but was instead preparing to alert the others who were sleeping. That or complain it was his turn to get some sleep.

I gave the instruction to kill right then, and as if timing was on my side. The guard was fully turned away from the general, and before he could even scream out a blade almost as thick as his neck passed from the back of his body to the front. The lifeless body slid off that blade like a doll and slumped to the ground. I forced myself to watch as that orange hue faded to nothing.

"Got him; wake the others." Lucas started to wake those still sleeping. Their bodies shook and their eyes showed fear as they woke. The thought of being hunted was on everyone's mind. Stomping it out now would save us from many sleepless nights, "We're leaving in five minutes," I said.

Jessica came up the stairs a moment later, "Is it done?" she asked. Presumably, she just was making conversation. She would have seen the marker for that person disappear from her tracking ability.

I gave a nod, "Have the other two guards moved?"

"No, they haven't moved at all," Jessica replied.

"Were we followed?" Maria asked while rubbing her eyes.

"We were, but we've taken care of it," I answered. "We need to move quickly though."

Alan was the last one to wake, and since most of us slept dressed, we were ready to go in under five minutes. "We take the backdoor and follow the fence as far as we can." I held the door open for everyone and when they were all through, rushed to the dead watcher's body.

It was a perfectly good corpse and half my skeleton warriors were currently dead. "At least you can become something." I held my hand and cast on the lifeless body. My squad repopulated around me and then vanished as soon as I stepped into the moonlight and cast Vast Shadow.

There was a bag on the ground there too that I hadn't seen from the upstairs window. I picked it up and realized it was the dead man's entire inventory. There was no time to check it now so I rushed back to the others. The root my skeleton general tripped on almost caught me as well; fortunately, given my bad leg, I stopped from tumbling over.

A pain shot through my thigh as I put all my weight on it. It was too dark for anyone to see my near fall, thankfully, and I quickly caught up with them all.

Chapter 24: Not all Passive Ability Gains are Welcome

Jessica led from the front as we walked near a fence and tried to stay out of the light. We took around thirty steps along the fence. I felt a growing unease building, until the hairs on my neck were standing on end, "Stop!" I said in a hushed voice, "something is wrong!" We were in danger, and if we continued to walk something bad was definitely going to happen.

"Do you feel anyone?" I asked Jessica. "Anything?"

"Nothing."

"Double-triple check please." I trusted her completely, but this feeling of mine hadn't let me down so far. My wariness put everyone on high alert as they scanned our surroundings. Given there were no monsters in the vicinity that Jessica could see, was the warning growing the further I moved away from the remaining two cultists for some reason?

Was this feeling caused by the game telling me to go back and kill those two remaining humans? It shouldn't be…My skill had never previously warned me of something that wasn't an imminent threat. More likely, it was a monster or human player that could somehow evade Jessica's tracking.

I started to trace every crevice, tree, and splotch of darkness in the distance. Eventually my eyes came to rest on a small farmhouse.

I could see it! An orange hue so small it was barely noticeable flickering through the window blinds on the second floor. "We're being watched," I said.

"From where? How can you be sure?" demanded Richard.

"Don't freak out," I answered him with sufficient volume in my whisper to be heard by everyone. "And don't all stare. But it's the second floor of that barn house at about two o'clock. I'm not one-hundred percent sure they've seen us, but I'm ninety-nine percent sure."

"We can make a run for it," Lucas suggested. "We could climb over the fence and disappear across the field. We don't have to fight."

"Yes we do," Maria said.

Jessica shook her head. "We should avoid a confrontation if we can, that's what we agreed upon."

"I understand that..." Maria paused. "I don't know about you all, but I hate feeling like I'm being chased..."

"I don't want to be looking over my shoulder non-stop either," Alan agreed with Maria. Eventually it was only Lucas and Jessica that wanted to run. Everyone else was for dispatching this threat, even Anna.

"I know I promised to only kill one person," I found myself wanting to explain my reasoning to Jessica. "But my skill is warning me this person is a real danger. If we don't act now...we will be followed. We might not get another chance to choose when to encounter them." My intuition was that if we moved on, in the future this person would be much more violent or bold in their assault. Either we were being watched by someone who was planning an ambush using their own special powers or they were waiting for more people to arrive. Both situations screamed bad news.

I could see the conflict in Jessica's eyes. "What's the plan then?" Slowly that conflict morphed into acceptance. Lucas came around shortly after, and with everyone in agreement we started to plan on killing another person this night.

"Remember, don't look, but he's on the second floor of that barn house just to our right, about a football field away." I wasn't even staring at the farm building myself. "As far as he's concerned, we have no idea of his presence."

None of my party members could see our enemy even if they tried, but at least they understood the location and layout. "I think we just pretend we are sneaking out in that direction and when close enough make a dash into the building. Jessica, hopefully as we get nearer, you'll get him on your tracker: we won't lose him then even if he runs." And that plan was as good as any. I just hoped he wouldn't dart the moment we moved in his direction. I really felt it important to deal with this threat while we had the advantage.

With Jessica and I at the front, we all moved forward at a cautious pace. Following an earthen path wouldn't take us directly to the barn house, but instead a diagonal that would bring us within fifteen feet. That would do.

"I can feel him now," Jessica suddenly whispered to me. "He's still there."

"I can see him too; he's watching us. If we were to walk on past, he'd alert the others and we'll have no end to our troubles." I reaffirmed that we were making the right decision.

"There's a blind spot for him after we move past the barn house door." Thomas muttered from behind me. "We can disappear from sight and then make our move."

That sounded like a good plan, but I was worried about how long it would take us to get in through the barn door if it were barred. In that moment, I didn't know if we should bait him to leave the house or just force our way in. If spent too long forcing our way in, he might be able to alert the others.

The upside was that we were now a decent distance away from the two sleepers. Our enemy would have to scream at the very top of his lungs, and even that might not be enough. Not from inside the barn house at least. Waiting for him to exit on his own also had its downfalls as well.

"I understand some of you probably don't want to dirty your hands with this," I whispered as we came closer to that sinister upstairs window. "I'll send my undead squad in, just be prepared for him to try and escape out of a window."

Hopefully, the time our enemy realized we were aware of his presence, my undead would be upon him. No matter how powerful he was, twelve melee skeletons should be able to overwhelm him in an enclosed space.

"Don't look up," Jessica muttered as we walked directly under the window. It was possible now to see him in plain sight by just using my peripheral vision: a figure peering from the shadows while half covered by the window shades.

It took several seconds of slow walking before we were no longer in sight of that window and everyone gathered at the side of the barn and crouched down. I didn't stop, however, and rushed to where I was relieved to see a back door, time was of the essence. He would be watching for us to continue our journey and come into view again. If we took too long he would be on high alert.

I cast Vast Shadows and grabbed the back doorknob. It jiggled in my hand but wouldn't budge. The door was locked; fortunately, the challenge was nothing more than a slight hiccup. I channeled

Decay and held it for nearly ten seconds, then grabbed the door-knob again.

I squeezed hard and twisted. The metal mechanisms inside had been rusted to fragility and the lock popped with a burst of red smoke: a mixture of decay and rust spraying into the air.

My skeletons flooded into the hallway and then raced through the house. I didn't know the layout, but it didn't matter. Once we were up the main stairs, they were like ants entering an enemy colony. There were enough of them to clear every room in mere moments.

It took five seconds for them to be upon our enemy. His shout of surprise was loud enough for me to hear, but wouldn't have travelled to the sleepers. Glass shattered and then something smashed into a wall. It sounded like he was cornered and throwing whatever he could at my troops.

My undead weren't intelligent, and I couldn't see through their eyes, but I did know when they had killed something. As soon as our enemy died I received a status message and my undead troops regrouped around me.

You have learned the Passive Ability: Blood Thirsty LV 1.

I wanted to check what this meant, but now wasn't the time. I took a brief look through the door. Bloodstains on the far wall showed where my undead had forced him and there was a body... of a woman in fact, in leather armor. There was bag floating above her, which I grabbed but disappointingly had only some rations and the most basic of daggers. Despite my sense of danger, it wasn't the gear of this person that had posed any the threat.

The prickling on the back of my neck had disappeared and I was pleased with the outcome. The others, too, seemed relieved when I came out and confirmed the enemy had been killed. We could now hope to shake off the cult and get away.

Jessica took to the front once more and led us through the fields of this once intensively farmed region. Every step was taking us away from the True Believers. Avoiding them was our number one priority for now.

Such a low population area like this didn't pose too much problem during the day, but at night it was a different story. There was a high density of monsters and even though they were only low level, we had to be careful. A goblin that was only level five or six could still toss a spear faster and stronger than an Olympic medalist. Offense and defense were not balanced in this game and a surprise attack against our lower members could prove fatal.

Even for Jessica, Alan and I, a critical hit from a javelin or arrow striking into our heads or hearts might mean death. And for everyone else, it probably wouldn't even have to be a critical. Fortunately, I could detect the life force of goblins, while anything I couldn't see that Jessica could track was an undead and she could keep us clear of danger.

It was over two hours of steady moving before the first ray of sunshine came over the horizon. An orange hue covered the land that illuminated a world so full of life and at the same time, so full of death. We pushed on until the sun was clear on the horizon and the day was bright.

"As far as I can tell, one should be following us," Jessica said as we came to a stop in a grove of trees, after making good progress, "I haven't felt anything besides monsters for the entire journey."

We'd been traveling through overgrown farmland and the occasional cluster of trees. Visibility around us on all sides was good.

"I've been looking back, nothing on our tail," Richard added. No one could have followed us without us seeing them.

The break wasn't for anyone else but me. My leg was still in dire need of rest, and I had pushed it too hard already. Bandages were useful, but it wasn't a cure all item. And the effect of Bandages was diminished as I gained more levels and HP. The damage done to me from those attacks was much larger than those items alone were capable of healing.

I took this brief moment of respite to open my stats and take a look the effect of Blood Thirsty.

Name: Mike Reynolds [27] Class: Necromancer Level: 22 EXP: 7%
HP: 1130/1130 MP: 35/460
STR: 5 Fear Resistance: 5
AGI: 2
DEX: 5
VIT: 29 +14
WIS: 27 +23
Available: 3
Skills: [A] Summon Skeleton LV. 9| [A] Summon Skeleton Mage LV. 2| [A] Decay LV. 3| [A] Reanimate Dead LV. 3| [A] Bone Armor LV. 2 | [A] Vast Shadows | [A] Temporary Grave LV. 1 | [P] Sixth Sense | [P] Bravery LV. 2 | [P] Mutated LV. 3| [P] Pain Resistance LV. 2 | [P] Skeletal Mastery LV. 4| [P]Intimidate Living |[P] Inner Calm LV. 2 |[P] Necrotic Vision|[P] Blood Thirsty LV. 1

It was there in the passive list, and I opened the description.

Blood Thirsty: You lose yourself in the carnage. Damage against human enemies +3%.

It was a positive trait, game-wise at least; I had worried it might be a curse. I thought on it a moment longer, is the implication that it has reduced my inhibition to kill humans? So killing other people would become easier and easier. I didn't know if that was a good or bad thing.

There were also the three stat points waiting to be used. I decided to hold onto them for now.

Jessica approached as I closed my character sheet, "Is your leg okay?" She didn't have the slightest inhibition, as she grabbed my thigh and felt the bandage for any blood leaking through.

"I'm fine, just a little sore." I said. "I'm sorry... I know I promised you." I had to take this burden to ensure these people around me were safe, so I was safe, so Jessica was safe. I knew she understood that.

"I don't know how to explain..." Jessica looked at me with sorrowful eyes. "It's not that I feel sorry for these people—I know they are bad people..." She paused. "It's more like...I'm scared...of what It will do to me."

That was when I suddenly had a realization. "Do you have Blood Thirsty as a passive?"

Her face showed surprise for a moment and then realization. She must have guessed that I probably just received the passive this morning. "I do... Level Two." She had killed more people than me, mostly during the Ghost Hand invasion. Her bow was as good as any gun, and when defense wasn't very strong due to low levels, each shot was basically a death sentence for anyone hit.

"What does the description say?" I asked.

"Bathe in blood. It's not just that…Inner calm is Level Four as well. The things I rationalize without even thinking is scary…Things that should tear my heart in two don't even make me flinch. Instead, I have to make a mindful effort to think about what decisions are still human."

"Is that why you shot the second True Believer in the thigh?" I asked. When they rushed us originally, she had killed one instantly and disabled another.

She gave a nod, "I'm scared of how fast it levels."

This was something I could see in her eyes when we were in the dungeon. There was a calmness that seemed inhuman, completely uncaring. I even felt this own way about myself, and my Inner Calm was merely Level Two. I never once saw those uncaring eyes look at me though.

"You're still you, and you're still human," I said. "You are in control of how you feel. It just makes the hard decisions easier." I couldn't be sure of that, but as of now I hadn't had any dark thoughts about my party members: at least not when I was mentally stable.

"I'm scared of what will happen if I have to keep hurting people." She somehow ended up in my embrace. "What if eventually Blood Thirsty creates a desire to kill? I don't want to be a senseless murderer." I could only hold her close and let her release her feelings.

We sat with Jessica in my arms for a dozen minutes, long enough for everyone to rest their legs for a moment. It was a good chance to ensure we weren't being followed as well, and no one came sneaking up on us during the break. Our goal now was to get our bearings.

Chapter 25: The Difficulty of Post-Apocalypse Choices

This entire region on the outskirts of the city was one large community meshed together. There was no main street, but just a winding mess of paths that went from one farm to the next: surely one of them would take us to a highway?

We eventually came upon a brick wall across our path. "Shall we just hop over and keep going?" I asked. The other option was to walk along in the direction of the wall to see where it led; both involved moving into the unknown.

"Let's keep going, we'll hit a road eventually," Lucas suggested, and no one disagreed. Jessica ran and leaped for the top of the wall, hauling herself on top and then assisting everyone else in turn. After I scrambled over the wall, I could tell we'd moved out of the farming district into a residential area of a very different kind.

"This is a trailer park," I said. The rows of homes were something I'd never mistake. The fake plastic paneling and the metal grating that did a bad job at hiding the underside of a trailer gave it away instantly. I'd grown up in a trailer park in my elementary school days. This one, however, gave off quite the cleanly vibe. "Probably a retirement community," I guessed.

Every trailer was white; the driveways were black asphalt. The homes were minimally decorated and most of the vehicles in the driveways were a newer model of car and didn't show many signs of being used. The whole feel of the place screamed that it had been used by the elderly. Confirmation of that came shortly after we had set off walking as a group.

Calm Waters Retirement Community. A white real estate sign stood in the front yard of a trailer for sale. Part of the problem with it being an old person's community was that most of the vehicles were small and therefore wouldn't allow us to travel as a group. There were eight of us and for that we needed a truck or minivan or SUV. Two vehicles would be a last resort.

"There are people here," Jessica said, "individuals, not a group."

"Survivors?" Richard and Alan asked in unison.

"Seems there are some people hunkering down in their trailers," Jessica answered, "more than I expected." We were barely a week away from the two-month mark since the apocalypse had happened. I guessed that this must be a low traffic area for mobs, where survival was more a matter of how much food and water you had stocked up than if you could fight back.

"We should take them with us," Lucas suddenly said. "We can't leave them here…"

"Wait a minute; don't decide that so quickly," Thomas said, "these are elderly people; we need to talk about this."

"How many?" I asked.

Jessica looked up. "There's six of them so far."

And we had merely walked two or three blocks. That was too much for us to safely take, accommodate, and protect already. This community could have dozens of people still in it.

"I don't want to sound cold," Richard said. "But we can barely care for ourselves. Are we expected to take in every stray we meet? They are old, they won't be able to fight or keep up."

It was a harsh reality, and Lucas opened his mouth to retort but it looked like he just couldn't find the words that reasoned with anything other than emotions. "I hear you, but they are people too."

"I understand where you're coming from, but we have to be rational," Richard said, "What about those in wheelchairs? Those that can't get out of bed? Are we meant to accommodate them too? Where do you draw the line?"

"There's no reason to argue over it," I said, "neither of you are wrong." It was a hard decision to make, and there was no right answer. "We don't have anywhere to take them if we 'save' them. This is probably the safest place they could be."

And what I said wasn't wrong either. The mob traffic here was almost non-existent. Goblins, ghouls, and zombies were a threat outdoors in these low population areas, but they couldn't break down doors, nor even tried to do so.

"So they'll just sit in their trailers till they die?" Lucas asked. "It doesn't sit right with me."

It was Jessica who responded to him, even before I could, "The other option isn't much better. Would you rather bring them along and watch them die one at a time to monster attacks we just couldn't stop? They can live out the remainder of their life here, as peacefully as possible."

We were on our way to Rotterdam to save our families. If the farm had still been intact, moving them there would be a priority and it wouldn't even be a question; but we didn't have a place to keep these residents safe and we couldn't provide for them. We had only managed to secure about a week's worth of Rations for ourselves from Withersburg before the True Believers came after us.

"And even if we did want to take them, how do we choose? There is bound to be more, so in the end you'll still be leaving some to die. All you've done is move the goal post," Jessica concluded.

"FUCK!" Lucas suddenly yelled. "I hate this shit!" And he stormed off.

Alan was going after him when Jessica caught him by the shoulder, "Don't. Let Lucas cool off. He was raised by his grandparents." That was something I had overlooked. Lucas's parents died young and his grandparents raised him. Leaving the elderly behind had to be hard to accept. "I can keep track of him, let's just follow behind him."

We walked a good distance behind Lucas, just close enough to keep track. All the low-level fodder in his path had been rushed and cut swiftly in half. All his worries, his anger, his regrets, he was letting them all out right now. It took twenty minutes before we came up to him, crouched down on the ground, seemingly done with his rampage.

Alan put a hand on Lucas's shoulder after we reached him, then extended an arm to help him stand up. Lucas took it with a firm grip, "Are you feeling better?" Alan asked.

"I'm not mad at you guys," he clarified, "I know we can't help the people here; I know it's not the right choice for us, but it isn't something easy to accept."

"There were more than we thought. We couldn't move this many people even if we tried. Jessica has counted thirty so far, and not all were friendly," I said. One of the trailers we walked right in front of had an older gentleman in the window, not only that, he was holding a shotgun. I caught his eye and he mouthed to me 'keep walking'. Not everyone even wanted our help.

It took us thirty minutes of slow pace to move to the opposite end of the trailer park, where there were finally some decent roads to give us options. It would be possible to find a highway and make our way towards Rotterdam from here.

Unfortunately, there were no suitable vehicles to take from the trailer park, and as we entered the suburban streets, I saw mostly destruction. More than half the vehicles were damaged and several were completely wrecked. We did check the bigger ones that had no obvious damage, but there were no keys in sight, and none of us knew how to hotwire a car.

There was a small shopping center across the street, and, contrary to what I expected, monster traffic was almost non-existent. Jessica didn't report any enemies at all. "Let's take a look," I said. If we could find anything of use then this was well spent time.

We moved swiftly across the street, checking every vehicle that wasn't completely wrecked or boxed in, before crossing into the parking lot of this little plaza. There weren't many vehicles here still parked, a few here and there. Specialty shops littered the plaza area and one grocery store.

It was funny to see human nature displayed so readily in front of our faces. The pawn shop, the cell phone shop and the PC repair shop's storefronts had been busted down and everything inside had been ransacked. Even at the end of the world, people cared about personal wealth and material goods.

"Let's check the grocery store before we go on. I'd love to eat something that isn't stale bread," Maria expressed a sentiment that was clear everyone shared. As useful as the Ration was, it just didn't taste good at all.

We pried open the electronic sliding doors and entered inside. It was pitch dark, and after Jessica confirmed we had nothing to worry about, we started to move through the aisles. The place was an absolute wreck, and most of the shelves had been knocked over.

Whatever contents they held had been spilled onto the floor, and the entire area smelled of mold and rotting food. We looked for where canned goods would be, only to find that area had been ransacked clean. In the end, after a good fifteen minutes of searching, we came out with a few containers of roasted peanuts and some boxes of cereal.

"Let's be smart about how we—" and before Lucas could even finish his sentence, Alan had already torn into a box of Captain Crunch. He tilted the bag without shame and let the pebbles fall into his mouth.

"My God that's sweet," he said while passing the box. "Taste it; was it always that sweet?"

Lucas didn't even bother to finish his sentence, and he had clearly given up on the idea he was about to express. He took the box from Alan and started pouring cereal into his mouth, "Yeah, it's actually so sweet it kind of ruins it for me."

"That's because you haven't tasted sugar in a long while," Thomas said. Eventually, everyone had a pass at the box with mixed feelings. The general consensus was that being able to taste anything was a blessing. Even little things like this could really raise your spirits.

We kept moving in the direction of Rotterdam while scouring the area. As quickly as the cereal raised our morale, our lack of luck with regard to a car brought it back down. "I swear to God, in the movies they make it seem like finding a vehicle is so easy," Alan complained.

"Yeah, but that's movies," Maria replied flatly. "What did you expect?" And he really couldn't retort. Everyone shared his pain. We walked for over an hour, scouring any vehicle we could see that would work for our situation, that wasn't ruined, that wasn't scorched, and that was able to get out of whatever enclosure it might be in.

"Where the fuck are the keys?" Richard nearly lost it. "Did these people just toss their keys into the wilderness after exiting their vehicle? Did the monsters eat the fucking keys?" Every time he went on a little rant about it, Anna couldn't help but snicker while covering her mouth. Seeing her was enough for Richard to realize he should cool off a bit.

A part of me still worried how the two would fit in, but so far there were no problems. Anna showed her emotions on her face, it was easy to tell if something was wrong. Richard was similar, and he just said what he was thinking without reservation. Someone who could come out and just say what everyone was thinking, regardless of how bad it was, was a valuable asset in my book.

It was early afternoon when we had our first real development, "Two strong enemies." Jessica suddenly said. "A block that way, not humans."

"How strong?" I asked.

"Elite level, similar to how the Children of Sobek felt."

"Should we take a look?" I asked everyone. It could be a potentially valuable leveling area for us. Time was of the essence; but being prepared was also important too. We still needed to get Anna and Richard some levels as well.

"Lead the way," Alan said and no one disagreed. Everyone was tired of walking without anything happening. Humans were so fickle in their mood swings; just yesterday we would have killed for this peaceful travel. Now we were pining for adventure.

We followed Jessica just one street to another small shopping plaza of three or four buildings. There was nothing we could see, "Behind the middle building." And so we made our way there by going around the back. What we found was not what we were expecting.

Behind the building was an open lot of dead grass and sand, surrounded by a fence that had been torn to shreds. Standing there were two large gorillas, or primates of some sort, at least eight feet tall.

"They don't look like they belong here at all," Anna observed, "is there a zoo somewhere nearby?"

"Look at the map, doesn't this seem familiar?" It was Thomas who helped me understand. There on the map, besides the manmade structures and the shoddily drawn roads, was a black doorframe.

"Is this the dungeon thing you were talking about?" Richard asked.

"I think so…" I said.

"Alright, are we ready to go?" Alan asked. He was roaring for some action, and I couldn't blame him.

"Wait a second, let's watch for a moment," I suggested. If this was a dungeon entrance, and the mobs were leaking into reality from within, then where did they go? They couldn't possibly just hang around here permanently. Surely there would have been a lot more than two if that was the case? It had been days since we received that message.

We took cover as best we could and watched the two apes. They didn't attack each other but instead moved around randomly, eventually one of them made it to where it spotted a zombie in the distance. As if it was a bull that saw red, the giant ape rushed the zombie and grabbed it by the torso before tossing it like a ragdoll into a nearby building.

The zombie exploded into blood and gore before sliding down the wall. After that, the primate just meandered away until we could no longer see it. "So they...just walk around? Is that why this area is so barren?"

We had wandered upon their spawn point, and this was too good of a situation to pass up. The amount of information, and potential EXP we could gain from this was incredibly useful.

"Let's grab the second before it runs off, yea?" Alan was itching.

"Stats?" I asked Jessica.

"Level Twenty-Six. Elite. Blood Ape," she reported, "should be easy enough." She laid a Quagmire trap in front and then prepared to pull.

"Richard you can just support for now, I don't want you anywhere in melee with something almost twice your level. Anna, you can just toss out spells as you see fit." They both nodded and Jessica pulled with a regular arrow.

Once the Blood Ape reached the Quagmire trap, Maria hit it with an Ensnaring Arrow for good measure and we pummeled it down in less than fifteen seconds. The ape didn't seem to have any skills, and was simply equipped with overpowering strength and attack speed. Alan ended up complaining for at least five minutes after that he couldn't even use his new sword in earnest.

The gorilla attacked with such fervor that doing anything other than holding his Steel Bulwark with both hands sent him hurdling backwards, and this was someone who had tanked a dungeon boss. That memory made me downcast at the thought that I couldn't reanimate Elite enemies, as they would make excellent vanguards.

"Let's stick around and figure out how fast these apes are being spawned into the world." I suggested. "After that, we should continue to Rotterdam. Risking getting stuck in a dungeon for a week or more could ruin our plans completely." It wasn't only that though. In four days, it would have been two months since this all started.

Nothing was set in stone, but new developments seemed to happen based on intervals of time, and typically there was some symmetry to it. Two months seemed as good a marker as any to unleash a bit more hell on the world.

"We can return to the dungeon in the future," Thomas reminded everyone, "the map has been filled in around the dungeon icon, so we don't have to guess anymore."

No one expressed any disappointment that we weren't going to try the dungeon right away. Anna asked several questions about our last experience, but considering she was only level 15 and the Elites coming out were 26, the dungeon boss here would probably end her with a single breath.

We passed the better part of an hour on idle chatter before more mobs spawned in. They appeared in the exact same position, which seemed interesting and definitely exploitable, but they weren't the same enemies.

Instead of two Blood Apes, there were four large black cats there. "Level Twenty-Three. Elite. Phantom Jaguars." Jessica gave us a quick rundown on the enemy.

"How long do we think it has been?" I asked. A quick consensus put it at anywhere from 45 minutes to an hour, which meant multiple elites were spawning every hour in this exact spot. There were probably more dungeons than this, too. The world was being flooded.

"Ready?" Jessica asked as she set her trap, that laser-focused attention was there again in her eyes.

Alan couldn't stop himself from jittering. His sword started to slap in his shield, "What? Are you a gladiator now?" Thomas poked fun at him.

"Ready!" Alan ignored Thomas and let Jessica know to pull. The bow sang and four cats the size of minibikes came rushing directly towards us. Alan held out his shield and prepared to rush in when something amazing happened.

The four cats in front of us suddenly turned into two, and then to one, and then three appeared. They were vanishing in and out of sight as they rushed at him. We'd never encountered an enemy like this, and Alan was at a complete loss on how to react.

All four of them lunged into the air at Alan and continuously disappeared from view. Even if you knew exactly what was happening, it still messed with your mind. Your reaction time would be off, or slowed, it created a vulnerability in your defense.

It created an opening for a mistake. The four jaguars created a vulnerability in just their first attack. "Shit!" Alan cursed. There was a long streak of claw marks on his left bicep. He had mitigated some of the damage, but the slash had still drawn blood.

The four cats landed and then circled looking for their next opening, the constant disappearing and reappearing almost made it look like two jaguars were simply teleporting around in front of our tank.

Fortunately for us, we had just the thing to deal with agility-based monsters. Maria had Ensnaring Arrow and I had an overwhelming number of summoned undead to pin them down. With those two things combined, we quickly surrounded the four jaguars. In the end, I lost half my minions and Alan needed to be healed for half of his life, but we took them down without much issue.

Unlike the Blood Ape, these monsters actually dropped items. In fact, we received a wrist guard for Anna and several more Rations.

Magister's Vambrace: WIS +2, VIT +2, Casting time reduced by 5%

This was a beautifully crafted wrist guard with a mixture of silver and gold decoration. Red gemstones circled around the cuff. Anna equipped it immediately then raised her hand high. The metal fit adhered perfectly to her wrist and went up her forearm. It would surely take a strong blow when she needed it to.

"This was kind of easy…" Anna suddenly said. "Isn't good gear supposed to be pretty rare?"

Jessica and I took for granted how difficult it actually was to get gear. Most people only had one or two pieces. For Anna, that was actually only her second equipable item.

"The EXP wasn't bad either." Lucas said. I opened my stats to check.

Name: Mike Reynolds (27) Class: Necromancer Level: 22 EXP: 37%
HP: 1130/1130 MP: 440/460
STR: 5 Fear Resistance: 5
AGI: 2
DEX: 5
VIT: 29 +14
WIS: 27 +23
Available: 3

Skills: [A] Summon Skeleton LV. 9| [A] Summon Skeleton Mage LV. 2| [A] Decay LV. 3| [A] Reanimate Dead LV. 3| [A] Bone Armor LV. 2 | [A] Vast Shadows | [A] Temporary Grave LV. 1 | [P] Sixth Sense | [P] Bravery LV. 2 | [P] Mutated LV. 3| [P] Pain Resistance LV. 2 | [P] Skeletal Mastery LV. 4| [P]Intimidate Living |[P] Inner Calm LV. 2 |[P] Necrotic Vision|[P] Blood Thirsty LV. 1

Wasn't bad? We had killed one ape and four cats with eight people and I had gained thirty percent of my level. This was as good as any place to rest. I needed to find some time before the walk to Rotterdam to recoup my leg, so why not here? "Should we maybe stay here for a few days and grind?" I threw the idea out there.

"Isn't time the reason we don't want to clear the dungeon?" Alan asked. "So is waiting really a good idea? I think—"

"This is a legitimate place to farm some gear and EXP though." Maria cut him off. "I know you want to clear the dungeon now, but I think it's better to do that later when you aren't trying to save your family."

Alan was about to open his mouth but stopped himself. He had probably realized that staying three days wasn't the same as entering a dungeon with an unknown number of floors. A dungeon like that could take weeks to clear.

"I need to find time to rest my leg, regardless if it is here or before Rotterdam. I just think it's more efficient to do here, where we can kill Elites on respawn with ninety-nine percent downtime," I said. When put that way, no one gave a retort. I also threw out something on my mind. "Four days from now will be two months since the apocalypse began."

"You think something will happen?" Jessica asked.

"It's been a while since we received an unprompted system message." I used the term 'unprompted' because our 'dungeon clear' message was most likely not based on time but our actions. That message had appeared when the first dungeon was cleared. "It would be as good a time as any to throw oil on the fire."

"Then we should definitely stay," Maria said, "more strength isn't gonna hurt us when we go to Rotterdam."

Richard seemed conflicted with the situation, but going as he was now would surely be a death sentence for him. The outer ring monsters in a city like Withersburg were already level twenty. Going deep into Rotterdam without some extra levels risked a quick death.

Chapter 26: Grind as Though Your Life Depends on it: it Probably Does

"If we're staying then we should establish a base. Let's split up in groups of two and move through these two blocks," I pointed to the position. "We want a vehicle; we want somewhere to sleep; and we want supplies. We have a little less than an hour before next spawn, so meet up here before then."

I ended up orchestrating the groups. I sent Alan with Maria, Thomas with Anna, and Richard with Lucas. Two blocks were within Jessica's radar, and we were all in earshot of each other. There was minimal risk of any problems, but at least these groups were balanced enough if something did happen.

After that, I just started to walk with Jessica on my side. This area had hardly been affected by fighting and yet was still a wreck. The road was almost completely blocked up by cars and all the good shops had been ransacked and broken into. Even the cars themselves had been robbed as glass covered the streets.

"I don't know if we're ready," Jessica said.

"For Rotterdam?"

"That, and for whatever is coming next."

"What's on your mind?" I asked.

"Another secret shop? The Fiend? More True Believers? There's so much. I feel like we've wasted so much time." It was true that we had spent so much time just moving around as well as in trying to start the farm and get back from the secret shop teleportation.

"We'll level here for a few days and catch back up to where we should be," I replied. But it was true that we had wasted a lot of time. If Jessica and I had simply hunkered down at Withersburg and ground out the levels, we could probably have been near thirty by now.

"I also feel that the choices that brought us here: they were the right ones."

I suddenly wondered if this was her Inner Calm talking. We protected those women. We liberated the farm from Ghost Hand. Those were good things we did, even if they weren't the most efficient use of our time. "I don't regret them," Jessica continued, "But more and more I feel like I need to prioritize us and not other people."

"There's nothing wrong with feeling that way. It's just the direction this world is going." I actually didn't think her thoughts were a result of Inner Calm. Putting our own group first was just a natural conclusion from living in a world like this. You constantly had to make real choices, and some of those raised you higher while stomping someone else down. Those that were coldhearted and ruthless probably made out the best, but in turn you needed to be willing to give up your humanity.

I hadn't reached that point yet and hoped to never have to make a decision between our progress and that of another group of decent people. Jessica wasn't there yet either, but somehow or another she had trapped herself in this loop of feeling the need to push on while wanting to help others. The demands of the situation conflicted with her morality, putting her in a spiral that only perpetuated itself further.

"You're in control of where you go," I said. "I'll be there, too." She nodded and forced a smile. I could only hope that my reassurances were doing something to help; but only time would tell.

Everyone was already waiting for us when we returned around an hour later. The elites hadn't spawned yet. "Wow, looking snazzy," Jessica said. Everyone but Jessica and I had taken the opportunity to acquire a new wardrobe.

"Is the clothes store near?" I asked. I was in dire need of new clothes. My pants were caked with dried blood and the shirt under my armor was greasy with sweat.

"Yeah, and there is plenty for everyone; you can probably find yourself a new pair of shoes, too," Alan answered excitedly. Alan obviously didn't recognize the genius that were my boots: the Corpse Runners. They may have been made of human remains and they certainly looked their three hundred years, but they gave me a level of Skeletal Mastery and made me move quicker.

"Richard found a vehicle as well," Lucas said, "an SUV."

Eyes closed, Richard couldn't hold back from making a proud face. If I had started clapping and cheering he would have walked like he was on a red carpet. Eventually, he opened his eyes in a squint to find everyone was looking at him. "Do you know what an Escalade is?" he asked.

"Where is it?" I asked.

"Second block at the end, I have the keys so it's not going anywhere."

"Good job." I said. Transportation was our number one priority, and we were only just now getting it. The SUV was going to save us at least a day or two of walking and made me feel a lot better about staying here for some days and farming the Elites.

"Our spawn should be about now," Alan said. He started to smack his sword into his shield in anticipation. I was about to tell him to knock it off when the next pair of mobs spawned. This time it was a troop of chimpanzees.

Two days passed by in a blur. By now, the overall theme of this location had become pretty clear. I felt like I was in a Jumanji movie, because nothing but jungle creatures were spawning. Even crazier was the diversity of the mobs – every kind of large jungle animal – and that sort of solidified my fear that there would be multiple levels within the dungeon. If the different mobs we encountered each had their own environment, that suggested that the place must be huge.

Only after fifteen spawns did our camp spot start spitting out repeats, but that was a lot of monsters. Not only had everyone leveled at least twice, Richard and Anna were in a more comfortable range to gain a share of our group EXP.

The speed of leveling was insane for the effort, and the drops were even better. Elites rained loot like nothing else, and I even worried that we were spoiling ourselves to the point of future ruin.

Name: Mike Reynolds (27) Class: Necromancer Level: 24 EXP: 2%
HP: 1210/1210 MP: 390/485
STR: 5 Fear Resistance: 5
AGI: 2
DEX: 5
VIT: 29 +14
WIS: 27 +26
Available: 9

Skills: **[A] Summon Skeleton LV.** 10l **[A]**
Summon Skeleton Mage LV. 4l **[A] Decay**
LV. 3l **[A] Reanimate Dead LV.** 3l **[A] Bone**
Armor LV. 2 l **[A] Vast Shadows** l **[A]**
Temporary Grave LV. 1 l **[P] Sixth Sense** l
[P] Bravery LV. 2 l **[P] Mutated LV.** 3l **[P]**
Pain Resistance LV. 2 l **[P] Skeletal**
Mastery LV. 4l **[P]Intimidate Living** l**[P]**
Inner Calm LV. 2 l**[P] Necrotic Vision**l**[P]**
Blood Thirsty LV. 1

We were grinding easily, without much thought, so I hadn't allocated my stat points. Summon Skeleton had reached level 10, which granted a third Skeleton General: something I had been hoping for desperately.

Besides that, Summon Skeleton Mage gained two levels and went to Level Four. I was hoping that some sort of Skeletal Mage General would come from levelling up, but that didn't happen when the base level reached 3. Maybe it just happened at a higher level than the regular summon skill on account of being a higher-level ability.

Other than those two skills and Decay, I wasn't training anything else. It also seemed that getting the next level of Decay wasn't going to come easy.

In between pulls was relaxation and scavenge time: I got myself a brand-new set of clean clothes.

The biggest upside from the grind was the loot. Our supplies were now well stocked, as each Elite pack dropped multiple Rations. The gear itself was insane too. Even Lucas, who had been with us from the get go, was still missing multiple pieces of gear. As a result of this camp, he had six and everyone had at least four items.

Apparently, I had been incredibly lucky with gear, as I had seven pieces going into the grind. In fact, the only slots I was missing gear for were a pair of gloves and an amulet. Funnily enough, a generic caster glove dropped that Anna – surprisingly – didn't need, which put me at eight out of nine equipment slots filled.

Gloves of the Serpent: WIS +3
A simple pair of snakeskin gloves.

The stat boost was literally all they did: there was absolutely nothing else special about them at all. They did feel quite nice on the hands though, and so I equipped them happily enough.

We also found six skill books, and two of them went directly to Anna and Richard.

Book of Frost Blades LV 1.
Cast Time: 1.5 Seconds
MP Cost: 18
Distance: 5 Meters
Shoots a blade of ice that lengthens as it travels outward. Deals less damage the farther it travels. Critical strike chance increases as distance is traveled.

Frost Blades seemed like an interesting skill, and it became even more interesting when Anna demonstrated it for us. When she cast, a fully formed blade of ice about a great sword in length shot out horizontally. As it traveled forward, the blade stretched and thinned until it was as thin as a razor blade. At five meters it was as thin and as long as it would become.

The skill demonstrated quite well what the tooltip said. It definitely held the most force and power when it first formed. As the blade grew thinner, it had an easier time piercing defense with how sharp it became, which is where the critical strike came in. The sweet spot was definitely going to change for each enemy you encountered, but that made for a more versatile ability.

Richard also received an ability, but his was more geared towards aggro control and tanking than damage.

Book of Holy Ground LV 1.
Cast Time: Instant
MP Cost: 25
Cooldown: 1 Minute
Distance : 2 Meters around the caster.
Duration: Five seconds
Creates a ground of unholy light around the caster that blinds and damages nearby enemies. Enemies within the holy ground burn for one percent of their HP per second and have their hit chance reduced by twenty percent. Affect is doubled against demon and undead enemies.

This was a fabulous skill that was multi-faceted. The blind effect acted as a defense, it dealt damage, and it could attract the attention of multiple enemies. Unfortunately, Richard really wasn't suited to be tanking packs of mobs: his skills shined in one-on-one encounters.

Richard and Anna had the fastest progress of anyone. At first we were taking most of their EXP from them, but as soon as they reached level seventeen, and were within five levels of Jessica and I, their EXP gain skyrocketed.

They were both nearly level twenty-one now, and the other four were level twenty-three. The EXP crunch was immense, which meant the requirement for the next level was going to get harder and harder.

241

Still, everyone was pumped up. The decision to stay till the fourth day was absolutely the correct one, and no one even hinted at wanting to leave. Even Richard, who had been on the fence, didn't voice a complaint about needing to hurry up to save his brother. In fact, no one mentioned Rotterdam after the first day.

Even my skeletons were getting fully equipped. My new skeleton general wielded a scythe that was as big as he was. If I could have given him a black cloak, you would have sworn he was the Grim Reaper incarnate. Besides that, a rapier had dropped, which I threw onto a regular skeleton warrior. I was within one of having every warrior fully geared with a weapon. The dream goal of equipping them all with armor, though, was quite far off though.

No matter what monster came out of the dungeon, we dispatched it with ease. The hardest part now was fighting off the boredom. The fights never lasted more than a minute and afterwards you needed to wait an entire hour.

During the downtime, we walked around all the streets near to the dungeon checking the shops and clearing the yard trash: an entire ten block radius had been swiped clean. We out-geared and out-leveled this place completely. "Enjoy it while it lasts! Haahha!" Alan said, while skipping down the road. He was a wild one, and was really starting to get a love for battle.

Eventually I worked up the nerve to ask him what happened: why had he changed so much? He explained that he had a passive called Battle Hungry, and apparently it was already Level Four. Jessica tried to hide it well, but I could see her flinch when Alan described the skill.

It was easy to see the change in Alan's behavior. He had been adventurous when we met him, but to this extent? Not even close. People do change, but this was drastic to the point where he was thirsting for battle; as if he faced death every day; as if he would die of boredom without mortal combat.

"It's just fun," he said. It wasn't a bad passive to have. I could tell it removed some of the fear he had for combat. He wasn't making the sole decisions here anyway – no one was – so it would be impossible for him to influence the group to make a bad decision for a pointless fight.

This is exactly what a party is for. I thought. We were a mesh of very different people that fit together well. We filled in the gaps of each other's weaknesses with our strengths. The sooner Jessica could see that, the sooner she would be out of her rut. Moreover, all the progress we'd made by grinding meant her stress that we had fallen behind the curve of the game's challenges lessened every day.

Chapter 27: The Voice of the Apocalypse

By the end of the third day, Jessica and I had gained another level to reach 25 while the others were all level 24 and 23. All the same, I felt that the fourth day couldn't have come too soon. This place had served its purpose, and done it well. We had gotten a few more pieces of equipment and many more rations. We were stocked for at least a month-long journey.

Despite that, I was about done with the grind. The EXP curve had climbed quickly, and two Elites per hour was no longer something that I could consider good EXP. It was fine EXP while needing to rest and recover, but by the third day my leg was in fantastic shape.

I managed to equip one more broadsword for a skeleton warrior, and Richard received an actual shield he could wield as well. There were some EXP UP potions and more stat potions as well, but the bulk of our spoils came in EXP and equipment.

"The Apocalypse started two months ago after midday," I said, "should we wait a couple of hours just in case of a new development?" I wasn't scared of whatever bad shit might be thrown at us, but I thought being organized as a group on the street was better than driving on the road. Decisions might change in a moment depending on what happened.

"That'll give us a few more spawns," Maria said, "might be more loot." She, most of all, had become addicted to finding gear. Anytime an item dropped that she could use, she was ecstatic to no end. The Sobek's Cuirass was the start of it all, and previously, just having that had made her content. She had never realized it could rain loot like this.

Honestly, we had created loot monsters in Maria, Anna, and Richard. Richard played it off well, but I caught him wiping off his shield like it was a new car, and even scraping any mess or gook off it in between fights.

Anna simply waved her gear around whenever she could, and loved to watch the sparkle from the gemstones encased in her magical equipment. I found it hard to blame them though, as I remembered how amazing it felt when I got my first pieces of gear. When you were a have-not, all you wanted was to be one of the people that have.

Time passed slower than normal, and as I waited my skin started to crawl. It wasn't a particular premonition, but my own feeling of worry and unease. I could still remember the day of the MMRPG Apocalypse perfectly: the exact events and what happened. It made me want answers.

Although I had anticipated that the two-month deadline might bring a new challenge, it still made me jump when a system announcement flashed up and was narrated by a deep, male voice.

**Greetings survivors! Two months ago we
tossed your world upside down, and yet
millions of you rodents have survived!
Bahahaha, that's such a beautiful
accomplishment, I almost want to shed a
tear. You should all be proud of
yourselves and how far you've come.
Because of your strong will and tenacity,
I've been instructed to provide some
cheese for you to nibble on.**

I suddenly found myself sweating bullets waiting for it to continue. This was nothing like the other voices we'd heard before. Those were... robotic, lifeless. Those felt like a preplanned message spoken by a machine. The style of past announcements had been part of the reason I believed we were on a schedule, a timeline, but this voice... it caused my skin to crawl.

There was tone, and pitch, it had life. The laugh gave me chills. The way it spoke about us was like we were playthings, insignificant and expendable. It was sociopathic. I glanced at the others only to see similar reactions: wide eyes and brows covered in sweat. Only Thomas looked any different, his face was a picture of raw fury.

**Sorry, I lost my prompt! Haha. To
clarify...we're not trying to kill you.**

"BULLSHIT!" Thomas suddenly yelled.

**You would do well to remember that!
You dying is just an unfortunate side
effect of the world changing. Now that
you know the world is changing, if you
die, you can only blame yourself, okay?**

The sweet tone of its speech made me want to vomit.

246

Now that I've established we aren't trying to kill you, the question is: how does this all end? I'm sure you're dying to know. Unfortunately, I can't tell you when or what that end is. What I can tell you though, is that there is an end, and if you are strong enough to make it there, death is not what awaits you. You can beat the game! Aren't you just so happy and thankful?
All you have to do is get stronger. Just kill monsters, kill your enemies, and kill each other! Isn't it so simple?

Everyone sat there in silence for at least a dozen seconds. We were all waiting for whatever fanatic words were going to come from the voice next. They never did come though…that was the entire message.

"I don't…know what to think," Lucas said. "This should be good news…but why do I feel so defeated?"

I tried to calm my nerves and think about it logically. There was information to be gathered from the message. "So, we can beat the game," I mused aloud, "it's not just about surviving until the end of our lives. There is an end. It's great news." Really, this was about the best possible news we could have received, and yet no one was smiling.

Jessica was frowning, "We have no idea how to get to that point. It could be ten years from now, fifty years from now. It didn't give any actual time limit."

"That's true, but there are regular events. It even confirmed that for us today as well. Maybe it's one year, maybe it's five years, but at least it's not all the fucking years of our life," I said. Thinking about the effort ahead of us made me tired.

"So we just keep doing what we are doing then—surviving and getting stronger," Alan said, "That's doesn't change whether we had to survive a hundred years or one year. Nothin—"

Maria cut him off. "Not true. It makes a huge difference if we aren't strong enough when that time comes. I'd imagine we'll die if we aren't. Delaying won't help us if it's the end-all be-all. You can't run from it, so we can only face it head on."

"What does everyone think about the last part of the message?" I asked. "Is that a clue about what the final encounter might be?"

"I hope not," Richard said, "if it is, then we might end up having to kill each other in the future."

"Richard! Have some decency." I'd never heard Anna reprimand him, let alone anyone.

"What? I'm just saying what everyone's already thinking. Kill each other is a pretty clear indication of player versus player combat."

"It's fine. It was something I was going to bring up as well. Your point is valid, but I'm going to choose to believe it means it in the sense of survival. If you have to kill someone, if it's you or them, then do so," I said. "As of right now, we are operating under the premise that we'll be party members till the end of days. Does everyone agree?" It was a hard thing to talk about, but letting that sort of thought brew was not good. If we started looking at each other as future enemies, we would grow apart, or even sabotage each other.

Everyone agreed without any reluctance; well, everyone but Thomas who didn't speak. He hadn't said anything at all. His face was still a mess of fury. "Thomas, do you agree? Party members no matter what?" I knew he was upset, but I needed him to say it for my peace of mind and probably the others felt the same too.

"I agree," he said.

"Good then. We're all in this together and we will continue to prioritize each other's strengths and growth. We can't make it to the end alone, so we have to work together." That was as good an incentive as any.

"Doesn't anyone care who was talking in that system announcement?" Thomas asked, and no one had an answer. His tone seemed hostile, but it seemed to me to be a foregone conclusion that we couldn't figure that out.

"What can we do even if we knew?" Alan asked, echoing my thoughts. "Snap out of it. I know you're pissed; I know you want answers. Survive, and get them." No one else could say those words to Thomas without the potential of him blowing up. I'd never seen him angry before.

"I'll do more than that if I make it to the end…" I didn't need to guess what he meant.

"Good, I'll join you when that time comes." Alan patted him hard on the shoulder. "Let's get going?" Alan had diffused the situation pretty masterfully if I was being honest.

"I'm driving!" Richard said while breaking into a run for the Escalade.

"No one but you wanted to drive anyway," Anna laughed. As I watched the mood lift, I felt encouraged by the amazing people around me; maybe things were gonna be okay.

We squeezed into the Escalade, which was a little tight and prepared to leave.

"Take as much time as you need." I told Richard while laying back. With the AC on, this was one of the few times you could feel like the world hadn't gone to shit. There was at least a seven hour drive ahead of us, and that wasn't including any hiccups.

"Might be a bit rocky to start; sorry in advance!" Richard called over his shoulder, and then a moment later the entire vehicle rocked up and down. He was driving over the median while snaking his way towards the highway.

It was indeed a bumpy ride for the better part of ten minutes as Richard skirted past all the encounters that he could. There were still almost no signs of regular monsters in the area, so the theory that monsters didn't spawn around dungeons might be true. Through farming Elites, we had gained a tremendous amount in these four days.

As much as knowing that someone or something was using us for entertainment pissed me off, it gave me a renewed hope. There was something to aim for, other than simply surviving. There was an end: one day we might be free of this hell. What that left of the planet afterwards I couldn't know.

"Best case we get there near sunset, worst case it'll be late at night," announced Richard. Presumably our progress depended on how hard it would be to move down the highway, and judging by how many abandoned vehicles I could see up ahead, it wasn't going to be a simple cruise.

Cars were packed up back to back, and Richard had to drive nearly off the highway, and sometimes on the grass bank to get through. We moved slowly, but it was still better than walking. Not only that, but as we traveled, we saw more other people than I was expecting.

Over the course of the first two hours of our drive there were multiple groups on the highway, some moving towards Rotterdam and about an equal number moving the opposite way to us.

It was after five hours, and after Richard had said we were more than halfway to the city, that we passed a number of alarming sights. There were several True Believer signs along the road warning of the Rapture. They gave the impression that Rotterdam was where the cult had its base, which would be a nightmare for us if true.

We also passed other signs and painted billboards intermittently through the journey: some were warnings to stay away from the True Believers and another in red paint said: Turn Back Now. Stay Out of Rotterdam.

"This is gonna be a headache, isn't it?" Maria sighed after seeing the sign.

"We're going in, whether the True Believers are there or not," I said. "We'll do our best to avoid them if possible." Even if this was their main base, Rotterdam was huge, and the chance that they were stationed all around it was unlikely. It seemed to me that avoiding the cult was a real possibility.

Our plan had already been agreed. We were going to get close to Rotterdam, spend the night outside the city at a safe distance, and then move into the city during the morning. From there we were going to get our bearings and start making progress.

Ahead of us would be days of careful maneuvering through Rotterdam, and we couldn't be sure if we'd even find a single person alive. None of us had seen what a big city like this was going to throw at us either. Still, we needed to try.

I felt a growing anticipation as we drove on. It was like I was being driven to the frontlines to participate in a war.

"About an hour or so left," Richard announced, "this is the road I always took to see my brother. We'll be able to turn off like five minutes before the city and it should be good to stay the night on a side street. There's a few houses there, too."

As we got closer to the city the sun set and Richard turned on the high beams. Despite the dark, we were setting a good pace because the highway here had been cleared of cars. No one speculated on why all the cars were gone.

Chapter 28: The Chase

"Dibs on a bed," Maria said from the back of the Escalade, "those of you who didn't end up scrunched back here can take last pick."

"Hey, that's not exactly fair: you're smaller than we are," Alan retorted

Maria gave a humph, "Doesn't matter. I called it first."

"Yeah? We'll see ab—"

"There are people in the road," Anna suddenly said, "slow down!"

"That's the religious fuckers and I'm not stopping." Richard put the pedal to the metal and I could hear the engine rev.

"What's going on up there?" I asked. "There's people in the streets?" I leaned forward to see dozens upon dozens of True Believers in a sort of blockade ahead of us.

"I don't know what they're doing, but I'm not stopping!" Richard kept driving at full speed towards their little blockade.

"TURN IT AROUND THEN IDIOT!" Anna yelled at him.

"And go WHERE?" Richard yelled back "There's NOWHERE TO TURN AROUND. LOOK, THEY'VE ALREADY SEEN US."

"Are we being attacked?" Maria asked.

Anna shook his arm. "So you're just gonna run them over?"

"I'm not doing anything but driving! If they don't move that's on them."

"Just stop!" Anna yelled.

"And then WHAT? They're going to kidnap us! IT'S US, OR THEM." By now we were just fifteen seconds from reaching their blockade. "HOLD ON!" Richard yelled.

"Strap in!" I yelled at everyone. "Just grab onto something." I turned back to Richard, "DON'T STOP." There was no turning back now. Into the lion's den…Everything was happening so fast.

"Fuck, fuck, fuck!" Maria was without a seat belt so she hunkered down, bracing herself, all her banter with Alan forgotten.

Time felt like it was slowing down as Richard plowed directly through the road block. The entire SUV shook and jerked to the left as he blasted through the front bumper of a small two-door sports car. I almost flew out of my seat, but my seat belt caught me by the waist and neck.

We were all tossed up, and I heard two True Believers tumbling over the roof on impact. The SUV rocked violently immediately after breaking through, like we were going to flip.

"HOLD ON." Richard screamed while grabbing the wheel for dear life. Two or three seconds passed that felt like an eternity, where it felt like we were going to roll. And then we stabilized.

"Jesus Christ!" Anna yelled, "you idiot!"

"HAAHAHHAHA," Richard was laughing like a madman.

"It's not over!" Lucas said. He had slid, so that he was nearly upside down, but could see out the back window. "They're chasing!"

I could see pairs of headlights appear one after the other as they started to pursue. "Fucking hell." I groaned. "Can't people just mind their own business?" I never understood why everyone needed to micromanage everyone else. This True Believer bullshit originated from a desire to control no doubt. "Try and lose them," I said.

"I am trying!" He was already flooring it, and I could see on the speedometer we were traveling over 100mph. "We're gonna have to go into the city."

"That wasn't the plan," Jessica said. "Just find somewhere we can pull over and lose them in the darkness, we can walk the rest of the way."

Richard looked back at us using the mirror.

"The rest of the way? We're about two minutes out! Look behind you, we aren't losing them." There were two cars gaining behind us. "There is no losing them."

I leaned over towards Richard. "Keep going. If we stop now it's a fight and they outnumber us two to one at least." There were at least a dozen people just standing in the street, who knew how many numerous others were resting in the vehicles. Did they have every major entrance to the city blocked up? The size of this cult was unbelievable.

It didn't take more than thirty seconds for the two chasing vehicles to be nearly side by side with us. The passengers waved through the windows as if that was going to get Richard to pull over, and when that didn't work they slammed their vehicle directly into the driver's side of our SUV.

"What the fuck is that?" Maria yelled. "Are they insane?" The whole vehicle shook and rattled. Richard had to slam the breaks to keep from crashing, and then he floored it again in order to rear-end one of the cars.

"Come here!" Alan grabbed Maria and kept her tightly tucked behind his shield. In the case of an actual crash she would have gone flying without his protection.

"Are you crazy?" Anna was nearly hysterical, and was worried about having her in the front seat. She was just moments away from grabbing the wheel and trying to forcefully stop Richard from driving.

"Anna control yourself!" I shouted, "Richard, do whatever it takes! Our lives are in your hands." I put that weight on him and Anna definitely heard it as well. There was a moment of silence from the front as she realized just how dire the situation was.

"Just thirty more seconds!" We were coming up to the border of where it would be considered Rotterdam. "These fuckers!" Richard said. The two vehicles on our side were swerving and threatening to smack into him. His knuckles showed white as he gripped the wheel and then swung hard right.

I felt my seat belt dig harder into my neck than before and we shook as Richard smashed into the chasing vehicle. The car to our right swerved wildly and then eventually completely turned sideways before rolling off the road and smashing into a metal fence thirty or forty feet in the distance. It was a brutal impact and I doubted the driver or passengers survived.

That gave Richard a moment of respite, but only a moment. Not even ten seconds later and another vehicle was coming up from behind. They didn't even bother to come alongside but instead smashed into our bumper. "Just a little longer everyone!" I yelled. "Richard, how are we doing?"

"GET READY FOR IMPACT!" he replied.

"Just pull over!" Maria said.

"I can't pull over, even if I wanted to!" And as Richard said that, the other vehicle smacked into us from behind again.

"It's fine, I got you," Alan said to Maria, "sit between my legs." She didn't argue and simply turned around before moving in between his knees and locking both hands around them. She wouldn't be flung around in case something bad happened, at least.

I grabbed at the handle that came from just above the side door. Holding it made me realize just how thick with sweat my hands were. I took a good look at everyone around me, every face. No matter what happened I'd not forget.

A moment after that thought we were smashed into from the side. The vehicle shook and wobbled as I bounced in my seat. Tires screeched and we started to spin. Weightlessness overcame me as I could feel myself flipping upside down. My ears felt like they were going to pop inside my skull as I swung wildly like clothes being dried. My brain was turning to scrambled eggs.

The stop came abruptly as the world around me exploded. Every window was shattered and sharp shards of glass flew through from every direction through the vehicle. We had smashed into something and rolled to a stop. "Is everyone okay?" I yelled as I tried to gather my bearings.

My hands fumbled for the seat belt. The strap was digging into my side as I dangled sideways. The vehicle was on its side fortunately and not completely upside down. One after another the others gave affirmation they were okay.

"Maria, help them out of their belts." She was the only one who wasn't restrained, and thankfully Alan had enough STR to keep her from flying. When we started flipping and I was thrown like a doll, he had planted his arms and feet so hard that he was his own roll cage. Jessica had done the same. Thomas and I weren't so lucky.

We quickly unstrapped and crawled up and out of the vehicle. Our feet landed one at a time on shattered cubes of glass. It was some store front we crashed into, and thankfully, the display had slowed our impact at least a bit. I couldn't be sure how badly we would have been hurt if the wall was a solid brick or concrete.

"We can't stop," Jessica said. "They're here."

"Let's just kill them!" Alan said.

"No, we can't win that fight!" I said. By the time we even finished off our pursuers, there would be far more arriving than we could manage. "Control yourself!" I said to Alan. "I can't use my undead squad right now!" My undead troops were an essential part of our battle force.

"This isn't time to argue!" Jessica said, "they're HERE." And as she spoke, I could see at least six vehicles pull up with four people leaping out of each.

"Lead the way!" I told Jessica. "Maria, buy time please!"

Maria seemed at a loss, but eventually understood. She pulled out her bow and shot an explosive arrow at the farthest of the two front cars that had crashed with us.

Her arrow struck directly to the gas tank, and she shot another two for good measure into the other vehicle. With the three going off together, it created a movie-level explosion.

The cover provided by the flame and smoke gave us a precious few sections, allowing Jessica to pull us out the back. "We have to assume they can track," she said and I was sure she was right. There was so many of them, it was unrealistic to think they couldn't. She started to run in the darkness, and God was it a nightmare maneuvering at a run.

Almost no light reached the alley we were in as we ran through pitch blackness. Necrotic Vision showed the endless number of auras around us as Jessica expertly brought us through the streets without triggering any mobs. Some of the auras I was seeing were on a level that was much higher than any I'd ever experienced.

"They're still right behind us!" Lucas yelled from the back. Our pursuers were close enough for me to hear them yelling behind us. They were insane, haphazardly aggroing the mobs they ran past with no care for their lives. I watched two of them get mauled down in seconds by a blur of teeth and claw. The others didn't even stop at the screams of their companions.

Jessica ran one block deeper and cut between a convenience store before crossing the street. We were directly in front of a twenty- or thirty-floor building, it was hard to see the top as it vanished into the darkness. Fortunately, moonlight was visible on the street just in front. I used Vast Shadows and pulled out my undead squad.

"Inside!" Jessica yelled at everyone.

During our flight we had aggroed a lot less enemies than the cultists had. It was clear now that they were probably too low level to be here. Even we were on the cusp of that breakpoint, and I doubted the majority of True Believers were even over level fifteen. They were pulling stuff from so far away due to their low level.

We had managed to trigger only three mobs, which was a monumental achievement and a testament to Jessica's quick wit. Unfortunately, each of those enemies was stronger than the Blood Apes that had come out of the overflowing dungeon entrances. Those and the True Believers combined were not a fight we could take.

"I'm last in." I let everyone rush past me as I looked back. The enemies that we had aggroed rushed in our direction while the True Believers were being repeatedly cut down by the train of monsters they had pulled. My neck had been prickling the entire time already, but seeing those lights of life being extinguished left a lingering fear in my heart. I got a brief look at one of the monsters chasing us, it was a wolf man—a Lycanthrope. As it entered the moonlight I could see an eight-foot frame full of power, and then it howled.

I rushed behind Thomas and Maria without taking a second look back. That thing was bad news at night. The feeling I got while looking at it was not pleasant. Fortunately, monsters had a tether range and as long as that also worked vertically, we could lose them by going up the stairs. The problem was everything was so fucking dark.

"Stairwell is here!" The situational awareness Jessica had developed was superhuman. The only thing I could see in front of me was Thomas's back, and she had somehow found the stairwell in a lobby that could hold at least a hundred people comfortably.

Thomas kept calling, "Here," just in front of me so I could follow his voice. It was thoughtful, but Necrotic Vision kept me from losing his trail. I raced behind him towards Jessica's voice. Her call echoed, and then a loud crash from the front entrance drowned it out of existence. The roar of the Lycanthrope behind us put me on edge, and put a fire under my ass.

We reached the door to a stairwell in a little under ten seconds, where Jessica was waiting and hurrying us in. She laid a Quagmire trap directly under the door and then slammed it shut behind her. "That should buy a bit of time."

We raced upwards, and had only made it three or four flights when the door exploded into a mess below. The sound of claws tapping into tile and slashing into metal echoed upward as the Lycanthrope rushed up the staircase.

My undead squad were trailing behind me, and so incredibly clumsy. I had taken them out in case, but they were almost useless here. It was clear, too, that the Lycanthrope was going to reach us before it tethered. "Can we fight?" I asked Jessica.

"No, there are two other powerful mobs a dozen seconds behind. It also seems like a few True Believers made it into the lobby."

"Keep going then!" I said. "Anna come to me."

Anna allowed Thomas and Maria to pass her. Once next to me we rushed up the staircase side by side. "You're gonna need to do what we did back in the Miasma," I gasped, "create a floor of ice."

"Right now?"

"In a few floors." We only had so much time. We were trying to ascend stairs in pitch black darkness. Even if the lights were on, we probably couldn't outrun this Lycanthrope, let alone given how clumsy we were now. "Jessica! Lay a Quagmire trap three floors up!" I shouted. Anna nodded on my words, she already knew what to expect.

We had gone more than ten flights of stairs already. What's three more? I thought. My lack of physical strength and endurance was becoming evident. I could hear Thomas and Anna breathing heavily along with me, so it was just a caster problem. No one else was struggling, and I wondered about using some of my stat points to help.

I suddenly felt a chill race up my arm that jolted me out of my thoughts. It was Anna pulling out the Staff of Piercing Ice, and I decided against any stat allocation. The situation was manageable.

"One more turn," I reminded her.

Anna gave me a nod and then rushed around the corner before ascending the last flight of stairs. She used her spell to coat the floor, until it was a solid slide of perfectly smooth ice. No amount of traction would get you up that ramp.

I positioned my undead just at the top of the stairs above the ice and we continued to ascend. They would be within my range there, and could fight it off for more time if needed. It took the Lycanthrope just a few seconds to reach our trap, and attempt to ascend.

We all listened in silence as the monster below us banged into the wall with great speed after slipping. Metal rattled as the werewolf went wild in the staircase. It eventually realized it could jump across the ice, but my undead were there at the top stacked together. The Lycanthrope landed in an embrace of swords that sent it hurdling backwards again, this time shrieking from its wounds.

"Here!" Jessica suddenly stopped at Floor Seventeen and opened the stairwell door. The curious stares she got were asking, 'why here?' "This is the only floor with no enemies," she explained.

"Wait, these things are spawning inside the buildings?" Lucas asked.

"Above; below; they are everywhere," Jessica replied. She didn't explain anymore and simply rushed down the hallway, we went past hundreds of rooms before she stopped. "The Lycanthrope and the other two enemies stopped chasing."

"So we're good now?" Richard asked before leaning against the wall and then sliding down to his ass. I wasn't the only one to let out a sigh of relief.

Chapter 29: Teamwork in a New and Dangerous City

"No one go too far," Jessica said, "the mobs around here are strong. I didn't get to inspect them yet, but they definitely have a more commanding aura than those we've fought so far."

"Let's just pick out a few rooms and bunker down for the night," Lucas suggested.

I agreed with him; we needed to get our bearings. Only Jessica really knew how far we had traveled while moving in the night. With the morning we could orientate ourselves properly.

"That was a nightmare," Anna said, "I'm sorry I lost my cool."

"No harm done." Richard seemed to let his earlier ferocious shouting slide off him like water off a duck's back.

"Good job, Richard." I gave him a pat on the shoulder. Not anyone would have made that call to keep going at such short notice, especially as it entailed having to drive into people. It was a tough call to make, but in hindsight it was the right one. The cultists would have already seen his high beams by the time we had spotted their blockade. If he had turned around they'd have chased us, and there was nowhere to run on the highway. Probably, we would have been caught and killed, especially if they tied us to the incident in Withersburg. Ramming through was the only right decision, and Richard had handled it flawlessly.

Honestly, everyone had done a good job. We hadn't panicked…much; we didn't fall apart and we made it through. Here we were in Rotterdam in one piece, and we were safe for now…relatively.

"I think we're good here," Jessica announced, "from what I can tell, the monsters here just patrol on their own floors. I don't know why Floor Seventeen doesn't have any spawns right now though."

Having recovered from the chase, we searched out some rooms for ourselves. We settled for two pairs of adjacent rooms opposite of each other. Each room was a double, and so every person got a bed. Maria and Alan still found some way to argue with each other about the arrangements though even though they ended up taking a room together.

As felt natural now, Jessica and I roomed together. I found myself exhausted despite having been sitting all day. The system announcement followed by the True Believers – hell I couldn't be sure I didn't have a concussion from that crash earlier – all of it meshed together into one big weight of bullshit on my shoulder. "What did you think of the system message?" I hadn't had the opportunity to ask Jessica about her take on it. We could definitely be more open with each other in private.

Jessica suddenly put her finger against my lips, "Let's not talk about that tonight." She walked me backwards with one finger until the bed chopped me at my knees and we fell into it together. I had no complaints about not being able to talk that night.

We woke in the morning to the sound of Maria screaming. I rushed into the hallway and saw everyone opening their door to see what was wrong.

"Aghhh! You're so annoying! Why can't you just listen to what I say?" Maria yelled.

I couldn't see Alan, but from behind Maria came his untroubled voice, he never seemed bothered by Maria. "Sorry guys. I think our argument probably woke you up." It seemed that whatever Maria was trying to achieve hadn't worked.

"Is that all?" Richard farted and then walked back without a care. It was probably a bit too early to be getting up anyway, and most everyone just returned to their rooms since there wasn't any actual threat. There were a few hours of sleep left to get.

"How many monsters are in this building?" I asked Jessica as we entered our room.

"It's hard to count exactly, more than fifty," she replied and then, obviously tired, went to the other bed and pulled the covers over her.

"How do you feel about using the Spawn Protection Stone?" I asked. This item was something we'd been sitting on for a while. Floor Seventeen had no spawns on it right now... but that wasn't something we knew for sure would remain the case.

My question was so out of left field she nearly tied her tongue, "Wai—you want to use it here?" she asked, "What would the point even be?"

"I don't know, but I'm just thinking about everything we have at our disposal."

"I think it's not off the table. It has three uses right? So we can put it down, and pick it up, twice, but it might be wasted here."

"The third time we place it we can't move it, but we have some leeway now," I said. "Just how far did we go last night? I could tell from a glance this place is no joke."

"We made it five blocks." It definitely didn't feel like that last night; but due to how dark it was and the overall panic, I had lost track. At least these tougher mobs were further towards the center of the city.

"That's a relief. I was worried the high-level mobs in this building were the yard trash."

"I think they are. As far as I can tell the rings of this city are just bigger than we're used to. I've not seen any difference in the monsters so far." Jessica put a damper on my mood instantly.

I recalculated, speaking my thoughts aloud. "We expected it to be a difficult trip, and as far as the stone goes I just worry that we might get an Elite spawn or something unexpected from the fact Floor Seventeen is empty. I was also thinking that a building like this as a base to level up from wouldn't be so bad. And seeing as we are off the ground, the spawn protection stone gives us its best value. Laying it where we are now will put a protection on the floor above and below us."

A Spawn Protection here would cover at least twelve rooms, each able to hold several people. Placing it on the ground as an alternative, and everything below ground level was lost: you ended up with a dome, instead of a sphere as it was intended. There were probably other nuances to be abused, but for now a building at least twenty meters off the ground level was ideal for its placement.

"I think we'll be using it to keep our necks intact," Jessica said.

"Honestly, you're probably right," I replied, "what of the True Believers?"

Four nearby, all hiding in the opposite stairwell," she answered right away. "The lobby is mostly safe, but there's a patrol that comes through about every forty-five minutes." Her ability to get an accurate read on our surrounding always surprised me even though I'd seen her do it time and time again.

266

"Did you pull that up instantly?" I asked. "Like, did you just know the second I asked, or do you have to focus and think about it?"

"I have to think about it, but I can feel the difference. It's like shining a flashlight in the dark and seeing the shapes that show up. Wherever I focus on, I get a read on what's there. You probably experience something similar with your undead squad? When you think about ordering them does that make you more aware of them?"

"Yeah." She wasn't wrong. My undead were still in the stairwell of Floor Seventeen. I could consciously ignore them, but the second I gave them the smallest fraction of attention, I could feel all my summoned undead, every single one of them.

Although by the way the world worked before the apocalypse it should be impossible, I could feel their distance from me, how many were alive, which ones were alive, the exact proximity between each other, what weapons they were holding, what spells they were going to cast. The amount of information that came through the link between us with that single thought was immense, and yet thoughtless at the same time.

That reality, that understanding, it was the reason why I could barely keep a hold of myself during the system announcement. The voice that had come through, the person speaking..., they had a power that transcended anything I could even fathom. A thought would be all it took to squash me or erase me from existence.

Living beings have wants, and needs, and feelings, and desires. That train of thought brought me to the harsh reality we currently lived: we were entertainment, an experiment, a toy, and when we became less fun…Well, probably the world would burn for their entertainment, and we would suffer and die in the flames.

"Do you hear that?" Jessica asked. There was a low thrumming that was increasing in intensity, ever so slight but it traveled through the building. A rumbling over the world, and it wasn't just us that noticed it. As I opened the door, the other members of the group came out of their rooms into the dark hallway, pulling on their gear and making for the stairwell from where the sound was coming. It was growing louder, until it was an incessant pounding.

Putting my undead into the lead, I climbed the stairwell upwards to the roof with Jessica just behind me. Staircase after staircase, turn after turn. I could never have managed it without a break before the apocalypse. We passed Floor Thirty, and then went one more flight. There was a double doorway waiting there, closed and chained shut through each handle. I channeled Decay and then brought ordered my Skeleton General to kick the door. The links of chain snapped and popped, sounding like marbles dropping on tile.

As we ascended, I had an idea as to what the sound was but only seeing it could I confirm my hunch. It was rain: an incessant downpour so strong that the sky might as well have been a waterfall. The impact of the water shook the very concrete we stood on, and vibrated us to our cores.

My Skeleton General held his shield out like an umbrella and I walked out on the rooftop with it above my head. As far as the eye could see, a dark sky hid the horizon, and curtains of grey rain obscured the view in every direction. I'd never seen rain like this, so strong that my skin stung from every impact. I had always assumed that the drought we were experiencing was purposeful, but maybe it wasn't.

I walked back to the stairwell and then cast Vast Shadows. My undead had been clogging up the place and the others could barely fit in. We were at a crossroads, and this rain could be a blessing or a curse for us.

"Richard, how far till we reach your brother's place?" I asked. We had talked through the route the day previously, and his brother was the closest and first stop. After that were Thomas and Alan's cousin, my parents, and then Lucas's grandparents.

"I don't know exactly, maybe fifteen or twenty blocks." There were hundreds of blocks in Rotterdam, but fifteen or more definitely would put us another ring closer to the center. From what I had learned in Sangeal and Withersburg, typically, normal monsters resided in the outer ring.

As you traveled inward, you reached a ring of exceptional mobs, and the occasional Elite. We'd never gone past that point before, and I could only imagine that next ring would be more Elites than exceptional enemies.

Beyond that, no one really knew. I doubted any group had ventured that far into any major city. I admired Richard for being so optimistic, but I could tell no one else had any real belief their loved ones were alive. My parents lived quite deep inward, and that location would qualify as a ring none of us had ventured into.

Everyone was waiting for me to make a call when I re-entered the stairwell, "Let's go down and make our move now," I said.

"In the rain?" Anna asked.

"This is as good a time as any. None of us knows just how the mechanics work on monster aggro. It's clearly not as simple as being only based on our level. This world is too complex for that." I had already decided that the mobs nearby were intelligent. Maybe they didn't seem so because they were tethered by some rule to a specific area, but they definitely had intelligence. The existence of the Fiend had solidified that for me.

With that being the case, they could definitely hear and react to sound. That meant sight played a role too, and probably other senses as well. This rain was coming down so hard that nothing could be seen or heard, the perfect cover for us to move swiftly.

I didn't know if it was overconfidence or some sickening determination, but everyone seemed more upset about getting wet than having to fight monsters. Alan was already itching to go, and we hadn't even seen what we were going up against. "Jessica will lead the front as before," I said. "Everyone else stay extra close. We want to avoid what we can and fight only when necessary."

We ascended the stairs as a unit and entered into the lobby moments later. The commotion we made seemed to alert the True Believers in the other stairwell. Their door to the stairwell opened as heads peeked out. I wanted to avoid a fight right now at all costs, "Just stay in your stairwell and you'll survive," I shouted at them.

They had no chance in a fight, and probably didn't want to lose their lives for nothing. As soon as their door shut Anna froze the entire frame closed. She was starting to think on her feet, and definitely seemed to have changed her demeanor since the previous night.

I pulled my squad from the faintest shadow and followed behind Jessica as she skirted along the building edge to stay dry just a bit longer. The howling wind had the rain coming down almost sideways. Vehicles in the street whined as the wind rocked and swayed them.

Richard gave Jessica a general idea of the direction and we moved across the street. The rain was no joke, and I used Bone Armor to stop the stinging hits from each droplet. "We have to fight here," Jessica said after two blocks. "Three mobs now and we can probably make it another two or three blocks.

"Level thirty-one. Exceptional, Medusa. And two level twenty-eight. Normal. Enslaved Lycanthrope."

Alan and Richard came to the front and stood by side on top of a Quagmire trap that had Jessica already laid. I knew none of us could see what we were facing through the rain. Jessica pulled, and this was the first time I'd not been able to hear the twang of her bow.

Three auras rushed in our direction and were just five or six feet in front of us when I could see them. Two Lycanthropes similar to those I'd seen last night, except they were a full head shorter and not as muscular. A spiked collar was on both their necks, the leash connected to a…Beautif—

"Don't look into her eyes!" Jessica's hand suddenly passed in front of my eyes, breaking whatever magic was being cast into them. I opened and closed my eyes a few times to shake off the slight confusion. The monster in front of us had the body of a snake with the upper torso of a woman, slithering snakes for hair hissed and danced around her shoulders, the lower half of her face held a seductive pair of lips. I didn't dare look higher again, "Don't look into her eyes!" Jessica yelled to everyone.

Alan and Richard had no time to stare as the two Lycanthropes rushed with teeth bared. Their shields held upwards blocking fangs and claws as long as kitchen knives. I sent my melee undead to surround the Medusa, allowing Lucas to find room to melee the Lycanthrope in front of him.

Anna moved just behind me and to the left and prepped her frost magic. I couldn't see her, but the wafting chill from her location penetrated my bones and caused me to shiver. I could suddenly see my breath in this dense downpour.

A coat of ice began to form around the Lycanthropes, whom were soaked to the bone. The hairs of their fur grew sharp and frozen. Even the joints of their elbows and wrist and shoulder started to encase in a layer of ice, slowing their movements tremendously.

Lucas and Alan continuously launched attacks that shed blood. Richard cast Holy Ground and took aggro for the both of them. With the Quagmire trap and the effects of Anna's frost magic, he could probably land some heavy blows with his mace, but opted instead to lock his feet in place and tank blow after blow.

His shield was white iron as every attack deflected off it, the sparks from claw slashing into metal lost in the brilliance of its glow. Freedom allowed Alan to be as battle hungry as he wanted, both Lycanthropes already sporting deep cuts on their chests and thighs, a result of Rend no doubt. Alan laughed like a madman with each attack, blood mixed with rain dripping down his face.

Lucas was no different than Alan in this moment. He still favored the Nodachi he had received that first day, and sent out brutal slash after slash. His demeanor was calm and collected but the look in his eyes said he was hungry for battle too. Wind Slashes chained together as a hairy and frozen arm went flying.

The front enemies were nothing we couldn't handle, and so I focused my full attention on the Medusa: she held both a shield and a bow, which seemed to contradict each other. My expectations were immediately flipped on their head as she pulled the bow back with the shield still on her forearm.

It was an impressive display of strength, and a terrifying one. An arrow raced several inches by my face and caused one of my Skeletal Mages to explode behind me. The yellow lights of its eyes disappeared as it collapsed into a heap of bone, the magic having left its body.

The Medusa then took the shield and smashed it single-hand-edly into a Skeleton Warrior, dislodging every bone in its body and sending the scraps hurdling down the street. A one hit KO on my minion was nothing to scoff at.

My undead repeatedly slashed and stabbed at her torso, their sharp weapons simply reflecting off that hard set of scales without leaving much of a dent. Fortunately, thick defenses were my new favorite target to break.

I started just below her breast, the line where human met snake, and started to channel Decay. The scales changed color rapidly, and then started to peel off in layers of white film like shed skin. The entire set of scales there eventually became white, so white the line between human and snake blurred.

That white soon became red as sword and rapier and axe focused attacks on the supple and soft skin. Even though her hair of snakes began to strike out and attack, they had no effect on my undead troops.

There was a flash of light that rivaled only Richard's shield on the face of the Medusa, then blood and gore could be seen dripping down those beautiful lips. The seductiveness vanished and was replaced with a brutal savagery.

I dared a sneak to see a gaping hole in her left eye socket, no doubt Jessica's doing. A fading howl came from the second Lycan-thrope as it fell—the upper portion of its body being bisected in a joint effort of Lucas and Alan. The first had no chance to howl. An explosive arrow from Maria had went straight into its throat and blew the entire head clean off.

Everyone prepared to focus their full attention on the Medusa when a wave of cold spread outward and past us. Frost Blade raced through the air from our left, cold enough to cause the rain around to harden into hale and shatter on the concrete below. The blade thinned until it was merely as thick as a razor blade, passed directly through the abdomen of the Medusa and kept going before shattering into an array of ice behind her collapsing back.

Blood splattered and rushed into the streets as the upper and lower body of the Medusa fell in different directions, the sound of her fall vanishing in this endless downpour. Deep red swirled in turbulent water and eventually ran clear, the drains doing their best to swallow the worlds sorrow.

"Is everyone good?" I asked. It was a quick fight, and our teamwork was on a completely different level. "Alan, grab the loot." I said. There was no equipment; it was a skill book and some supplies.

"Good, but freezing." Was the consensus I got back.

"Let's get moving then so we can warm up a bit." I said and then turned to Anna, "But can you put that away please?" She was sticking right by my side and the staff truly was turning her into a walking freezer. Somehow that didn't affect her at all, but it was clearly the system's doing.

I walked up to the three corpses and helped myself to their bodies. I reanimated a Lycanthrope and the Medusa, and opted not to repopulate my skeletons. I had lost one warrior and one mage, and couldn't replenish them both in the same cast. I'd wait for a better opportunity.

Chapter 30: A Tank too Eager for Battle is a Headache

I continued forward in the rain in a much better mood. That first battle was under our belt, and the enemies we had anticipated might be incredibly tough were well within our abilities. They were clearly a step above the monsters outside the city, but we had outpaced their growth.

Our party of eight was a force to be reckoned with, and there was no real gap in our defense or offense. Another magic dealer or a second healer would be ideal, but Thomas was a professional. I didn't know how he was so good, but his healing was always on point.

"Inspect leveled up," Jessica announced, "I can see if an enemy has any passives now. Oh, it seems I can also see what level another player is." That…was fantastic news. Being able to tell what level another player was incredibly useful, potentially overpowered. Jessica would make a fantastic partner for an assassin if she ever decided to go that route.

We only made it two blocks before Jessica stopped us again. We faced the same encounter again. It seemed every Medusa had its own two slave Lycanthropes. The Lycanthrope I saw last night was a different beast altogether then.

Jessica told us their passives, "Stone Gaze: Enemies cannot stare into your eyes without turning to stone. Lethal Attraction: Your beauty makes it hard for others to not stare at your face." Although we already knew this about the Medusa, being informed about the passives of monsters would be incredibly useful in fights in the future. "Slave Bond: You cannot disobey your master. Pack's Fury: Twenty percent increased damage done per pack member fighting alongside you."

It was actually useful for us to know the Lycanthropes' passives now. The effect of Pack's Fury hadn't been discernible in the last fight, but now that we knew the nature of the buff, we all focus-fired the Lycanthrope's down one at a time. It wasn't necessary to do so to win, but was good practice.

Jessica kept us on the right track with a route that probably felt safe to the others: they couldn't see what I was seeing. They didn't realize just how many mobs we were walking past to get through this mess. It wouldn't be an understatement to say that without the cover provided by the rain and Jessica's tracking, we'd be fighting 5 or 6 times as many monsters as we were now.

I was sure we could handle nonstop fighting, but we hadn't come to Rotterdam to level and gain experience. We were here to try and save any family members we may have had left. There was the most basic of plans set in place after that: survive until the next challenge. So with that goal in mind, Jessica knew to avoid encounters as much as possible and press on to the residential area where Richard's brother might be found and then, nearby, the address of Lucas's grandparents.

The rain continued to pelt down on us; the incessant droning and being permanently wet irritated my nerves and made keeping track of time difficult. We came to a stop where Jessica stood in thought for some time.

"Is everything okay?" Lucas asked.

"Have you ever played Frogger?" she asked. "I need to focus." That was her saying to Lucas and us all, in the politest possible way, shut up. I knew what Frogger was, but some of the younger ones may not have. The point was, she now had to find the pattern for us walk across the street without aggro. I could see the auras patrolling, and it wasn't at all easy to find a path that did not involve fighting.

After two minutes, it became clear there was no such path to cross, and we would have to pull. Jessica explained this and all the stats on the key monster that we'd have to remove from the route. "Level Thirty-Two. Elite. Dual-headed Ogre Brute. Quick Wit: Having two heads gives you increased reaction speed and decision making. Ogre Race: Natural Strength increased by fifty per cent. Mace Specialty: Mace attacks have a twenty-five per cent chance to stun enemies.

"Ready?" Jessica asked while nocking an arrow.

Alan couldn't contain his excitement as he rushed forward without even waiting for Jessica to place a trap. "We don't need Quagmire, just pull!" he said. I wanted to reprimand him, but between the rain and him smacking his shield, I knew he wouldn't be able to hear me.

Jessica looked back at everyone and then her bow twanged; another shot lost in the torrential downpour. Richard moved forward to Alan's side and his iron shield glowed white; if it weren't for the rain constantly pattering into it without a hiss, I'd have been convinced it was several thousand degrees in temperature, it glowed so bright.

The ogre came stomping through the street in our direction, and I felt its movement before I could even see it. Eventually it pushed through the grey curtain of rain and appeared in front of us, a towering giant.

The monster was at least ten feet tall standing there. Its arms were chiseled and muscular while its gut protruded laughably around its waist. Its shoulders sported two heads, each with one gigantic eyeball; its hair was braided back into a ponytail and disappeared behind its laughably small heads. Each arm carried a mace that a normal person would need both hands to hold.

The passives that the ogre had indicated it was a strong enemy versed in melee combat. This fight would be on Thomas and the three tanks while the rest of us simply pelted it from a safe distance. These were always the easiest enemies to deal with, almost a pure stat check encounter.

Alan rushed forward with a charge and Richard struggled to follow him in. Alan slashed out at the fat gut of the ogre only to find two maces coming down like missiles on his head. Fast! The ogre had reacted at an insane speed, even if it would allow Richard to slice across his stomach.

There was no chance of a proper defense from Alan, his arm being extended outward in an attack. He raised the shield high as he could as the two maces came down. The first sound in our fight that I could hear through the rain, was the clang of metal. Alan's arm gave way instantly and he smashed into the concrete so hard blood exploded outward from his mouth.

His health dropped to 30% percent in that single exchange, and my heart went into my throat. Only a second had passed since the fight began. My minions hadn't even reached the target; Richard was moments away from him. Alan lay there stunned on the ground.

Maria's Ensnaring Arrow hadn't landed yet and there was no Quagmire trap in place. The maces rose again and were going to turn Alan into meat paste when Lucas arrived. His Nodachi pierced directly into the armpit of the ogre, completely stopping one hand from swinging. The other hand that was going to smash Alan instead changed course and swung sideways ready to pulverize Lucas instead.

Richard arrived just then with his shield raised and Holy Ground cast. He took the hit for Lucas and found himself sliding across the ground. The interference by those two gave Alan enough time to get out of the stun and roll along the floor to safety.

"Are you satisfied you idiot!" Maria yelled at Alan. I could tell she cared for him; not that I could understand it. My squad of undead fighters and her Ensnaring Arrow reached the Ogre at the same time, giving a bit more reprieve to the three fighting in melee.

Thomas threw out heal after heal onto Alan to top him off and Richard also aided with an instant cast heal as well. Despite the close call, Alan didn't seem discouraged at all. He cast Battle Shout and then charged back in to melee range. This time he wasn't alone.

Anna sent out Frost Bolts repeatedly focusing on the ogre's shoulders, while Jessica and Maria shot at the monster's eyes and took away its vision. Within ten seconds it was blind and immobilized. Between the hacking by my minions and Lucas sending out devastating slashes, the ogre no longer stood a chance and fell just fifteen seconds later.

"You are so stupid!" Maria ran up to Alan and punched him in the arm.

"What was that for?" He jerked back.

"You…you idiot." She sobbed. "You could have died!"

"I was fine!" He looked at everyone. It seemed it took him a moment to see the looks of worry and disappointment on our faces. "…sorry," he added.

"You were about as close to dead you could have been and still made it," I said. "If Lucas hadn't risked himself to save you, you would have been brain matter washing down the drains." I had no doubt in my mind he would have been squished beneath his shield with no chance to retaliate.

"Let's be smarter about it," Lucas said, "no matter what we think of the enemy, full preparation every fight. That means a Quagmire, an Ensnaring Arrow, and not rushing in like a maniac on your own.

"Alan, you're not fighting alone," I added, "Richard and Lucas are both there, so work with them." He already knew this, but he was blinded by hubris, or more probably his passive Battle Hunger. I was feeling a headache coming on. The passives were starting to be a problem, too.

No one else had anything to say about Alan's little episode. Now we could cross the street on Jessica's word, and we made it through two more blocks without encountering a single enemy.

Richard pointed to a furniture store. "I know where we are. My brother's house is just three more blocks east." I was thankful that it wasn't necessary to go much further in towards the center of the city. I could feel we were on the cusp of walking into that territory where only Exceptional and Elite monsters roamed.

It was definitely much harder to skirt past those, and we would have tough battles ahead of us if we continued onwards. Instead, we turned to our right and carefully made our way with Jessica leading the front. Encounters were scarce, and those battles that were necessary went smoothly. Alan didn't act up again, this time patiently waiting for Quagmire and Ensnaring Arrow before charging in.

The ogre elite seemed to have knocked some sense into him. We spent fifteen minutes making it past those three blocks, mostly because of our new outlook on safety, and we were now in a residential neighborhood. Richard could see his brother's home, and we had to stop him from rushing to it like a madman.

"Five more minutes won't kill you," Anna said. "Let Jessica do her job." Everyone was excited; everyone was anxious.

This rain was saving us days and days of time, despite chilling us to the bone. If Richard's brother had holed up and was still alive, what were our options? We could travel back to the hotel and give him a room on Floor 17. If I needed to use the spawn protection stone then, so be it. On the other hand, if he was only level one then bringing him with us anywhere was a massive risk: if any of these monsters so much as breathed on him, he'd fall over.

After careful consideration by Jessica, she announced that there was no way across to our goal without pulling another elite ogre. This time Alan redeemed himself, letting us set up properly and pull the mob through our traps. It was noticeably slower and Alan was ready for the initial double blow, putting all his effort into deflecting them with his shield.

During the fight, I got the opportunity to test my reanimated Medusa. I had hoped that her Stone Gaze would still be in effect against opponents and although that hope was faint, it still sucked to see my new passive didn't work on the ogre. A passive like Stone Gaze would have been overpowered on a reanimated minion so I understood why it didn't work, but damn it would have been good to have had it for PvP.

After the ogre went down, Alan was like a vacuum cleaner as he slurped up all the loot without a care. No one was in a position to use any new skills; the only items we needed to check thoroughly were the pieces of gear. Unfortunately, none dropped. Perhaps that was a reflection of the challenge: eight people around level 25 had no issue dominating a level 32 elite.

When the path was safe through the block, no one could stop Richard from rushing to his brother's home. I followed him with a mix of emotions. I wasn't sure what to expect, and I imagined in that moment what it would feel like to be able to meet my parents. It had been two months, and despite my skepticism that anyone could survive by hiding, I didn't rain on his parade.

Chapter 31: Even After the Apocalypse Clouds can have Silver Linings

From what I could see through the downpour we were in a pleasant residential neighborhood: long clean driveways with expensive vehicles parked in them; once-maintained lawns filled with green grass and bushes that needed trimmed but were no doubt beautiful additions to these mostly two-story homes. I could see what it once was, and all of it came together with a roundabout at the end that screamed 'community!'

I knew the result before we even entered the house but didn't crush Richard's hope. If another human was present, Jessica would have said something. We shared a look and I could tell she agreed with me. The excitement visible on Richard's face said no amount of cold reason would keep him from searching the house for his brother. I could only shake my head and follow Richard inside. How fickle life was now...

"Mark! Are you here?" Richard yelled through the home, pushing open doors and checking bathrooms. In the end, he accepted that Mark wasn't there, but at least there were no bodies or evidence of any attack. It was too clean.

"It looks like no one was here when the Apocalypse happened," Jessica said. The clothing, the shoes, everything was in a neat order.

If you were abandoning your home surely you would take a small bag or some belongings with you.

I didn't want to say it, but if Mark was out when this all started…the chance of him being alive was next to zero. While the original mobs spawning here wouldn't have been level thirties, the sheer number of zombies and ghouls and goblins in this area with the population so high…it would have been a bloodbath.

Inspecting the homes across the street and around the area showed that clearly. The neighbor just two doors down had a massive hole in his front door. Dried blood was caked along the entrance way as if someone had been dragged out. It was the same story for most of these homes in fact.

"He's alive, I know so;" Richard insisted, "his car isn't even here."

"There's a chance, but we don't know where to look," I replied. "We have to keep moving while we can."

Richard was frustrated with that, but there was nothing to do about it. We couldn't go on a wild goose chase.

"Next stop was our uncle, yeah?" Alan asked.

"How far is it?" Lucas asked.

It was Thomas who replied, "I don't know for certain, maybe thirty minutes from here on foot if we had no obstacles? His shop is only five or six blocks from here, though." The Apocalypse began midday, so their uncle was probably working at the time. It was unfortunate Richard didn't know where his brother worked as if there was any trail to his whereabouts and possible survival, it would begin there.

"His shop?" I asked.

"Yeah," Alan said. "I thought we told you guys that he's an engineer. He works on cars and he has a garage he runs." That…was an incredibly useful skill to have in the Apocalypse. It was still early, and even if we had to go 5 blocks or 20 blocks, there was enough time in the day as long as we could avoid endless encounters.

Previously, Richard had told us finding his brother was more important than his own life, which left me wondering what he was going to do now. He was silent, almost hollow as we left the house and moved back onto the street. I wanted to give some encouragement, but realized shallow words would probably just piss him off more.

It was actually Alan who stepped up, finding the right words to say. "Once this is over, if we haven't died and got all we needed to do done—I'll help you find your brother."

I could see that Richard didn't know how to react, but eventually his face morphed from confusion to a smile before he grabbed Alan and gave him a hug. After that, some of the energy in his step returned and we were back in business.

Alan and Thomas's uncle was the next priority, and would probably be our last trip for the day. Still, our progress was faster during this downpour than it would be in good weather. It got me thinking that having someone specialize in stealth or camouflage would be insanely good for our group. I didn't know if that was even a skill, or if there was a class that specialized in stealth, but it definitely got me wondering.

It took us five minutes to make it out of the neighborhood and return to the street we originally traveled. Thomas said it was easier navigating from here, as he had traveled this road many times before. We needed to go five street lights and then take a left, and head one block deeper into the city. From there we would find his shop on the right-side corner of a small plaza.

We were smooth sailing already; I had full confidence in Jessica's abilities. She got more efficient as we moved, so much more so that

I wondered if her tracking ability had improved. I wasn't sure how it leveled up, because it seemed she was almost always using it.

Three blocks later we came to an abrupt halt. Jessica peered around the edge of a building corner. I wondered if she was having another Frogger moment. "Guys, what is this?" Maria suddenly asked. "And why is it so sticky?"

We all turned back to take a look at what she was talking about. Maria was standing there, and on her right shoulder was a strip of cloth, or fiber. It was some sort of fabric or bandage type material about the thickness of typical gauze. "I can't get it off my clothes," she said while grabbing it and pulling at it.

There were no enemies around, and so none of us were on alert. Like everyone, I assumed she had just walked into some random debris that was left over from this mess. There was trash every-where—well, not such much with the downpour nearly sweeping the streets clean—so it could have been anything.

Alan came to take a look at it and Lucas cut straight to the chase—literally. He pulled out his Nodachi and shot a Wind Slash at the fabric. What I expected to happen didn't happen, though. It didn't cut and instead the Wind Slash did nothing.

"This…looks like spider web," Lucas stepped closer to study the material.

"Where did you get stuck on this?" I asked hurriedly. "How long has it been on you?"

"Just now…right here," Maria answered in confusion. We all looked around for more threads, and as I moved only four or five feet from where she was standing, I realized the entire street was covered. The webs had gone from one building and all the way across the street to the other, and climbed an unknown distance into the air.

We were near a giant web that climbed over sixty stories up, one that would put even Spider Man to shame. I looked at Jessica and so did everyone else, "I don't feel anything," she shrugged. "Just cut her sleeve off; we can find you a new one."

Alan took out a knife. "Stop wiggling, stay still."

"I'm not wiggling idiot, just cut it!" Maria barked back.

"Someone hold her still then! Look how much it's moving."

Lucas was holding onto the web with some wet newspaper, "I...don't think that's her." The web was shaking sporadically and violently now, as if something was crawling across it.

"Enemies incoming!" Jessica said, "Cut the damn shirt already."

Care with Maria's clothing was the last thing Alan's mind now. He stuck the blade into the shirt hole and slashed upwards, mangling the cloth but freeing her from the web's clutches. The web whipped back a few feet where it was attached originally and started twitching violently.

We rushed back to known safety and prepared for battle. We couldn't see or hear our enemies approaching, but Jessica filled us in, "Four strong mobs; at least elite level." Alan and Richard moved forward and prepped their shields in front of them.

Everyone was completely still. My heart was in my throat as we waited for our enemies to appear. Less than ten seconds passed from when Alan cut Maria's shirt when the monsters started to come through that grey curtain of rain: four towering insects.

Spiders as large as two-door vehicles crawled from the street in our direction. The front legs were the first thing I could see: hairs and spikes thicker than pencils atop their carapaces. Then it was their eyes, a deep purple that penetrated the soul, life-sucking. Something about their eyes was so archaic, so innocent and yet deadly.

We were nothing but food to them: something to satiate their hunger. Their sharp fangs dripped a deadly green liquid that would no doubt assist them in doing so. Droplets of poison fell from the fangs and vanished with a sizzling smoke that was eventually washed away in the downpour.

Their abdomen was thinner and more elongated than I'd seen on any spider, the far tip of it containing two pincer-like spikes. It also seemed like their legs were longer than usual, despite them sitting so low to the ground. They reminded me of a water spider in some ways.

"Level Thirty-Four Elite, Prong Spider," Jessica announced. "Just one passive. Venom Splasher: Your poison is explosive."

"What does that even mean?" Maria asked frantically.

"I...don't know." I confessed. Poison was a nightmare to deal with. We didn't have any item that cured poison, and standard healing probably wouldn't remove poison affects. Four level 34 elites, each of which could probably spit venom from multiple locations on its body. "I think we need to run." Even as I spoke I felt this was the understatement of the year.

"Jessica, lead the way!" I shouted while sending out all my undead. They were fodder now, and I fully expected to be using Shallow Grave to replenish them. This was a fight we could maybe win, but at what cost?

Anna began casting spells before I could say anything more, placing a Harrowing Storm in between us and the Prong Spiders. Quagmires were laid and Ensnaring Arrows were released. Everyone was already thinking on their toes.

"Stay behind me!" Jessica said before sprinting into the wall of grey. I was the last one to turn and follow, my necrotic vision ensuring that I wouldn't lose them even in the bleakest of conditions.

Fleeing was the right call, as my undead all perished on combat start. I turned in time to see why: a skeleton general covered in poison exploded like a grenade had gone off. That explosion not only sent boney shrapnel flying in all directions but took out three skeletons just in proximity of the explosion itself.

The poison was unbelievably potent. It melted through metal and bone like hot water and sugar. I didn't think an antidote would even be useful in that moment because the afflicted flesh would simply shave off.

"LOOK AHEAD!" Thomas yelled. He was right. Someone falling or tripping now would be a death sentence.

This was a fight not worth taking, and I breathed a sigh of relief as the curtain of rain came between us and the monsters. Thirty seconds of running was all it took to make it four lights, and for the Spiders to give up their chase. They weren't very mobile off their webs, at least not enough to keep up with us when we were using the alleyways and stacked cars to our advantage.

"We've lost them." Jessica said while scanning the surroundings. "It's relatively clear here, how close are we to our goal?"

"Only about a minute away," Thomas replied. The excitement on his face was visible, a welcome change from the gloomy look he had maintained since we all heard the latest announcement. Alan was always bouncing off the walls lately, but right now he was still. He did his best to hide the jittery excitement he was no doubt feeling.

"We can make it directly there then," Jessica said while taking to the front. We walked one block inward and a plaza became visible through the rain. A welcome sign contained the names of at least twenty stores and even a movie theatre; it was not a small plaza by any means.

After thirty seconds Jessica stopped us. "Two people ahead." She hadn't given any warning previously, so this was definitely promising.

Thomas could barely contain his excitement and broke into a run.

"Slow," I said, "We have to be careful above all else."

It was unlikely there would be two True Believers on their own out here, but I couldn't rule out that possibility completely. We slowed our pace even more, and eventually found ourselves outside of an auto-repair shop.

"They are inside." Jessica stopped. The rain was the perfect cover for us as we approached, and there was no commotion or movement inside. We walked the outer edge to the door, only to find it had been barricaded from within.

It was eventually Thomas who broke the silence, "Is anyone in there?" He yelled out.

"They moved." Jessica let us know they were aware of our presence.

"Uncle Glen?" Alan yelled a second later.

A weak voice came from within, "You know me?"

"It's Thomas!"

"And Alan!" The two were shouting in unison.

There was an excited commotion from within, barely audible through the rain but we could hear it clearly: the sound of metal being hustled out of the way, and another hushed voice asking Glen to be sure of what he was doing, if removing the barricade was the right call.

Eventually, there was no barricade between us, and the door opened revealing the two men inside. One man wore a mechanic's outfit still dirtied from oil. His face held a thick beard that barely hid obvious signs of malnutrition. The other man waited further back, out of the light and much more concealed.

Glen's expression was of disbelief, while Thomas and Alan could find no words. They opted instead to rush him and squeeze him where he stood. So much so that a few groans escaped his mouth.

"How did you survive?" Thomas asked eventually.

"You call this surviving? We're barely living here." Glen managed to joke. Alan didn't wait to pull out Ration after Ration and stuff it into Glen's hand. "These are Rations?" He asked. "We had some of these originally, when the monsters were goblins and zombies, things changed quickly though."

"They're both Level Six." Jessica whispered to me.

"Mark, come on up here," Glen said, "these are my nephews." I could see Richard suddenly twitch when the name Mark was said, and suddenly I felt like a coincidence this big couldn't be possible.

The man walked forward out of the darkness, and like Glen his face was covered in hair, barely able to hide his hunger. He scanned over everyone, and the rations, and then his eyes went white and round as saucers, "R-Richard?"

Richard couldn't even find the words. Instead, he just started crying. It was the most ugly cry you could possibly imagine. He was howling along with the wind and rain for a dozen seconds before Mark was hugging him.

This was an emotional reunion, and it took a good few minutes before everyone was settled enough to calmly sit down and talk. Mark and Glen were both given multiple Rations, which they snacked on while telling their stories.

They were both in the shop when it started. The two managed to close up the shop and fight off the goblins and zombies that came their way the first few days. Other people came too, intent on robbing the tools, but a stern warning and the blood from the monsters splattered about the area made any with weak stomachs think twice about trying their luck.

They barricaded themselves in and eventually realized there was no more easy prey. Killing enemies for Rations or levels no longer was an option, not with just the two of them. The enemies changed from goblins and ghouls and zombies to much stronger foes and they had fallen too far behind. Initially though, the Plaza had plentiful supplies to keep them going.

Besides the two vending machines Glen had on site, they had ransacked several others. About a week ago though, things got way too rough and it wasn't possible for them to venture outside. The two of them hadn't eaten anything since then.

Mark then went on to explain to Richard how he was here. He was having car trouble, and found Glen's shop by chance while going to the movies. He brought his vehicle in the day of the apocalypse, and was actually waiting for his ride home when it all started. Needless to say, the two had become good friends since then.

They had survived two months in this small little shop on what they could salvage from vending machines. They had saved water for some time, but when the drought came they were barely making it by on just a few sips per day.

This rainstorm had given them renewed hope, at least enough to keep going and trying to survive, as bleak as that was. Another week though and they would have both kicked the bucket no doubt. Our arrival in time was a silver-lining to the farm being ransacked and burned, albeit a dark one.

Even a few days of extra waiting may have been the difference between Glen and Mark surviving, and us reuniting with them here instead of finding two fresh corpses.

Chapter 32: A Somber Veil Over the Post-Apocalyptic City

"What do you think?" I looked to Jessica.

There were a few options now on what to do. I knew that Richard, Thomas, and Alan didn't want to be apart from those who they could truly call family, but it currently wasn't safe to bring Mark and Glen along with us. Both of them being level 6 meant they were probably one-shot kills for any of the monsters roaming the streets.

On the other hand, moving them now might just be our best and only option. The curtain of rain was probably the only thing stopping that mobs from aggroing in numbers that we couldn't handle. Maybe keeping them in a pocket as we moved back to the hotel could be a solution.

'I'm not sure,' Jessica replied, she gave a slight shake of the head as though imagining the worst outcome.

Jessica and I weren't the only ones contemplating our best move, and it was actually Richard who suggested a decent solution, "Let's just go to Mark's place. It is relatively safe and near the edge of the city. We also had no run-ins with Believers there." That was a good point about the Believers. My idea of using the hotel had overlooked the fact there were multiple Believers inside, and potentially more coming.

The word Believers drew curious expressions from both Glen and Mark.

"Crazy religious fanatics," was all Richard needed to say, and neither bat an eye at his short but sweet description. They had seen enough crazy shit to worry about humans forming a mindless cult.

In the end, the consensus was to head back to Mark's place. Our spawn protection stone could be placed there, and could supply the two with enough rations to last them over a week. Their bodies were in a state of starvation already, and so just half the normal dose was enough to satiate them for the entire day.

Our only option was to back track along our path and pray the Prong Spiders had disappeared into the upper regions once again. Other than that, the monsters we had dispatched on the way should not have respawned yet, or so we hoped.

"Richard, you take the back and ensure they don't get lost. We don't know how mobs will react to their presence, so we start slow. If we must fight, we do it defensively, making sure to screen Mark and Glen. And if we can't fight, we run with them in the middle," I said. I had full confidence in our abilities as a group, but I didn't have enough information about the mechanics of aggro ranges. It was possible that level difference was a factor and that hordes of monsters could pour down upon us once they got a sniff of low-level players.

The expression on every face in the room was stern. We were walking into uncharted territory, and no one wanted to be the person to bring up the obvious. There was a very real possibility Mark or Glen would die today.

We walked outside moments later, back into the torrential downpour that quite possibly was our only lifeline. Without it, I'd have not dared to move Mark and Glen before seriously clearing this area of any enemies. There were also the True Believers to worry about and time was of the essence in staying clear of them.

Going back out into the rain caused me to shiver, but Mark and Glen relished the cold shower. They raised their faces to the sky and scrubbed vigorously. Their long hair and thick beards were filled with dirt and grime and even blood. This was their chance to clean up. They swallowed the rain without a care as it pelted against their faces.

"Let's move." Jessica got everyone moving in the right direction and we quickly backtracked several blocks without incident. When we returned to the site of the Prong Spiders, however, we became especially wary.

I finally got to see the result of the short encounter we had with them. The road was a mess, and many cars had been totaled and thrown off into the buildings by the spiders in their short but vicious chase of us. The poison they used was strong enough to melt the metal frames of the vehicles, and shiny debris from the resulting explosions gleamed from underneath rushing streams of rainwater.

"Anything?" Alan asked from just behind me. We were huddled as a group, waiting for Jessica to make a call. There wasn't much I could contribute in this situation; Necrotic Vision couldn't compare to the range Jessica's tracking ability had. My concern was that the Prong Spiders could wait outside of her range but be sensitive to signals coming through the webs.

Hopefully, though, as long as we were careful to avoid any webbing, they wouldn't be interested in having a peek down here again. We waited for several minutes in silence, and that time crawled as if limbless.

"I think it's safe," Jessica assured everyone at last. It was never safe, that was the world we lived in now. Everyone knew that

295

already but Mark and Glen. Their faces were all smiles, a mixture of happiness and ignorance. They had avoided the darkest features of this world so far.

Backtracking was much faster than we expected, and the rain didn't let up in the slightest. The streets were flooded now, and the drains could not keep up with the resulting flow. It seemed like the possibility of venturing further today was possible.

We needed to move further in and not skirt the edges. Our encounters would be more difficult, and I wondered whether we should take the rest of this day off, make sure Mark and Glen were settled, and then push in the morning.

The thought of relaxing tempted me, and I had just about persuaded myself of the idea when Jessica turned and said urgently, "There's people all over, twenty or more. They're moving in this direction while dispatching mobs."

We were at least two blocks further towards the center than the hotel. These had to be cultists, which meant they had taken control of that block and were now clearing towards us. "How fast are they moving?" I asked what everyone wanted to know.

"Not super fast, but they are clearing rapidly through the mobs." With over twenty of them dogpiling a single enemy, even if they were merely level 15 it would be a cakewalk. Power in numbers was a very real thing in this post-apocalypse MMRPG.

It would be possible for them to move even faster as they picked up on our route, too. We had cleared a few elite enemies, no doubt something a tracker could pick up on. They would be directly on our trail, rain or not.

"Do we go back?" Anna asked anxiously. We couldn't just walk into the cultists, yet they were just a block away from where we would turn to head to Mark's place. Avoiding them while making it there was probably impossible with a group of our size.

"We have to go back," I said, "we can't fight them." By now I was convinced there was something wrong with this situation. Fanatics and crazy people weren't uncommon, but this just made no sense. We meant no harm to them, and the lengths they went to deal with us was abnormal. It was as if these people chasing us were subject to a hive mind that needed to keep increasing the number of its subjects. Whether that mind was a human player with a powerful ability to charm others or a mob, I couldn't say. A human would explain the religious side of the movement, but why the obsession with us?

The rules of this world were so fresh it could be any number of things. There was no ruling out any option, which didn't exactly get us anywhere. The most thorough and brutal response was the only response: Destruction of the True Believers. I told myself I'd sacrifice my humanity to protect our group, and this was another test of my resolve.

"Let's use the Prong Spiders," I announced. There was a brief confusion and then some light bulbs went on.

"You want to lure them and feed them up?" Anna asked. I was expecting a retort of some kind, but instead she calmly contemplated my proposal without a fuss.

"Essentially." It was good in that we wouldn't have to be the ones doing the killing either. Progressing our passives scared me right now, and until there was some way to protect our mental health and humanity from them, I wanted to avoid being the one holding the knife.

"Good idea," said Jessica. "It will be all about the timing, but I think we can do it."

297

We backtracked once again to the area with the Prong Spider webs and took a good look around. The area we originally entered was merely the outskirts of their lair, and with some skillful maneuvering we could see just how large the affected area was.

Five square blocks were covered in thick sticky webs. Not a single other monster remained in sight, and while I wasn't sure if they would cannibalize each other, I started to think it was a very real possibility. We had witnessed the apes killing zombies, but never using them as food.

No one wanted to be the bait bringing the spiders down while the true believers waited close by, and it was actually Glen who found a solution. The front hood of a car had been ripped off in the previous chase and, with careful maneuvering, it was lowered onto a thick cross section of webbing.

The rain was making the sheet of metal lightly hum and vibrate... but an arrow shot from either Maria or Jessica would make it rock back and forth like struggling prey. With the right timing, it would bring the Prong Spiders descending for a meal, just as the True Believers ran into the area.

Everything was set in place here, and the biggest risks were clear to us now. First, would be something going wrong with our signal through the webs, and our being caught by the True Believers; second, would be getting caught by the Prong Spiders if they aggroed us and not the cultists; and third, would simply be the Prong Spiders not showing up and somehow having the True Believers right on our tail.

After a brief discussion, I found that the consensus was that I should be the bait. My Bone Armor was a solid defense, and my squad of undead would work as shields and could also slow down the enemy if something unexpected happened. Although I hadn't planned on this, I couldn't complain. It was also possible a few of the cultists would recognize me specifically and throw any caution to the wind and chase.

Only Jessica and Maria had a role to play in this ambush. They would shoot arrows into the metal plate to try start this whole spider ambush. Everyone else waited safely in a spot we had previously cleared, and as long as no mobs respawned, they would be fine.

As I gathered my squad around me, rain still pouring heavily I had no complaints: the rain provided a big contribution to the surprise factor. Take a few steps back and the spider webs were nearly invisible, they blended in perfectly with the curtain of grey. Hopefully, I would been spotted as simply a stranded person ripe for death or recruitment and they would be none the wiser as they entered the area of the webs.

We waited for about fifteen minutes before the True Believers moved a block closer. By now they had already cleared most mobs along the path leading to us. Their speed would be picking up now, as this area was devoid of spawns as a result of the spiders and our own efforts. Further towards the city center would be more mobs, but they could safely avoid them and probably wouldn't choose to fight for no reason.

Another block for them and they would spot something was wrong. With a good tracker they would be able to pick up our trail by the gaps in the pattern of spawns.

"I'm going," I announced. It was important to make this work before the cultists had the slightest hint something was untoward. The plan was about as simple as could be, 'accidently' stumble into the True Believers, and then run like hell.

The rain continued to pour down relentlessly, casting a somber veil over the now post-apocalyptic city. I questioned to myself while

I walked towards my fellow humans whether this was okay, was it the right thing to do? I couldn't give myself a yes or no answer. It just... had to be.

Us or them: that thought repeated in my head enough times for me to believe it wholeheartedly. The rain beating down couldn't drown out the ever-thumping echo of my heart in my ears. People were going to die if things worked out in my favor, a lot of people, and I wasn't sure they deserved it: the circumstances surrounding the existence of the True Believers was still a mystery.

With so many odd and unknown abilities, it was impossible to know if they chose this path willingly or were manipulated in some way. In the end, it didn't change anything. As of right now they were mortal enemies, and I would always choose us over them.

I reached the street corner just moments later. There was only this single intersection and one office building between myself and the pursuers. I could only wait, as walking further from our trap was not part of the plan. My outfit didn't exactly make me look the part of stranded or helpless civilian, but it would have to do.

The beat of my heart started to fade as I rationalized the last bit of humanity out of my thoughts. This was the right choice, the only choice, and even if it wasn't... us or them. The tribe mentality was dangerous, but it would keep us alive: anything to survive. That was the way of the world now.

My eyes focused to a break in the buildings across the street. I could hear shouts and cries through the dense rainfall. Seconds passed like minutes as figures walked out and appeared on the sidewalk across from me. For a moment my heart stopped in anticipation. They would see me in just a few moments.

They called back and forth amongst themselves for a dozen seconds and then I could feel the stare of danger. One of them noticed me, and then they quickly alerted the others. The talking stopped and they eyed me like a pack of hyenas. My neck hairs stood and my Premonition told me what I already knew: they were bad news.

Chapter 33: Release the Spider Trap!

I didn't try to interact with the cultists, instead I just turned and sprinted towards our trap. There was no need to incentivize them further, they had no plans of letting me go from the moment they set eyes on me, that much I could feel through my passive. What did they wanted to do with me? I didn't know, and didn't want to find out.

The whole street was flooded well past my ankles by now. Moving fast was more challenging than I had expected and water splashed soundlessly into the air with every step I took. Wading was so much easier than forcing my feet through this city river.

They were right on my tail, and I could hear the shouting behind me: telling me to stop; telling me they weren't my enemies; wouldn't hurt me. A slew of sweet nothing whispered into my ear that might have enticed an unknowing victim on their last legs. I knew better and kept running.

It was a short thirty seconds that felt like five minutes. Time seemed to slow down in my head when my heart was pumping this fast, no doubt the adrenaline coursing through me, stronger than ever.

I reached the hanging door and moved past it a dozen feet, maybe more, and then 'fell' on the road. My body crashed into the water and I turned instinctively while fumbling backwards inches at a time—the believers were just twenty or thirty feet away and closing in fast.

There was a low gonging sound as I witnessed an arrow pierce through the car door. The shaft of the arrow rested halfway through the metal frame, and the whole thing wobbled up and down like a board on a spring. The web was twitching like a snake come to life, and any commotion was drowned out by a subsequent crack of lightning. The resulting thunder roared like nothing I'd ever heard before.

Even the True Believers chasing me stopped in their tracks and stared into the sky, which gave me just enough time to get to my feet. I was facing them already, and they approached carefully. I eyed them with caution, and not like a group about to be spider snacks. A quick count put their numbers at fifteen, and those were only the ones in front of me. Jessica said twenty, so there must be more nearby, or simply observing from safety.

"What do you want?" I asked. I didn't want them coming to close to me. They were the perfect distance away, and just a few feet behind them were stretched those nearly invisible spider webs. Any closer and they would have a chance to run.

They didn't respond instantly, and no one even stepped forward to answer. They eyed me eerily, and that feeling that something wasn't right about them prickled my thoughts. It was almost inhuman how they acted: us or them.

"Come with us." That was what was said. Not a question, not an inquiry. It was an order, and it made my skin crawl.

"Who are you?" I stalled for just a few more seconds. The door was wobbling out of control, and if any of them hadn't been eyeing me so closely, they would have seen it. The Prong Spiders arrival was imminent, and so was my escape.

Several cultists took another step forward without answering my question. Alarm bells were ringing and I pulled my undead squad into the world and they flooded the street in front and behind me. The appearance of all these skeletal monsters was enough to stop the True Believers in their tracks.

"You're the Necromancer we heard about," a tall man said confidently, and then he followed it by pointing at me, "get him." All my undead were sent forward to intercept them. Little good they would do to stop their assault, but I could see the Prong Spiders now with my clear vision. A few seconds of delay would be enough.

There were more of the arachnids this time: a total of six of them, perched twenty feet above us and descending slowly. I turned tail and started to run as fast as I could. The venom they could spit was an instant kill if it landed on any vital area, and I was not interested in testing how strong my bone armor was now.

A rush of cold flew past my face as I turned; Anna had cast blizzard in between me and the cultists. Two different arrows as well, one exploding and sending a geyser of water into the air, and another created a massive field of entangling vines. The multiple surprises caused my pursuers to stop, and then it was too late.

There was an ominous hissing that I had not heard before, not having been close enough to hear before. I turned back against my better judgment to see a pool of green acid fly outward from a Prong Spider's maw and send a True Believer tumbling into the water screaming in agony.

Another spider stabbed out with its weird abdomen and pierced a different believer before pulling it to its face and biting their body clean in half. The sudden sight caused a rush of nausea to wash over me. Inner Calm did its best to suppress that urge, but my stomach churned.

The cultists tried to run in all different directions, but the spiders were at such close quarters that to turn from one was to run into another. The water ran red and green with acid and blood alike, and when all was said and done I supposed that no more than three or four True Believers would make it out.

Turning back, I reached the others to see that only Jessica and Alex could manage to keep their eyes open and watch the slaughter. Everyone else stood behind the wall with their backs facing away from the massacre. Even the rain wasn't enough to drown out the screams. This was nightmare fuel.

We waited a dozen minutes in silence before Jessica gave the go ahead. They were all dead, or if there were any still alive, they had fled far enough to not be in her radar. The spiders had gone too, no doubt with full stomachs. In the aftermath of that experience, I walked with bated breath, alert to danger.

So much damage and so fast, the entire battle lasting no longer than two or three minutes. The remaining ten minutes we spent nearby was to ensure the spiders were finished with their meal. I was glad the rain and thunder drowned out any crunching we may have been able to hear. I didn't need that in my memories, too.

Bodies were strewn about the road, pushed by the flow of rainwater until jammed up against an obstacle. The corpses that hadn't find a car tire or wall to wash into were long gone now, and who knew how many were eaten whole. I couldn't help but look at the carnage.

Alex was shameless about it. He rushed over to the nearest body and turned it over. His hands went through pockets. Then he went on to the next, even looking under cars for remains of the cultists.

It took a few moments before he scooped out every little bit of loot they had remaining, which oddly wasn't much.

"Doesn't this look weird to you all?" Lucas said suddenly. He wasn't scouring for loot, but he was looking over the bodies. Maria and Anna didn't approach, but the rest took a gander at what he was talking about. It was the neck of a True Believer, the backside at least.

There was a circle there, like the flesh was bumpy and swollen at one point. It reminded me of a ringworm mark I got as a kid. "Looks like a bug bite or something." Alex said.

"It does, but that's not what I was getting at." Lucas pointed at another True Believer, both were fortunate enough to keep their heads. "The same mark is on this one, and this one." He pointed at another.

We looked at seven bodies that had intact necks, and each one had the same mark. "Can't be a coincidence." I said. Something had stung them or infected them.

"Look away if you don't like gore." Lucas warned everyone. I wanted to look away, but my curiosity got the better of me. He took the tip of his Nodachi and dug it into the odd wound. Blood didn't run as I expected it to. My stomach churned again as the flesh began to wiggle and jiggle.

I suddenly had a bad feeling, "Careful!" I warned him, and just as I did a worm the size of a finger with a mouth of teeth burst forth from the dead flesh and nearly dug into Lucas's palm. He managed to fling the piece away with the worm still inside it. The whole thing vanishing down the city river.

"What in the actual fuck was that?" Richard asked. It was like something straight out of an alien movie.

"I don't know but can we please please please get out of here." Maria begged. No one had any objection to her request. We all rushed to the sidewalk and well away from the bodies. Jessica led the front as we discussed it while walking.

"Was it a parasite?" wondered Lucas.

"It could be a skill," I speculated. "Maybe some kind of druid player able to infect people: that seems to me just as likely as if they were planted by a monster. If it's a monster taking control of people with parasites that would be the more dangerous scenario: it wouldn't stop until everyone was under its control, which it seems like the True Believers are all for.

"Having said that, if it's a player then that person is extremely dangerous." The level of power for someone able to control large numbers of people with class abilities was immense. If it was a player who was able to do this, that person was essentially a necromancer who dealt with humans... and the living. A livingmancer? I didn't even know what I would call that. It was essentially a form of mind control, via those worms.

Either way, this meant these people were most likely innocent in this. The thought of that would have made my stomach churn before, but now I felt just a twinge of guilt and nothing else. I opened my stats to check on Cold Hearted, the likely culprit.

Name: Mike Class: Necromancer Level: 24
EXP: 27%
HP: 1210/1210 MP: 440/485
STR: 5 Fear Resistance: 5
AGI: 2
DEX: 5
VIT: 29 +14
WIS: 27 +26
Available: 9

Skills: [A] **Summon Skeleton LV.** 10 | [A]
Summon Skeleton Mage LV. 4 | [A] **Decay
LV.** 3| [A] **Reanimate Dead LV.** 3 | [A] **Bone
Armor LV.** 2 | [A] **Vast Shadows** | [A]
Temporary Grave LV. 1 | [P] **Sixth Sense** |
[P] **Bravery LV.** 2 | [P] **Mutated LV.** 3| [P]
Pain Resistance LV. 2 | [P] **Skeletal
Mastery LV.** 4| [P] **Intimidate Living** | [P]
Inner Calm LV. 2 | [P] **Necrotic Vision** | [P]
Blood Thirsty LV. 1 | [P] **Cold Hearted LV.** 1

It was there in my skill list, and a simple inspection gave just five words: You are harder to move. Move? I assumed it meant the word in an emotional sense: that shocks would not disturb me as much as they would have before. How much of an affect this had was not listed in a percent or value, but it was enough that the feeling of killing those people before had left me so uneasy, so torn, and then afterwards I simply felt sick to my stomach.

Would I even be human when all of this ended? Would any of us still be human? Even scarier was the thought tickling my mind that I just didn't care to know the answer to that question. We were all being morphed into monsters, every day and every passive at a time.

"All of those people now dead were victims of this system," I said.

"It's not something we could have done anything about," Anna was the person who replied. "They are innocent in the same way zombies are; they're still trying to kill us." Maybe kill us wasn't the right word to use, but no one corrected her.

As far as I knew, whatever ailment that worm brought about was permanent. Losing my free thought was as good as being dead, at least to me. I'm sure others had a similar thought. The information gained was gold though. We couldn't use common sense to determine what they might be capable of—they weren't rational. Not anymore.

We walked two blocks closer to the hotel before Jessica stopped us, "Someone in front." She said. "A single person." She pointed with an arrow that she had nocked and raised. The group mimicked her, all of us preparing for an encounter. No one spoke a word.

Twenty seconds later we turned a corner to find a True Believer leaned up against the wall of a candy store. His head slouched down lifelessly, and yet he was clearly still alive else Jessica could not have detected him. "Careful." I whispered.

Jessica walked forward slowly with bow fully drawn, and only when we got closer could we see the state he was in. His entire right side was melted badly by acid. The cloth he once wore was now a part of flesh that bubbled and smoothed in odd ways. There wasn't a clear demarcation between cloth and flesh anymore—just a mesh of white and red and green that smelled like death.

I hadn't encountered a situation like this before, and everyone stopped in their tracks to look at me. Us or them. I almost found myself telling Jessica to release the arrow and end it right there, but curiosity and a bit of rationality won out. "Let's take a look and see what we can learn, just be careful," I said.

The cultist wasn't even conscious. It didn't look like he was in any shape to move, let alone fight. Eventually we formed a circle around him in silence before I worked up the courage to move forward. I grabbed the shoulder that wasn't melted by acid and gave him a shake.

A groan escaped the True Believer's mouth but his eyes remained closed, which bolstered my confidence. "Come help me." I beckoned at Lucas. We leaned him on his side and turned him flat on the ground, which got no lack of agonizing moans. His red face and cheeks led me to believe he was fighting a bad infection and was probably delirious.

The mark was there on the back of his neck as we expected, just the same as the others, except he was alive. "Can we cut it out?" I asked. I wasn't sure if there was any other way to get that worm out of him. I wanted to know what that worm did, and how they got infected by it.

"Won't that kill him?" Thomas asked.

"Probably," I said. "But it's likely he dies anyway." There was likely no saving him in his current state.

"Well, he'd need to be awake for us to know anything," Lucas said. "Can you heal him?" He looked at Thomas.

"Is that a good idea?" Maria asked.

"It's not a good idea, no," I said. "But it might be the only option we have."

"Remove the worm first and then heal him." Jessica added. A good idea, since as long as he had that thing inside him he wouldn't be open for any discussion.

"Wait, can I try something?" Anna asked. She had remained in quiet contemplation up to this point.

"Why not? Before or after we heal him?" I asked.

"Don't heal him yet," she answered, "can you make a slight cut in the middle of his neck wound?" Anna looked to Lucas.

Lucas agreed after a moment's thought. He urged us to hold the cultist tight and then made a small cut directly in the center of his neck, right where the wound was. Not too deep but enough to split flesh and make blood flow. After that, Anna wielded her Staff of Piercing Ice and then placed her hand on the wound.

"That's disgu—" Maria started.

"Let her work," Alex cut Maria off and pulled her back and away.

The True Believer let out low moans for a moment and then began to squirm uncomfortably while groaning. Fifteen slow seconds passed before Anna jerked her hand away from the wound. The skin there was purple and clearly cold, bordering on frost bite. She shook her hand in disgust before vigorously scrubbing it in the city river.

The skin of his neck wiggled and squirmed frantically despite the chill. Blood started to spurt and ooze out of it with each beat of his pulse. The True Believer suddenly let out an agonizing scream as the flesh split apart—a parasitic worm the size of a middle finger burst from within and flew into the air.

Ever alert, arrow taught on her bowstring, Jessica sent a pinpoint shot directly through the worm splitting it in half. The two pieces fell soundlessly and disappeared into the water below.

"Jesus Christ, that scares me so much when I see it," Richard muttered.

"Can you heal him now?" Anna asked. The worm was out and somehow or another the wounded man was still alive. Thomas gave a nod and poured two or three heals into him. He even went a step further and bandaged the side of his body still bubbling with acid burns. The damage was extensive enough that all of this probably wouldn't save him, just provide him some relief.

I could tell Thomas was reluctant to even heal him, and for good reason. The cultist was going to be in extreme agony after waking up, and we were simply extending his agony for the sake of trying to learn something that may or may not help us at all.

Mark and Glen had been watching this entire situation in eerie silence. This wasn't the time for idle chatter, and they were clearly

311

shell shocked. "How long till we reach your place?" I looked at Mark. That was our destination, and we would need to take the True Believer there.

He fumbled in confusion for a moment, still processing what he just saw. "Uh, uhm probably ten minutes if traffic is good?"

Richard let out a chuckle and even Anna gave a rare smile.

"Sorry, no traffic." Mark shook his head.

Richard stopped him from speaking before he could say anything else. "Let's get back and rest for the day." I had originally wanted to continue, but now was as good a time as any to call it. The rain had provided great cover, but we couldn't keep moving through it like this.

Being wet sapped your energy quickly. We were all burning calories crazily trying to stay warm in this downpour and we couldn't tote around a True Believer as cargo either. The other option was leave him with Mark and Glen, but there was no telling how that would turn out once he woke up.

We carried him back with us and put a hold on our recovery mission. This person might have incredible information for us, and it was paramount we knew exactly what the True Believers were up to, and why.

Chapter 34: A New Announcement from the RPG Gamemaster

The rain didn't stop the entire night, and we all had to cramp themselves upstairs to avoid the flooding on the first floor. It wasn't comfortable at all, and the True Believer constantly groaned throughout the night. Mark mumbled about his beautiful home being flooded, but eventually stopped after Richard reminded him the world was basically ending and it didn't matter. To me, it just seemed that everyone was dealing with the shock differently.

The rain let up early afternoon the following day. Seeing a color in the sky other than a dark and gloomy grey was a surprise, and it brought everyone's mood up. The flooding would take hours to clear up though, so we stayed hunkered down regardless.

We made a basic plan in the meantime: find out what the True Believer experienced or knew, and determine whether he was a threat or friendly. If he was friendly we would do our best to make his passing as comfortable or quick as possible, and if not...well his death would be even quicker.

After that, Glen and Mark could bunker down here and we would continue moving through the city and do our best to not die. I didn't have any expectation of finding my parents or Lucas' grandparents, but until Lucas made the call to stop we would do our best to make the attempt.

It was around dusk when our 'captive' woke up. I was outside standing off the front porch and enjoying the remaining sunlight. The water had receded just enough to not swallow my shoe, but it would probably be another night before the flooding was gone.

"He's awake!" Maria yelled while racing through the house. She had been watching the prisoner closely the entire time, mostly because the parasitic worm scared the shit out of her. She somehow believed there were more lurking inside of him, which meant she couldn't leave him out of her sight unless she was sleeping.

I brushed past Mark on my way inside. Mark was using a broom to sweep any water he could out—there was nothing else to do to pass the time anyway. My feet splashed with every step as I rushed up the stairs to find everyone else already huddled in the guest room around the bed.

"What's the situation?" I asked before focusing my eyes upon the True Believer. He was slouched over and vigorously rubbing his eyes and forehead while groaning.

"He hasn't said anything." Maria said in a hushed whisper.

The cultist continued to rub and groan until he fell backwards onto the pillow once again, "...Where am I?" He mumbled out, his eyes remained closed. "Ahh, it hurts so bad." He moaned. I wasn't even sure he was aware we were in the room with him. "Why can't I remember?" His groaning quickly turned to tears as he grew frustrated with himself.

I moved to Thomas quickly, "Can you heal him?" A healing spell would probably provide some relief, which would in turn calm him down. The injured man wasn't in great shape, so suddenly flailing about in a rage would definitely be counter-productive to what we

314

wanted to achieve. Thomas nodded and healed him twice in quick succession.

The frustration and pain on the captive's face disappeared in a flash. He let out a light smile and then moments later was fast asleep again.

"That's it?" Alex asked reluctantly.

"Let him sleep," I said. "This is good progress, there was always the chance removing that parasite would turn him into a vegetable." He had mumbled about his memory, though—which wasn't good news. We would have to wait and see what was left of his old personality.

"I'll keep watch." Maria reminded everyone as if it was a valiant and sacrificial job.

I knew her real motivation in monitoring the True Believer was fear, but I still said, "Good job, you're doing great. Keep it up." Maria gave a big smile and then plopped back onto the chair.

I turned to walk back outside, Jessica quick on my tail. She had her bow nocked the entire encounter, which I didn't blame her for. That night at the gas station and our first fight with other people had removed every ounce of naiveté she had in her. "Are we doing the right thing?" she asked.

"I hope so." I didn't have the answer, and I don't think she even expected one. We walked out onto the porch in time to see the orange hue of the sky. Something that would have been beautiful months ago now worried me. Those could actually be flames on the horizon, or some worldly phenomenon coming to kill us. "Anything?" I asked.

"No traffic at all," she replied. "Respawns appeared last night, but they haven't wandered this way." This was great news for us. The plan when we left was to drop the Spawn Protection Stone here

315

and leave Mark and Glen with enough food to hunker down a while. But the stone might not be needed.

After this mission was over, I felt that things were going to change. If Mark didn't want to level up and come with us to face the challenges of the world, then Richard would probably acquiesce to that, and we would lose a tank as he stayed behind. I didn't know about Alex and Thomas, but I believed Thomas wanted to continue to progress, and Alex as well. How much of that was his passive, I couldn't be sure.

Ever since the incident with the ogres, Maria seemed to have been able to keep Alan grounded. His wild side showed through occasionally, but not usually until after the battle had begun and the room for mistakes was a lot slimmer. As long as he didn't go overboard, Thomas would always be able to heal him.

Jessica and I continued to watch the sunset for around fifteen minutes. The sky was growing dark fast, but the stress of everything started to subside as the day was coming to a close. No one had died today, nothing untoward happened. It was a good day, relatively speaking.

We turned to enter back inside when we heard something that made my skin crawl.

Ahem, I don't like to normally do this, but special circumstances have arrived. It seems that some of you think that you can hide in the most remote locations and just be fine. Unfortunately, this possibility was not intended and is going to be patched right now. You may feel a little sting. Just kidding! Do your best. Oh, I forgot to mention that we have added a few new classes, so it isn't all bad.

"That doesn't sound good," I said. They had just added something to the world that clearly was meant to kill those humans who were trying to get away from the RPG. I wondered if this meant an increase in the density of spawns, even in the most remote of places. Jessica had a different idea.

"Have they added more flying mobs?" Jessica speculated. "It would only make sense. Monsters that can fly are fast and they aren't restricted by the terrain. You would never be safe in the open again and if they had a long enough range, they could find all the communities currently trying to hide out."

"I hope you're wrong." This was all I could muster before turning back inside. Fighting off flying monsters sounded horrible. Granted we had great ranged capabilities in our party, but if you had fled the cities and were low level, you would have a terrible time of things.

The mood was dreary when we got inside. Not a single face had a smile on it: and Richard in particular was pacing anxiously in the corner. It was a side of him I had not seen and I wondered if it was because he had been planning to live quietly with his brother.

"Should we talk about this new patch?" Lucas asked. "It doesn't seem like it's going to affect us right now, but we should be prepared."

"Jessica reckons it might be the addition of some sort of flying enemy." I said, making sure to give credit.

"Don't say that!" Maria chimed in. "Don't bring that into existence."

I looked over and probably had an expression of surprise. I hadn't taken her for the superstitious type.

"That's possible," Lucas nodded, "something that can fly or something that can track, or both." His logic brought him to the similar point Jessica made earlier.

"The announcement did mention that it was for people trying to avoid populated areas," Alex added. "So perhaps it won't be a problem while we are moving through the city."

Anna chimed in, "Right, but we were just doing the whole non-populated reclusive thing days ago. Six or seven hours from here is pure farmland and small towns. I'd think that would qualify for 'low population' in their definition."

"What about the new classes then?" I asked everyone. "That should be a benefit at least." I couldn't help but look at Glen and Mark. Both were level six and primed for becoming a new class—which, if the logic of most games followed here—would be something incredibly useful.

"They didn't really give us anything to go by, but if they're forcing us into populated areas or out of the countryside, they should give us some benefit through the classes," Thomas said. I had a bad feeling the challenges we faced were going to be changing drastically in the coming weeks or days. For the better or worse? I couldn't get a read on it until I found out about the new classes and the new encounters, but the spirit of the beings creating the RPG was ultimately hostile to humanity.

I looked at Maria, "Is he still asleep?"

"Sound asleep." She spoke with uncertainty then raced back upstairs. We wouldn't have any parasitic worm incidents with her on watch.

"What's got Richard so anxious?" I whispered to Lucas. He was still pacing in the corner of the room, and hadn't joined in on the conversation at all.

"He was already jittery before the announcement, but as soon as it happened, he went white as a sheet and started pacing," Lucas answered. This made sense: it was likely the patch had foiled his plan. I didn't fault him for wanting to settle down somewhere and try to live safely with his brother, but it didn't seem like that was going to be an option for him now.

It was the same for us though, too. My plan of starting a community and settling down had probably been ruined for now. Which meant an alternative must be opening up. I speculated about the new classes. What classics hadn't we seen yet? The possibilities were endless, and putting too much mental power into it wasn't worth my time.

A sudden rush of panic washed over me. Was I stagnating here? Were things suddenly going to speed up and leave me and everyone else behind? My passives, my skills, they weren't exactly advancing very quickly now. Should I be focusing on my personal growth?

My thoughts spiraled down that path until I rationalized it some more. Forcing everyone into more populated areas meant more human interaction. Power in numbers was the best way to survive, and that's what we were doing currently.

Sure, there were probably people more powerful on an individual sense, but how much would that do if eight or nine people slightly under your level were to come at you? You probably didn't have much chance of surviving.

The True Believers were a perfect example. They couldn't be more than level fifteen, and some probably even under level 10, and yet a group twice our size would give us a fight to the death, and we definitely wouldn't come out unscathed even if we did win it.

I still needed to focus on my personal growth, and that was something I would do as soon as we found a way to set up a grind.

I didn't feel good about knowing very little about myself right now. The way the passives affected me, my mutation, these were things I'd spend extensive time on as soon as I was able.

"I'll take the downstairs bedroom tonight." I said. The water had receded enough that the first floor was usable again, and Mark had been hard at work trying to get the water out. We wouldn't be as crowded tonight, especially since our captive had his own bed.

Jessica followed me in, her face the picture of quiet contemplation. "How much larger do you think we should get?" I asked her. This question was on my mind, and my earlier anxiety had left it deeply embedded in my thoughts.

"Party size?" she asked. "Not much larger." I was in agreement with her. It was hard to micromanage even this many people, to make decisions for this many people. It was also hindering our individual growth. There was no room for selfishness as of right now, though.

"I think core party size shouldn't be much bigger than what we currently are," I agreed. "If we add any more people, maybe it's not to party, but an association: a guild or a raid. I wonder if the menu will have tools for something like that." If I was being honest with myself I didn't want the game to allow big groups, because I couldn't be personally responsible a lot of people. I wasn't confident enough or equipped to deal with crowds. Maybe Lucas could.

Instead of a massive group, would it be possible to create something along the lines of a guild or association? An overarching structure with multiple people in positions of power, and not one person making every decision? Even if the menu didn't have those tools, we humans could figure something out. Mainly, I wanted an association because I didn't want the responsibility of leading large

320

groups and witnessing people die under my command. This was something I resolved to discuss more with Lucas in the future.

"A guild would be nice." Jessica said, "But we don't exactly have somewhere to stay at... like a guild house or something." That was also a problem, which is why I didn't want to dive too deep into it right now before getting everyone's opinion. I could bounce ideas around with Jessica though. It was easy to share with her.

"I hope tomorrow brings some good news." I said while winding down on the bed. The new classes weren't going to outweigh the downside of new mobs or intensity of spawns. We hadn't planned on what we would do once we finished here, but the obvious plan would to base ourselves somewhere with less traffic: which arguably might be more dangerous than a populated area like this. At least here there were set spawn zones and pathing for enemies... Jessica lay on the bed with me and that interrupted my thoughts. Now I was overwhelmed by warmth and softness.

Chapter 35: The Story of a True Believer

I woke to the sound of yelling sometime around five or six in the AM. I could see the slight hue of a hidden sun coming through the curtains, which meant it was around dawn. The entire house was stirring with shouts.

"What's the ruckus?" Richard yelled from behind me on the stairs. His voice was loud and abrupt enough to almost make me trip.

We found Maria with an expression of worry at the end of the hallway on the second floor. She was pacing back and forth when an agonized yell came through the door in front of her. "The Believer's awake," she said, biting her nails, "but it's not good."

"What's the problem?" I asked.

"He's in a lot of pain." Maria opened the door for us to see. Inside was our 'captive', face red and covered in sweat. His fists clenched hard into the comforter and pulled up and down with each wave of pain. His eyes opened rarely. His face grimaced constantly with each clench of his teeth and the squinting of his eyes.

"Get Thomas, fast," I told her.

Alex came through the doorway just as Maria rushed out to get Thomas. "Doesn't look good," he said.

"No, it doesn't," Richard added angrily. More people started to clump upstairs, I let Alex and Richard deal with their questions.

I entered the room and walked closer to the True Believer and spoke in a hushed voice. "Can you hear me?" No response, closer now. "Can you hear me?" I asked again.

There was laborious breathing followed by an unhappy exasperation, "I can hear you." He groaned, "Who are you? Why am I here?" Each word was spoken as if forced through a dirt sieve.

"You don't remember me?" I asked him. It was likely he could see me, but I couldn't be certain. "The Necromancer?"

His eyes turned clear in thought for several seconds. "I don't know..." He gripped hard at his face with a single hand, as if the process of trying to remember caused extreme pain. "I remember bits of something." He paused, "I don't know?" his head fell to the back of the pillow in exhaustion.

"What do you remember?" I pressed.

The Believer started to ramble almost incoherently about seemingly irrelevant information, but as he went on it became clear to me that he was recounting his Apocalyptic experience. From the very start till now.

The beginning was chaos and death, barely scraping by. He skipped through those times, as if it was all a blur. It was the sort of experience I expected most people to have, and he barely lived by the skin of his teeth. It was the next part of his story where things got odd.

He started to mention a certain person a lot—'my friend'—too much in fact. Even more odd was that this occurred after the Believer and his friends got their class changing stones as a group. Which meant it was most likely that My Friend got a skill that made him the dominant person among them.

Thomas showed up in the middle of the Believer's narration and healed him. His exhausted face showed some relief, but the heals weren't going to help him in the long term. I wasn't sure if he was aware, but his entire side was badly infected. The comforter was already soaked through with a disturbing red and green color, and it smelled as bad as it looked.

Thomas sat down next to me and began listening to the account as well, "Don't mind me," he urged the prisoner, "keep going." The heal seemed to have gained us some goodwill, and even a smile in response, and the Believer got back into his tale.

My Friend, whom he had met after the Apocalypse, already grouped up, was the sole subject of every recollection. The Believer began to do everything for him, and somehow didn't seem to think this was out of the ordinary. He dictated gruesome actions that he'd carried out with no sense of responsibility or remorse. Even more worrisome was that he just referred to him as 'my friend'. To me it felt like how I treated my undead squad. They did not have names, they were just mindless followers. My Friend seemed to have been treating the group around him in the same way.

The actions the Believer said they did…I almost couldn't bear to look at him until I understood his perspective. Everything he was telling us was fiction. It was literally a dream: a story in his mind that had never happened. He had lived in a fog that felt completely out of his control, which it may have been.

There was a theme to his recollections: item collection. Everything they did as a group was in order to secure more items. That included killing and robbing, but also doing absolutely stupid things. People died constantly from badly managed encounters and poor engagements. All the items they collected they brought right to My Friend, and only items they had earned before meeting him did they get to keep. Anyone they recruited would also go meet him immediately.

"So, they are item collection slaves?" Thomas summed it up about right with a glance at me.

"It seems so," I agreed.

"Item collection slave? What are you talking about?" the Believer asked.

"Do you know what you were going to do next?" I asked him instead.

"We...were going to fight something called a fiend. We were clearing for it." He said with some uncertainty. "That's kind of weird..." He mumbled, "I shouldn't know what happens next in a dream, right?" His hand went to his face as he scrunched it up in pain.

I waited a dozen seconds before the groaning stopped and he refocused on us. "Everything you told us happened." I said. I wasn't one-hundred percent each thing happened or he remembered perfectly, but I was convinced most of it was true if not all of it. He looked at us with a deadpan expression of disbelief. "Are you okay?" I asked.

"...That can't be," he said. "I...murdered people?"

"You did...but didn't," I said, "You weren't in control." His head fell back on the pillow and he didn't even bother to close his eyes. He just stared up at the light hitting the ceiling from the incoming sunrise. "Sorry." It was all I could muster. "We'll try and keep you comfortable till the end."

Thomas stood with me and cast another heal. There was no happy expression or smile this time. Just an empty shell of a human there in the bed now.

"That's depressing." Thomas said.

"Very." I agreed. It was pretty much confirmed now that those people were not in control of themselves. They were victims of circumstance just like anyone else. Still, I didn't regret the spider ambush. We had to fight for our lives even if the enemy was unable to help themselves.

"Did you find out anything?" it was Jessica who leaned into the room, with Anna and Maria close by behind her.

"Item collection slaves," Thomas said.

"The True Believers are being used to farm items. They have no choice in the matter." It was a sad situation all around. One that was so big now I didn't know how to fix it. The number of followers My Friend had now was unknown. They always traveled in large groups, too.

Without taking him out directly I didn't see a solution. We had no name, no face. Was he even with his followers? How far could he be away and still control them? Was there even a distance?

I assumed there must be some distance over which the parasitic worms could no longer contact or responded to My Friend, but maybe that was naïve. There was obviously a limit, but after a certain distance it didn't matter. To search for My Friend would be like finding a needle in a haystack.

"Was there anything else?" Anna asked.

"The cult leader is going after the fiend." I told them. Something I didn't want to involve myself with. The fiend was something I'd see in my dreams occasionally, and it was never a pleasant dream when it showed up.

In a big city like this, I could only imagine every True Believer going was like a lamb to slaughter. The outcome of that encounter would be terrible for the humans.

"Is it nearby?" Jessica asked anxiously.

"No idea," I said, "there wasn't much information relayed besides that they had the fiend as a goal." Her agitated response confirmed my own feeling—we didn't want anything to do with the fiend.

"Good," she said, "let's steer well away from it then. In fact, we should be leaving as soon as possible. With the True Believers moving so much in the area, the fiend is probably somewhere in the vicinity, or had been spotted at least. That put us at risk."

"If the weather holds, we can leave as early as today," I said to everyone present. No doubt that message would get passed down to the others gathered on the staircase.

"What about the True Believer?" Anna asked.

"He probably won't last a more than a few hours at this rate." Thomas said. "He's in bad shape, even worse since our talk." His passing was never a matter of if, but when. Everyone knew that, but it was still nothing to be happy about.

It came sooner than expected, though. Not even an hour passed before Maria found us downstairs discussing our next course of action. "He's gone," she said. Her face a mixture of sadness and relief.

"And with him, so did your responsibility." Alex had followed her down the stairs.

Richard had also cheered himself up a little, "Finally joining us you lovebird?" He poked at Alex in response to him poking at Maria, which surprisingly didn't get any reaction.

"Yeah, so who is going to explain what the fiend is?" Alex asked instead. Only Jessica and I had experienced that monster, and the one we had encountered didn't amount to what a fiend would be like in this city, or if it was even the same creature here as it was at our home city.

We took turns dictating the tale. The feeling of being trapped in that apartment building. Thinking that it could read my mind or sense us from much further than a typical monster's aggro range was.

"So it's like a free-roaming, self-aware monster?" Lucas asked.

I got what he was getting at. "Yeah: it seemed to not be held down by any imaginary tethers."

"That doesn't necessarily mean intelligence though." Thomas added. "It's possible its pathing is just the entire city, which gives it a unique appearance, but that would make it no different than any other mob."

"Does that even matter?" Alex asked. "The thing can fricking camouflage. Does anything besides that REALLY matter?"

"It was also much, much higher level than us," Jessica added, "and that was more than two weeks ago."

"Add on the fact this city is much more populated..." Maria pointed out.

"WAS more populated." Alex corrected her. The populations of all the cities had definitely dropped to a very low number.

"Right, it's probably much higher level here. It may even be in the high thirties or low forties in level." Which meant it wasn't something we could hope to take on without casualties. I wasn't interested in risking anyone's lives for some EXP or loot, at least not in this situation. This was one of those 'stupid' ideas the True Believers were being forced into.

"That's why we should leave as soon as possible." Jessica said. "it's a hunter, and with so many people moving through here. It's bound to find us out, if it already hasn't. I don't want to be a target."

"Two hours then," I said. "Let's be on foot and making our way out of here towards Lucas's family."

"Should we just leave the city instead?" Lucas suddenly asked. "I don't think it's possible my grandparents are alive."

He was looking at me, and not at anyone else. I could surmise why—I was the other person that still had potential family here.

"I agree with you," I said. I thought finding the words would be hard, but they came so easily. "I don't think my parents could have fared any better." Looking at Mark's neighborhood, seeing the broken-down doors and blood splattered entranceways...

They lived in a very tightly packed suburb, and their homes definitely weren't as high quality as this. Single story, made in the early 70's. There was nowhere to go if something like this happened, and if they ended up being stuck at home...that was that. If they were alive, they would have miraculously made it out—but finding them would be like finding a needle in a haystack.

Not to mention...they were much further in, and in this ring tiered system...I was not sure we could fare very well going too far too quickly. Add on the situation with the True Believers and the fiend. The feeling prickling at the back of my neck had been present so long I almost wasn't aware it was there.

We were in constant danger, and it was definitely not going to get any safer by continuing a hopeless quest. It seemed Richard agreed; Mark and Glenn agreed, even though they didn't say it out loud. The mention of leaving caused an instant change in their demeanor.

The two absolutely didn't want to be left here alone, if something happened to us, they were as good as dead after their rations ran out. Richard also didn't want to split from his brother either.

"Let's be on our way out within the hour then." I told everyone, we could move faster without the weight of heavy future planning. Leaving should be easy...

Chapter 36: When Two Impossible Forces Line Up to Fight: There May be Loot

"How about we go to find somewhere between the two cities," I proposed. "With this new change, I don't know if going to a secluded area is safer than living nearby."

"I'll check the map," said Lucas, "an actual map of this area I mean, not the system map. The most ideal situation would be if we can get ourselves secured by high walls and fencing. Even if there were lots of mobs around we could be secure."

After spreading out his map and studying it for a few minutes Lucas pointed to a housing complex just south of the city. On foot it was at least a day's walk as we would have to skirt around the edge of the city and avoid True Believers. Still, it was extremely promising as a place to start some sort of base camp. With the spawn protection stone we could essentially secure ourselves in the middle of enemy territory.

The housing community was gated, and had two different lakes on one side. Natural human traffic should be low as it didn't lead to anywhere, it was just its own enclosed living area. It looked pleasant enough too, with single family detached homes that should be spacious enough for everyone.

Some of the doom and gloom I had been feeling vanished as we talked about getting out and finding a more secure place. It felt like a new chapter was going to be starting for us shortly and we could actually start working towards surviving.

As much as I wanted to know for certain what had happened to my parents, I had a group of people depending on me. Truthfully, from the beginning, I never thought we would be strong enough or quick enough to venture as deep into the city as was needed to reach where my parents lived. The only hope that they were still alive was if they had gotten out, and if they did do that—I couldn't find them right now anyway.

Soon we were gathered outside on the street with our bags. Before setting off, there was a consensus that we should scavenge the local stores first. An extra pair of shoes and some fresh underwear went a long way when showers weren't commonplace. We stayed in Mark's neighborhood as we went in search of useful gear.

The area didn't see many spawns or patrols, and the three enemies there were we dispatched with ease. They were all lycanthropes, which were no longer any threat. Fortunately, they were the most common mob in this outer ring of the city.

Even while inside the stores, we made it a rule that everyone had to be within earshot of Jessica at all times, for safety reasons. And it was just as well that Jessica had insisted on that rule, because after only a few minutes of scavenging she raced to my side. "Fifty plus people moving two blocks away from us." She spoke in a hushed whisper.

"Okay, you get everyone from that side and I'll get this side. Be quick." I sprinted off to alert those who had gone inside stores on my side of the street. They responded well to my urgent calls, dropping clothes or stuffing them hastily into a bag. It took under two

331

minutes for all of us to meet on the sidewalk about a block away from Mark's home.

"True Believers are moving nearby en masse," Jessica explained. "So far over one hundred people have crossed two to three blocks away, heading inward."

"Is it to battle the Fiend?" Alex asked.

Richard nodded. "Probably."

Looking around, I saw a mixture of excitement and unease in the expressions of our group, and Anna put into words the question that everyone was thinking, "So, what now?"

I truly hadn't expected hundreds of True Believers would be sent to fight the Fiend. This was something we could potentially take advantage of. "Well, we have two options…" I began, "we can use this window to leave without the fear of encountering any True Believers."

"Or?" Maria asked a bit anxiously.

"We can follow them from a distance and take advantage of the situation, maybe grab some drops." There was a two-birds-with-one-stone sort of situation developing. "The Fiend and the True Believers are bitter enemies…and if they fought and weakened each other, or even better wiped each other out…"

"The amount of potential loot…" Anna was salivating.

"And experience…" Alex agreed.

"It's a huge risk," Lucas pointed out. "We could be wiped out by either side, but especially the Fiend." I agreed with him. I had made it fervently clear how dangerous the Fiend was, as had Jessica. On the other hand, if the True Believers won at great cost, removing the survivors now could save us from tremendous future problems, especially since we wanted to create a base nearby. Maybe too, the Fiend wouldn't respawn and this would be an unrepeatable opportunity to rid the world of it?

"Jessica, how far can you track now?" I asked.

"Four blocks maximum." She had been using her tracking continuously since we had arrived at the city, and even before that. Four blocks was an incredible distance, and that would give us at least thirty seconds head start for anything untoward coming our way.

"We can watch from four blocks then, find a defensible position and wait."

"What if it isn't the Fiend they are after?" Mark asked.

"Well, if it wasn't the Fiend, they would probably spread out looking for us instead of marching by like that." In fact, it wouldn't have surprised me if they had detected us. Two blocks wasn't that far away. It was a range that Jessica could do almost from the get go and we knew they had trackers. It really did seem like we weren't the priority at the moment.

"What does everyone think?" I asked. This had to be a group decision.

"What about Mark and Glenn?" Richard cut in.

"They can come along if they want, although it should be safe enough here now that the True Believers have congregated and marched past," I answered.

Richard looked at Mark while both Alex and Thomas looked at Glenn.

"We'll be fine for a few more days," said Mark.

Glenn nodded. "Yeah, we'll stay here. Don't worry about us."

I couldn't tell if they actually were as confident as they sounded, or if they simply didn't want to be a burden that affected our group decision.

Anna and Alex had no reservations and immediately indicated they were in favor of tracking the cultists, and the others agreed after a few moments of hesitation. Only Maria was unconvinced. Ever since her near-death dungeon experience, she had been very reluctant to do anything too risky. Loot or progression didn't entice her, and she was completely fine with remaining stagnant but safe.

That was a problem in and of itself, but maybe time would fix it. "We'll be as careful as possible, I promise," I said to her. "Four blocks, we don't move unless the situation is overwhelmingly in our favor. We retreat if things look in any way odd."

She seemed conflicted, and her eyes wandered to find Jessica. But it only took a nod and a reassuring smile for her to agree, "Okay, but keep your promise," she said sternly.

I looked at Jessica. "Lead the way."

Jessica gave a nod and then ran through a backyard before jumping the fence, "Keep up!" she yelled back.

Richard was the last of us to make the jump, staying back to ensure his brother and Glenn had everything they needed for the next few days. "Everything good?" I asked him when he reached the other side.

"All good. Just being careful." I gave him a nod and then signaled to Jessica to keep moving.

The area was barren of mobs. The swarm of Believers had cleared the area for several blocks. It was a leisurely stroll for us, and then we came to an abrupt stop after just ten minutes. "They're congregating ahead," Jessica stopped us, "hundreds of them."

"Hundreds?" Anna asked.

"So many it's hard to count," Jessica said in confirmation.

"Find a roof." Alex urged everyone. We were surrounded by buildings, but after short consideration, only one would do. It was a block inward and tall enough that we wouldn't have any line of sight issues with buildings on the way.

The Believers had moved through these streets like a swarm of locusts clearing a farm, and even that block inward was devoid of spawns. It was as if they had cleared this entire area and turned it into one giant arena for the battle with the Fiend.

The building itself was still filled with monsters, but the east stairwell was sealed and clean all the way through to the roof. So after a few straightforward encounters, we found ourselves looking out over the whole city: a beautiful and yet terrifying sight.

Every street the Believers hadn't cleared was infested with monsters. Months ago, you'd never imagine anything other than humans walking and driving along these streets. Now it was pure hellscape. The rain had cleaned up much of the trash, but the downed power lines and heavy metal from torched and destroyed cars still littered the street in a chaotic landscape.

I couldn't help but think this was the kind of view every person needed to see at least once. Once you saw this, there you knew that humanity was no longer top dog on the planet anymore, and this would remain the case for the foreseeable future.

"There's so many of them," Richard said, "Disgusting." It took a moment to realize he was talking about the True Believers and not the monsters.

"That's easily several hundred people," I confirmed. Even more eerie was what was happening. They were all just standing there motionlessly. It was nothing like a normal gathering of people. They stood...in silence...and waited.

Unfortunately, that's all we could do as well. Sit and wait for whatever was to come.

"How can we take advantage of that?" Maria asked skeptically.

"I'd also like to know." Anna chipped in. Those two seemed to always piggyback off each other when it came to being skeptical. Not that there was anything wrong with that.

"As sad as it is to say," I replied, "we wait for the Fiend to take care of that." I pointed at the clump of people standing like mindless zombies in the distance. The guilt from it washed over me like water off a duck's back.

This was happening whether we intervened or left, and as far as I was concerned we were completely neutral...for now. If an opportunity arose that allowed us to grasp some benefits and maybe weaken the True Believer camp, I was all for it.

"You think the Fiend will put up a fight against that many people?" Richard asked earnestly.

"I think it will do more than that." I responded. I was less confident than my words suggested, though. I didn't know how it would fare against hundreds of people, but it should do a decent amount of damage... If it didn't, well we could simply descend and be on our way in a few minutes.

Time crawled. There was no shade upon the roof, and the morning sun started to pound down from above. The recent cloudy and stormy weather was nowhere to be seen, and our only solace was a nice cross breeze that made this bearable.

"Do you think we're in for another drought?" Thomas asked. There was a bit of weariness in his eyes. He hid it well, but I could feel the anger he held just beneath the surface, waiting to explode over. Holding onto that for so long...it surely wore you out and slowly ate you up? Finding Glenn had definitely helped appease some of that, but his suppressed rage was still there bubbling.

Alex was curled up in a ball in a corner of the roof. Only half of his body was protected by the light overhanging shadow from the

roof's ledge. "I hope not!" he yelled out. His hands constantly fid-
dled with tiny bits of gravel that he tossed into the air.

"We'll be okay with just the Rations." I reminded everyone.
Others weren't so lucky, but for now we had the fighting power to
sustain ourselves by grinding Rations if we needed to.

All at once, my hair started to stand on end, as if I was being
electrically charged. The vibrations across my skin made me think
I'd be struck by lightning at any time, but I knew what it meant.
"It's here," I said.

Chapter 37: The Fiend Versus the True Believers

Everyone who wasn't already paying careful attention the Believers jumped up and raced to the building ledge.

"Are you sure?" Jessica asked me.

Until I had spoken, Jessica had remained quiet, presumably keeping a careful track of the surroundings. Our lives were in her hands at the moment. The intel from a tracking ability was invaluable, and any lapse in her judgment could lead to monsters, or worse, True Believers, locating and trapping us upon the roof. No amount of human enhancement could survive more than a forty-floor fall, at least for now no single person in our party could manage it.

I nodded to her and focused my attention beyond the True Believers. If she couldn't track the Fiend, that meant it was on the far side of them to us, and that was good news.

I watched with bated breath for a dozen seconds, anxiously waiting for what might happen. In those short moments, time stopped, the wind stopped, and the world stopped spinning. It felt as if only my heart beating in my chest existed, and nothing else.

That serenity lasted only a moment, and then came hell. A screech louder than anything I'd heard in my life blasted outward from across the True Believers. A pulse of sound so loud and fast the air moved, and it was visible to see.

My hands were at my ears before my brain even registered what had happened—PAIN. My head felt like it would pop any moment, and all I could do was squeeze my ears harder and clench my teeth till I felt my cheeks were full of blood and my eyes were bulging. Then the sound was gone as fast as it had come, but the damage it had dealt was already evident.

My hands fell and I looked around. The sounds of the world around me came in muffled. The words coming out of my mouth were spoken as if underwater, and the world sped up again. "Is everyone okay?" I fumbled out.

My eyes raced around the group, happy to see everyone still standing. Their faces were red, eyes bloodshot, and Maria and Richard and even Anna had blood dripping out of their ears. The rest of us had held on through sheer ability, or were fast enough in putting our hands on our ears to mitigate the damage.

Thomas used an AOE heal to top us all off and I quickly assessed the situation below. It was astonishing, and yet at the same time the sight pointed towards my expected outcome for this encounter. Thirty percent of the True Believers, give or take, were lying motionless below. The scream of the Fiend had killed outright a huge chunk of their force.

The cultists rushed together like ants defending their colony and prepared for battle. I couldn't see the Fiend, but I could feel it. My eyes traced the building I suspected it to be on, where it had been watching and waiting, and as I did, I felt alarm bells go off. If I focused hard enough on a spot that screamed danger, I could see it ever so faintly.

It suddenly propelled off the building and jumped hundreds of feet, landing on the top of a large tree just twenty meters from the mass of True Believers. The tree shook like hurricane winds had come through, and the top leaves rippled as if the air was as hot as for a desert mirage. I couldn't see it clearly, but it was now obvious to everyone where the Fiend had taken up position.

"We watch and don't get involved unless we are certain it's the right move," I said. "Pay attention. We aren't just monitoring what happens with the Fiend. If we can spot the person in control of the True Believers—put a face to this monster—we might just be able to really kill two birds with one stone."

I doubted anyone could look away at this moment even if I'd told them to. Every eye locked upon the top of that tree waiting for the impending battle. The Fiend too seemed stuck in place, as it rested upon the tree without motion. I had expected it to slaughter ravenously, but it was the True Believers that started the battle.

Dozens of spells were launched in succession, so many that they momentarily blocked off my vision. The amount of spellcasters was staggering to behold. The top of the tree became a mess of colorful magic that fully concealed the Fiend within.

It was quiet after the barrage, and when the magic faded and cleared, a cocoon rested where the tree once was: clearly the result of some magical spell. Now those True Believers who specialized in melee moved forward one step at a time, slowly encroaching upon the cocoon from all sides. The Fiend, somehow trapped inside, remained motionless.

The brown cocoon was eight or nine feet long and half a man's height off the ground. It was cylindrical in shape and had protruding ridges every few feet. Needless to say, it wasn't all that pleasant to look at. I couldn't tell how tight the encasement of the Fiend was.

"Is it over that fast?" Maria suddenly asked.

"Not possible," Jessica replied, then hinted with a nod to keep watching.

The True Believers had weapons drawn and pointed at the cocoon, but stood waiting. It seemed that even they had no plan for this situation, of the Fiend putting up almost no resistance. Their spears and swords would probably have trouble piercing the leathery shell of the cocoon, which raised the question—do they cancel the magic spell and start attacking?

The cocoon suddenly started to vibrate and then buzz. The True Believers raised their weapons in response. Those who had shields moved forward and extended them in preparation for the Fiend breaking free.

It was amazing, and yet scary, to see the coordination possible when one person could dictate the commands of all these people with a single thought. The shields slammed down at the same second, and the resulting sound echoed even here to the rooftops, and was incredibly intimidating.

This was the kind of prowess that would scare almost anyone, and would definitely make an imposing force think twice about fighting a battle. Unfortunately for them, the Fiend wasn't a human force, and definitely would not be intimidated by this display of coordination.

The vibration of the cocoon stopped as suddenly as it started. It wiggled just once, and then a screech even stronger than the first burst forth. The nearest True Believers were blown back several feet by the shockwave, some of them never getting up again.

Even the cocoon, which no doubt had considerable holding strength, burst like a popped balloon. The Fiend appeared from within, then dashed through a crowd of melee, sending two heads flying. Nothing could match it in this moment. It was on a rampage.

The sudden confusion left the ranks of True Believers rattled and confused. Even though I was looking from on top of a building four blocks away, I could barely get my bearings for several seconds. Those in the vicinity were probably temporarily deafened and confused, perhaps they were afflicted by the Fear status.

The Fiend's screech was overbearing, and it was able to slaughter without resistance for nearly thirty seconds. That was how long it took for the remaining melee to band together and put up a united front. I estimated that by this point, around fifty percent of the original numbers of the cultist army had perished. That was hundreds of people dead.

It seemed like this mass death had taken place over a long time, but in fact it must have merely been a minute since that first deadly howl. In a single minute of battle, over one hundred people had died. I wiped the sweat from my brow and had to question what we were doing here.

I looked at Jessica in that moment and could see she was thinking the same thing. We weren't going anywhere near that thing unless it was seriously weakened. I was starting to think we'd be leaving empty handed, as the Fiend was going to mop the floor with them.

Yet the cultists were no longer stunned and it was impressive to watch the brave actions someone could undertake when they didn't care about their own life. The melee fighters had no fear at all, and pushed forward towards the Fiend regardless of the risk. Soon the monster was fully on the defensive.

The spellcasters in the back seemed to be freely pummeling the Fiend with whatever spell they knew. Collateral damage wasn't an issue either. Everyone there was expendable, which created a terrifying fighting force.

An inferior monster would have perished immediately from such an assault, but the Fiend seemed to have some level of intelligence. Its attacks weren't repetitive in the slightest, and there was no pattern to its offense or defense that could be exploited. It weaved through the melee, making sure to take a head or two with every attack.

The reasoning for its successful attacks was that it outclassed its opponents and must have had far greater stats. The difference in levels meant no single person there could even touch the Fiend. Trying to defend was pointless, and if you tried to defend, well you couldn't attack. The Fiend could attack and retreat before even fearing retaliation.

This would have been a death sentence for a normal group. For us, it would have been an impossible decision to be in: give up defending and fight, knowing that you would die. And worse, you knew even that sacrifice would not deal significant damage. Self-preservation was too strong for someone who'd never been in a life-or-death situation to make that call, let alone execute it.

The True Believers, however, could give up their lives to chip away at the Fiend. The person in control had been practicing some level of self-preservation, to avoid losing his fighting force, but I could tell that he'd now switched to a zerg strategy: overwhelm the enemy with lots of small damage.

Given that the cult leader had realized the issue so quickly, he was most likely here, watching close enough to see the problem. I scanned the crowd for anyone out of place, but came up empty.

The fight turned in favor of the True Believers with that simple change in tactic. The melee and tanks didn't try to defend at all. If the Fiend came in to attack, they all attacked. It was like the Fiend was attacking into a cactus. It took several heads with each attack, but it couldn't dodge the barrage of swords, spears, arrows and magic.

The Fiend wasn't completely helpless in this battle. After an attack it usually relocated, and very frequently used a flick of its tongue killed a spell caster. It was hard to see with the naked eye, but they were constantly falling. Jessica was the one who realized it was the tongue and not some sort of bullet.

By the time the melee and caster force were cut in half, the Fiend was missing a limb and its body was badly burned. Arrows stuck out of its back and it seemed to me that the several hundred people force was too big of a hurdle for the Fiend to overcome. Still, it had done considerable damage already. The True Believers numbers were dwindling fast.

"Should we start moving?" I asked. Things were developing fast, and if we waited any longer the opportunity could slip out of our grasp.

"Is it really time?" Anna asked, and from their expressions it seemed everyone else shared the implied thought that it was too soon to get involved safely.

"We need over a minute to get there. If we're too late, the winners might be alert and recovering." It would be terrible if the Fiend won and then escaped while we were on the way. In the same way, it would be awful if the True Believers defeated the Fiend and then recuperated. We needed to strike during the confusion.

"Look at the Fiend. Its movements are fast, but no longer so fast it can't be followed with the naked eye. It is sluggish, and a lot of damage has clearly accumulated. On the True Believer's side, there are around twenty melee, and twenty or so spell casters left. We can nearly take them now, let alone after they've had more losses."

That wasn't to say the Fiend was a pushover in this moment. It still sent heads flying with every attack, it just couldn't do it as quickly as before.

"Let's go then," Alan said. His resolve had hardened with my words. And he set the mood for the whole group: if things went awry, Alan was the one who would be tanking the Fiend.

Richard gave a nod that he was ready and they rushed down the staircase. Jessica was directly behind them, followed by everyone else. I was glad going down the stairs was easier than going up. The feeling of impending doom I felt right now was stronger than I'd felt before.

My heart was beating so fast in reaction to that feeling, it seemed like blood was rushing to my head, and if I was going up stairs instead of down I'd probably have passed out. My body sorted itself out when I touched the sidewalk. This was not the time for any mishaps.

Chapter 38: Teamwork at the Highest Level

Jessica raced ahead and we made quick haste. All in all, it took us a little over a minute to reach the location of the battle. We found some vehicles to the side with a good vantage point and took cover.

The fight had slowed down considerably. Both sides were tired, and it seemed five or six more people had fallen on the True Believer side. Still, the Fiend wasn't in good shape either. Judging by the fight though, there was a chance the Fiend would be able to finish this cleanly if we didn't intervene.

That was the best-case scenario for us. By that point the Fiend would be on its last legs and we could dispatch it with due care. At least that was the ideal situation we were looking for. The feeling of impending doom I felt didn't leave as we watched, and of course… things could never just go right.

The Fiend took the head of another melee class, and during its repositioning, sniped another spell caster with its tongue. This time when it landed, something odd happened. The melee didn't rush to attack and encase it after it fled, and the spell casters stopped bombarding it with abilities. It was like time had stopped. The True Believers were all frozen in place.

I suddenly had a bad feeling, could it be? The Fiend was also too confused to attack. Its head turned from side to side as if wondering was this was a ploy to bait it into attacking: perhaps it was questioning whether to strike these stationary enemies would cost its life.

"I think the person in control of the True Believers just died," I said aloud.

"Had to have been," Thomas agreed instantly. "They all stopped moving at the same time."

"What happens now then?" Maria asked.

"We wait a bit longer…" Jessica said to everyone while giving me a warning glance. It was all we could do. Safety was the number one priority.

The Fiend remained poised for action for what felt like an eternity, and then rushed a tank who had been giving it considerable trouble. The head of the tank flew clean off with no reaction and the Fiend suddenly became emboldened. It didn't know what was happening, but it behaved as if a light at the end of the tunnel had arrived. It was going to rampage again.

The True Believer it was flying towards suddenly moved, just before their head was sliced clean off. This movement again gave the Fiend reason to pause. The other cultists were starting to wake. Once more the Fiend watched and waited. It did have intelligence, but not enough to know these humans had once been controlled. Probably nothing about this situation was making sense.

One after another the players started to move and come to their senses, and the sight wasn't pretty. They groaned and spoke in muddled confusion while looking around. As they saw the carnage and bloodshed all around, their eyes showed unimaginable fear… and then they started to run.

Those who had woken up and regained enough self-awareness started to run like hell. The Fiend didn't chase them, and instead started to kill those still in a stupor nearby as it grasped the crux of the situation at last. This was its last chance, and ours as well.

"If we are going to fight it, we have to strike now," I looked at everyone. "If we wait any longer, it's going to finish them off and disappear. Should we go for it?" I asked.

"It's still incredibly strong," Jessica warned.

I had come to terms with the possibility of leaving with nothing, so right now it was truly a toss-up for me. In the end, the fight hadn't panned out as I had hoped, and the amount of power left in the Fiend wasn't known. It was weakened—maybe even on death's door—but how many HP it had left was hard to gauge for sure.

"It's okay to say 'no,'" I spoke loudly enough for everyone to hear. But even as I said that, the option of declining the fight seemed to be taken away from us.

A female True Believer who had woken from her stupor came sprinting in our direction and having spotted us hiding behind the vehicle, she started yelled like a maniac. "HELP ME PLEASE!"

I looked at her and then the Fiend, while putting my finger over my mouth. It seemed her self-preservation skills remained poor, because she didn't heed my warning and kept screaming. "PLEASE HELP ME, PLEASE!"

She wasn't even half way to our vehicle before the Fiend, attracted by her yelling, sent a tongue directly through the back of her head. It then jumped to perch on a vehicle just ten feet away from us, and clearly had no intention of letting us walk away for free.

"Alan, Richard, GO!" I yelled.

They rushed to the front without a word, shields extended to the front. The rest of us took cover, either behind them or the vehicle between us and the Fiend. That tongue attack would be a one-shot to anyone in view. My undead squad poured forth to join Alan and Richard at the front.

Jessica cried out, "Too high level! I can't get any stats or skills on it." This was expected, but we at least had an idea of what it was capable of from seeing it in battle. The scream was a terrifying aoe ability that I prayed it wouldn't use right now. Besides that, the tongue attack was deadly.

At least the Fiend's terrifying melee prowess was only a fraction of what it had been at the start of the fight. At our current level we could just barely deal with its weakened state. It eyed me with a venomous stare: no doubt it was weighing its options.

"Use all the magic we have!" I told everyone. Elixirs came out of inventories and were popped back-to-back. Our farming had given us quite the haul of usables and now was no time to be stingy.

Alan and Richard threw back an Elixir of every stat, while the rest of us just had Elixirs for our main damaging stats. Whether the Fiend understood what we were doing or not, it was clearly hesitant of jumping into melee against opponents who were once again behaving differently to what it was used to.

Perhaps the weird actions of the True Believers had made it question what it knew about humans. It wasn't logical to attack without self-preservation in mind. That was something ants, or bees, or beings that only lived for a collective colony did.

Previously, its interactions with humans would have shown us to be timid creatures who cared about self-preservation more than anything. The people it would have met would have fled or tried to hide, and I could imagine how even when death was guaranteed they still crawled as if there was hope at the end of their fingertips, just out of reach. Today, it had met a human army acting to maximize the collective damage by sacrificing individuals.

Alan slapped his shield with his sword, and that meant the Fiend had no more time for contemplation, "Support me!" he cried, then cast Battle Shout and charged directly at the Fiend. Richard rushed behind him to assist. Alan was fully heated up now, and there was no turning back.

My undead warriors rushed forth like a tidal wave and quickly wrapped around the Fiend, lashing into it with their blades. The Fiend was completely encased in a circle of undead with Richard and Alan at the front opening. My spell casters were constantly firing magical bolts through the openings between our fighters.

Maria shot an Entangling Arrow and Jessica prepared some Quagmire traps in several directions. Given its high agility, the Fiend was going to be moving quite quickly. Hopefully, some of the Quagmire traps would prove useful as the fight progressed.

Lucas sent out a Windslash between Alan and Richard, but otherwise waited from a safe distance. As the only other melee, he needed to bide his time so as to not end up in the way, or worse, dead. Anna, Maria, Jessica and I had it much easier, all sending ability after ability towards the Fiend from a safe distance. The only thing holding us back was our MP limit.

Our teamwork was a beautiful orchestra to witness. I'd have believed it a fluke that every projectile reached the Fiend as Alan was just arriving to attack. It wasn't a fluke though. It was synergy gained after fighting hundreds of battles together.

As Richard swung like a madman towards the Fiend, the Fiend also struck back. Its claws flashed out towards his jugular in a strike that had decapitated a hundred people already this day. The result that the Fiend must have expected, however, did not happen.

Richard's head did not fly from his shoulders. No, a sword dug into the Fiend's flesh instead as Alan parried the attack, sliding the sword across the top of his shield for stability. Not only that, a magical spell and two arrows shot into the exposed arm, the fiend's only remaining arm, as it tried to attack.

The Fiend attempted to kick off Alan and retreat while tearing our tank's belly open, but Richard was balanced to fend that attack off, too. His shield, glowing like hot iron, proved the defense against the kick of the Fiend, fully protecting Alan.

My horde of undead were raising their weapons and in another moment would have left the Fiend riddled with wounds. Despite its horribly damaged state, though, it launched off Richard's shield as if gravity didn't exist, fully breaking out of the enclosure of undead and repositioning itself with a furious glare towards Richard.

As it flew away with great force, it left a mist of blood hanging in the air from the wound inflicted by Alan on its arm. Nor did the bleeding stop. No doubt this was a result of Rend from Alan's special sword.

"Careful of that tongue! Stay low!" I warned everyone while sending my undead after the Fiend in a frenzied chase. It always sent out a tongue attack with each repositioning, and I fully expected that scenario to repeat itself. Hopefully, everyone was fully concentrated and in their peak state, ready to duck if they were the target.

In anticipation of this moment, I had the forethought to position my casting skeletons between the Fiend and Jessica and Maria. The tongue did come, but it merely smashed into the skull of one of my casters before retreating as fast as it had come. Lucas had sent a Windslash in anticipation of the tongue attack, hoping to remove

351

such a devasting and risky weapon. Unfortunately, the tongue was just too fast and it escaped the spell.

My warriors reached the Fiend just a moment later, as did Alan and Richard. We couldn't give it a moment of reprieve. We all knew what happened when it was free to go on the offensive. Heads would fly. Even one loss would be devastating, let alone the fact that as soon as we began to go down, we could easily all be wiped out.

Fully surrounded on all sides, the Fiend lashed out with an almost break-dance type move as its back legs twirled. With its remaining, terrifyingly sharp claws, it probably expected to see slit throats or torn bellies on all sides.

Instead, it had simply sliced along the bones of each melee undead. Alan and Richard had cleanly parried its attack with their shields. Despite the ferocity of its move, it had failed to damage our melee classes. It knew a counter-attack was coming, and so the Fiend jumped again.

It jumped, but instead of finding a new vantage point for a tongue attack, the Fiend landed in a Quagmire trap. Its movement became sluggish and as though weighed down. A moment later there were vines covering its body as well. The damage done by the True Believers before our involvement had truly put the Fiend on death's door. Its mobility was greatly weakened.

When the Fiend had looked at me, in its eyes I could see that it thought it would effortlessly finish off the remaining runners, and then have time to recuperate. Instead, it was being outclassed while in its weakened state. Now it writhed and faced away from us, clearly wanting to escape, but found that it almost couldn't move from the floor at this point.

The air around it was frozen solid, and even the blood on its body crystalized and stiffened to a point every movement caused it to scream in agony. The Quagmire trap effect and Ensnaring arrow must have felt like chains heavy enough to restrain even a god.

The Fiend could only watch helplessly as magical spells flew at it and bombarded into its body constantly. It must have had a very high magic resistance, because the spells did not seem to cause much harm. Physical attacks however, were different.

The Fiend had taken almost all of its damage from physical attacks, especially when the True Believers had given their lives to deal damage to it. Because of that, I could see that it paid careful attention to arrows and melee weapons.

So now, when there was a fiery arrow shot directly towards its head, it did everything in its power to dodge. Despite the numerous restraints and terrifying damage, it twisted its body and bent its neck at great peril to its open-wounds. The Explosive arrow from Maria rushed by its head and exploded on the ground behind.

The world seemed to be in slow motion. I dreaded the fact that the Fiend had a moment to counter-attack: it was opening its mouth, preparing to strike with its tongue, and then suddenly its face exploded into gore. Through the blood and gore, I could see the confusion and dismay, the questioning: What had happened?

It was Jessica's Godless Arrow, masked perfectly behind Maria's Exploding Arrow. To something intelligent, this situation would be utterly baffling, and terrifying. To feel the enemies' attacks could not be dodged, or to feel you'd done something correctly but the result was wrong.

It must have been terrifying for the Fiend, especially when the wrong result meant death. It managed a jump away from us, perhaps in hope of regaining its bearings and understanding what was happening. Unfortunately for it, it landed in another Quagmire Trap. The vines came, and so did the chill. We had created a recurring nightmare that the Fiend couldn't escape from.

The Fiend was now riding a tiger and couldn't get off. By skillful foresight from Jessica, perhaps based on observing the kinds of landing spots it preferred, it had landed in the second Quagmire she had laid. We would have a few seconds more before it could try to jump again and escape.

"A final effort!" I yelled to everyone. The effects of Quagmire on the weakened Fiend were astonishing, and it made landing the chill from Anna and the vines from Maria easy. Jessica was able to target one of the Fiend's eyes with her arrows and blind it. The battle power we were unleashing right now was miraculous. We were executing the combat almost as efficiently as the True Believers, and we weren't of one mind.

Maria shot another Explosive Arrow directly at its face in anticipation of the tongue attack. The Fiend was not so bewildered as to let it hit, dodging a different direction than previously. All the same, there was a new hole blown its face. This time however, it didn't come away confused.

Its good eye was focused on Jessica and I had a grim intuition that it had noted the way she had released the string of her bow without an arrow flying from it. That eye glared with hatred at Jessica. It knew she was the main threat to the Fiend. She was the culprit. There was resolve in that look and I feared for Jessica.

Somehow or another, as the fight went better and better for us, the feeling of impending doom only grew worse for me. We were winning, but the feeling prickling my neck made me dizzy. The Fiend was on death's door. A cornered animal with nothing to lose was most dangerous.

The fight reached a crescendo. Alan and Richard were moving in again, as were my undead warriors. Within seconds the Fiend would be surrounded and pummeled again. Contrary to expectations though, the fiend didn't dodge or leap away from our encirclement. Instead, its tongue flew out lightning fast directly towards Jessica.

I looked at her face—her eyes were closed in concentration. She was no doubt using another Godless Arrow. My casters weren't in the way this time: as the battle had turned by half a circle, they were out of position to our right. There was no time to berate myself for not having devoted a second of my mental focus to relocating them.

My alarm bells were ringing danger, and even without thinking about it, my feet moved. Not out of the way… but in the way. My world seemed to stop as I stared at the Fiend and that growing blob of pink. Just before the tongue tip completely blocked out my vision, the Zweihander-wielding Skeleton General cut the Fiend's head clean off.

My neck started to burn like fire that oddly didn't hurt at all. I reached down with my hand as my vision started to close in on itself. There was warm blood covering my entire hand. I looked at Jessica one last time before I collapsed.

Chapter 39: Ahead of the Curve

Why was it so peaceful? My life started to pass before my eyes. Images of my parents, my childhood. The good and fun things I enjoyed early in my life. Nostalgia and longing engulfed me.

The feeling was so warm and embracing. Like I was wrapped in the most soft and comfortable blanket on the coldest night. Suddenly, there was a light. It was a white light in the distance that drew me towards it.

It grew larger and larger, and I realized it was not approaching, but it was I that was moving towards it. I was not scared, not afraid. This was the most peaceful and stress-free I'd felt in years and years.

I welcomed the light as I approached, even basked in its welcoming glow. Walking through would bring me endless bliss, and so I kept moving forward. It grew closer and closer, just a few more steps, and then suddenly it moved back.

I started to feel panic as the white light raced away from me into the distance. My way out...my endless bliss. The feeling of warmth disappeared momentarily, and the darkness enveloped me once again.

"Mike!" The faintest of sounds echoed in this black world, reverberating like an echo in a well that rushed over me constantly.

"Don't die! Wake up!" Another voice brushed past me. The darkness around me started to shake and I suddenly felt something.

I felt my eyes in my head, the weight of my eyelids as I slowly opened them.

Blurry vision greeted me, and then it was my comrades. Huddled around me in a circle staring down, some of them with blood covering their hands. Vertigo assaulted me the moment I tried to lean up and I felt a stabbing pain in my chest.

I groaned in agony before letting my head fall back down. "Careful." Jessica said softly. I could see the redness of her eyes in a single glance. Guilt accompanied the vertigo as I looked at her, unsure what to say.

"What happened?" I muttered. I had a rough idea, but I needed to hear it from them.

They paused for a moment, and then Thomas spoke up, "You died," he said. "You were dead for over two minutes."

"I died...?" I asked. That confirmed my sense that the white light calling out to me was the end of my life.

"You were really, really dead," Maria said. Her face had choked up a bit as she wiped away a tear.

"Why does my chest hurt so much?" I groaned in agony as Thomas helped me lean up.

"Sorry," Thomas said. "Your heart stopped and I just banged on it hoping it would do something." The pain was horrible enough to make even taking a breath hurt.

"The Fiend is dead then," I said. I saw it die, but who knew what kind of miraculous survival abilities a creature like that had.

"Yeah, it's dead," Alan said.

"Drops?" I asked.

"It didn't drop anything." Anna said rather regretfully.

"Huh? Nothing?" That was deeply disappointing. "If you're going to bring me back from eternal bliss, it should at least be for an epic Necromancer drop."

Despite the pain in my chest, I managed the joke and it was worth it to see the smiles on faces that had been so concerned.

So there was no loot on this monster. Was this just by design or did the people toying with us not expect something like the Fiend to die so early?

"We got two levels each, though." Jessica said with a rather hoarse voice. I checked my level curiously and sure enough it was true.

**Name: Mike Reynolds Class:
Necromancer Level: 26 EXP: 42%
HP: 1290/1290 MP: 440/485
STR: 5 Fear Resistance: 5
AGI: 2
DEX: 5
VIT: 29 +14
WIS: 27 +26
Available: 15
Skills: [A] Summon Skeleton LV. 10 | [A]
Summon Skeleton Mage LV. 4 | [A] Decay
LV. 3| [A] Reanimate Dead LV. 3 | [A] Bone
Armor LV. 2 | [A] Vast Shadows | [A]
Temporary Grave LV. 1 | [P] Sixth Sense |
[P] Bravery LV. 2 | [P] Mutated | [P] Pain
Resistance LV. 2 | [P] Skeletal Mastery LV.
4| [P] Intimidate Living | [P] Inner Calm LV.
2 | [P] Necrotic Vision | [P] Blood Thirsty LV.
1 | [P] Cold Hearted LV. 1**

I was now level 26 with 15 available stat points, and halfway to the next level simply from the numerous enemies we fought on our trip. There had been no notification popup at the time of the Fiend dying, most likely since I passed out almost immediately.

There it was in the log.

Congratulations! You are part of the first group to defeat a Tier 1 Fiend. As a reward you have been granted two levels.
Congratulations! As the player who contributed most to the encounter, you have been awarded an extra skill slot.

I paused hard for a moment. An extra skill slot? But how did I contribute most to the encounter? I wasn't even the most valuable person...The Fiend was already on death's door when we killed it. Not only that, Jessica had done a fantastic job putting it in a corner with her Godless Arrow. Was it because my undead warrior got the finishing blow?

Even if my squad of undead had done the most damage among my group, they would still have done a lot less that the mass of True Believers. But perhaps the contribution of the cultists was wiped clean on death.

Glad to have the extra skill, regardless of whether it was justified, I noticed a subsequent message in the notification log.

You have fulfilled the conditions for mutation.

I glanced over my skill sheet and realized Mutated no longer had a level next to it. It simply said Mutated. Was it because I had died?

That had to be the only explanation. I was fearful what it would now say if the requirement was death…

Mutated: You looked death in the eyes and now walk among the undead.

There were lines below that explained what it did as well as many question marks.

You are immune to poison. Hunger is now satiated by slaying enemies.

??

??

??

And the question marks continued downward. Whatever effects they were, I guessed I didn't fulfill the requirement for them. Whether that was my level, or if Mutated had levels, or some other metric I didn't know about yet.

What I did know was that going forward my life could never be a peaceful one. If I needed to kill enemies to sustain myself, I could never take a break. Rations had been a source of food I could trade for or buy from a secret shop: some people were probably doing that now, hoarding rations and secluding themselves hoping to wait this out.

I grabbed Thomas' arm. "Help me up." Alan took my other arm to help him scoop me off the floor and I got my bearings once more. I could feel Maria behind me, brushing the gravel off my tattered shirt as I fought the vertigo.

"Did anyone else receive a new skill slot?" I asked. I got a resounding 'no' as everyone shook their head. "Apparently I did."

Which meant I would have 4 skills in just four levels. I also needed to find a skill suitable for me in the meantime.

There was also the fifteen stat points to allocate. I would do so as soon as I got my next ability. Right now, we needed to evacuate this area before respawns started happening. We had a plan in place already.

Jessica gave me a strong hug from the side, "Ow, ow, ow." I groaned. My rib cage was probably broken. Despite the bandage and heal from Thomas, it would take some time to recover.

"Are you well enough to walk?" asked Lucas. And when I nodded, he ushered everyone southwards. "Let's head back."

With the area being completely devoid of spawns, Jessica was allowed to stay back and support me. The rest hurried forward, led by Richard. Being away from his brother for a few hours was already long enough for him. This world was too cruel.

I realized as I walked that my sense of freedom as I approached the white light was something I would miss. There were no monsters around, but compared to how calm I had felt in the face of death, I was on edge all the time now. The experience of that blissful feeling made me realize just how much my responsibilities in the post-apocalyptic world were weighing on my shoulders.

It didn't take for us long to return, where we fortunately found that Glenn and Mark were safe. They were anxious though, reporting to us that many people had rushed by in a frenzy. There had been a scary possibility that someone may have discovered them. Richard let out a sigh of relief that this hadn't happened.

Those ex-True Believers were confused, but who knew how they would behave once they realized they held power over someone else? It was very possible they would continue to be player killers. Fortunately, that risk hadn't been put to the test.

"Let's head to 'home base,'" I said. That was the plan now, take over a walled community we had identified and start working towards making this existence a livable one. We set off through the streets with me safely packed away in the back.

Jessica could no longer support me, which was a letdown. Instead it was Glenn and Mark on either side making sure I didn't take a tumble. There was no rush now. The mobs only got weaker as we made for the city exit. Not only that, True Believers were no longer breathing down our neck.

I wasn't even required for the battles now. Two levels were a major strength boost to everyone present which brought me some comfort. I already knew this party was sufficient enough. Everyone had grown into their roles fantastically.

"How long on foot?" I asked Lucas. He was the orchestrator for this idea.

"Around two hours if you can sustain this pace," He answered. "We aren't traveling very far. We just need to take a few detours."

It made sense to avoid encounters that weren't particularly dangerous but which would slow us up. "Sounds good," I said. We had about two hours before the sun would set and visibility would drop. A good feeling suddenly filled me. It was expectation: and some of that stress and weight washed off my shoulders.

For the first time in a long time I actually enjoyed the walk. Despite the pain I was experiencing while moving and breathing, I felt confident our group could meet the challenges ahead and the ease with which they pulled and destroyed the occasional mob in our way was a pleasure to see.

Eventually we approached a two-meter-tall community gate. There was a booth on the side, no doubt someone used to sit in there and allow entry and exit. Now was empty and only had broken windows remaining with a bit of dark blood inside.

The sun was setting in the distance as an orange hue shined over the fence and basked all of us in its glow. I couldn't help but smile, "Welcome home everyone," I said.

Alan rushed forward and kicked the gate as hard as he could. The latch broke and it swung open in a miraculous display of his strength. He had destroyed the mood I was trying to set. I could only sigh, while Jessica came over to me grinning.

Taking my head in both her hands, she kissed me full on the lips, careless of the applause and cheers from the others. After a second I didn't care either.

At last she broke away. "You did it Mike. You kept us ahead of the curve. And with the Fiend gone, there's nothing in the local vicinity that need cause us fear. Let's enjoy this time while we can. Until whoever is controlling the game ups the challenge levels, we can live happily."

"Three cheers for Mike," shouted Lucas. And as the others joined in, I found myself blushing and also deeply touched. I'd lost my old way of life and my old family. But I'd found a new one.

End of Book Two

Jeremy Chambless was born in Deerfield Beach, Florida and studied Psychology at Florida Atlantic University. Gaming has always been a part of his household: as far back as he can remember, he was holding a NES controller. His own gaming passion has been focused on MMOs and RPGs. Jeremy is an avid LitRPG reader turned writer. A love for RPGs sparked his desire to create *The MMRPG Apocalypse*.

If you have enjoyed Jeremy's MRPG Apocalypse series you'll be glad to know he's completed an earlier LitRPG series: *The RPG Apocalypse*. And you can follow his progress with book 3 of this current series on Royal Road.

Level Up publishing specializes in LitRPG and GameLit books. You might be interested in our other titles, which can be found at www.levelup.pub/books

To join our mailing list for news about forthcoming books and opportunities to be an ARC reader, just fill in the form on that page.

You can also find us on:
Facebook @LUPublishing
Twitter @LevelUpPub
...and by searching for Level Up WhatsApp group